A Psychiatrist, Screams

Also by Simon Parke
Pippa's Progress: A Pilgrim's Journey to Heaven
A Vicar, Crucified: An Abbot Peter Mystery

A Psychiatrist, Screams

An Abbot Peter Mystery

Simon Parke

ABBOT PETER
A HABIT FOR CRIME

DARTON·LONGMAN + TODD

First published in 2013 by
Darton, Longman and Todd Ltd
1 Spencer Court
140 – 142 Wandsworth High Street
London SW18 4JJ

ISBN 978-0-232-53020-9

A catalogue record for this book is available from the British Library

Phototypeset by Kerrypress Ltd, Luton, Bedfordshire.
Printed and bound by Bell & Bain, Glasgow.

To the flower
who grows through the wall

My thanks to Shellie Wright, Elizabeth Spradbery (the Queen of Commas) and David Moloney, who were all kind enough to read and comment on the text along the way.

And to all at DLT for their various and remarkable skills ... and their madcap willingness to venture further with Abbot Peter.

'Neurotics complain of their illness but they make the most of it; and when it comes to taking it away from them they will defend it like a lioness her young.'

Sigmund Freud in a letter to Martha Bernays

Act One

*The goal of psychoanalysis is the
movement from misery to ordinary human
unhappiness.*

Sigmund Freud

One

Stormhaven, England
Halloween night
early twenty-first century

Although seven clowns started the evening alive, only six still breathed by the evening's end. And while everyone saw the murderer and knew the murderer, no one knew their name.

The Lord of Misrule had seen to that.

They'd seen to everything at the Feast of Fools.

Two

❧

Shiraz, Persia
1389

'Believe me, Behrouz, death is a favour to us!' said the plump Hafiz, seated on the divan.

'If you say so, master.'

Behrouz was glad of a break from his inky toils and the concentration they required.

'Your disbelief is poorly disguised, Behrouz.'

'I speak as I find.'

'Then clearly you haven't found very much.'

A gauntlet was laid down, which Behrouz picked up.

'I've just never regarded death as a favour.'

How could death ever be a favour? It was a ridiculous idea. His master may write fine lines – very fine, some of them – but that didn't mean he had to agree with him. It was a professional relationship, poet and copyist. They must concur over text and punctuation, but not about the mystery of death. If you had to agree about death, who really would you be friends with?

'Then in what manner have you regarded death?' asked the poet in his flowery silks of red and gold.

'Not as a favour, that's for sure.'

'Already established, I think.'

'Definitely not as a favour.'

Patience, Hafiz, patience.

'So how?' asks Hafiz gently.

'No sane person regards death as a favour.'

4

The poet was a joyful presence, almost always, perhaps content more than joyful, for who can always be joyful? But he was distracted today, with much on his mind.

'Well, that is most strange,' he says.

It was strange to Hafiz that someone should not regard death as a favour.

'Why would I?' comes the firm reply.

Behrouz has been getting bolder of late. When first employed, he was in awe of this smooth-skinned wordsmith, but lives now in another land, a truer land, a land of respect, trust ... and constant disagreement.

'Why would you, Behrouz?'

The tone is incredulous, as though the answer is sitting on his lap in a robe of bejewelled gold.

'Death is the end of our painful marriage with cruel beauty! A most divine favour, surely?'

The calligrapher looks out across the courtyard and ponders his evening meal.

'Perhaps for poets but not for copyists,' he says.

'We are no different.'

'You are different. There's no fancy longing for death among tradesmen, believe me.'

The poet shakes his head.

'You need more delight in your life, Behrouz.'

'I'll settle for more wine.'

'God's beauty is a great deal more intoxicating.'

'So you keep saying.'

'And no hangover, no demons in your head the day after!'

'I find the red very adequate.'

For the first time in a while, a long while, concern crosses the face of the poet – a blue sky touched by cloud. And he has his reasons.

Hafiz has been court poet for more years than he can remember – not true, he remembers them all and not all have been easy, far from it. But as he sits with Behrouz sipping rose sherbet, he does ponder what it all means. These moments come, not often but sometimes, moments when we breathe deeply and wonder: what does it all add up to? Or was subtraction a better approach to the meaning of life? What must he take away or lose to see things more clearly?

Hafiz was sixty-four years of age – imagine it! Sixty-four years of breathing this earth's fine air and now celebrated by many for his wonderful words – oh, yes, this Persian poet could write, very popular around town!

But behind his words lay much unresolved, much unhealed; and too many times in these palace rooms he'd quite failed to redeem the

5

present from his sadness. That we'll return to, sadness can always be postponed. But for now, here in this moment, the harder edge of fear cuts at his life.

'My life's work is under threat,' as he'd said to Behrouz just yesterday and he believed it. There were rumours, plots and grudges out there, poison brewed and stirred. As courtiers have always known, forget the dark forest – a royal palace is the most dangerous place to live.

'So how are we doing?' he asks, with a deliberately casual air. No pressure.

'Do you mean "How am I doing"?'

Behrouz is definitely standing up for himself more these days, Hafiz has noticed; in fact he barely ever sits down. And this independence is to be applauded by the poet, if not always with great merriment. You can get used to wide-eyed admiration and miss it when it's gone.

'It's a partnership, surely?' he says. 'I compose the poems, you copy them.'

'Then we're going as fast as we can.'

'That's good, very good,' he says, pondering the minaret skyline.

'You press more than usual,' says Behrouz.

'You think so?'

'You do not usually press in this manner.'

'Then forgive me – but perhaps work harder nonetheless.'

'I do believe you're worried!'

'Worried? Maybe. If I press – and I do press, I know; I know I press – I press because these stiffening hands of mine cannot hold a pen for more than a minute … and because of that dear bastard Karim.'

'Karim – is he the slight one?'

'In body but not influence – and he snarls at my heretic heels.'

'Not a good enemy, I hear.'

'A bad enemy, brim-full of hate. And I suspect – no, I'm certain – there's no time to lose. They are coming for me, Behrouz, I smell it in the air.'

'I'm writing as fast as I can.'

'Of course you are, so who could ask more?'

'You?'

Hafiz smiles.

'Well, maybe I could ask for a little bit more. Speed is of the essence.'

'But speed must share the carriage with legibility.'

'You become a poet yourself!'

Behrouz is quietly pleased with the line. He would use it when next with colleagues.

'Our deadline?' he asks.

'By tomorrow night, please.'

'Tomorrow night?'

'Possible?'
'I will try.'
'And then your journey starts, my friend.'
'I know, I know.'
'Even if mine must end.'

There is fear in his words. Death may be a favour – but it doesn't mean we have to desire it.

Three

Monday, 3 November

'So what does "*Mind Gains*" mean to you?' says the pushy female over the phone.

'Mind games?'

'*Mind Gains.*'

'*Mind Gains*?' says a male in a monk's habit that still contains desert sand. 'Well, it's a mental health clinic recently opened in Stormhaven.'

'Of which you are a trustee?'

'I am, yes.'

'So you know the place well?'

'I know the place to a degree. I'm not sure I know it well.'

'Why do you have to qualify everything?'

'I prefer accuracy to headlines.'

'It's irritating.'

'Good.'

The inquisitor, with an urgent agenda this morning, returns to the matter in hand. Her agenda is always urgent.

'So what do you know of *Mind Gains*?'

'A better question, more open.'

'And the answer?'

'One AGM so far, a wander round its premises in the remarkable Henry House, a few chats with users and staff … a very nice cleaner there called Pat.'

'You fancy her?'

'She should probably be running the place.'

'You do fancy her.'

'She's a leader.'

'Only held back by the broom in her hand and a complete lack of qualifications?'

The inquisitor likes her qualifications, something of a personal treasure, something for the mantelpiece, for display.

'And I suppose,' says the man, reflecting further on the clinic, 'I'm an occasional shoulder for Barnabus Hope to cry on.'

'Barnabus Hope, co-director?'

'The same.'

'So you know him well?'

'I know him quite well.'

Not this again. Is a straight answer a sin?

'And why was he crying?' she asks.

The question is fast out of the blocks, like an eager whippet. The *Mind Gains* clinic is important but Barnabus Hope even more so.

'Oh well, nothing really. It's a metaphor.'

'You mean he wasn't crying?'

'Oh no, he was crying – but crying on the inside.'

'On the inside?'

'I'm not sure if that counts as crying, though it's common enough.'

'Why?'

'Why do people cry? How long have you got?'

'I mean, what made Barnabus cry?'

Now there's an intimate question.

'He has certain difficulties at the clinic, but -'

'What sort of difficulties?'

'For God's sake!' thinks Peter. Too many questions, one after another, like some long and tedious form to be filled.

'Oh, the usual sort in the mental health trade.'

'And what are the usual sort? It's not familiar territory.'

'Well, obviously it's never the clients who are mad – it's the staff.'

'Any in particular?'

'As I've said, I'm really not an expert on the internal relationships at the clinic.'

'You see everything, Abbot – stop obfuscating.'

'You've bought a dictionary since we last met.'

'Tell me.'

'Relationships at *Mind Gains*?'

'In your own time.'

'It's not an easy relationship between Barnabus and his fellow director, Frances Pole.'

'Why not?'

Was this how it was on *University Challenge?* He'd seen the programme, his first experience of TV, while house-sitting for a nun last year. How she came to have a house, he wasn't sure, but then he was an Abbot and he had a house, though not a house as nice as the nun's nook with its aromatic oil sticks and huge TV. And as for *University Challenge*, what really was the point? He'd sat watching in increasing bewilderment: knowledge for the sake of knowledge, knowledge without understanding, endless questions fired low and hard for no other reason than points on a board and the limp applause of family and friends. Questions were worth more than that, and he'd been glad to return to the silence of his own front room. Back with the inquisition, however, he was now attempting an answer:

'I suppose Frances comes from a different therapeutic tradition to Barnabus.'

'Psychologists at war?'

'Maybe. There are different schools in the world of mind health and that can create tensions. Remember Freud and Jung.'

'No.'

'It's of no great consequence.'

He shouldn't have mentioned Freud and Jung.

'It may help me to know,' she says, sensing his reluctance.

The Abbot sighs.

'They started as master and pupil, father and son, in a way. But difference of therapeutic approach began to divide them as humans.'

'What sort of difference?'

'Where to start?'

'The beginning?'

'There isn't one. But Freud believed the principal driving force behind men and women's activities was repressed sexuality.'

'Everything's a penis?'

Ignore that for now.

'So for Freud, it was unfulfilled sexuality that led to pathological conditions, whereas Jung, his former disciple, cast the net a little wider, believed that sex was just one of the many forces that drives humans.'

'Ambition?'

'Maybe. Jung saw the human need to achieve individuation as the most important drive.'

'Indi what?'

'Individuation, the search for full knowledge of the self. The goal of the therapist, according to Jung, is to help the client recognize the work of the unconscious and thereby guide them towards becoming a more whole person.'

'You're losing me.'

'Why don't we leave Freud and Jung in their graves?'

'Good idea. We need to get on.'

She was all for leaving people in their graves, especially if their dug-up bodies held up an investigation.

'We were talking about Barnabus's difficult relationship with Frances.'

The Abbot's mind returns to Henry House and the *Mind Gains* clinic.

'Sometimes we simply struggle with people.'

'So it wasn't just rival theories with these two?'

'Our wars are never about our theories, they're about ourselves. We may buy the same newspaper as someone or share a passion for Persian miniatures – but somehow, and for some reason, we simply don't get on. And that's how it is between Barnabus and Frances ... who can, I know, appear a rather unhealed soul.'

A slight pause, hardly a pause at all.

'What are you doing now?' she asks.

'I'm sorry?'

'What are you doing now?'

'Holding the phone. Though really, who isn't?'

'Who isn't what?'

'Who isn't a rather unhealed soul?'

'Well, me for a start!' she says.

The Abbot laughs.

'I applaud your self-confidence Tamsin, even if I weep for your self-awareness.'

Abbot Peter is in his early sixties with a heart rate of forty-one beats per minute, due to a strange passion for running. He likes running, always has, even in the desert. He'd completed the Saharan marathon on six separate occasions and one day, and may it be soon, his nervous English doctor will stop sending him to hospital for yet another heart scan, and just accept that he's fit for his age.

Doctor: 'Your pulse rate is low.'

Abbot: 'Yes, I run. It often is low with runners.'

Doctor: 'Even so.'

Abbot: 'It's been low for many years.'

Doctor: 'Perhaps a check-up would be wise.'

Frustrated Abbot: 'Another one?'

'We just want to be sure.'

'I think we are, aren't we?'

'Feeling okay otherwise?'

'Fine.'

'You seem tense, there could be something more here. Can you locate a specific pain?'

Peter could, but it would have upset the doctor; and like all truly dangerous people, she meant well.

In between hospital visits, he was an Abbot in retirement from the desert, and spoke now with Tamsin Shah, both a Detective Inspector here in East Sussex and his recently discovered niece. Twenty-five years of Peter's life had been spent in the rock and sand of Middle Egypt, where he'd been Abbot of the monastery of St James-the-Less. But life is change and sometimes the change is surprising. Like the nun, he too had a house, a small affair on the seafront in Stormhaven. It had been the unexpected gift of a deceased relation he'd neither heard of nor met; but being homeless in the desert at the time, it was one received with gratitude. He'd now been a resident on the south coast of England for two years and was growing to love the sea, as he'd once loved the sand.

He continued with his reflections on Barnabus Hope, co-director of *Mind Gains:*

'And of course there's a fragility to him that can lend itself to victimisation.'

'Interesting choice of word.'

There's a pause on the phone which some, fearful of the void, might feel obliged to fill. But Abbot Peter is not a member of this society; he can live for days in the void.

'Having said that,' he adds, 'Barnabus is a fine therapist in a wounded healer way. Very fine ... a discerning and kind listener ... he's helped many when the wheels have come off their lives and I can give you his number, if you're seeking help.'

'Me?'

Why else was she ringing?

'You sound shocked.'

'Why would I be seeking help?'

'Everyone needs help sometimes, Tamsin.'

'Only the mad.'

'No, strangely the mad never seek help, have you noticed that? You have to be sane to realise things are not right.'

'How do you mean?'

Infuriatingly, the Abbot's answers lead only to more questions.

'Visit an acute psychiatric unit and you'll not find any there who imagine they need help. Quite the opposite, they're Jesus, Napoleon or some other grandiose concoction. The mad are quite oblivious to their illness or their need.'

'Then everyone is mad.'

'I couldn't have put it better myself.'

A dismissive female laugh comes down the line.

'There's no shame in it, Tamsin. Or aren't Detective Inspectors allowed to be vulnerable?'

The unspoken answer is 'No' and one well-heard by the Abbot.

'You look after your body, Tamsin – so why not also look after your mind?'

'Can we get on?'

'Care of one, without care of the other, has always struck me as perverse. And Barnabus is a good port in a storm. You should speak with him.'

'I'm not sure that will help,' says the police woman.

'How do you know until you've tried?'

'Because he's dead.'

'Who's dead?'

'Barnabus Hope.'

Silence.

'He was found yesterday morning in the office cupboard in Henry House.'

'In the cupboard?'

'Dressed as a clown.'

From a standing start, Peter's imagination slowly creates the scene:

'Dressing as a clown isn't normally fatal.'

'He'd been stabbed … repeatedly …and his skull smashed.'

Further silence.

'And do we know why he was dressed as a clown?'

'I'm coming round to see you now,' she says. No more stupid silences. 'We can discuss it further then.'

'And if it isn't convenient?'

'I'm still coming.'

'I have someone here.'

'Then ask them to leave.'

'I could ask them, but – '

The phone line is dead in his hands. The Detective Inspector is coming to call, while Peter's mind swims with images of a clown in a cupboard, his old friend Barnabus Hope, who'd always hated fancy dress.

Four

Hafiz stood at the centre of the world.

And let us be clear, this was no cheap boast but indisputable fact – and yes, one which brought responsibility. A poet on the edge of the world, dwelling in some smoky cave or dreary wood, will be declared a god for simply being able to write. But at the centre of the world, with everyone so knowing and closet poets themselves, rather more demanding targets were set. He was a wordsmith in a country of wordsmiths.

And if Persia was the centre of the world, then Shiraz was the jewel in its turban. How to describe it? A city of poets, literature and wine – yes, the local grape, named after its home, was really very fine ... though Behrouz must be careful, and Hafiz had told him so, for an excess of wine can make the hand shaky, not helpful in his profession. But that said, this ancient metropolis was a remarkable city and his home – his adopted home, adopted long ago, when brought here as a child, young Shams-Ud-Din, (his former name), from Isfahan. In that sense, the city had not been a choice ... but then few things are. What do we really choose in life?

And until now, it had been a city to be proud of. The equal of Isfahan in trade and grand capital of the Fars region – yes, the river of civic pride ran wide and deep through the streets of Shiraz. But more glorious still was its cultural and artistic magnificence. Was not Shiraz called 'The House of Knowledge' and perhaps even better, 'The Athens of Persia'? And here Hafiz had found powerful patronage, the ruler Shah Shuja no less. He'd also found celebrity and condemnation, affection and hate. Celebrity and affection among the common people, who heard love in his words; and condemnation and hate from those who smelled in his lines the wretched stench of blasphemy – and who wished to stop the evil flow at source. The man thought he was God! What more was there to say? How could he be allowed to live?

So if the poet was a little distracted today, and demanding more from the quill of his copyist Behrouz, this was why, this was the reason, the shadow of the net, a net of harsh orthodoxy, knotted and strong, waiting to drop, trap and entangle him before the final kill. When would it fall? He didn't know. He knew that it would fall and that he'd be caught, but how long did he have?

A wandering Dervish walked past his window, plenty of those around, hovering at the back gates of the rich, holding their kaskuls, their begging bowls, with arms aloft to facilitate donations from upper windows, as they passed. For once, Hafiz offered nothing but pondered instead his journey to this point, to this moment. How had he come to now?

He was noticing such moments more these days, a sign of old age and the uncertainty it brings. Because really, when he thought about it, what else could he have done? That was the opening line of his defence. What else could he have done given that experience, that extraordinary moment of revelation? So was it sane to start punishing himself now – because, if he could go back and live it all again, would he really do it differently? In a way, he'd spent his whole life wondering.

Some called him a fool, understandable of course, and he'd limped ever since the revelation, that was plain to see: a hobbling man is a hobbling man. But the question again: what else could he have done in the face of such beauty? He'd simply had to go mad, there'd been no choice in the matter, just as there'd been no choice in his exile. Ah yes, we should mention the exile. This adopted child of the city was kicked out of Shiraz for a while, expelled from the Athens of Persia, forced to return to Isfahan for a few years – and all because Shah Shuja took offence at a perceived insult and got unreasonably aroused. And, although he'd not been there at the time – this was long long ago – Behrouz still blamed his master.

'You can be rude,' he said, on hearing the story.

'Just so long as I am accurate, Behrouz. If accuracy is rude, then let me be the rudest man on earth.'

And he had been accurate in his own estimation and done nothing wrong unless truth is wrong! If truth was wrong then he was a very bad man for he'd mocked the city's inferior poets, a mocking wholly deserved, they were both talentless and smug, an unpleasant combination – only to discover the Shah was one of their number.

'You should have known,' said Behrouz. 'Everyone in Shiraz is writing that great poem. Draft after draft in the cabinet by their bed, their flying carpet to fame and glory.'

The Shah's punishment of Shams-Ud-Din, son of Baha-Ud-Din, coal merchant, had been instant: he'd been exiled before sunset, not the Shah's finest hour, a ridiculous decision and still stupid in Hafiz' estimation, despite the passing of years. Looking back on his hurried eviction from court, he remembered travelling light, carrying only a candle, an amusing aside he'd used more than once when recounting the story, though sometimes listeners were slow, a candle, travelling light … never explain a joke.

It was a great shock at the time, oh yes! At the time, his exile was the collapse of his world and the end of everything, he'd been quite sure of that in a dust storm of youthful self-pity. Yet now, all these years later, it was a barely remembered thing. And if it was remembered, it was remembered only for its irrelevance, as an event entirely dwarfed by beauty, by cruel beauty … well, his 'uncomfortable marriage to cruel beauty' to give the story in full, and the reason why death is a favour to us.

'So how did it happen?' Behrouz had once asked him, because Hafiz spoke of this moment in so many ways and on so many occasions that you had to ask in the end, if you wished to understand the man.

'I remember the force,' he replied, and as he spoke, he felt it again, the force of her dragging him in shock to the altar, that's how it happened, a boy made helpless by her presence. And with Behrouz scribbling again – sunset tomorrow was his deadline – there was time for reminiscence if he dared, and if he was brave; for sometimes one must be brave to look back, to return to the left long ago, for it was not always left in happiness. And even now, he could feel her; feel the quivering and madness in his bones.

So let the remembering begin, because God knows, he'd tried to be orthodox. While his teenage friends drank sherbet on street corners, he'd sat at home memorizing the entire Koran, an extraordinary achievement, as he was often told, and he'd done it by listening to his father's recitations, night after night. But when after a long illness his father died, he left a family in debt and a mother fit for little but grief and the harsh judging of others. His two elder brothers left Shiraz to find work and escape the judging, while Shams and his mother moved in with his uncle. Things had changed. He was now the provider of income – when he wasn't at school – taking an evening job in a bakery.

And the stage was set for the great revelation, when …

A loud banging on the door! Hafiz is jerked back to the present. Bang, bang! Angry voices outside. It's the lovers of orthodoxy demanding entry. Bang, bang! They must not see Behrouz and his copying, this is his first thought.

'Behrouz!' he whispers as loud as whispering permits.

He would get rid of them, tell them to call back. This was just a skirmish; the war was to come.

Five

Stormhaven
Six months earlier

'The Feast of Fools,' said Frances, 'is based on the Roman festival of Saturnalia, Barney.'

'I don't want you to call me Barney,' thought Barnabus.

Frances Pole and Barnabus Hope were co-directors of the *Mind Gains* health clinic but he didn't want her to call him 'Barney' and he needed to say something rather than just think something. Thinking something was not a great act of courage in the circumstances, and the circumstances were getting on his nerves. The reduction of his name was presented as affection, but never felt consensual, had the feel of rape about it, something about power, about becoming what she wanted him to be. She'd call him Barney and he'd have to accept it – or be regarded as 'way too sensitive, Barney Boy!'

Frances continued to explain: 'It was in medieval Europe that it became known as the Feast of Fools. You're familiar with that, I presume?'

Frances Pole was forty-ish, had short hair, polished skin, silk scarf, tight trousers and a penchant for the leather jackets which often accompany mid-life crisis. And here she was in lecture mode, which Barnabus, on this occasion, would allow. It was what she did and he could never do.

Barnabus was happiest sitting alone with a client, this was his strong hand. His weak hand was lecturing people and being a salesman, promoting the *Mind Gains* clinic to the world outside, the purpose of this current meeting. Frances seemed to have it all sorted anyway. Could it be – and here was a thought - that she'd make a better administrator than a therapist? The idea had often crossed his mind.

'I have heard of the Feast of Fools,' he said. 'Wasn't it the time when social norms were reversed for a night?'

'Correct, Barney.'

Barney again.

'So I won't despair of you completely!' she said.

Why would she despair of him at all? He was always on trial with Frances, that's how it felt.

'You do have a negative worm inside you,' he said.

'Barney, don't get moody on me. I was complimenting you if anything!'

'Really?'

'In the Graeco-Roman world, the festival of Saturnalia, as you say, was characterised by role reversals and complete behavioural licence. Role-playing, mask-wearing or "guising" as they called it, rampant gambling, over-eating, over-drinking, over-everything – imagine it!'

'These days it's called "Christmas".'

But with notes in hand and spectacles applied, Frances was driving the idea on: 'In what Horace called "The December Liberty", slaves were treated to banquets usually reserved for masters and allowed to show disrespect while remaining exempt from punishment.'

'I can't imagine that.'

'How do you mean?'

'I'm just wondering how it worked.'

'I don't see your problem.'

Frances didn't see other people's problems, which he felt was an unfortunate trait in a therapist.

'Well, you can't just put the genie back in the bottle.'

'Why not?'

Barnabus smiled. There were plenty of genies bottled up in Frances, each gasping for air.

'Do you seriously imagine that last night's barbs were all forgotten the morning after? Imagine it, Frances: you're a dishwasher and you've called your boss vain, pompous and insecure over dinner, because they are – and the following morning it's somehow all fine and dandy? It may happen in a parallel universe but not on planet earth. Very few of us forget, particularly the powerful.'

Frances wished to get back to the point – and the point was saving *Mind Gains* from early extinction.

'The thing is, Barnabus – and this is our point of entry – it's an evening that creates this arena for psychological disturbance, for the breaking of established behavioural patterns.'

'I can see that's possible.'

'I mean, think of the material there for the therapist!'

'I'm never short of material, to be honest. And I'm now remembering, from some dark corner of my mind, that not every Roman was keen on the idea.'

'Pliny?'

'Yes, that's the man.'

'Pliny would lock himself in a secluded part of his villa throughout the festival – a fact you remembered, Barney, because like him, you're a killjoy.'

'Just a different joy perhaps, Frances. Quiet joy is not the same as no joy.'

'So you say.'

Barnabus decided on a further observation:

'I know you have to binge, Frances, seek the path of alcoholic annihilation – but it's not true of us all.'

'This isn't a therapy session, Barnabus.'

'Who said it was?'

She closed her notebook and put it back in the drawer.

'We're going to use the name, going to call it "The Feast of Fools".'

'This is your idea for publicity?'

'It's a therapy package, Barney, a promotional one-off. It'll get us some local press, get people talking about us and, my God, how we need that!'

'We do need something.'

'So we offer one session for participants before the evening, live the evening itself and then offer one session after the event, to work with the material that came up. It's brilliant!'

'So it's an evening of disguise, social chaos and alcohol.'

'Indeed. But with one wickedly demonic addition.'

'What's that?'

'The Lord of Misrule.'

'You've lost me.'

'You didn't know about the Lord of Misrule?'

'No.'

'The most important figure at the Feast of Fools! The evening subverted the ordinary rules of life, but the whole affair was conducted by a Master of Ceremonies, the Lord of Misrule, the purveyor of darkness.'

'Sounds a little disturbing.'

'They were disturbing, Barney, with the power to order anyone to do anything during the Feast!'

'Interesting and dangerous in equal measure. What a fine role for any psychopath in our midst.'

'I don't know about that. Most just used the position to mock their masters.'

'While others no doubt used it to abuse the weak.'

Barnabus wasn't sure he liked the Lord of Misrule.

'He's just another ambiguity in the mix, Barney, another source of confusion and alarm.'

Barnabus nodded.

'And how is this Lord chosen?'

'By lot.'

'So it could be anyone.'

'Indeed.'

The idea for a Feast of Fools seemed both brilliant and irresponsible, mainly the latter. But beyond sticking cards in newsagents' windows, or paying for a full-page spread in the *Sussex Silt*, he didn't have a better one.

'You couldn't sell a drink in a desert,' his mother had once said, so how on earth was he to sell mental health in Stormhaven?

And then there were the financial pressures. They'd bought Henry House at a reasonable price – more reasonable than they dared expect – but they had to be paying their way within the year, or give the whole thing up and go back to … well, Barnabus wouldn't be going back anywhere. He was a Non-Qualified Teacher whose qualification period had just run out. If he wanted to teach, he'd have to start the training all over again. *Mind Gains* just had to work.

'And did you have any dates in mind?' he asked.

Frances clearly had.

'Saturnalia was celebrated at the Winter solstice in December, but that's no good for us – it would just get lost in Crimbo.'

Barnabus winced.

'So I wondered about Halloween night, something to give it a little edge: the time of chaos in heaven, when danger stalks the earth.'

'Beats trick or treating … just.'

'Oh come on, Barney Boy, let's have some human enthusiasm here! Your name's Hope not Despair!'

Barnabus said he was happy to proceed with the idea. A bit of a gimmick but harmless enough, and who knew what might arise from it? 'Not even God can steer a stationary car,' as his old vicar said. So why not drive the car recklessly and see where we get?

'I'm happy to handle the sessions, Frances, if you look after the organisation of the Feast.'

He felt the need to go, the need to be moving, to be somewhere else, away from here and away from Frances … the sea air of Stormhaven would be nice and he moved towards the office door.

Frances: 'I'll do better than that: I'll instruct Bella in the matter.'

'Who's Bella?'

His departure is postponed.

'I've been a little naughty, Barney,' says Frances, as she mimes slitting her throat. 'The *Mind Gains* clinic has a new administrator!'

'What?'

'Yes, and before you say anything, she's going to be just what we need, I know it.'

Barnabus finds a chair and sits down.

'You've employed someone without my knowledge?'

'Barney, don't take it all so seriously! Lighten up!'

'I'm noting you telling me to do something you wish you could do yourself.'

'Look, she just rang me up and offered herself – along with her fantastic CV, I might add, and we could do with one or two of those.'

This was a veiled attack, without much veil. Barnabus had only a limp diploma in counselling from a year-long course in Brighton. It wasn't the Institute of Psychiatry, not a qualification on any brass plaque in Harley Street.

Frances continued: 'And I knew if we didn't snap her up, someone else would very quickly.'

'She sounds like the messiah.'

'There's no need to be bitter.'

'Why not? I feel it's the least I can do in the circumstances.'

'And you've been away, of course.'

'Only for a week.'

'Life goes on.'

'As does recruitment apparently. How are we going to pay her?'

'Trust me, Bella will be excellent.'

'And my question about pay?'

'She seemed to know all about us.'

This puzzled Barnabus.

'All about us? No one knows all about us. We barely exist.'

'She gets it, that's the thing. She just gets *Mind Gains.* And she'll free us to do what we do best.'

Was this the first time Barnabus scented danger? Possibly. And now he was thinking of Abbot Peter, though he wasn't sure why. How strange that their lives had crossed once again amid the peeling paint and seagull cries of Stormhaven. After all, they'd first met years ago beneath the blazing desert sun, in the rocky arms of the monastery of St James-the-Less.

'And what do we do best?' asked Barnabus. 'I've temporarily forgotten.'

'We rid people of their demons.'

'I don't believe in them.'

'You will after the Feast of Fools!'

Six

And news of the Feast of Fools did reach the people of Stormhaven, though the idea was not always greeted with warmth. Virgil Banna-ford heard about it from a friend, because he was having trouble with his marriage. It was going the same way as every relationship had gone in Virgil's life: Suzanne didn't seem to understand him anymore, leading to excruciating conversations:

'You can't even look at me, Virgil,' she'd said.

'Not true.'

'It is true.'

It was true. He couldn't look at Suzanne.

'You look at Emily, you can manage that,' she added.

'She's my daughter, for God's sake!'

'And I'm your wife.'

'I know.'

'You're supposed to be able to look at your wife.'

Virgil knew Suzanne might say that, and yes, you ought to be able to look at your wife, it's expected, a traditional view of marriage and he was all for tradition – but she was making it pretty damn impossi-ble.

'You used to be able to look at me,' she said.

What could Virgil say? There had been a time when he could look at nothing else, when Suzanne was everything to him and he'd been everything to her.

'So why is it so hard to look at me now?'

He couldn't really say why, merely confirm it was so. And this wasn't ideal. So Virgil had moved out of the family home – well, he was pushed really, that's how he saw it, and now lived a mile away but visited twice a week for Emily-time: tea, bath and bedtime sto-ries. And Suzanne hoped he'd return, she really did, she liked Virgil, though things were getting worse not better. They now talked through their daughter, through the five-year-old Emily: 'What does mummy mean by that, I wonder?' That sort of thing, and not good for anyone.

Why couldn't Suzanne just love him and think he was brilliant like she used to?

'The courtship was magnificent,' a mystified Virgil had confided to a friend called Justin.

'It usually is,' said Justin.

'But marriage? Marriage feels like one long judgement, she used not to judge me, she used to adore me!'

'And you her, no doubt.'

Virgil adored anyone who adored him.

'And what happened to the sex?' he continued.

Justin waited to be told.

'I mean, it isn't about the sex, Justin – well, not all about the sex, but it's a sort of barometer, isn't it? I mean, the old sex bit matters somewhat!'

'You need to see someone, Virgil.'

'You mean a shrink?'

'Why not?'

'I'm not bloody seeing one of those.'

'*Mind Gains*, it's a new clinic.'

'*Mind Games*? Yes, well that says it all. The last thing I need is any bloody mind games.'

'*Mind Gains*. I read about it in the *Silt*.'

'*The Sussex Silt?* That rag? You're not selling it to me, Justin.'

'They're organising a Feast of Fools, along the lines of the old medieval practice – which being an historian, you ought to know all about.'

'Feasting, boozing, dressing up and the inversion of social norms for one night of the year.'

'Plus free therapy, before and after.'

'A strange mix.'

'Maybe, but what's to lose?'

Virgil thought about Emily. He could walk out on an ungrateful, griping woman – but his daughter?

'*Mind Gains,* you say?'

'I don't know if they're any good.'

Justin was back-peddling slightly.

'Therapy is run by the mad for the mad,' declared Virgil. 'You pay someone to tell you how rotten you are – don't need it!'

Justin was losing interest. He'd done his best, but Virgil, as ever, was all over the place and stubborn in his dysfunction. He'd known him since their Eton days and he hadn't changed, still the same ball of confused and garrulous energy.

'So where are they, the *Mind Games* people? Lewes probbers! They like that sort of nonsense in Lewes. Is it Lewes?'

'Stormhaven – well, Henry House.'

Virgil went quiet.

'Are you all right?' asked Justin.

'Fine, fine!'

'Another drink?'

Silence was so rare with Virgil, you noticed it when it appeared.

'Might give it a try,' he said.

'The wine?'

'No, I mean the other thing.'

'Mind Gains?'

Virgil nodded.

'I think it's the Halloween weekend,' said Justin, surprised. 'So it could be a treat!'

'And if it's a trick, I'll bloody murder them … a seasonal murder by the sea.'

Seven

The seventeen-year-old Shams-Ud-Din, schoolboy and breadwinner, had returned home in shock, elation and terror. And one thing was certain amid the collapse of everything else: nothing in his life had prepared him for such beauty. And another thing, for these were confusing times: nothing would ever be the same again, absolutely nothing, so all in all, not an insignificant evening for young Shams, with two astounding certainties catapulted into his life by Shakh-e Nabat – yes, he now at least knew her name. Well, he knew more than that. He knew of her beauty and knew where she lived, so that was three things he knew, three more than a couple of hours ago. But if that was clarity, the rest of his life was confusion. What now to do with the religion he'd faithfully learned and followed? And what now to do with the sweet girl to whom he was engaged? For the past year, these had been the twin pillars of his life, the pillars of every young man's life. But they'd collapsed in less than a moment, dissolved by the presence of a woman who did not say a word, nor acknowledge him in any way at all.

What had happened? The desire to make sense of no sense had him retracing his steps. He'd turned up for work at the bakery after a dull day at school. He'd hung around for an hour doing not very much, and had then been sent to the rich quarter of the city to deliver some Barbari bread to a new customer – and gone gladly, because he preferred work to standing around. He'd arrived there at dusk, elegant streets, different from his, and approached the house, thinking of something, he couldn't remember what. She'd stood in the porch – the woman in question – looking across the Musalla Gardens, but made no move as he climbed the steps and left the Barbari bread on the table beside her. There must have been a moment when he noticed her, a point in time when he perceived her green eyes, elusive scent, flawless skin and the serene life beneath the skin. And then suddenly, nothing he'd ever known meant anything anymore. His legs buckled and his arms locked as he placed the bread by her side. The metal tray seemed to crash and bang unnecessarily, how could he be so clumsy? And then a loaf fell to the ground and he sweated with embarrassment as he returned it to the tray, muttering to himself and perhaps to her.

Would she now turn and greet him? He fervently hoped not, while wishing she would. But she never moved, why would she, no movement at all, perhaps a slight glance towards him as he made his awkward exit, his body disturbed with the noise of passion and awe.

'You look like you've seen a ghost,' said his mother, as he crept in later.

He'd walked and walked and then walked some more, knowing only the chaos of his heart. He'd returned to the bakery, declared himself ill and been sent home. His boss had also said he looked like a ghost, so he must look like a ghost, not that anyone had ever seen one. So he looked like something that no one had ever seen.

'Just a late delivery,' he said to his mother. 'I went to the rich quarter.'

'What was it like?'

The rich quarter would not be well known to the widow of a bankrupt coal merchant.

'Wonderful,' he said.

'Don't start imagining money will make you happy.'

She imagined this every day.

'I wasn't.'

'All those big houses. It can turn a young man's head.'

'Not mine.'

'You'll never be rich.'

'I'm the richest man on earth.'

'I hope you haven't been drinking.'

*

'Do you believe in love at first sight, Muhammed?'

Muhammed Attar was the only person Shams-Ud-Din could ask. And it was a question that needed asking, such was the inner turmoil.

'Love is a ridiculous word, Shams-Ud-Din – though you may speak of beauty.'

'I speak of both.'

'Then you are too confused to speak of either.'

Muhammed Attar was like that: unforgiving of human emotion and profoundly suspicious of passion. God help Gulalai, his wife! Shams could imagine it:

'I love you, Muhammed!'

'And I contemplate you too, Gulalai.'

28

A seller of fruit and perfume, Muhammed was a quiet man 'who kept himself to himself', as they always say of the odd; and a man who invited no one beyond the shop front of his life. His love of privacy had created its own set of opinions on the streets, most opting for 'dullard' or 'idiot' – descriptions they'd shout down the street and then run.

'And what is an idiot?' he'd once asked Shams, as a further insult hung in the dry air.

Shams had thought carefully and replied by saying that an idiot was someone who was stupid, adding hastily that he didn't think Muhammed was stupid or an idiot ... even if others said that he was.

'It is a word from ancient Greece' said Muhammed, stacking the purple grapes with care.

'Really?'

How did a fruit and perfume seller know about Greece? But then this was the Athens of Persia.

'A word used by the Greeks to describe a private person uninvolved in public affairs.'

This seemed strange to Shams.

'Why is such a man an idiot?'

'The Greeks thought, and not without reason, that a free man who took no part in politics, who failed to interest himself in his own present and future, was stupid, an idiot.'

Shams could find no polite way out of this conversation, for if this was an idiot – a man who took no interest in politics or public affairs – then yes, Muhammed was truly described. He didn't get out a great deal and was not in the front row at public meetings – or indeed any row. Muhammed seemed to sense his line of thought:

'But what if public affairs are themselves mad?' asked Muhammed. 'Who is the idiot then, eh?'

Shams thought he must answer, but it turned out he didn't – for it was a rhetorical question. Shams had never heard of such a thing but learned of it that day: a rhetorical question is a question that demands awe but no answer. This was definitely an idea he could use in his poetry.

Oh yes, he was becoming a poet. He wasn't telling his friends, but he was now writing poetry, and idiot or otherwise, he liked Muhammed, the only adult to listen to him as he grew up. Never a father-figure of the warm, loud and hearty type – he wasn't cold, just not hearty; but always there when his own father died, a significant rip in the fabric of his young life. They would sometimes talk as he washed fruit or sniffed the perfume. And then one day he'd met him on the banks of the Ruknabad river, but when he greeted the fruit seller, Muhammed had hurried on, saying they must not be seen talking here ... as if he was scared of something or someone.

Today, however, his question to Muhammed was simple: 'So what must I do?'

His house had been burgled, he said, and his sanity stolen by the beauty of Shakh e-Nabat. So what must he do?

'Go home and carry on with your life,' said Muhammed.

'And if I can't?'

'You can.'

'No, I can't.'

'What do you mean, you can't?'

'I mean I can't!'

Muhammed winced a little at the passion displayed. But the boy continued:

'I cannot eat, I cannot sleep – and I have begun to write poems about her.'

Muhammed winced again, a deeper pain.

'Poems?'

'Poems!'

'Each of which will give you exquisite embarrassment in later years. God spare us from the poetry of young men.'

But the boy was rather pleased with his work and had even bestowed on himself a new name to accompany this calling.

'I write now under the name of "Hafiz".'

'What's wrong with your own name?'

'We need something more timeless.'

'We?'

There was nothing quite as pompous as literary ambition in the young.

'And you're embarrassed by your family?'

'Not at all, not at all.'

Silence.

'A little perhaps.'

'Hafiz, you say?'

'That is now my name.'

'And a name for those who have learned the Koran by heart.'

'Which I have,' said the boy with strange authority.

Muhammed stared into his eyes, drilling for gold. He then put down the melon he was slicing, looked around the street, up and down, long ways and sideways and ushered the boy beyond the shop front, through the work tent and into the small courtyard beyond. Hafiz had never been this far before. No one had been this far before! He was then guided up some stone steps which led to an upper room with nothing but a few old cushions scattered around the floor.

'Sit,' said Muhammed and Hafiz obeyed.

How strange this was! As if he'd passed from one world to another, as if something had changed between them, as if he could never go back to former things. Muhammed didn't look like an idiot now and Hafiz didn't feel like a boy. It was as if, when he walked past the fruit into the courtyard and climbed the stairs, Shams had become a man.

'Would you like to touch beauty?' asked Muhammed in a matter-of-fact sort of a way.

'Touch her? I would like that more than anything.'

'Then consider the promise of Baha Kuhi.'

'The Master Poet of Shiraz who died in 1050?'

'The same – and keep your voice down.'

'But I have memorised many of his poems!'

Muhammed looked mildly interested.

'I was learning one last night!' added the boy.

'Then consider his promise.'

'His promise?'

'The promise of Baha Kuhi. Now go – Hafiz.'

The boy was confused.

'But what is his promise?'

Eight

Monday morning
3 November

'Do you always leave your front door open?' asked Tamsin.

She stepped thankfully out of the gusting south-westerly, fresh from the Atlantic and God knows where else, into Abbot Peter's simply furnished front room.

'I didn't want you ringing the bell,' said Peter quietly.

Too quietly.

'I'm sorry?'

'The bell. I didn't want you ringing it.'

'Why ever not?'

'Ssshh!'

Tamsin wanted to be noisy now. As soon as someone said 'Ssshh!' she longed only to march around the room playing a trombone. And how bloody typical of Stormhaven to have issues with doorbells – noisy things, disturbing the peace in this seaside graveyard. Tamsin was not a fan of the town, seeing here only a collective loss of the will to live.

'She doesn't mind voices,' said Peter, as he finished cleaning up ash from the fire place with a dust pan and brush. 'But the bell disturbs her.'

'Disturbs who?'

'You're very welcome of course!' said Peter, with a smile. 'Long time no see.'

There followed an awkward hug between the two, neither familiar with the practice. No one hugged in the desert, and the desert had been as near as Peter got to a mother ... and maybe Tamsin was the same. As a girl, she was hugged neither in love nor in pain; love was absent and pain drew only the instruction to get on with it. And this she had done, she'd got on with it with some success, she'd got on with getting on – but she was always uneasy with physical contact. What was the point? And anyway, she'd come here today as a copper, not a niece. She had a murder to solve and this man was going to help her, despite the 'long time no see'.

'Almost a year,' she said in a matter-of-fact manner, putting down her bag. 'Which in uncle/niece relationships is probably not that long,' said Peter.

If there isn't a funeral, just when do family meet?

'Any coffee coming soon?' she asked.

'Just keep your voice down.'

Trombone thoughts again.

'You sound a little flustered, Abbot,' she said playfully.

But beneath the play was a message well-heard by Peter: he was not 'Uncle' today but 'Abbot'. She was definitely here on business and not for the first time.

*

It was just eleven months ago that she'd arrived as an unknown on his doorstep and left him stunned with the revelation that he had a niece ... and that it was her. For reasons of messy history, Peter's family was a scattered community, fragments of which could be found all over the world; all knowing much, but all ignorant of each other. And without much ceremony, Tamsin had drawn him into the sad case of Stormhaven's murdered vicar, the Reverend Anton Fontaine, crucified in his vestry. She'd stayed with Peter for the duration of the case and, on leaving, had promised to remain in contact. Well, you do make promises as you leave – otherwise how would you ever get away?

'Speak soon!' she'd said.

But time passes, promises fade, eleven months sped by and he'd heard nothing from her, until she rang him half an hour ago to pester him with questions about the *Mind Gains* clinic and announce the death of Barnabus Hope. She'd said she was coming round, and now here she was on this grey November morning, demanding coffee and probably something else.

'I see you haven't had the decorators in?' she said, placing herself down in the one comfortable chair, left by the previous owner.

'Not to my knowledge.'

'And furniture still provided by Beachcomber Furnishings?'

This was an accurate observation from the detective inspector. There were persistent echoes of the shingle beach in the house, for the simple reason that most of the furniture had come from there, in one way or another; but not the black buggy in the corner, which was clearly new.

'What's that?' asked Tamsin.

She wanted to get on with the murder. SOCOs were finishing at Henry House even now, she needed to be there herself, she wanted Abbot Peter to be there also, she'd get to that – but first, another mystery to solve.

'It's called a "buggy", I think,' said Peter. 'Don't ask me why, but it's a remarkable contraption, never seen anything like it.'

There was a little sigh across the room.

'You're not a father are you?' asked Tamsin.

'Me?'

'I wouldn't think the worse of you.'

'Is that possible?'

'You were a long time in the desert, after all. Who could blame you if you wanted to make up for lost time, wild oats and all that?'

Wild oats?

'I'm not a father, no.'

'Why am I disappointed?'

'Just a novice in the repulsive baby-care industry. The more unnecessary the item, the more expensive it is, as far as I can see. It's a new world to me.'

'The Bedouin branch of Mothercare has yet to open.'

'Indeed,' said Peter, enjoying a digestive. 'How have they survived for the last seven thousand years?'

'And why's it here?'

'The buggy?'

'The buggy, yes.'

'Where else would Poppy sleep?'

'Poppy?'

'It's a rather long story.'

'Then feel free to edit savagely.'

'I'm part of a local fostering network.'

'Sounds like an exposé waiting to happen. Does the *Sussex Silt* know?'

'Not proper fostering, of course.'

'It's getting worse.'

'I just give young mums the chance to get out for the day, whether for shopping, a job interview, that sort of thing. I have Poppy twice a week to enable Sarah to work for a business diploma.'

'Sarah?'

'Nice girl.'

'All very cosy.'

'Only to a mind soaked in the fearful juice of suspicion.'

'I need to talk with you.'

Tamsin's interest in toddler tales had waned; it was time for work.

'She's just gone down, so we have an hour or so,' said Peter. 'As long as we talk quietly.'

And so they did, talking in the warm, while outside the gusting south-westerly blew, and above them, circling the white cliffs, a seagull rested on the wind, wings strong but still, its only work to rest in the strength of another.

Nine

Earlier the same day, Monday 3 November – three days on from a bloody Halloween – various conversations had occurred in Storm-haven, the first when a man had forgotten his lunch when leaving for work … though lunch was hardly his greatest concern.

'You've forgotten your lunch, Gerald!'

'Have I?'

Gerald appears in the kitchen doorway.

'Wake up, dearie,' says Kate, his wife of twenty-three years. 'Get some sort of a grip.'

Gerald picks up his sandwich box, while Kate swans around like a resentful prima donna when make-up is taking too long. He is awake, so why does she say that? He had to be awake with four maths classes to face, as well as a parents' evening; so he's wide awake, awake enough to survive, which will make it a good day – survival equals good for Gerald. But neither equations nor parents are the matter now on his mind.

'I put an apple in,' says Kate.

Gerald is disappointed.

'No bananas?'

'I'll get some. Apples are better for you anyway. Do you know how many calories there are in a banana? It's why tennis players eat them.'

What has that got to do with anything? He's a teacher not a tennis player. Kate can go hang, he loves her in a way – but sometimes … ?

'How did they find out?' he asks.

The tidying prima donna knows what he means and pauses for a moment. This isn't a tennis question.

'We've talked about it and it's sorted, Gerald.' she says. 'End of discussion. End of.'

'How?'

'Let's just say that the Feast of Fools therapist proved very help-ful.'

Gerald looks through her, motionless.

'Well go on then,' she says, 'you'll be late!'

Ye gods, get yourself together, Gerald! This is what she's thinking. But Gerald is struggling to get himself together … not easy at the best of times and this is one of the worst, for while the discussion is over for Kate, 'end of' as she says, the fear for Gerald is just begin-ning.

Beginning all over again …

Ten

'He just said he was going out,' she said.

'And you didn't ask where?'

Why had she not asked where? As his mother, she should have asked where he was going.

'He just said he had to collect something from a friend's house before school.'

'And you didn't ask which friend? Or what he might be collecting?'

Rebecca felt bad for not asking, she should have asked Michael where he was going, but then again, why should she have asked him?

'He's seventeen, Ezekiel, I don't feel I can just – '

'Assert some discipline?' came the sharp reply.

Sometimes Ezekiel despaired of his young wife, and not that young anymore … yet not learning, not growing in the Lord, this was his view. As pastor of the church he needed a mature and godly wife, an obedient wife under his headship, certainly, but also a stronger force for discipline in the home. Michael, their son, had left the house while Ezekiel had been at a prayer breakfast with the church elders. This is what he'd discovered on his return. And it was unusual behaviour for the boy, a committed student at school and a role model in diligence, which his elder sister had never been. Michael had even preached at Sunday worship when he was only sixteen years old, never done by anyone in living memory in the church … and many had commented on how well he spoke.

'The apple has not fallen far from the tree, Ezekiel!'

That was one comment from the congregation, and while guarding against the sin of pride, Satan's sin, Ezekiel had high hopes for young Michael.

And before this news, the news of the boy's unexplained departure, it had been a good morning for Ezekiel, a time of blessed assurance among fellow believers, folk who shared his certainties. The Feast of Fools had been a strangely unsettling evening, a great shock of course, as the ways of the ungodly are; but he'd done what he had to do, he'd had no choice, though what to do now, he was unsure.

Eleven

So what's the problem?' asks Frances Pole, co-director of *Mind Gains* but presently denied access to her place of work by a young policeman approaching puberty.

'There's no entry, madam,' he says.

He's keeper of the gate this Monday morning with clear instructions in his head: 'No one to be allowed in to Henry House – understand, Brightwater?'

That's what the sergeant had said, and he'd made it clear to the lady: no entry.

'I can see there's no entry,' she says. 'But why?'

Police tape is stretched across the gates and her car parked by the side of the road.

'I'm afraid I'm unable to say at present, madam.'

He didn't know, hadn't a clue and hadn't thought to ask.

'I work here,' she said.

'Not today, you don't,' he said, before realising his mistake, before realising she deserved better than his playground response. But then he'd only been a policeman – 'Little Barry, a policeman, would you believe!' – for six weeks, and you don't suddenly know how to do these things, because he'd never had this conversation before, never in his life, never been at a crime scene – and he'd blanked out the role plays at training school for good reason. He also quite fancied this forty-ish woman, large earrings and all, dressed all trendy, too good for Newhaven, his home town, so he felt sheepish and asked about the purpose of her visit, to which she replied, 'to work', at which point he called over to his better-looking colleague:

'She works here, Sarge!'

The better-looking colleague indicated he'd be over in a minute, and the constable, PC Barry Brightwater, indicated to madam that his sergeant would be over in a minute which madam already knew, while noticing Bella, her new administrator, twenty yards away in deep conversation with another policeman ... well, not deep, because Bella didn't do deep, but she did do persistent, and she was persisting with them now, not giving up, half coy little girl, half Miss Pushy.

And then noise on the drive way.

'Stand back please!'

Scene of crime tape was being wound back to allow a police car out of Henry House, the small crowd scattering, allowing a change of partners, PC Brightwater now dancing with his sergeant.

'Who was that?' asked Brightwater, watching the car drive through the gates and head west.

'DI Shah,' said the sergeant.

'Oh,' said Brightwater, who still didn't know who anyone was.

'Tamsin Shah. Cold bitch but tasty.'

PC Brightwater was over the moon with this banter.

'So she's handling the case, is she?'

The sergeant nodded, young himself and grateful for the naivety of this PC who rendered him a battle-hardened veteran by comparison.

'So she works here?' says the sergeant, looking across at Frances.

'Yes, Sarge.'

Frances is now talking with Bella, seeking information:

'So do you know what this is all about?'

'They wouldn't tell me.'

'No clues?'

'I think it's a burglary,' says Bella. 'It must be a burglary.'

'But they didn't say that?'

'No, they didn't say that, but no one's been here since Friday, so how could it be anything else?'

'That's true,' and as an afterthought Frances adds that everything was fine when she locked up after the Feast of Fools.

The events of last Friday had left things slightly frosty between the two of them, unresolved obviously, but this wasn't the place to sort all that out.

'Apart from Barnabus,' says Bella.

'Sorry?'

Frances had been eyeing the sergeant. She had an eye for authority ... and attractive men.

'Well, he might be in there.'

'I suppose.'

'Perhaps something's happened to him,' says Bella, who looks more concerned than the co-director of *Mind Gains*.

'I don't know what his plans were for the weekend,' says Frances, vaguely.

'He didn't like the feast very much – *fact*.'

It feels like a dig.

'Perhaps he should have pulled himself together and got on with it. Anyway, how would you know, you weren't even there!'

'Hello ladies,' says the better-looking colleague. 'My constable tells me that you both work here.'

His eyes rest happily on Frances, who confirms that they do, as the car carrying DI Shah and Chief Inspector Wonder makes its smooth way from Henry House to the police HQ in Lewes.

'Well, I've seen some bodies in my time,' says the Chief Inspector, 'but never a clown. Not much for him to smile about, eh?'

'Isn't the clown smile just painted on?'

'Never liked them as a child,' says Wonder, 'always frightened me those clowns, can't be doing with masks.'

They travel on in silence. The Chief Inspector could share his childhood fears with Tamsin, but she wouldn't be reciprocating. Never give ammunition to anyone, certainly not your colleagues … and she used the term loosely. Her childhood fear was not being as good and brilliant as her mother expected her to be, but what did that matter now? All that mattered now was the case in hand, the murder of a clown at Henry House, recently acquired by a therapy clinic called *Mind Gains*.

The case had arrived on her desk yesterday. A morning call from a phone in the house had alerted police to a body in the office cupboard. No idea who made the call, a disguised voice, 'a bit croaky' said the desk sergeant.

'Bring in all known frog impersonators,' said Tamsin.

'Yes, Ma'am,' said the desk sergeant before realising.

But the body was there right enough, a clown without the comedy, sprawled sideways, smashed skull – there'd been no Sunday lunch for forensics.

'So we'll need to ask some questions about Barnabus Hope,' said the Chief Inspector, offering fatherly wisdom to his young DI. He was old enough to be her father, though perhaps best that he wasn't, given some of the thoughts in his head.

Tamsin didn't answer. Wonder may have meant well with his advice, but frankly, she didn't need to be told that questions would have to be asked about Barnabus Hope. What did he think she was going to do? Write him a get well card?

There was something she did need, however – or rather, someone.

'I'm going to ask Abbot Peter to be Special Witness again.'

'The monk fellow?'

'He knows this place apparently.'

'The *Mind Gains* thingummy?'

'He's a trustee.'

'Well, it's your call of course, Tamsin –. '

'I know,' she said, before he made it to the 'but'.

'But whether a monk can seriously be of assistance to a modern police force – .'

'He can.'

'Not sure he was much of a help last time.'

'He helped.'

He did more than help, but the Chief Inspector needn't know that.

'Well, if you say so – .'

'I do.'

'It's your case, your reputation.'

Tamsin Shah was aware of the fact, as the Chief well knew and he saw the fear. He could still frighten her a little, so he hadn't completely lost it.

'Just keep me informed,' he said as the car pulled into HQ.

Twelve

The brick through the window was a surprise – they're always a bit of a shock. But the most surprising fact was that no one had thrown one before. The *Sussex Silt*, a popular but demonised local paper, was not short of enemies. And neither was the demon who ran it.

Martin Channing, editor, was a pink-shirted demon today and sitting with his deputy editor, Rupert Brooke ... not the poet, though perhaps he'd like to have been. Rupert had always possessed a turn of phrase and won endless essay competitions in his teens, when the world lay at his feet. But that was a long time ago, and things had changed. Suffice to say that for Rupert Brooke, the *Silt* was not how he wanted to be remembered, not at all; while the man opposite him – an old friend from Fleet Street – seemed quite uninterested in legacy.

As Channing once said: 'I've never understood how being remembered could possibly interest the dead!'

Martin Channing wanted only to be busy with something, preferably five things – juggling, shocking and earning in equal measure ... like a child terrified of being bored and of his pocket money being late.

'You're a literary snob,' he'd once said to Rupert, when he'd turned his nose up at a tasteless story.

'I'll take that as a compliment in this particular office.'

Even a demon can be kind, however, for Martin had rescued Rupert from the financial oblivion of publishers' small advances, for one last and moderately well-paid hurrah in the newspaper trade; and Rupert had been briefly grateful. There were newspapers and newspapers, however, and then there was the *Silt*.

'I'd sooner read toilet paper than the *Silt,*' groaned Rupert's new lady friend, president of the Chaucer Society in Lewes.

'The sport isn't so good,' replied Rupert.

If you didn't laugh, you cried, because something died in him every day of his working life at the *Silt* ... while something also paid the mortgage. Rupert was taking self-hate to new heights.

'You were keen to run something on the Feast of Fools at the *Mind Gains* place,' says Rupert. 'This weekend, wasn't it?'

Martin nods but looks mysterious. Rupert says:

'You did go, I presume?'

And then the brick, smashing through the office glass, a shattering rudeness, narrowly missing Cheryl the receptionist, who screams loudly while Martin and Rupert make for the savaged window.

No one out there ... or no one they could see. There must be someone in the shadows, someone who doesn't like them. Who cares, though? You give the people a local paper they actually read, and this is how they repay you! Martin, at least is thinking this.

'Oh yes, I went to the Feast of Fools,' he says, as they return to their desks, hoping Cheryl will pull herself together and ease up on the hysterics. 'Unusual evening ... really, very unusual.'

'In what way?'

Thirteen

Tamsin and Peter drove in silence through the lashing rain of this Monday afternoon, 3 November, no words muddying the air until Tamsin had to speak:

'I can't believe a murder investigation has been held up by a baby's sleep routine.'

Huge frustration.

'There was her lunch as well,' said Peter calmly. 'Where would you be without sleep and food?'

Trees bent and swayed in the whipping wind, leaves ripped from their grasp and sent swirling in the sodden air. Their destination was Henry House, a fine Elizabethan manor on the edge of Stormhaven. It had recently become the home of *Mind Gains*, a new venture in the well-being of the mind: 'Mental wealth is the best investment of all,' as their slogan reminded everyone.

And Peter's presence in the car was quite straightforward and not in any way a mystery: he sat here because he'd said 'Maybe'. That's how it had started nearly a year ago, and he'd said it again today. Tamsin had knocked on his door, asked him to take the role of Special Witness in a police murder investigation and he'd said 'Maybe'.

'It's like last time,' she said.

'Remind me about last time.'

He remembered the case, but not the exact nature of his employment.

'It's an idea being trialled by the Sussex police.'

'That bit I remember. You were ground-breakers, I seem to recall bringing the community into the enquiry.'

'Well, nothing's changed. An individual with special knowledge of the murder scene is co-opted onto the investigation. They sign a confidentiality agreement, receive a small allowance and effectively become a detective, under the leadership of the DI handling the case.'

'Which is you?'

'Which is me, yes – who else is there?'

It was a joke … just.

'I'm responsible for finding the murderer of Barnabus Hope and I want you to help me.'

'Well I'm certainly with you in spirit. He was a good man.'

'I'm not interested in that side of things.'

'You mean the good?'

'And I need a little more than your best wishes.'

'You want my very best wishes?'

'Uncle, you know the set-up at *Mind Gains*, you know the deceased and you know your way around the sick world of psychology.'

'The glorious flag of prejudice run boldly up the mast!'

They were driving past wet sheep, seeking shelter in a crowd of soggy wool.

'And you know people,' she added.

'I know no one. My list of contacts is shorter than a rhino's temper.'

'I'm sorry?'

'A rhino's temper – it's very short.'

'Really?' said Tamsin with mock interest – but she wanted this man on her side. 'What I mean is, you know people, you sense their inner … whatever. Most people see from the outside, but you see from the inside. My God, I'm beginning to believe your own publicity.'

'It's a gift I've accepted with great reluctance,' said Peter.

'So will you do it?'

'Do what?'

'Join the investigation as Special Witness?'

'I did enjoy the allowance.'

Peter had happy memories of the brief income.

'It's only small.'

'Not to me.'

'I'm glad you enjoyed it,' said Tamsin, though remembering his home, it was hard to see what he'd spent it on.

'I've never really earned money, you see,' said the Abbot. 'Strange, isn't it? Sixty-one years old and I've never earned a wage. I've been looked after by the money of others, but never earned it myself. So to be handed some bank notes of my very own … '

'I thought in your world everything belonged to God?'

'I now take a cut.'

But would he take the case? Peter was thinking it would be nice to buy Poppy a Christmas treat, he could ask Sarah's advice in the matter, as he wouldn't know where to begin. And something had awakened in him during the last investigation. He'd become a hunter in pursuit of justice and enjoyed the chase. And he'd find pleasure in cornering the killer of Barnabus, who a long time ago, when his brief marriage ended, came to the desert for six months to ponder the emptiness of life – and where better for that than St James-the-Less? Not that Peter had seen much of him while he was there; that wasn't how it worked in the sand. Apart from meal times and work in the monastery garden, Barnabus had spent most of his time in the library reading ancient texts. He'd returned to England with a deep tan, stronger arms and a fresh sense of purpose; but, while he had been happy for the young man's soul, Peter had thought no more about him until six months ago, when a letter arrived out of the blue:

> *'Remember me, Abbot Peter?' it said. 'Barnabus Hope here, brief refugee with you in the desert all those years ago. But would you believe I'm in Stormhaven now? And I'm a shrink!'*

He'd given Peter a number to ring.

'Well, will you?' said Tamsin once again, returning him to the present. 'We don't have much time.'

Fourteen

It was true, they didn't have much time. They were approaching Henry House and, if this was the parting of ways, the time was now. Tamsin had promised him an immediate lift home in another, less comfortable, police car if he decided this wasn't for him.

'You never have much time, Tamsin.'

'So?'

'Time harasses you unduly.'

'It's because I have a job. You should try it one day.'

'Yes.'

'Yes, what?'

'Yes, I will be Special Witness.'

'Good. I knew you would.'

'I proved rather effective last time, as I remember.'

He'd practically solved the case single-handed.

'Last time doesn't exist in my book,' said Tamsin.

'Selective amnesia.'

'There's only now.'

The Abbot was impressed.

'A profound thought, Tamsin.'

'I wouldn't be asking you, though, unless you were some use.'

Some use? Praise indeed from Tamsin. Truly this was the age of miracles and perhaps they'd need them.

For Henry House then came into view.

Fifteen

Henry House seemed unmoved by murder.

'It does spook me a little,' said Tamsin, as she turned the car through the large stone gateway and proceeded slowly up the drive. Dark windows were Tamsin's first thought as the house came into view, a grey-stone silhouette against the cold sky, chimney stacks in threes, classical columns on high. There was something of the Italian renaissance on display; but something else as well, something resistant, a place old enough to make its own rules and not care.

Tamsin continued: 'As one obsessed with the origin of things, I suppose you know its history?'

'I know a little,' said Peter.

This was usually a sign that he knew a great deal.

'Built in the reign of Henry VIII? Or is that too obvious?'

'The obvious is sometimes right.'

And Tamsin liked getting things right.

'Though not on this occasion,' added Peter. 'A little later, around 1590.'

'Elizabeth?'

'Indeed. Henry House is Elizabethan.'

'The one with the ginger hair and white face?'

'Lead-based paint and highly toxic – a fashion accessory for rich women, one which sometimes killed.'

'Everyone has to die of something.'

'But not of make-up, perhaps.'

Henry House sat in four acres of lawn, rhododendron bush and scattered clumps of trees. Beyond such domestication of nature lay the flat lands of sodden field, static cows and horses in muddy coats … and the ravens, of course, hopping awkwardly on the wet lawn, sitting like sentries on the chimney stacks, big winged, black beaks, famous residents of Henry House and recently in the news for killing a lamb in a nearby field. The farmer had told his story to the *Sussex Silt*, and Stormhaven was appalled by the fact that a bird had got to the lamb before they did. The *Silt* had stirred disgust, posting an online petition in favour of a cull of the killer ravens.

'How do ravens kill a lamb?' asked Tamsin.

'They attack the face.'

'They're carnivores?'

'Omnivores.'

'A bird for all seasons?'

'Carrion, insects, berries, mice, food waste, they're survivors. Maybe that's why they were the first animal to be released from Noah's Ark.'

'Or maybe Noah just didn't like them very much,' said Tamsin. 'I don't like them.'

'You'll have to get used to them while here.'

And they would be here a while.

Sixteen

'So we're looking at posh Elizabethan?' said Tamsin, gazing again at the house.

'Very posh, yes. In the sixteenth century a stone house, rather than beam and plaster, spoke of significant wealth. There was in fact very little building towards the end of Henry's reign, for the simple reason he'd bankrupted the country. The once wonderful wool trade was no longer delivering, which left little money for architects' fine schemes.'

'Every cloud and all that.'

'But under Elizabeth, the country's economy began to revive.'

'It takes a woman.'

'Wealth created mainly around farming, certainly in the Storm-haven area, and once again there was cash for building projects like Henry House, named in memory of the dear queen's father.'

'Why would anyone want to remember him?'

'I'm not rushing to his defence.'

'Misogynist pig.'

'Ruling a misogynist nation.'

'Don't we each have to take responsibility for our actions, whatever the era?'

Peter enjoyed Tamsin's rare excursion into moral certitude.

'I always knew it, there's a priest in you!'

'No, there's a judge in me, patrolling the borders of anarchy and order.'

That shut Peter up.

'A very striking image,' he said.

'And that's the trouble with therapy, you see.'

'Oh?'

'No lines – no lines clearly drawn. And you have to have lines.'

Tamsin parked the car alongside two police vehicles. Peter returned to the 'Henry' in the House.

'It was probably a pitch for royal patronage. Perhaps the Rowse family, who built the place, thought the queen would like to see her father honoured and thereby look upon them favourably in some way.'

'Burn the farmer next door for heresy and grant the arse-licking Rowse family his lands?'

'No, that wasn't Elizabeth's style.'

'So what was her style?'

' "I see, and say nothing",' was her motto.'

I see, and say nothing. As Tamsin contemplated the merits of this approach, strengths and weaknesses, the Abbot continued:

'So after 274 burnings under Mary Tudor, when simply being a Protestant was a crime, there were just two burnings in the very long reign of Elizabeth – two Flemish Anabaptists.'

'That is quite a change.'

'There were eleven of them sentenced to death, but she commuted the sentences of the other nine.'

'Not much help to the two who died.'

'Mercy grows slowly.'

'And particularly in Henry House.'

Suddenly they were back with the present.

The entrance to Henry House was its most ornate aspect, all heraldry and ornamentation, and there, beneath the large carving of a Tudor rose, the tasteful bronze of the *Mind Gains* sign. It declared this place a centre for life and health; but not today ... today Henry House was a tomb and a keeper of death. Inside, stashed away in a cupboard, dragged there and dumped, lay the body of Barnabus Hope.

'There's something Dutch about it,' said Tamsin, sighing as she looked through the car window, safe from the rain. With the engine quiet, they both knew this small moment was the calm before the storm.

'It's the curved gables, isn't it? Elizabethan architects clearly holidayed in Amsterdam.'

There was a pause. Tamsin looked at the edifice and felt its resistance again. Near the drain, a raven was picking at the carcass of a rat.

'They deserve each other.'

'Sorry?'

'Nothing. Shall we get to work?'

Act Two

Neurosis is the inability to tolerate ambiguity.

Sigmund Freud

Seventeen

A week before the Feast of Fools
Late October

Barnabus Hope pondered the list of clients given to him by Bella Amal, the new administrator for *Mind Gains*. She'd been appointed in his absence, against his wishes and had been busy ever since, with her straight black hair and slightly flirty skirts for a woman in her late thirties. And then there were the clickety shoes on the marble floor in the hall ... though her dress code was not the issue for Barnabus.

The big news, big in these parts at least, was that the Feast of Fools, grand publicity stunt for the struggling *Mind Gains* clinic, was finally going to happen. The brainchild of co-director Frances Pole and organised by Bella Amal, it was now the moment of truth. Four people had signed up to take part – not quite the numbers they'd hoped for, and not quite the public interest they'd craved. But it was workable and better than had looked likely at one point. After all, there'd been no takers at first, a bleak silence that echoed daily through the dark-wooded rooms and tilting floors of Henry House. Bella, however, had remained a bundle of energy and optimism.

'There's no way we're giving up on this,' she said. 'I think the Feast of Fools is just the best idea.'

Encouraging.

And Bella's confidence had proved a daily reassurance to Frances, and she'd worked tirelessly on the preparations. Whatever else Barnabus felt – and he felt a great deal about her arrival – she was a most efficient administrator. But you needed more than efficiency to stir the people of Stormhaven, this was well known, and at the beginning of September there'd even been talk of dropping the idea.

'You can't have a Feast of Fools if there are no fools,' observed Frances glumly.

Barnabus withheld his amusing reply, with Frances not in the mood.

'God help the good idea conceived in Stormhaven,' she said in despair, 'for it shall be aborted before it is born!'

'We can only do what we can do, Frances,' said Barnabus gently.

Frances was no stranger to self-punishment and he could see her going there now.

'So what are you doing?' she asked aggressively.

'I'm doing what I can do,' said Barnabus.

'With your little diploma.'

Barnabus had looked at her in amazement.

And then two things happened. First, Frances contacted the *Sussex Silt*, the popular if disreputable local paper. On a quiet news day, they'd printed a predictably irreverent piece on the event entitled: 'Therapy clinic wants to make a fool of you!'

And second, Frances decided to offer the experience free of charge.

' "Loss leaders",' that's what supermarkets call them, Barnabus.'

'I'm familiar with the idea.'

'Products sold below cost price, simply to get footfall in the shop. We take the short-term hit to make a long-term splash.'

Within a week, four clients had signed up and a fifth was thinking about it. And then Barnabus had surprised Frances with a remark:

'Therapy is better when people pay,' he'd said.

He and Frances had walked together with their coffee from the large kitchen into the hall and then up the slightly misshapen stairs. They stood now in the gallery, surveying their Elizabethan kingdom. They looked down on the large entrance hall, with its striking black and white marble floor in chess board patterns, while behind them was the Long Room, where the Feast of Fools would take place.

'Much better!' said Frances. 'You can't bank good will.'

'No, I mean it tends to be more healing.'

'More healing? What are you talking about, Barnabus? How does parting with cash help anyone therapeutically – apart from yourself?'

'It's something someone said to me once and I agree with them. Experience shows that people work harder when they've paid money, they value it more.'

'Oh I see.'

Frances felt strangely reassured.

'It doesn't need to be a lot, just something; there's usually more honesty, more risk taking. They don't want to waste their money.'

'And I don't want us to waste our time, Barney, so let's keep our eye on the ball here.'

Brisk change of direction.

'Which particular ball do you have in mind?'

Eighteen

So what did Frances want to say? She wanted to say something and from the locking of her jaw, it was apparently awkward.

'Well, obviously the clients matter, Barnabus.'

'They do – it's a basic principle of therapy, I believe.'

'So the client is king, the client is queen and all that.'

'Indeed.'

'So we're taking that as read.'

'I sense a "but" Frances, so shall we save time and make our way there now?'

'But on this one occasion, more important than all that – . '

'More important than the client?'

'More important than the client, yes, is the publicity for *Mind Gains*.'

There, said it.

'More important than the client is the publicity?'

'Spare me the shocked look, you pompous prick!'

Henry House had been acquired cheaply. An alcoholic doctor had retired to Somerset and wanted to make amends for years of misdiagnosing patients.

'I want to put things right,' he'd said to them. 'And I don't need the money.'

And Henry House was a wonderful space. Downstairs, the house offered a large entrance hall, kitchen, utility space and toilets, two offices, a counselling room and a dark dining room. Upstairs there were four bedrooms, one presently inhabited by Barnabus; a bathroom, another counselling room and the Long Room, the social hub of the old house.

And then there was Bella's little nook. This was more an alcove than a room, a recess in the entrance hall but large enough for her administrative needs. They'd offered her one of the offices but she'd felt it better to be visible for people who arrived. In fact, she'd been quite insistent about that.

'It's best if I see all comings and goings,' she said, and it did make sense. *Mind Gains* had an administrator who missed nothing and no one.

'So you're ready for the clients?' said Frances to Barnabus, draining the last dregs of caffeine from her cup.

'Yes, I see two tomorrow, two the following day and then it's the Feast on Friday.'

'For which preparations are well in hand. Bella's been a marvel.'

She had been very good, there was no argument there.

'And Bella tells me that we're all to look alike,' said Barnabus.

Frances nodded knowingly.

'Very alike indeed.'

'With clown uniforms and voice disguise?'

'Thrilling, isn't it?'

Barnabus was managing to keep his excitement in check.

'At the heart of the Feast of Fools were three things,' she said. 'Disguise, role play and excess. Hopefully we can manage all of those.'

'We can't just meet as the people we are? That's too far-fetched, I presume?'

'Not interesting enough, not for the publicity. You've got to think of the stunt-value.'

'One of Freud's lesser known sayings.'

'Lighten up, Barney! We'll meet not as the people we are but as the people we'd like to be! We'll live out our dangerous fantasies!'

'None of mine include a clown suit.'

'So what do they include?'

'A confidentiality clause.'

'Shame. But imagine if the inner monster was released!'

'That's a genuine health and safety issue.'

It was at this point that Jung suddenly came to life, chirping merrily. The *Mind Gains* budgie, constant resident in the hall, was thought by Frances to be therapeutically helpful.

'Budgerigars are relaxing,' she'd declared, and that was very much that.

Bella had taken to feeding Jung, which was probably just as well, as Frances thought only of the Feast and was presently proclaiming the importance of anonymity, absolutely crucial, Barney, absolutely crucial to the liberation of people from old repressed patterns of relating, do you see that, you must see that?

Barnabus: 'You're beginning to sound like a sociology lecturer from the 1970s.'

'Thank you.'

'It wasn't a compliment.'

'I won't let you be a wet blanket, Barnabus, I really won't!' She was telling him, someone had to. 'Get on board or get out!'

Nineteen

There was a pause as they stood with their empty coffee cups in the gallery of Henry House.

Barnabus: 'I think we both know that my "getting out" would have a significant impact on the clinic.'

'Not as significant as you imagine.'

Barnabus took a deep breath; Frances looked flushed.

'This is perhaps for another time,' he said.

'Another time, yes.'

'For now, we do it – and I will give it my best.'

It was a declaration of peace, after which Frances excitedly declared:

'And as the flier says, "At the Feast of Fools, there are no rules!".'

She sounded like a naughty little girl which explained Barnabus's next remark:

'Rules must oppress you very much, Frances.'

'Well, it is rather fun to break them occasionally – I can be a great rule-breaker, believe me!'

Barnabus did believe her.

'And God knows how these voice-altering pills work,' she said, speeding on. 'Bella's got them from somewhere and they're effective for up to four hours apparently.'

Barnabus did his best with a 'Fancy that!' expression as Frances continued:

'Yes, if what I'm told is true, you and I won't be able to recognise each other!'

'How will we survive?'

'The clown costumes will re-shape us and who knows what we'll sound like?'

'So we'll be able to speak – but sound different?' says Barnabus, seeking clarification.

'That's the shape of it, guys!'

Bella had appeared in her flirty skirt and clickety shoes from the Long Room.

'And height?' asked Barnabus, now the organiser was here and available for questions. 'How on earth do you disguise height, apart from beheading?'

'We did contemplate that,' said Frances, with a knowing smile towards Bella. 'But then we thought we'd give you one last chance!'

'Part equipment, part luck,' said Bella, with a bright-eyed, clever-girl smile. 'There's an online store called *Show Shoes* – they sell shoes that enable you to play with people's heights. And from what I've seen, there's no great height difference among those coming anyway.'

'You know people's heights?'

'I know more than that, Barnabus, which, if it's helpful, I'll be passing on to you for your sessions. I've got all their personal details.'

'Shoe size doesn't matter hugely in therapy.'

Frances leaps in playfully: 'Oh, everything's material, Barney boy, everything's material. Or didn't they tell you that on your little diploma course?'

His little diploma course?

'I'm not sure the Buddha had any letters after his name,' said Barnabus, trying to stay calm, though he'd like to hit her, knock her over the balcony and watch her fall and shatter on the cold marble below.

Why did he feel so uncomfortable? Because there was no safe ground here and if it wasn't Frances, it was Bella. Why couldn't he just get over his issues with her and accept what was? Wasn't that what he encouraged his clients to do? Embrace the moment, lean into the pain, walk through your fears?

'And I mean look at us,' said Frances. 'Here's the three of us looking each other in the eye.'

Bella was a couple of inches shorter than the other two, but not in her noisy shoes.

'In disguise, we are free!'

'In disguise, we are dangerous.'

'Don't worry, guys,' said Bella, with a mischievous smile. 'I'll try and behave myself!'

Twenty

Hafiz walked as one in a daze.

In the few weeks since their first encounter, he'd written twenty-one poems about Shakh-e Nabat; twenty one poems of love and intoxication and he knew it was twenty-one because he'd counted them and kept copies, which took a bit of time, but what else was time for?

And it wasn't as if he'd had a choice, because he'd had to write them, just as he'd had to deliver them, each one taken personally to her house on twenty-one separate visits, not including the visits which weren't visits, times when he was merely passing, when he just found himself in the rich quarter of Shiraz and ever-ready with the line, 'I was just passing, fancy meeting you, did you see my poems?' should they meet.

But they never did. She seemed to have taken against the veranda of late, she never appeared there, though on one occasion, he did believe she'd pulled back the curtain, a slight but perceptible movement as he turned to leave after placing a poem on the table – a desire to catch a glimpse of the mysterious poet perhaps? It was possible. He'd like her to wonder about the mysterious poet, he'd like that very much, like her to be losing sleep over him, asking around, 'Who is this man?' And he had heard, in a second-hand manner, possibly third, that she'd received each of his poems and was not entirely unfavourable towards them. She'd held his poems and quite liked them! If that was so, then he could die.

But he also wanted to live, which was why he now walked away. Knowing what he must do, he walked away from beauty and away from Shiraz. The promise of Baha Kuhi, the promise first spoken of by Muhammed Attar, was also revealed by the same, a promise now etched in his mind like engraving on a tomb; and the words shaped each step of the way, as he left behind everything he knew.

He'd discovered the promise more easily than anticipated. He'd expected a battle with Muhammed, a war of attrition, for in his experi-

ence, the enlightened do not like telling you anything – they prefer you to find it yourself. Muhammed released knowledge with extreme reluctance, as though you were asking him to cut off his arm. He believed most people were unready for knowledge and if given it, would only ruin it, twisting it to suit themselves.

But not always: for when Hafiz had approached him the following day, he'd pushed at an open door.

'So tell me the promise of Baha Kuhi.'

Muhammed was unloading melons.

'The promise of Baha Kuhi?'

'It's a simple request.'

'Help me with the melons and I will tell you the promise.'

Hafiz could not believe his luck. Here was a fair exchange, melons for a promise, and as he sweated with the large fruit, too full of water to be light, Mohammed kept his word:

'The promise is this: 'If anyone can remain awake for forty consecutive nights at my tomb,' said Baha Kuhi, 'then I will grant you three gifts: the gift of poetry, the gift of immortality and the gift of your heart's desire.'

The three gifts were quickly and securely remembered. Memory was not a problem for Hafiz in those days; if you can learn the Koran you can learn anything and with the words repeated and established in his mind, he'd finished with the melons and taken his leave, knowing what he must do.

And so here he was now, doing it – leaving the woman and leaving Shiraz, to walk the four miles to the tomb of Baha Kuhi, with the three gifts on his mind. Well, this was not entirely true. The first two gifts of poetry and immortality were of no consequence. After all, he was a poet already with little to learn there; and as for immortality, it was too far away to concern one so young. But the third gift, the gift of his heart's desire, this could not wait. Hafiz walked towards the tomb of Baha Kuhi with a mind focused on one thing and one thing alone: the possession of that vision of beauty, the beauty that had been killing him daily since he'd delivered Barbari bread to the rich part of town; the beauty expressed in the body and soul of Shakh-e Nabat.

He would keep this vigil, no matter what the cost. He would draw a circle in the dust and remain there for forty days without sleep. This was all perfectly fine, this he would do. Someone said it would send him mad, but how could that be so? Hafiz was mad already.

He remembered the words of Muhammed Attar: 'Like a moth dying in the flame, much of us is lost in pursuit of the light.'

And if that included his sanity, then so be it.

Twenty One

Monday 3 November
Three days after the Feast of Fools

'So this is Henry House?'

'Yes, rather fine really.'

Tamsin and Abbot Peter stood in the cold-stone entrance hall, polished black and white marble beneath their feet. They were overlooked by a first floor gallery, criss-crossed now by blue-coated forensics tidying up and readying to leave, cutting edge modernity on sixteenth-century floors.

'The body's in the office, Ma'am,' said a young officer.

Tamsin ignored him.

'Thank you,' said Peter, on her behalf.

'And your friend Barnabus both lived and worked here?' she said.

'Friend is a bit strong.'

'Why are you so frightened of the word 'friend', Abbot?'

'I'm not aware that I am.'

'You should see a therapist.'

'I believe I'm about to.'

Tamsin laughed in shock. Her uncle could still surprise her sometimes.

'But he did live here?' she said.

'Temporarily, yes. He had use of one of the bedrooms.'

'And the run of an Elizabethan manor after dark?'

'I suppose so.'

'Well, don't sound so mealy-mouthed. It's not a bad bachelor pad, is it?' Tamsin was aware that the small flat she'd left that morning would fit comfortably into the hallway of Henry House.

'Possibly,' said Peter. 'But Barnabus wasn't that type of bachelor.'

'So what type of bachelor was he?'

'Strange.'

'Why was he strange?'

'No, I was just thinking … it's strange how a bachelor sounds so much more fun than a spinster.'

'I sense he was gay.'

'Barnabus? Oh, I wouldn't know. He had been married of course.'

'And look what happened there.'

'Marriages do end for other reasons.'

'But you're saying he wasn't happy here?'

'He might have changed his mind, but when I last saw him – which is a couple of months back – he was looking for somewhere else to lay his head; he had no desire to live above the shop.'

'And now he doesn't,' said Tamsin.

'No.'

'So it's not all bad news for him.'

Peter felt embarrassed at the remark.

'And on Friday night there was something called The Feast of Fools?' he said, picking up a flier from the table, and reading : ' "At the Feast of Fools, there are no rules".'

'A grand publicity stunt apparently,' said Tamsin. 'A cry to be noticed.'

' "An evening of disguise, role-reversal and excess",' continued Peter. 'Sounds appalling.'

Tamsin looked puzzled.

'Just where did they get that idea from?'

'Well, I'm assuming it was based on the medieval festival of the same name. It might explain the clown's outfit.'

'Yes, they were all wearing clown outfits, I'm told.'

'And each hidden behind a mask, no doubt.'

Henry Hall suddenly felt chill and Tamsin saw only dark corridors and small latticed windows, heavy with lead to keep out the light.

'So what happened here, Uncle?' she said.

They were suddenly the words of a frightened girl.

'That's what we're going to find out, Tamsin, if we can persuade this ancient space to give up its secrets.'

'And do you think it will?'

Peter smiled and Tamsin remembered why she'd wanted him alongside her. His arrogance was reassuring.

'We'll find some coffee,' he said, 'and reflect on our cast of fools – because one of them has been rather clever.'

Twenty Two

A short while later, they sat in the large kitchen with coffee and a tin of soft biscuits. Someone hadn't put the lid on properly but there were greater crimes to consider.

'So, how many fools were invited to the feast?' he asked.

Tamsin consulted her notes.

'Eight in all. The two directors, Frances Pole and Barnabus Hope; the administrator, Bella Amal; four clients of the clinic: Ezekiel St Paul, Kate Karter, Virgil Bannaford and our dear friend Martin Channing – .'

'The editor Martin Channing?'

'The very same.'

'This'll be interesting.'

'Won't it just – the editor of the *Sussex Silt* for once not inventing the story, but one of its lead characters.'

'A slippery eel would be sticky in comparison,' warned Peter. 'Anyone else?'

'The clinic cleaner Patience Strong, your favourite, was also there. Surprised a cleaner was invited.'

'No, that makes sense. The Feast of Fools was all about servants and masters coming together as equals, breaking all social conventions.'

'Including the right to life.'

Peter looked out the window as the rain continued to fall. It had been the wettest autumn on record.

'Not good for the rats.'

'What isn't?'

'They don't like the rain.'

'Who does?'

'They seek the dry in times like these. They come inside.'

'Why are you talking about rats?'

'It must be the setting.'

Abbot Peter cast a casual eye into the store cupboard.

'Are you the rat warden or something?'

'In the sixteenth century, rats ferried the plague-carrying fleas from town to town.'

'Shall we get back to the humans?'

'And they're dealt with by understanding what they most desire: warmth and food.'

'Rats or humans?'

'See that outhouse?'

Peter was pointing through the window. He continued:

'It's the tradition here, in the winter, to keep it warm and full of bird seed, poisoned.'

'Why?'

'The rats can't get to their own execution quick enough.'

'Is that true?'

'Ask the gardener.'

'No, I can't be doing with the working classes, not for conversation, anyway.'

It could have been a joke, hard to tell.

The Abbot continued: 'So why did our rat enter Henry House? They wanted something.'

'Now you're getting creepy.'

'Our little rodent, surreptitious and crafty, crept into Henry House to kill Barnabus Hope. But why? What did they want?'

The question hung for a moment before Tamsin remarked that it was hard to see why anyone would want such a harmless nobody murdered.

'Revenge? Money?' she ventured.

'You're staying with the traditional.'

'Or perhaps ambition? That's all I'd kill for.'

'Remind me not to stand in your way.'

'I really don't see that happening.'

There was a pause.

'Or silence?' said Peter. 'Therapists do know things, often embarrassing things, revealed in the moment and then regretted.'

'It's a big coincidence that Barnabus was killed so soon after his first meeting with the four clients.'

'A coincidence the size of the moon.'

Another pause, and then Peter spoke:

'Of the 435 males killed in England and Wales last year, 249 knew the main suspect.'

'How do you know that?'

'Looked it up before we came out.'

'Never had you down as a criminologist.'

'I hope, Tamsin, you never have me down as anything. Labelling kills.'

'Don't get all pious.'

'I just don't want to be trapped in one of your categories.'

'Then you shouldn't wear a habit.'

Peter took the hit, adding:

'But only twenty one were killed by their partners or former partners.'

'All of which, like most criminology, takes us nowhere very much. Barnabus knew all the clients and he didn't have a partner – or not a partner that we know of. I still think he was gay.'

They sat quietly, the moment interrupted by clickety shoes and then a girlish figure at the door, coy and simpering.

'Just wondering who was in here,' she said.

'And you are?'

Twenty Three

'Bella Amal, the *Mind Gains* administrator,' she says, by way of introduction as she takes a few steps further inside the kitchen.

'Ah.'

'Well, Director of Administration to be precise.'

'You obviously like a title.'

'Oh it isn't me, it's Frances.'

'She likes a title?'

'I don't mind what I am, it's not why I do it.'

'And why do you do it?' asks Peter.

Bella is a little caught out.

'Oh, I just believe in it. Really believe in everything *Mind Gains* stands for.'

Peter nods appreciatively.

'Have you ever been in therapy yourself?' asks Tamsin.

'Me?' Bella is embarrassed and giggly. 'No, I'm not crazy!'

'So why do you believe in it?'

'Sorry?'

'Well if you've never experienced it yourself, how do you know it's so good?'

'I don't know – I just do, I suppose. I mean, it's got to be good, hasn't it?'

'Having never tried it, I'm as ignorant as you, Bella.'

Embarrassment.

'So Frances likes a title?' says Peter, offering Bella a path out of the hole.

'She likes things to appear professional, yes, and "Director of Administration" looks better on the website than "Administrator", I suppose.'

'And don't tell me,' says Tamsin, 'you have your own business card?'

'Oh yes.'

'Thought you might.' Tamsin rolls her eyes in a dismissive sneer.

'Would you like to see it?' asks Bella, unaware of the scorn.

'No, that won't be necessary – now or ever.'

The only business cards Tamsin came across were those handed out by failed coppers who'd found a second career in police training. Only the desperate or the bent handed you a card with the invitation to 'stay in touch'.

'As I say, everything must look professional for Frances,' says Bella. 'Well, you have to these days.'

Peter: 'But though you organised the Feast of Fools, you weren't there yourself?'

'No, I wasn't.'

'Odd.'

'I can explain.'

'I'm sure you will. But we're sitting here now because while seven fools were alive at the beginning of the evening, only six finished it in the same state.'

'Yes.'

'That wasn't part of your planning, I presume?'

'Hardly!'

She giggles again.

'And tell me, Bella – who was the Lord of Misrule?'

'The Lord of Misrule?'

It was as though she'd never heard the phrase before.

'The one who had all the power on Friday night – that must have been part of the planning, surely?'

'Oh no, not at all!'

Slightly hysterical.

'You mean there was no Lord?' persists Peter.

'Well, I suppose there was, but it was all done by lots on the night.'

'Oh I see. So there was definitely a Lord.'

'There was – I mean, there was meant to be, yes, it's what Frances wanted – but I had no part in it.'

'So the Lord of Misrule was a random appointment.'

'That's how Frances wished it to be.'

Peter continues: 'Which may mean that no one actually knows who the Lord was.'

'It might I suppose. I wouldn't know.'

'As you keep saying,' says Tamsin.

People who keep saying things are always lying.

'I mean, if the disguises were good enough, it might,' says Peter.

'If they were, yes.'

'And I'm told they were very good.'

Bella: 'Why do you ask about the Lord of Misrule?'

Tamsin is wondering the same thing.

'Because if we find the Lord of Misrule,' he says, 'we'll probably have found our murderer, Bella.'

Bella looks to be in a state of some shock.

Twenty Four

∾

It was the thirty-ninth day of the 40 day vigil, and Hafiz sat staring at the tombstone of Baba Kuhi.

The scene was not glorious, with dry wood, stones and excrement his only companions in this wasteland … apart from the black-beaked ravens who hopped and strutted impatiently. They were companions in a way – but those intent on your death can hardly be called friends.

Here in the circle of death he'd remained, unshaven, unwashed and increasingly unhinged. Sometimes he rang the changes. Sometimes he walked the circle, round and round, one way one day, the other way the next day, shouting at the sky and then singing to the stars and then doing neither. And sometimes he was in the court in Isfahan, where people spoke of such feasts, he'd heard them, such exquisite culinary excess, great rice dishes, elaborate sherbet cordials, opulent casseroles, succulent meat dishes and extravagant sweets of sugared delight. Sometimes he visited the Isfahan court as many as twice, three times, four times a day. It was hard to say 'no' to the meat and cordial, though for now, on this thirty-ninth day, he rocked back and forth, sitting but rocking, moving his hands in strange ways, twisting his arms, wrenching his shoulders, straining every sinew to remain conscious, to fend off sleep and stay awake, to fulfil the challenge and gain the promise, the gift of his heart's desire.

His mother had brought bread and water until he told her to desist. He could see the pain the visits caused her … and an eight mile round-trip was hardly right for an older woman or for one so doggedly concerned for the girl to whom he was engaged.

'People do enquire, Shams.'

He knew what 'enquiring' meant. It meant people telling her that Shams-Ud-Din, her son, was mad, irresponsible, immoral or all of the above.

'It's Hafiz now.'

'What is?'

'My name.'

'Hafiz?'

'Yes.'

'You've just decided to change your name?'

'I haven't just decided.'

'The name you've had all your life suddenly is not your name?'

She spoke as one who'd swallowed a fly.

'If anybody asks,' he added.

'If anybody asks?'

They might, thought Hafiz, they might quite easily ask; but apparently not from where his mother stood:

'People who have known you since you were a child, are unlikely to ask your name, Shams.'

'From here on, Hafiz.'

'The family name is not good enough?'

What was he to say to that? You grow out of clothing, you grow out of toys, you grow out of people, so why not also grow out of a name?

'You will understand if you are always Shams to me.'

Hafiz nodded, and then said with solemnity:

'And I will understand if you stop visiting.'

His mother took appropriate offence.

'It is a strain for you,' he explained.

'And a strain for you?' she countered.

Hafiz had not been going to mention that – better for the strain to be hers.

'I will be home soon enough,' he'd said, which was true in its way, though in another way, he would never be home again. And he'd watched her go, a stooped but determined frame, taking an age to disappear in the dusty expanse. And while he sensed something ending, he felt no great grief and no great loss, perhaps that would come another time, they did say – or he'd heard it said – that we feel things when we are able, rather than when they occur.

And there was always Muhammed Attar, who also brought supplies, a melon or two dried figs … his perfume would have been a waste in this place. But he came only by night. He said he had a shop to run by day, but Hafiz suspected he liked the cover of darkness, being a man with one eye constantly over his shoulder.

He appeared for the last time at sunset on the thirty-ninth day. He sat quietly for an hour, said that the stars looked kind tonight, sat silent for a further hour and then left. So really, why had he come?

And then the occurrence – or the happening – which shaped his life from there on: but how to speak of it? Well, it's best not to speak of these things, or perhaps tell one person but no more … more than that and

76

you begin to lie or invent, you elaborate a little to ensure reaction, this is what Hafiz thought and so he told only Muhammed Attar. And what did he tell? He told of the moment, on the thirty-ninth day of the vigil, when the Angel Gabriel appeared to him, which is not something easily dropped into conversation:

'I bought a new camel today. And you?'

'I met the angel Gabriel.'

'And tomorrow I'll hear back from the shoe mender. He told me not to give up hope on my sandals.'

'The angel gave me my three greatest desires.'

'I've only had them a year. But you can't tell with sandals these days.'

But the angel did appear to Hafiz, a fire-figure of orange and red, purple and gold, distinctive in the beige surrounds of night fall. He was certain it was Gabriel, though the two of them had never met before. Hafiz had been otherwise engaged in his life, memorizing the Koran, studying the great poets, wasting time at school, avoiding the judgements of his mother and making bread deliveries. So when had there been time to meet an angel? But he knew without doubt it was he, for whom else could it be in this place, at this time and holding such a cup? Yes, the fire-figure held a silver cup and offered it to the parched lips of Hafiz.

'The water of immortality' said Gabriel and Hafiz drank thirstily.

'Thank you,' he said, wiping his mouth and wondering what immortality he had just drunk.

The angel then placed a quill in his hand, his touch burning without disfigurement.

'The gift of poetry', said Gabriel. 'Your pen shall pour light into lives that are dark.'

'I have learned from the best.'

It's best to be humble with angels, thought Hafiz, especially as they're made of fire. Humility at all times, they'll think better of you.

And then the pause which felt long, nearly eternal: it was, after all, the third promise he had come for. Immortality and poetry were fine, to be received with due gratitude, but these were not why he had come.

'There was a third promise, I believe' said Hafiz, both hesitant and insistent.

'And what was that?' asked Gabriel.

It was a slightly weak voice for an angel of flames. Had he imagined fire speaking, which he hadn't, but if he had, he might have imagined something more impressive.

'It concerned my heart's desire.'

'And what is your heart's desire, Hafiz?'

And this is when everything went hopelessly wrong – or wonderfully right; to his dying day, he'd never quite decided. But something changed beneath the inky sky and shimmering stars as he gazed on the angel figure before him – and he did gaze, for here was a figure of such extraordinary wonder that, for a moment, he forgot even the beauty of Shakh-e Nabat. Yes, impossible! But it happened. And the thought occurred to him:

'If an Angel of God is so wondrous, then how much more wondrous must God Himself be?'

'I want God!' declared Hafiz in his filthy madness.

The fire-figure bowed as if something was settled and then spoke:

'Return to Shiraz and go the house of Muhammed Attar. He will teach you and you will learn from him.'

'Muhammed Attar?'

'He will teach you.'

'But what does he know? He sells fruit and perfume! And looks constantly over his shoulder!'

But he obeyed the angel.

Twenty Five

Two days before the Feast of Fools

'Welcome to *Mind Gains*, Kate,' said Barnabus.

First impressions of Kate Karter: a fight with age, hair dyed blond, late-50's, large earrings, clothes of tossed-on elegance and weary-eyed make-up, like some former film star 'glad to be out of the whole wretched business, darling'.

'And all blessings and felicitations on you, young man.'

Barnabus felt the polite pushing away; the mannered declaration of distance. 'That's quite a greeting.'

'One does one's best.'

One? Royalty – or simply someone unsure of their identity? It would tie in with her surname, for really, who was called Karter with a 'K'? Changed presumably for attention. As Frances said, everything is material for the therapist.

'Do sit down.'

'A rather wonderful setting.'

'It is, isn't it? We're very lucky.'

They sat in the Long Room on the first floor, its dark wooden floor covered by occasional carpet. It was the lightest of the rooms in Henry House, catching the sun in the afternoon, as much as the leaden windows allowed. Elizabethan houses – and windows – were built before anyone thought a view was important. A good view was a roaring fire and a roasting pig, both of which tended to be indoors. Barnabus liked the room for the sense of space, a good climate for therapy.

'Come far?'

He'd chosen not to look at Bella's extensive documentation on each client. He preferred to risk the insight of the moment.

'And there was me concerned the questions would all be rather problematic!'

'That's not something I can predict. What's tricky for one is easy for another. It depends how familiar we are with self-exploration, I suppose. Is self-awareness a path you've been on for a while?'

'All nonsense in my book.'

Kate Karter was the first of the clients taking part in the 'Feast of Fools' package.

'So what brings you on this strange adventure? Given, as you say, that it's all nonsense.'

Kate was looking for something and nothing in her bag which she still held, both shield and comfort.

'Well, it isn't a cry for help, if that's what you're thinking!'

'Okay. Is that something you don't do, cry for help?'

'Why would I?'

'No cries for help from Kate.'

Kate snorted.

'Gave up on those a long time ago, darling. CWT!'

'I'm sorry?'

'Complete Waste of Time.'

Barnabus allowed a pause.

'Have I thrown you?' she asked.

'No, why do you say that?'

'You went all quiet on me.'

'I like quiet.'

'I like the radio on.'

'I think silence gives space for things to grow.'

'Hah!'

'You don't agree?'

'It doesn't grow anything in me. Silence is a very barren land, darling. Well, that's a face!'

'The one I was born with, unfortunately.'

Kate looked in her bag again.

'You seem very interested in what I'm doing,' said Barnabus. 'Why do you think that is?'

'You needn't screw it up, that's all. I'm not that bad!'

'I was just wondering something.'

'Wondering what?'

'Wondering why you gave up crying for help?'

She looked down again.

'Nobody came.'

She spoke the words quietly, to the arm of the chair.

'Nobody came?'

'It doesn't matter anyway.'

She was keen to hurry on.

'It would matter to me, if no one came when I cried,'said Barnabus. 'It's all in the past, done and very much dusted.'

Tears were building in her eyes.

'Still powerful though,' said Barnabus. 'The past makes the present we now live.'

'Shall we move on?'

She dabbed at her eyes, resuming control.

'So what made you cry?'

'Don't we all, dear?'

'I don't know if we all do. I can only speak for myself.'

A short pause.

'I'm no different from anyone else.'

'You must have been sad.'

'I wouldn't call it crying.'

'Is it difficult to be sad?'

'Long time ago, young man; it's all a long time ago and I'm getting bored of talking about it.'

'Okay. Though you haven't really spoken about it at all. It must feel frightening.'

'Onwards and upwards is the best way.'

'Is that what you say to yourself?'

'Cast off dull sloth and joyful rise to pay the morning sacrifice!"

'Is that your line?'

'A hymn we sung at school.'

'Very bracing.'

'Pretty good advice for those thinking of topping themselves.'

'And are you?'

'No. Much too busy.'

'So you keep yourself busy.'

'Best way. Can't be doing with all this sitting around.'

'So does it feel difficult to be sitting here now?'

'We're not going to be long, are we?'

'We'll be together only for as long as it suits us.'

'I can't stay long.'

'Who knows, the time might be a gift to you.'

'I'll need to collect my husband soon.'

'And his name?'

'Gerald.'

'Gerald.'

You learn a lot from the way someone says a name.

'I collect him from school and don't worry – he's a teacher not a pupil! No toy boys for me!'

'No.'

'Well, you do hear stories … terrible stories.'

'You look sad.'

'I don't do sadness, young man.'

'Why's that?'

'Sadness is not allowed!' she said in a voice that came from somewhere else. It was almost military in inflection, hard, as she looked at her watch.

'Need to keep a check on the time,' she said. 'Gerald doesn't like it when I'm late.'

She paused before adding:

'Though really, who cares a fig what he thinks?'

She was fiddling with something in her bag. Barnabus watched her agitation. Freud believed that the analytic gaze must be 'without memory and without desire'. There must be something innocent and neutral about the therapist, always refusing to categorise or solve. Instead, he advised, create space for the surprising discovery.

'So how did you feel when no one came,' he gently asked. 'If you didn't feel sad, how did you feel?'

'You need to get some new questions.'

'Oh?'

'Definitely some new questions.'

That military inflection again, the other voice.

'What's wrong with the present ones?'

'They're annoying me, darling.'

Twenty Six

'Therapists are just expensive friends, isn't that what they say?'

Barnabus felt the assault of Virgil Bannaford straight away. Chunky and unkempt, blond hair and embattled eyes, he sat restlessly in his chair, braced for conflict.

'Well, not on this occasion. I don't believe you've paid anything.'

'A free offer to draw us in, hoping for the big *Kerching!* down the line, eh?'

'How about just a free offer?'

Barnabus heard his own hypocrisy … Frances would love some *Kerching!* But then he'd never imagined himself a messiah. And a little sparring was fine … it drew people like Virgil out from behind their defences.

'Free offers don't exist,' said Virgil.

Appearances can deceive in therapy. They sat quietly together as the winter light dimmed gently across a room of faded sixteenth-century elegance. But it had the feel of a boxing ring, an illegal fight house, a sense of blows traded, bare knuckle and bloody, in a quest for domination.

'That's an interesting observation.'

'It's just how it is.'

'That's how you feel, Virgil? That no one's ever been kind to you, simply because they like you?'

'Everyone wants something, that's all I'm saying.'

Virgil disappeared behind his defences again; Barnabus felt the drawbridge raised, with him on the wrong side of the moat.

'And what do you want?' asked Barnabus.

'Nothing.'

'You've come here for no reason?'

'There's nothing you can give me, old fellow, if that's what you're asking.'

'Fair enough.'

There was an obvious question hanging in the air.

'So why are you here?'

Virgil looked at him in a between-rounds sort of a way.

'I'm not a fan of therapy, as you might have gathered, complete load of tosh.'

'I had picked up on some aggression in you.'

'Who's being aggressive?'

'I'd say you are.'

'This isn't aggressive, matey!'

'I'm not feeling great warmth towards me.'

'I haven't started on you yet!'

'There's more to come?'

'Therapy is just the indulgence of the worried well.'

'Is that so?'

'It bloody is from where I'm standing.'

'Perhaps you've had bad experiences in your past and now want to destroy me.'

'Bit strong, old man! Who's saying anything about destruction?'

'I'm only saying how it feels to be talking with you.'

'I've given it a try, I can't do fairer than that.'

'You've given what a try?'

'The therapy thing. I've been open-minded, came in here open-minded, always open to giving things a try.'

'You imagine you came in here open-minded, Virgil?'

'Of course.'

'From where I'm sitting, you haven't given anything a try.'

'Your opinion.'

'My feeling, yes. You've talked at me but not with me.'

'Again your opinion.'

'It feels as though you want to destroy me and I was wondering why?'

Virgil lurched forward on his chair.

'Look, if you can't take the banter, chummy, then you're in the wrong job.'

'This is banter?'

Virgil smiled wearily.

'And what's this banter about, Virgil?' asked Barnabus.

'Banter's not about anything, matey! You should get out more, you really should.'

'Matey' could be such a hostile word.

'That may be true, Virgil.'

'Been making a dishonest living for too long!'

Barnabus breathed deeply, took the hit and calmed himself as the pugilist in the other seat waited.

'Though from what I know about banter,' continued Barnabus, allowing the hostility to pass through him, 'at its heart is relationship, as opposed to attack. Do you have anything to offer apart from attack?'

Virgil contemplated him with turbulent eyes.

'Look, I've ballsed up and I want my wife back,' he said.

Big change of direction.

'She's gone away?'

'She wanted me out, I had a bit of business, nothing really.'

'An affair?'

'Total over-reaction on her part.'

'Your wife was unhappy about the affair?'

'Women!'

'What about them?'

'Over-reacting, I mean what's the point?'

'Was this the first time?'

'I don't see what that's got to do with anything.'

'I was just wondering why she was over-reacting, as you say.'

'Not an endearing quality; give me a woman who doesn't over-react. It pushes you away.'

'Do you feel pushed away?'

'She pushes me away and then wonders why I wander a little! Crazy. She's a Medusa!'

'So this wasn't the first time?'

'What's this – the inquisition or something?'

'Not a rack in sight ... just a question.'

'You're supposed to be on my side.'

'I am on your side, Virgil, and committed to your happiness – but the facts of the story are important.'

'I'm giving you the facts.'

'No, you're giving me interpretations of the facts, your interpretations which are important; but the facts themselves matter too. Perhaps, for instance, if you've been repeatedly unfaithful to your wife, it explains some of what you call her over-reaction.'

'Total over-reaction.'

'So you say.'

'This is going nowhere.'

'Why do you say that?'

'I get more sense from my bloody milkman.'

'Do you mean our talk is making you feel uncomfortable?'

'I'm not uncomfortable. I just don't see what it's achieving.'

'What do you want it to achieve?'

'I want my wife back.'

'That's not in my power.'

'Let's be honest, nothing much is in your power, matey.'

Matey again, as a weapon – but he hadn't finished.

'You're about as effective as the Elizabethan doctors who wore the ground-up remains of dead toad round their waist, to ward off the plague! Thought themselves so bloody clever – but they didn't last long!'

'You sound angry,' said Barnabus.

'I'm not angry. I don't get angry, no point in getting angry.'

'You sound angry.'

'I'm a peaceful guy. It's you who seems to be having all the problems.'

Barnabus paused again.

'So you're full of peace and I'm full of problems?'

'I wouldn't want to be paying for this, put it like that!'

Virgil celebrated a clean punch through the defences of his opponent, like scoring a try from behind a ruck on the playing fields of Eton.

Barnabus sat quietly, heart beating hard, but again allowing the hit to pass through.

'So as a guy who's so full of peace, where do you put your rage?'

Nothing in Barnabus' experience prepared him for the hostility that now contorted the face of Virgil Bannaford.

Twenty Seven

The three beards sat opposite Hafiz, black opposite red and gold, a table in between.

On the left was the Karim Khan, neatly bearded, precise fingertips attending to detail; on the right, the large lawyer Mubariz Muzaffar, who must have missed a fast or two along the way, sweating through his robes; and in the middle, a dead-eyed young man unknown to Hafiz, too still to be well, locked inside another world, where he was right and he was king.

Hafiz was here to be questioned, and the first enquiry came from the smiling Karim:

'So good of you to meet with us.'

'A pleasure,' said Hafiz. 'So far, at least.'

'And you must tell me, because everyone wants to know: are you a poet or a mystic?'

Hafiz smiled in return. He'd been promised a chat about nothing and everything. How had the offer gone?

'We must sit and talk Shams-Ud-Din, just to clarify things, nothing more,' – this had been the tone of Karim. 'Misunderstandings can arise, oh and how easily, and we don't talk enough, we really don't!'

And then came a suggested time for their chat, 'after prayers, we could meet after prayers, fresh from the prostration of our unworthy selves before Allah. Share a coffee perhaps? Shams-Ud-Din, tell me you will join us?'

And so two days after the battering on the door, the interrogation began, interrogation by invitation and with a smiling question about whether he was a poet or mystic?

'Is water liquid or wet?' replies Hafiz.

Karim looks at Mubariz. The man in the middle looks at no one, still king in another land.

'It would be foolish to declare for one above the other,' says Karim, smoothly.

'Indeed,' says Hafiz.

Karim allows his opponent a small victory in the opening skirmish; he would not be a victor for long. The forces of orthodoxy were gaining strength in the court, leaving the poet an isolated figure. And of course his patron, Shah Shuja, had other things on his mind right now, much on his plate, so it seemed a good time to deal with the poet – God's moment, you might say.

'It's a delight to see you, of course,' says Karim.

'Then perhaps you should remind your friend.'

Hafiz looks at Dead-Eyes.

'The delight would appear to be passing him by,' he adds, 'which is a shame. I'm all for delight. And you, Mubariz?'

Twenty Eight

The large lawyer stares neutrally back at Hafiz. Delight is not his concern.

'We find ourselves in some difficulty,' says Karim, fingering one or two pieces of parchment on the table. 'So many attacks on our faith, both beyond our borders and within.'

'I'm sorry to hear that.'

'The most worrying of attacks.'

'Not from me, Karim, I assure you. It's my business to celebrate God rather than assault him.'

'I said "faith", Shams-Ud-Din. It is our faith under attack.'

'Ah, then I cannot help you, my friend. I am in love with God, not faith.'

Karim looks puzzled.

'But God is found and defined by faith, surely?'

A tightening of the screw.

'No,' says Hafiz, 'God is found and defined in a barking dog, in the ring of a hammer, in a drop of rain, in the face of everyone I see. God is even found in my friend who sits between you – he who lives in a land that does not border sanity.'

'You show an unfortunate contempt for religion,' says Mubariz.

His voice is deep.

'Loving God is not enough?'

'Religion is God's guardian.'

'I thought only minors needed guardians, those still finding their feet in the world. I've never believed God to be one of those.'

Mubariz does not offer further opinion. They are happy for Hafiz to hang himself and the poet seems eager to oblige.

'The idea of anyone presuming special knowledge of God's needs has always seemed a strange one to me,' he says.

'Then perhaps you're forgetting the opening lines of the Koran which you claim to know by heart.'

'Guide us in the Straight Path, the path of those whom thou has blessed, not those against who thou art wrathful, nor of those who are astray.'

Hafiz is word perfect. Karim claps in mock praise and responds:

'It would appear you condemn yourself. In noting those who stray, religion is surely God's guardian?'

'More often God's jailer in my experience.'

Raised eyebrows among the beards, which don't come down as Hafiz points out that those who imagine they know what is good for others, are the most dangerous of people.

Mubariz moves restlessly. Here is a lawyer more at home with a fist buried deep in the abdomen than the niceties of theological dispute.

'Are you aware of the blasphemy law, Shams-Ud-Din?' asks Karim.

He asks the question gently, a polite enquiry, the tone of one asking the way to the fruit market.

'I know the Koran doesn't mention the word "blasphemy" so neither do I.'

'Your innocence is charming.'

'Thank you.'

'But dangerous.'

'My innocence is true.'

'In the ninth sura of the holy book' – Dead-Eyes hands Karim a copy – 'we read, let me see, where are we now? Ah yes, "When the sacred months are over, slay the idolaters wherever you find them. Arrest them, besiege them and lie in ambush for them everywhere." '

He hands the book back to Dead-Eyes and continues:

'It would appear to be fairly clear in the matter of blasphemers from that reading.'

Hafiz replies: 'And in the second chapter we read, if my memory serves me correctly and it usually does: "Let there be no compulsion in religion".'

'As for unbelievers,' declares Mubariz reading again from the holy book, "God has set a seal on their hearts and on their hearing, and on their eyes a covering, and there awaits them a mighty chastisement".'

'And then in the seventh sura,' adds Hafiz, "My mercy embraces all things".'

There is a pause in proceedings. Karim fingers his parchment again and Mubariz leans his sweating frame forward a little. Hafiz speaks again:

'There is little to be gained, my friends, from throwing verses at each other like fighters with their punches. Trading verses really is one of the dullest pastimes in my experience, akin to throwing excrement at one another. Both activities leave a nasty taste in the mouth.'

'You will not deny that in the Koran, Allah has friends and enemies.'

'Indeed.'

'That at least we can agree on.'

'And we will know his friends by the delight in their life!'

A further silence follows, broken by Hafiz:

'People find in the scriptures exactly what they are in themselves. Did you know that, Karim?'

'I did not know that and still don't.'

'Then take it from me.'

'An unlikely event.'

'So those who are angry or unhappy or hateful find a God of similar mind. This is why people's scriptures always agree with them.'

If a poisoned atmosphere can get worse, it does at this point.

'You mentioned coffee in your invitation,' remarks Hafiz, briefly craving its bitter strength.

'That poor man last week,' says Karim, ignoring him.

Coffee would have to wait.

'Which poor man was that?'

Hafiz didn't follow the news as closely as he might. He'd learned that from Muhammed Attar.

'Did you not hear about him? I'm surprised.'

'I see many poor men in this city … so many to choose from.'

'I refer to the one found guilty of blasphemy.'

'Ah.'

'Tragic.'

'And an increasingly familiar tale, sadly.'

'Though, of course, this old man stayed silent throughout the proceedings. Didn't he stay silent, Mubariz?'

Mubariz nods.

'And that was a problem?' ventures Hafiz.

'It was perhaps unwise.'

'In my experience, noise is a cruel ruler,' he replies, and then, remembering the poem from which he drew, continued:

' "Noise is a cruel ruler
and always imposing curfews.
While stillness and quiet
Crack open the vintage bottles
And awake the real musicians within".'

The beards are unimpressed. Music had recently been banned among the faithful and Karim continues:

'He was finally condemned to death on the charge of "finding fault with a belief or practice that the community has adopted".'

Hafiz ponders the words.

'And that is blasphemy?'

'Indeed it is.'

'Then it is a new law for a world already weary with them; and as I say, one beyond the knowing of the Koran, a book I learned by heart in my teens.'

'You learned nothing, Shams-Ud-Din.'

'Is that why you struggle to use my name, "Hafiz"?'

Their refusal to call him by his adopted name rankled.

'You learned the words, but not obedience to the commands.'

'I learned the spirit behind the words, wherein lies true obedience.'

'Oh, so now you go behind the words, Shams-Ud-Din? You go behind God's words?'

'I prefer flowers to fences and God to laws.'

Was he saying too much? Should he mind his tongue?

'Then beware for your health, Shams-Ud-Din.'

Hafiz contemplates the threat.

'My health? Well, I cannot skip like I used to, and I do widen a little round the waist, but still enjoy a walk in the Musalla Gardens. It is good for the heart, I'm told.'

'We will not talk of punishment today,' says Karim.

'And in that choice we imitate God.'

'But if we did speak of punishment, not that we will, but if we did, we'd note that correction for blasphemy starts with fines and imprisonment but moves quickly on to flogging or amputation.'

Karim allows the words to sit for a while.

'And that would be a tragedy, Shams-Ud-Din. No, really, imagine a poet losing his hands. How would he then write for his adoring public?'

'Rest assured, I write mainly with my heart.'

'And then, of course, in extreme instances – and it is not what anyone wants, but what truth sometimes demands – there is the beheading of the blasphemer or, as the poor man last week discovered, the tightening noose of judicial hanging.'

Dead-Eyes moves, slightly stirred, a half-glance at Karim.

'He will be a freer man now,' says Hafiz.

'We must hope so, because I believe you once knew him.'

'I knew him?'

'Oh, I think so.'

'He spoke of me?'

Hafiz tries to sound calm, though his chest tightens.

'He didn't need to; others did that for him.'

'And the name of this man?'

'The fruit and perfume seller, Muhammed Attar.'

A terrible rage swamps Hafiz. He thinks of Muhammed cutting melons, sniffing the perfume and then swinging on a rope. He thinks of his dear friend and master, so frail and tired, patient teacher, eyes over his shoulders, a secret life now public, swaying in the sun on the end of a rope.

'Yes,' says Karim, picking up the story with some glee. 'We – how shall I put it? – encouraged one of his students to tell us what went on in that secret little room up the stone stairs – stairs, I imagine, you're familiar with, Shams-Ud-Din.'

'I may have met him,' says Hafiz with indifference. 'I like fruit and have lived in Shiraz a long time.'

'And, of course, alongside your love of fruit, he was your teacher for forty years, which makes familiarity a strong possibility, don't you think?'

Hafiz breathes in deeply.

'I fancy a walk by the river,' he says. 'We could breathe God's beautiful air together.'

Now big Mubariz speaks, entering the ring late, with his opponent already on his knees.

'The blasphemer Muhammed Attar lacked the patronage you have so far enjoyed,' he says.

'He enjoyed God's patronage, I believe.'

'Muhammed Attar had no Shah to hide behind, which made him vulnerable, poor man. You must feel bad about that.'

'Why so?'

'He was the real thing, Shams-Ud-Din, a brave man, living with a daily threat that you – the pampered court poet and so-called celebrity of words – have never known, not even close! Until now perhaps.'

Muhammed Attar had taught Hafiz everything; or rather, created the climate in which he'd learned everything. Muhammed didn't offer spiritual flowers but worked the soil that gave life to them. Beyond the fruit and perfume the seller had been a spiritual master; and beyond the shop front, a gathering of seekers sworn to secrecy, aware of orthodox eyes. Whenever the meetings ended, with hasty goodbyes exchanged, there was always the feeling, as they stepped out into the night, that this could be the last time; that next time, Muhammed might not be here. And now he wasn't.

And then the conversation further muddies its boots. It's Karim who speaks:

'It was Sultan Baybar, of course, who made legal the use of torture on apostates.'

He delivers the words as one commenting on the weather.

'Do you have an opinion, Shams-Ud-Din? An opinion on torture?'

Twenty Nine

'An opinion on torture?'

An unfamiliar request for Hafiz and he hesitates.

'You know how we value your words,' says Karim.

'Well, I'm for sane ideas rather than mad ones. That's where I start, I suppose. I always favour the sane. And one sane idea is not to bring a cocked gun into a meeting. It's better to leave it outside in a field. Brought indoors, it can make for a tense atmosphere, and may well go off.'

'But on the matter of Sultan Baybar and torture?'

'An interesting figure,' says Hafiz. He knew what he would say: 'A man who legalised torture, as you observe; yet also the first Sultan to allow the Christian order of Franciscan monks to set up communities in the Holy Land. Is there such a community arriving in Shiraz any time soon?'

Hafiz notes the bearded irritation across the table, but continues. He is angry:

'Our heroes, you see, don't always behave as we might want them to. So we pick and choose what suits us.'

'You would have blasphemers in our midst?'

'Oh, I think we're done, are we not? I think we have travelled as far as we sensibly can.'

He added that he'd learned so much from God, that he could no longer use the old religious labels. Christian? Hindu? Buddhist? Muslim? Jew? Neither these, nor any other tags, meant anything, Man? Woman? Angel? 'All inside me is ashes,' he says, 'and all inside me is freedom.'

The four men sit silent until Karim speaks:

'We are a ship you would be wise to sail in, Shams-Ud-Din.'

'A good picture, Karim.'

'Thank you. I like to think there is a poet in me as well.'

Doesn't everyone?

'And all the great religions are ships, Karim, there we agree, ships moving slowly and purposefully through the water.'

'Moving with God's purpose, I believe.'

'Yet do you know what? Every sane person I've met, has had in the end to dive overboard – with Muhammed Attar kindly handing out life belts here in Shiraz.'

There is no going back now. And anyway, what does he have to go back to? 'Expect a visit soon, Hafiz.'

'I look forward to it.'

'I don't think you do.'

And they were right, he didn't. Behind his smiling eyes were fearful feelings and then Dead-Eyes spoke:

'So now you know the fear the blasphemer Muhammed Attar knew for sixty years.'

Such intensity, such venom.

'You're very precise about that,' says Hafiz.

'And why not, Shams-Ud-Din?'

'My name is Hafiz. And you ask why not? Because you simply cannot know these things about another. You cannot know what he feared.'

'A son might know these things of his father.'

'Possibly.'

'And I am the son of Muhammed Attar.'

Thirty

The day before the Feast of Fools

Barnabus pondered tomorrow's Feast of Fools and today's clients. Neither prospect filled him with joy.

Yesterday he'd seen the mannered Kate Karter and the aggressive Virgil Bannaford. Later today he'd see Martin Channing, the newspaper editor; but first, the quiet, suited man before him now, the Reverend Ezekiel St Paul, Pastor of the Seraphimic Church of the Blessed Elect in Uplifting Glory. And he was nothing like he'd imagined.

What had he imagined? Barnabus had expected a hell-fire preacher, an ebullient figure filling the room with his wide-eyed presence. But the Reverend Ezekiel was no such a man. A small figure, he barely filled his chair, let alone the room, and presented as a thoughtful soul and polite. Nigerian religion was not always so irenic, but after Virgil Bannaford, Barnabus could do with some serenity. Later that evening, of course, he would squirm at such misjudgement and appreciate once again how even therapists can misread the psychological weather to come.

'A warm welcome to *Mind Gains*, Ezekiel. Is that what I call you?'

'May I ask a question?'

'Certainly.'

'Are you under the blood, Mr Hope?'

'I'm sorry?'

'Are you under the blood?'

His first thought was to look up to the ceiling.

'I'm not sure I'm with you.'

'Under the blood of the lamb?'

'Which lamb would that be?'

'One of the elect?'

'Ah!'

Barnabus rebuked himself for being slow. Jesus as the Lamb of God, a truly repulsive idea, its throat cut for the sin of others.

'I'm not sure I'd put it quite like that, Ezekiel.'

'Reverend.'

'Reverend.'

'So how would you put it?'

How would Barnabus put it? He wouldn't put it at all.

'It's not imagery I find helpful.'

'Is that so?'

'I suppose we all have different ways of making sense of the world.'

The Reverend sat quietly, moving his lips a little, looking down and then up, in some private religious transaction.

'What are you thinking?' asked Barnabus.

'I wonder to myself by what authority you speak?' said Ezekiel, with a half-smile.

'That's quite a question.'

'You say you don't find the blood of Jesus Christ helpful – so by what authority do you speak?'

Not an inquiry he received every day.

'By what authority does anyone speak?' he offered back at the precise moment the answer flashed before his eyes, the right answer, which the Reverend then gave him:

'When I stand in the pulpit to address my people every Sunday, sometimes twice, I speak with the authority of God.'

Why didn't Barnabus think of that? Probably because he didn't believe it or perhaps assume it, didn't assume he was God's mouthpiece on earth. Though who knows, perhaps sometimes he was. By the law of averages ...

'And so I wonder by what authority you speak?' continued Ezekiel, like a polite but determined drill.

Dreams of a serene afternoon lay in ashes, but Barnabus gathered himself and looked for the steel in his veins. You do on occasion need to gather yourself as a therapist. And first of all, he needed to escape this therapeutic log-jam of self-righteousness ... he needed to dislodge the sticking logs, so the river of communication could flow again. That would be helpful.

'By what authority do I speak?'

The Reverend nodded. The witness had correctly heard the prosecution's question.

'And tell me: did you come here today to ask me that question?'

'I do not think it an unreasonable one.'

'Neither do I, Reverend, I think it's a very good one.'

They smiled at each other, a brief moment of connection.

'And I suppose my answer would be,' continued Barnabus, 'that I don't locate the authority in myself.'

'No?'

'No, I locate my authority in you and your will for health and in this unfolding moment between us, this present conversation.'

Ezekiel did not hide his puzzlement.

'That's how talk therapy works,' continued Barnabus. 'If we can make it to now, to the here and now, I mean, to who you are in this moment, honestly acknowledged – then something truthful might emerge.'

The Reverend nodded politely, tolerating the inadequate response and fingering a small leather tome he had withdrawn from his pocket.

'The psalmist says, "Unless the Lord builds the house, those who labour, labour in vain".'

Again the sense of interrogation, the sense of self-righteousness, which, therapeutically, is impossible to work with.

'Who said the Lord isn't building the house?' asked Barnabus.

'I do not hear you mentioning his name.'

'Those in the sea don't have to talk about water.'

Ezekiel was quietened for a moment, and so Barnabus continued:

'Perhaps the Lord is at work – but in a disguise that hides him from your eyes?'

Barnabus felt the satisfaction of a counter-thrust hitting the mark. But he was more concerned at the combative nature of the exchange so far. Truth travelled best through relationship, and this wasn't relationship but debate.

'I do not come for myself anyway,' said the Reverend Ezekiel.

'So who do you come for?'

A new line of enquiry?

'I come about my daughter.'

Ezekiel's jaw tightened.

'Your daughter?'

'She is not well.'

'A doctor may be better than me.'

'I don't think so.'

'I work mainly with the mind.'

'My son is a fine young preacher at only seventeen.'

'That is very young to be preaching,' said Barnabus.

'A good boy, Michael, he knows right from wrong and respects his father. Are you married with children?'

'Neither of the above.'

Ezekiel acknowledges this failing.

'God has been good to me, I know,' he says, 'truly blessed in the fruit of my loins. But my daughter, she has a demon.'

'A demon?'

'She goes her own way.'

'And how old is your daughter?'

'She is – nineteen.'

'Then she's still young, Reverend, with a lot of maturing to do. I don't believe we reach the age of responsibility until we're twenty seven or twenty eight, by which time we've seen a little of the world and been able to distance ourselves from our parents.'

It seemed Ezekiel was not keen on distance.

'Do you believe in demons, Mr Hope?'

Barnabus paused. He was aware of strong feelings arising inside him, but wary also of embarking on another confrontation. He looked for a bridge to bring them together, rather than a bomb to blow them apart.

'I know the power of an un-well mind.'

'With all due respect, that is not an answer to my question.'

'The hard-wiring of the brain takes place in the first few years of life, Reverend, in response to the nurture offered. That is when the mind patterns are formed which we take into later life. I understand why people talk of demons because we can be very destructive, both towards ourselves and others. But maybe the real demon is our nurture; or in this case, simply a teenage girl in a religious household beginning to wonder who she is.'

The Reverend Ezekiel St Paul sat politely enough, with the beginnings of a smile.

'We've tried to beat the demon out of her.'

Barnabus felt rising anger again.

'And did that help?' he asked.

'The elders say she must now suffer greater punishment to be freed.'

'Greater punishment?'

'It is a kindness, believe me.'

He didn't believe him.

'Really?'

'They must do what they must do. I would not be a good father if I did not allow that.'

Was this the hint of a cry for help? Was there something in the Reverend that wanted Barnabus to name this for the nonsense it was?

'And we all want to be good fathers,' said Barnabus.

'You have no children.'

99

'But if I did.'

'If you did, they would be godless,' he said.

But Barnabus wanted to stay with fatherhood, with Ezekiel's fatherhood.

'And as her father, how do you feel about the "greater punishment" you speak of? How do you feel about your daughter suffering in this way?'

For a moment the Reverend's eyes watered, like a weak fire in the ice; but then he looked down and squeezed his bible.

'You're not happy about this, are you?' said Barnabus. 'And why would you be?'

'The godless cannot help the godly, Mr Hope,' replied Ezekiel, closing the issue.

'Maybe that's so, and maybe it isn't. But in the meantime, I sense you don't feel the godly are helping much either.'

Barnabus was aware of a slight crack in the Reverend's well-patrolled defences. Just for a moment, this man had touched on true feeling, evidenced in the tiny tear, the struggle for words. Which way now? Would he lift anchor and risk more; or drop anchor in terror and panic. Barnabus had his answer soon enough.

'The demon will be choked out of her,' said Ezekiel, as though it were something quite settled.

'Choked out of her?'

'How else to make her God's temple once again?'

'But that's child abuse.'

There was a pause. The judgement had slipped out, darting past the barriers of professional code. He'd never been sure how far to take acceptance, but felt a line had been crossed.

'I will be consulting my lawyers,' said the Reverend.

'I beg your pardon?'

'I will be consulting my lawyers, Mr Hope. I thank you for your time but wipe the dust off my feet as I leave. Tomorrow, I am told, we shall meet as fools.'

'Indeed.'

'So there is no need for you to dress up.'

Thirty One

Barnabus Hope knew of Martin Channing by reputation and would need to forget this when they met. There was no place for preconceived judgements in the therapy room. 'Hitler's just a man when he walks in that door,' as his tutor would say.

The editor of the *Sussex Silt* was not Hitler, but excited strong reaction, intrigue and loathing. Even those who didn't believe in demons believed Channing to be one, perhaps the devil himself. Majoring on the criminal, the snide, and the cess-pit of celebrity, the *Silt* left the reader infected with negativity ... yet somehow gasping for more. Sales were booming and Martin Channing, former editor of a middle-England national, was greatly enjoying his new 'hobby', as he called it – though with his keen eye for remuneration, no one doubted it was a hobby that paid very well. And he was sitting with Barnabus now, who opened with a cheery line:

'When your paper ran a feature on our *Feast of Fools* package, I didn't expect the editor to be one of the participants!'

Martin settled himself in his blue cord jacket, pink shirt, crisp denim jeans – and smiled.

'And neither did I.'

Referred to as the only reptile on earth in a cravat, Barnabus did wonder if he was being set up by Channing. Normally it's the client concerned about confidentiality, but on this occasion, the fears went the other way:

'I mean, whoever trusted a journalist?' thought Barnabus. 'He could destroy my reputation!'

'I did suggest that our features editor Susie give it a shot. I mean, it all sounded rather fun and I used to know Frances at university – in the way you know anyone at university, which isn't at all. I mean, you have sex but you don't know them.'

Barnabus's mind was swimming.

'I expect you've got psychology degrees falling out of your pockets!' continued Channing happily.

Barnabus didn't, and suspected Martin knew that he didn't. Battle lines being drawn early.

'And, well, I suppose I just wanted to give Frances a helping hand – do what I can for the community.'

'You know Frances.'

Barnabus left it somewhere between a statement and a question.

'But then Susie had to pull out, God knows why, flaky girl, and I thought, "Free therapy? Why not?".'

'And so here you are.'

'Safe in the hands of an expert, I'm sure.'

Was Barnabus getting paranoid or was this another dig? He was always suspicious of comments in therapy delivered with a smile … a sign of evasion or attack.

'So what do you think you might get out of therapy?'

'I think it was the word 'free' I found most appealing.'

Barnabus allowed this deft and witty evasion.

'Though I imagine you must be comfortably off, Mr Channing … not someone who needs free offers.'

Challenge him on the reality of his last statement, jerk the reins of control from his clever grip.

'Is that a therapist using their privileged position to be nosy about the financial affairs of others?'

'No, it's a therapist wondering where your survival fears come from. Wondering why you invent financial insecurity, why you find the world such an insecure place?'

'Well that's telling me!'

'It's not telling you anything.'

'The therapist's revenge!'

'I have no interest in revenge, Mr Channing, and no reason for it. I was just reflecting on your words.'

'Hah!'

'You don't believe me.'

'I'm trained in spotting hokum.'

'So you're a suspicious soul.'

'Perhaps I'm just too sharp.'

'Suspicion helps you as a journalist, but perhaps not as a human.'

'Explain.'

Progress?

'Suspicion can cut you off from personal truth,' said Barnabus. 'Suspicious people are frightened people and frightened people don't dare look at themselves.'

'Everyone has an interest in revenge,' said Martin, as if it was self-evident.

'Do you?' asked Barnabus.

'Take the therapist.'

'We're not really here to talk about me.'

'But what do you do in a session, if a client makes you angry?'

Barnabus decides to go with the flow.

'The first thing is to notice I'm angry.'

'No, I'll tell you what you do.'

Aggressive, thinks Barnabus.

'You twist the knife in some way.'

'And you know that because?'

'Don't tell me you just smile and think "That's okay".'

'I recognise the client's aggression for what it is.'

'And what's that?'

'It's called transference and it lies at the heart of talk therapy.'

'Of course! Our old friend transference! Now what would the definition of that be these days?'

It was a word from his past, but now lay in the attic of his mind, under layers of dust.

'It's simply the unconscious process whereby attitudes, feelings and desires of early significant relationships get transferred onto the therapist.'

'Of course.'

'You're doing it now … projecting your shadow side onto me, with this talk of knife-twisting desires for revenge.'

'Nonsense.'

'Transference occurs in all relationships, to some degree. But in the hands of a good therapist, it's not a bad thing but a good thing … uncomfortable but good, a life-shifting occurrence if handled well.'

'So what if the transference gets violent?'

Barnabus felt trapped.

'One thing I try and avoid,' he said, 'is a session becoming an interview or discussion.'

'What else is there?'

'We're here to help you listen to your life.'

Channing offered a withering smile.

'If one of my writers used that phrase, I'd put a line through it and tell them to replace it with plain English.'

'So the phrase is a problem for you, which is revealing in itself.'

'I have absolutely no problems with the phrase, none at all, other than the fact that it's gobbledygook.'

'But the only reason to be here is to listen to your life.'

'You have no idea about my reasons for being here.'

'It's the one good reason: to listen to your life in the company of another.'

'I'm not sure I'd choose yours.'

Ignore.

'Therapy is less a discussion – more a contemplation of the mystery who is you.'

'That all sounds very dull.'

'Are you using the word "dull" instead of the word "frightening"?'

'Frances was right.'

'I'm sorry?'

'It doesn't matter. And I need to be getting on, twenty-four hour news cycle and all that.'

Barnabus sat quietly for a moment, mortified. He felt like crying.

'Why do you need to be getting on?' he asked, as the editor made to leave.

'We'll meet tomorrow in rather different circumstances, I'm told.'

'They will be a little different, yes,' said Barnabus.

'Clown outfits.'

'Yes, I must get over my fear of people in masks.'

'Ah, physician heal thyself!'

'Well, it's good to be honest about our fears, Martin. I'm not sure how honest you are about yours. I sense you're running from something, something painful.'

'Ooh! A parting shot!'

'Why do you perceive everything as an attack?'

'I don't perceive anything as an attack.'

'Remember how transference works, Mr Channing.'

'That's your big word today, is it?'

'It describes something dangerous, yes.'

'Then let's hope it keeps away from the Feast of Fools – or something very cruel could happen. Goodbye! Things to do!'

Thirty Two

Later that night, Barnabus sat alone in his room in Henry House.

The space was small, a preponderance of beams and sloping floor, with bed and small desk. Perhaps it had once been the changing room for the lady of the house. The master bedroom was next door, with its own four-poster bed and grand window looking out on the gardens. But Frances had thought it best kept for special guests, though none had so far come. Frances liked the idea of special people arriving, and being put up in style by *Mind Gains*, famous people, people of substance; certainly people more important than Barnabus. For a socialist, Frances was a Grade One social snob, and it hadn't crossed her mind that Barnabus might be hurt by this stance. In her eyes, he was lucky to be getting a rent-free room; and the fact that he didn't pay rent had, in truth, become increasingly irksome for Frances. Yes, *Mind Gains* had an on-site caretaker free of charge. But did Barnabus really deserve free accommodation? Everyone else had to pay for where they lived, didn't they? An unresolved sense of wrongdoing left resentment, a hard feeling to hide. Barnabus, for his part, viewed it differently. He felt he earned his keep via the countless small jobs and inconveniences that devolved to him because he lived on site.

'Barnabus can do that,' Frances would routinely say.

The truth was, he felt more trapped than grateful.

But now he sat worried at his wobbly desk – blame the floor, not the desk maker – and wrote in blue ink. It was a nameless anxiety, elusive as mist, but cramping his breathing, squeezing it tight; and these lines were the best he could do. Simple lines, short lines, lines which took him back to another place, a warmer place, a safer place, memories … but not for long, he wouldn't dwell, and with his work complete, he sealed and addressed the envelope, put on his coat, trod the creaky stairs down into the hallway and having locked the front door behind him, stepped out into the chill of the late October night.

It was a clear sky on the south coast of England with a fat smuggler's moon to lantern his way to the letter box at the bottom of the drive. He wasn't sure the postman came every day, but there was evidence he came some days and that was enough. The day's sessions had been difficult, no question about that; and they'd left Barnabus wondering about his performance. He always wondered about his performance, it was hardly something new. He'd been wondering about his performance for as long as he could remember, but he particularly wondered tonight.

The Feast of Fools package – with just two sessions – demanded a more aggressive style than usual, this is what he felt, a deliberate attempt to create ripples, waves even ... but the clients had created the turbulence as well. What was it Freud said? The therapist should be opaque to his patients, and like a mirror, show them nothing but what is shown to you. It was a passive approach, in which the therapist offers back to the client only what the client offers to them. Had Barnabus been opaque enough? Not always, no; transparency had broken out once or twice, his own colours revealed. But then sometimes he liked to be naughty and put a stick in the psychological spokes; just as sometimes he liked to be an angel, and encourage the suffering soul. Freud would have allowed neither ... he didn't encourage relationship, naughty or angelic.

But he must leave the encounters now. The meetings were recorded and best left to soak in their own juices, until next week. A lot could happen in a few days, in a few seconds even, and he felt better for walking, he often did. And while it wasn't easy to pull the spears out of his back after sessions, he usually found they dissolved of their own accord, if left kindly alone.

'It's not personal,' as the manuals said: 'transference is never personal.'

Of course, transference was one of Freud's most significant discoveries. When he started out on the talk therapy path, he never anticipated he'd become emotionally important to his patients. He imagined himself a detailed observer, handling the new science of the mind with some detachment. In the early days of psychoanalysis, it wasn't about transference, but about tracing the patient's psychosexual development. The patient's relationship with the therapist was regarded as secondary ... the patient was an individual on a singular journey. So Freud was surprised, very surprised, when patients started expressing both love and hatred towards him. It was a problem, and one he referred to, initially at least, as 'a curse'.

These days, however, it was different. Transference was regarded as an essential tool of psychoanalytic treatment and offered rare common ground between the fighting followers of Jung and Freud.

So that was the theory: transference isn't personal. But tonight beneath the cold moon, walking down the drive alone, professional manuals be damned, because the spears of hostility felt lodged deep within, rusting in his veins, unyielding and highly personal – a curse indeed! He felt again the cold distance of Kate Karter; the restless aggression of Virgil Bannaford; the divine judgement of Ezekiel St Paul and the dismissive cunning of Martin Channing. And what had Channing meant when he said 'I see what Frances means'? What had she said about him? What was the relationship between the two of them? And perhaps one day he would accept Bella's appointment, made behind his back, but it hadn't happened yet.

He pushed the letter through the post box, heard it fall into the empty metal cage and then turned back through the large stone gates. He walked for a while, gazing only at the dark ground. When he looked up, he saw Henry House waiting, like someone angry, an angry parent, as if he shouldn't have left, shouldn't have posted that letter, shouldn't have written what he'd written, shouldn't have felt he could ever escape.

Thirty Three

And a little later that night, on that eve of Halloween, a strange dream for Barnabus in his Elizabethan holding; for in his dream, he heard partying downstairs, lute and madrigal, pig on the spit merriment, hearty guffaws, shouts and the drinking of ale. And then voices raised, no music now, madrigal crushed, angry sounds, rage, clamour and suddenly the hallway filled, a surging ale-fuelled crowd, a struggle on the stairs, a victim manhandled, a rope prepared, hasty work outside his door in the gallery, a struggling figure, a harlequin in Irish green, a baying crowd below, the harlequin noosed, pushed forward and thrown over the rails, the crowd cheering, a twisting body, fighting to save itself, how he fought! And Barnabus disturbed, out of bed, he must save him, free him from the noose, running through the corridor to the gallery, but ... no one there, stillness, just a dream, a mad dream, an empty hall below and Jung the budgie covered and quiet. He stood panting in the darkness and felt some-one pass him, a shadow of silk, that's how it felt. He looked round, but there was no one there.

He returned to his room, heart beating hard, and then his phone rang. Who could be ringing at this time of night?

Thirty Four

'You must go now,' said Hafiz.

He looked at the small bag of provisions made ready for the escape.

'But I haven't finished.'

'Then you must go unfinished, Behrouz, take what you have, for you have much and much is enough, there's no time for more.'

The words are firm but sad.

'Just give me a few more hours.'

'Our hours have run out. They will be here today, Behrouz, any moment! I know this court, I can read the signs. And if they find you here – well, a great deal is lost, my friend. I have lost my wife, I have lost my son – and I do not want to lose these children as well.'

His poems were his children, conceived in love and pain, but must now be given away.

'I have worked as fast as I could.'

'And you have worked wonders, believe me. You have the fastest and finest hands in Persia – and I want you to keep them.'

'There were more amputations last Friday.'

Hafiz did not want to dwell on the amputations.

'You must head west, Behrouz, make for the deserts of Egypt. They will be safe there.'

'Egypt?'

'We need distance between these words and the competing empires which surround us.'

There was a banging on the door.

'We're too late!' said Behrouz.

'Quick, hide.'

'But they'll find me.'

'Behind the screen.'

Louder banging.

'How will I not be found?'

'Hide!'

Behrouz moved awkwardly towards cover, made slow and dim by fear. He was a copyist not a bandit.

'I am coming, I am coming!' called out Hafiz. 'You interrupt a man at prayer!'

More banging.

On opening the door, he faced two stone-faced guards and behind them, Dead-Eyes, son of Muhammed Attar.

Thirty Five

'We have orders from the Grand Council to search your apartment,' said Dead-Eyes, holding up a piece of parchment, with the distinctive seal attached.

'Which you are most welcome to do, of course,' said Hafiz. 'And if you find God in a cupboard, then dance a little but carry on. Less is more when it comes to worship and stupid devotions make him ill.'

'Out of the way.'

'And do you have a name?' asked Hafiz, not moving.

'Why would I give my name to a dog?'

'Because the dog is your friend?'

One of the guards moved forward but Hafiz stretched his arm across the opening, confidentially.

'Just one thing.'

'Move aside.'

'This is Hafiz being kind, being very kind, a miracle I know. But I'm thinking of your heads' – he pointed to them – 'presently enjoying union with your necks.'

'I won't ask again.'

'And here's the kindness: to maintain this happy connection, I strongly advise you come back in an hour.'

Puzzled looks.

'Why?'

'The Shah's son is about to arrive for his writing class.'

'Is that so?'

Dead-Eyes was somewhere between belief and derision.

'It's quite so; there are some things even a poet cannot invent. Well, there probably aren't, but he's a fragile boy, nervous in the company of adults. It might be best if, on his arrival, you and the guards were not here – and that I was. He's young and easily frightened.'

He smiled as best he could, thinking only of Behrouz's bag of provisions, surely in view behind him?

'Of course, you could forget common sense,' he continued cheerily. 'I know I do! All the time! You could allow the Grand Council's command to make you stupid, allow the blood-rush to your head, push your way in, you have the strength, of course you do.'

He sensed them about to move.

'But Shah Shuja is a family man, as I'm sure you know; upset one of his children and you tend to upset him.'

There was a moment as the guards looked to Dead-Eyes for guidance, and Dead-Eyes stared straight through Hafiz. Surely he could see Behrouz, who was far from small?

'Do you fear death?' he asked.

Definitely, thought Hafiz.

'No,' he replied, 'for beauty has slayed me already. It slayed me once in a porch with some Barbari bread, again by the tomb of Baha Kuhi and has slayed me many times since. In fact, beauty keeps laying its sharp knife against my soft neck' – he mimicked a knife against his neck – 'so if you wish to murder this corpse again, you must wait your turn. Sadly, Hafiz has only one neck to offer – and there appears to be a queue of assassins.'

Another pause.

'We will be back in an hour.'

'The pleasure will be mine.'

Hafiz watched their retreating shapes disappear down the corridor and through the colonnades. Only when they were quite out of sight did he close the door. He allowed himself brief relief and a quick dance of delight, before firmly pushing the bookcase across the entrance, should there be a change of mind.

'Behrouz!'

'Yes?'

He appeared from behind the screen, still uncomfortable from crouching.

'You must go, now!'

'I understand.'

'Take your provisions and the poems and leave by the garden window. That is an order.'

Behrouz nodded, finally convinced of the need for speed. The conversation at the door had terrified him. Sweating behind the screen … he'd felt real fear for the first time in his life.

'And here is money. You will need money. Travel with the tradesmen, you are a man in search of work.'

'They are beautiful,' says Behrouz.

What is he talking about?

'I'm sorry?' says Hafiz.

'They are beautiful.'

Hafiz doesn't understand, so the copyist pats the sheets of parchment in his bag.

'Beautiful.'

Tears well up in the poet's eyes. Behrouz is not a man given to ecstasy; and Hafiz, not good at goodbyes.

'They are my children,' he says. 'And I don't want them burned, I want for them the best of lives and the freedom to make new friends.'

'I will protect them, believe me, master.'

'I know you will.'

'I will find a Caliph to keep them safe.'

Hafiz looks out the window, watching movements in the court yard. And suddenly something is clear.

'No, find a monastery.'

'A Christian monastery?'

'You make it sound like a whorehouse.'

'And aren't they?'

Hafiz sighs.

'There are plenty in the deserts of Middle Egypt, thanks to Father Anthony in the fourth century; and a monastery always has need of copyists and calligraphers, particularly one of distinction like yourself.'

Hafiz senses discomfort, attempts further encouraging words:

'And on your way through the Mamluk Sultanate, you may get to see the magnificent Koran of Sultan Baybar!'

'Seven volumes written entirely in gold by master calligrapher Muhammed ibn al-Wahid,' says Behrouz in a monotone.

'In that cursive script, what's it called?

'Thuluth'.

'Ah, yes.'

'I am familiar with the work.'

'I thought you might be.'

'And could have done it better.'

'Of course, of course!'

Behrouz is not for calming, but Hafiz will try once more.

'And in Cairo you can visit Sultan Hassan's new mosque. Mamluk architecture at its best, I'm told.'

There's an uneasy pause.

'You would have me give these poems to Christian dogs?'

Hafiz laughs loudly.

'So that is your problem?'

'How can it not be a problem?'

'It may have escaped your notice, Behrouz, but it's a Muslim dog who's trying to destroy them.'

'Better the dog you know.'

'No, Hafiz likes all dogs, believe me – but doesn't trust any of them.'

113

Behrouz ponders the Zagros Mountains, in whose generous arms the city of Shiraz was built. He was aware he'd not gaze on them for a while … if ever again. How hard it is to say goodbye to a view.

'We must all camp somewhere, master.'

'Maybe so, and you will place your tent where you choose, Behrouz. When it comes to religion, no one can place your tent for you.'

'And where is your tent?'

'I have not written for any particular camp's shrivelled revelation, Behrouz – but towards a more charming and expansive light. A camp is temporary shelter for the desperate … we should never imagine it to be more.'

'I will be gone, master.'

'And no more "master", please. Those days, like many days, lie in our past. From here on, your kindness, skill and bravery make you the master of me.'

'Never!'

'And remember this, Behrouz.'

He pulls his copyist closer, and looks deep into his eyes:

'When the journey is hard and your spirits are low, remember this: a long time ago, I met an angel, a figure of fire.'

'You have spoken of him before.'

'Quite a meeting, yes, and I'm still recovering, still singed, still singing. The angel was magnificent! But know this: on my deathbed, or wherever I meet my end, I will thank God more profoundly for the day I met Behrouz, for the day I met you!'

Two wet-eyed men hug and then one leaves by the window, watched by the other. He slips quietly into the crowd, a convenient melée of servants on their way to buy provisions from the market. Behrouz disappears wonderfully; a copyist by trade, but also a craftsman in the art of becoming unseen. The palace guards barely gave him a glance, and why would they?

And so it was that Behrouz and his strange cargo slipped out of Shiraz and headed west … into the unknown.

Thirty Six

Barnabus woke first, in unfamiliar surroundings. He felt the deep comfort of the four-poster bed, set in the simple elegance of the master bedroom. He was at first confused, then guilty and then happier than he'd been in years. The room was a deep dark, thick velvet curtains keeping out the awakening sky. It was their first night together, and Barnabus hoped against hope – his name was suddenly true, perhaps for the first time in his life – that it wouldn't be their last. Pat was a coming home.

She'd rung him late, very late, he'd been asleep, well, woken by a dream, or maybe dreaming he was awake, wandering fearfully in the gallery trying to save a man from hanging, a man who wasn't there. Though someone was there, that's how it had felt, at least. And then the phone call and Pat saying she was sorry it was so late, and how she'd understand if it wasn't possible, but she needed to get out of the house.

'Were you asleep?'

'Me?' he'd said, 'No, not at all! No, just a final check of the gallery before turning in.'

It was almost true.

She'd come round on her bike while he'd got dressed, and they'd talked in the kitchen, watched half a film on the small kitchen telly, before she suggested the four-poster. Yes, it had been her idea, not being the sort of thing Barnabus would suggest … nor Freud probably: 'The great question that has never been answered,' he once said, 'and which I have not yet been able to answer, despite my thirty years of research into the feminine soul, is: 'What does a woman want?' Barnabus was equally unsure but Pat had known what she wanted, and as it turned out, Barnabus wanted it too.

'I don't understand why you don't have this room anyway,' she said, bleary-eyed in the morning dark.

'Frances thinks we should keep it for VIPs.'

'But you're a VIP.'

Delirious happiness passed briefly through him.

'Not in Frances's book.'

'So?'

'For her, I'm probably little more than an investment partner; and now the money's safe, I'm not even that. In fact, I may be running out of uses.'

'You're a VIP to me, anyway.'

They kissed.

'And I've always wanted to wake up in a four-poster … particularly this one.'

'Why this one?'

'I've cleaned and dusted in here for the last six months. There comes a moment when the cleaner starts to dream.'

'I don't think dreaming is part of the cleaning contract.'

'I do it off-premises.'

'I'm glad to hear it. Dreaming on the job is a serious abuse of company time.'

They laughed happily, snuggled up together and Barnabus wondered how this had happened.

*

He'd met Pat at work, here in Henry House, met her without realising he was meeting her, the best sort of meeting in a way, nothing planned, nothing nervous, nothing 'Oh my God, does she like me?'. Just Barnabus lifting his feet as Pat cleaned around him, and sometimes in the kitchen or on the stairs, some joke or other, or perhaps he'd perform an extravagant Elizabethan bow. And once they'd shared a lunch sitting at the outdoor table in the garden, curtains twitching no doubt. But they'd never shared a bed, until now.

'You're the happiest cleaner I know.'

It was almost a reproof, as he lay gazing heavenwards from his pillow. Happy people could be a threat to therapists.

'I am the singing cleaning woman in my elegant green rags!'

For some reason, Frances had decided the cleaner at Henry House should wear a dowdy green outfit. And suddenly, Pat was out of bed, dancing naked and singing, pushing an imaginary broom. It was immediately arousing.

'You must have something the rest of us don't,' he said, as she climbed back beneath the duvet.

'I don't understand.'

'Well, who's happy as a cleaner, for God's sake? Aren't you supposed to be bettering yourself, ambitious for more?'

'I'm a queen in God's Kingdom.'

'And that's enough?'

'It's more happiness than you seem to know, in your very clever job.'

Barnabus laughed, remembering his recent sessions:

'I didn't feel too clever yesterday, I can tell you.'

And still Barnabus wondered how he had got here. They'd turned out the kitchen lights, he remembered that, walked through the dark corridor in to the hallway and then, hand in hand up the stairs, like many couples down the years. But had any of the men felt as lucky as Barnabus, with such beauty and vitality by his side? He doubted it. And on the stairs he'd kissed her hand and spoken things, said how he wanted to be alone with her, to walk the desert for a thousand years with her, to stand on the edge of the planet, beside her, inside her, neither of them afraid, stepping over the edge and free-falling together into God knows where.

Barnabus loved his Brazilian despite her denials.

'I'm not Brazilian!' she'd say.

'Don't tell me, tell your skin,' he'd answer, running his finger across her sweet cheek. 'Your skin is definitely from Rio.'

Thirty Seven

And an hour or so later, it was time for work. Pat was leaving, a goodbye kiss on the stairs, a long kiss, the changing of the guard at Henry House as Bella arrived on Halloween morning, the morning of the Feast of Fools.

Pat and Bella exchanged some words in the entrance, Bella irritated, Pat unconcerned and then she cycled away, singing but clothed, back towards Stormhaven. She'd be returning later for cleaning duties before the evening's festivities, to which she was invited and how could it be otherwise?

'The Feast of Fools is all about the least,' she'd said. 'And the cleaner is the least of the least in Henry House – Frances makes sure of that!'

'She does like her hierarchies,' Barnabus had said.

'Oh yes.'

'So perhaps the cleaner will be the Lord of Misrule? That would be most appropriate, would it not?'

'We'll see.'

But with Pat gone, it was now Bella demanding his attention.

'Are you okay?' he asked, as she finished a brief call on her mobile. 'You look a little harassed.'

'It may have escaped your notice, Barnabus, but I have a busy day ahead of me,' she said, placing some files on her desk in the recess. 'And it just got more complicated.'

'I'm sorry.'

'Nothing I can't handle.'

'I know you're carrying this thing almost single-handed.'

'Oh, that's the least of my worries – as long as you don't do a disappearing act.'

'I'm sorry?'

'I'm aware, Barnabus, that you've been dragged screaming into this by Frances; wouldn't want you running away again.'

'Again?'

'You don't always face up to things, Barnabus, as you well know.'

He was in a good mood today and received the observation with grace. How untouchable one becomes in love! He'd be back in his small room tonight, but somehow the four-poster no longer felt like forbidden territory.

'I'll be at the Feast, Bella, Scout's honour.'

Perhaps they could be friends?

'To be honest,' he added, 'it's the sessions after the Feast, when we're out of disguise and back to ourselves – it's those meetings that are more of a concern to me now. I haven't had an easy time of it so far.'

'Then you must just live for today,' said Bella, as she began to open the post.

'My guiding thought this Friday,' he replied, as he turned towards the office.

'Tomorrow may never happen!' called out Bella cheerily.

'No, I want tomorrow to happen,' said Barnabus, surprising himself. 'I want plenty of tomorrows!'

When did he last say that?

Thirty Eight

The fire burns bright in the brazier but the market square is subdued; for once, the street traders are unhappy at a crowd.

Mubariz, fat lawyer and master of ceremonies, stands on a raised plinth:

'Bring the blasphemer forward!'

From the crowd emerge four soldiers escorting an old man whom many know, pulled forward by his rope-tied wrists. They pass the fiery brazier and come to a halt by the large block of stone.

'The prisoner Shams-Ud-Din, disgraced son of the coal merchant Baha-Ud-Din, has been tried and found guilty of blasphemy. Does the blasphemer acknowledge his guilt and beg forgiveness?'

Hafiz lifts his eyes from the common ground. He gazes across the square to where Muhammed Attar had once stood, slicing melons and sniffing perfume. He remembers his words on a particularly dark day, when, overcome with despair, Hafiz had spoken of giving up on his poetry:

'What's the point?' he'd wailed.

Attar had pinned him against the wall with surprising force:

'Some day, my sweet Hafiz, all the nonsense in your brain will dry up like a stagnant pool of water in the sun – and your belly become pregnant with the seed of the universe! And then you will give birth to wonderful words, enlightened words!'

Had Hafiz stayed with nonsense, rather than the enlightened, he might today be keeping his hands. As it was, the sun would set this Friday – the day for all amputations and beheadings – on a poet with two stumps with which to wield his quill. Dr Saad, the court doctor, would perform the amputations. He had visited Hafiz the night before, to reassure him of his competence:

'I use a special knife, curved, sharp – not a sword.'

'And I am to be encouraged by the quality of the weapon?'

'When I cut off a hand, I cut it from the joint, clean.'

Clean – but not without messy consequence; the dark stone in the market square was made so by the blood of thieves and blasphemers. Hafiz had seen it all before: the amputated limbs held high for all to see, then thrown to the ground and left for the ravens.

'Does the blasphemer acknowledge guilt and beg forgiveness?' bellows Mubariz again.

'I confess to being God, yes,' calls out Hafiz.

Gasps from those around.

'We have heard it from his own lips!' squeals Mubariz in the dry air.

But the hysteria is quashed by the cry of another.

'Because try as I might,' continues Hafiz, discovering a voice he didn't know he had, *'I cannot separate myself from his love.'*

'He claims to be God!'

'And you are God too, my friend, don't forget yourself – his love is remarkably un-choosy.'

Karim slaps Hafiz across the face. There is a hush in the square.

'You'll enjoy this,' he says to Hafiz.

Hafiz looks him in the eye, but no words come.

'Has the poet run out of material?' taunts Karim.

'I've always tried to weave light into my words, but maybe silence is the brighter path now.'

'Then you will enjoy the fire.'

The flames in the brazier are busy with their destruction.

'I was concerned we'd run out of wood, Shams, but suddenly we discover a whole forest! It's amazing what kindling you can find if you look hard enough.'

A stooped servant appears, dragging a sack across the market square and Hafiz understands. The labourer stops by the flames and then guided by Karim, empties the sack on the ground, bundles of paper, small logs of tightly-bound parchment, scrolls he knows well, pitifully falling to earth. No one moves.

'Let the blasphemer step forward!'

Thirty Nine

'It is you who will stoke our fire,' says Karim, eyeing the brazier.

'I burn my own poems?'

'It seems only right that your sinful hands perform one last task before separation.'

Hafiz looks at his fingers, perhaps for the first time in his life. He'd never looked at them quite like this before … he should have noticed them more often.

Karim again, the quiet voice in his ear: 'I like the symmetry; your own hand destroys the evil your own hand created! See, I am the poet again!'

'It is best not to get carried away with yourself, Karim. You may quickly arrive in the dark alley of delusion.'

'Poetic justice for the poet, Shams-Ud-Din – and who knows? Perhaps the first step on the long road of recompense. Allah is compassionate.'

'Allah is not my problem.'

Hafiz is jerked forward by the ropes, and now stands by his poems, his passion, his endlessly demanding life's work, spilt carelessly at his feet. Could he really place his children in the flames? He'd heard nothing from Behrouz since he left, and that was a year ago now. In the current climate, it was hard to imagine a safe place for his poems; and even harder to imagine Behrouz finding it. A fine copyist – but an adventurer?

And once again, Hafiz is in the past, sitting in Attar's upper room in the circle of disciples.

'We must not mistake desire for love,' said Attar.

Confused, he'd asked a question:

'And what is the difference between love and desire?'

'Love could let go tomorrow,' Attar had replied. 'Desire will cling for eternity.'

'We're waiting,' says Karim.

Love could let go tomorrow, so why not let go today?

'How rude of me,' says Hafiz with a smile, and bending down picks up the first batch of poems. With captive hands, he begins to cast them into the fire, more gasps from the onlookers, a scream from one, sobbing behind her veil. Hafiz looks into the crying eyes. He remembers words of Muhammed Attar, when insults and mockery became more commonplace towards him, more casual, more careless:

'It is a naïve man who imagines we are not engaged in a fierce battle, Hafiz, for people fall around our feet in excruciating pain, and the mad are the ones most heard. But don't harden your heart against the cruel arrows, my friend. Rather, soften your heart that the arrows might pass through.'

And now in the market place, Hafiz feels and speaks from those words again:

'We shall relinquish sadness, my friends!' he cries, tears spilling down his cheeks. 'And let my poor work feed the flames of hope! Just think: with my poems gone, there's more room in the world for love!'

With such words, he continues in his task, one batch after another tossed on the eager fire, dancing through the parchment in hysterical delight. Hafiz is ashes within, everything lost, everything crucified, as around him a quiet wailing holds these mad, sad moments.

Again the voice of Mubariz is heard, reading verses from the Koran: 'The punishment of those who wage war against Allah and His Messenger, and strive with might and main for mischief through the land, is execution or crucifixion or the cutting off of hands and feet ...'

Hafiz sees Dr Saad standing by the dark stone and feels the tug of the ropes pulling on his wrists. Time to go, time to make his way to the stone, where the knife is curved as the good doctor had said. He could see that now, could see the turquoise handle. And it would be clean. I cut it clean from the joint, he'd said, and you can trust a doctor. Maybe all executioners should be doctors, men with a keen eye for health, as they disfigure you, kill you.

With luck, he would be allowed a little wine, a kind anaesthetic and the cauterizing blessing of hot tar ...

Forty

Monday 3 November

Done!

Tamsin and Abbot Peter had now spoken with all those who attended the Feast of Fools at Henry House on Friday night, the night of Halloween. Peter had chosen the smallest of the counselling rooms for these conversations: dark wooden panelling, thick door and small window.

On entering, Tamsin had not been impressed: 'I see the cupboard – but where are the brooms?'

'It focuses the mind,' said Peter. 'Nothing too ornate to distract.'

'Nor air to keep alive.'

'Life is full of hard choices.'

'I prefer to have everything.'

They had not been long interviews, hastily arranged and fitted around commitments this Monday morning. And while the suspects were no longer dressed as clowns, there was something of the circus about it all, something of the absurd: each one of them so full in their recollections, yet so ignorant of who was who; each so confident about events, but so stupid about identities. And in a murder case, identity tends to matter.

Tamsin and Peter knew more than they had at the start … that at least could be said. With words spilled and recollections remembered, they now had a rough picture of the evening, as well as the fingerprints of those who attended. A thick veil of mystery remained however. As Peter had said as the final suspect left the interview cupboard: 'Well, that's all clear as mud.'

'It's not great.'

'But with the house locked and no sign of forced entry, amid all that we don't know – .'

'We've probably just spoken with the murderer, yes, I was thinking the same.'

'So brief reflections on the evening?'

'I have an idea,' said Tamsin.

'You've cracked it already? An investigation is traditional.'

'How about we sit somewhere else?'

'Is that necessary?'

'I'm beginning to feel like a broom.'

'The human need for beauty.'

'The human need for air and light.'

'How about the Long Room and some coffee?'

The positioning of his mid-morning coffee remained an issue for Peter … even when pursuing a murderer.

Forty One

With coffee in hand and notes on their laps, Tamsin and Peter now contemplated their material in the larger air and more generous light of the Long Room. So just what had been revealed?

They remembered a pathetic, if slightly unhelpful, Kate Karter.

'You seem to be having trouble remembering the evening,' Tamsin had said.

'Why would I want to remember, darling?'

'Because someone got murdered?'

'I remember sherry, I remember wine, too much of both, I remember trying to get people singing just to lighten things up a bit, get some life in the place.'

'And who was the Lord of Misrule?'

'Well, it wasn't me.'

'No idea who it might have been?'

'None at all, could have been anyone, those costumes – they were very … clever.'

'Anonymous?'

'Scarily so, especially when you're drunk.'

'You didn't hold back?'

'I'm not used to it, not normally a drinker me, I can do without … but then the Feast of Fools wasn't normal.'

'You needed some Dutch courage, perhaps?' said Peter.

'Something like that.'

'And which farmyard animal did you impersonate?'

'What?'

'At the meal, we hear the Lord of Misrule made everyone impersonate a farm yard animal and run round the Long Room in character. We were just wondering which animal you chose?'

'God knows.'

'Possibly. But you?'

126

'You'll have to ask the others, I can do a good horse, I may have done a horse.' Kate Karter neighed. 'It was probably that.'

It was a good horse.

'But there's nothing else about the evening that feels important to mention, like the meal, for instance?'

'I ate nothing, not hungry.'

Tamsin left a pause. She'd learned it from Peter, the therapist's pause she called it, deliberate space into which honesty must leap.

'Oh, I remember banging on the office door, when I couldn't get in.'

'Really?'

'That was during the game of Sardines, locked door, very suspicious.'

'The office door was locked?'

'I was suddenly very angry, unaccountably so, must be the drink, not my finest hour, bang-bang-banging on the door I was!'

'And inside the room, while you banged, Barnabus was being killed.'

'Apparently. Terrible thought.'

'You can't help us with that?'

'No.'

'Did you like him?'

'Barnabus? Hardly knew him, darling. Asked me a few stupid questions in our session, and that was that. Seemed a harmless fellow.'

Peter noted the 'harmless' epithet used again about Barnabus ... though not harmless enough to be allowed to live.

Forty Two

The interview with Ezekiel St Paul stumbled initially, but ended with Tamsin pulling a grand rabbit from the hat.

'So you had no alcohol throughout the evening, Ezekiel?'

'Reverend.'

'Reverend,' echoed Tamsin, with enormous self-discipline. She hated all instructions. 'Do you not like your name?'

Ezekiel offered a smile, but little else, closed to spontaneity like a polite but secretive crab.

'So you had no alcohol – Reverend?'

'No.'

'And your memories of the evening?'

'It was informative.'

'In what way?'

'To see the godless at play.'

This felt like an evasion to Peter, something untrue.

'For a similar experience of the godless at play, you could have gone to, well – you could have gone to a brothel?'

'You probably do,' thought Tamsin, eyeing the self-contained little man opposite her, in his shiny lime green suit and dog collar.

'Yet you chose the Feast of Fools,' continued Peter.

'The scriptures say, 'You are to be in the world, but not of the world.'

'That isn't really an answer.'

But Tamsin is stirred and takes the questions down another track:

'And this was you being in the world?' she said to a nodding Ezekiel. 'But not of the world, as you say, not drinking, not laughing, not enjoying yourself, that sort of thing? Which farm yard animal were you?'

'I was a cock.'

Peter avoided eye contact with Tamsin.

'You are a good cock impersonator?' asked Tamsin.

'It is of no consequence.'

'But it can be useful at parties to have an animal in us ... a cock in us, or whatever.'

Tamsin's self-discipline appeared to be cracking ... but appearance lied.

'And how was prison?' she asked.

The green-suited crab almost betrayed surprise.

'A three-year sentence for dealing in Class A drugs,' said Tamsin, referring to notes in slightly theatrical fashion. 'But not all bad, reduced to ... let me see, eighteen months for good behaviour. So well done there.'

'Repented of long ago.'

'So that's all right.'

'In God's eyes.'

'We'll have to take your word for that.'

'No, we can take God's Word for it,' he said, tapping his bible and smiling.

'Nevertheless,' said Tamsin, putting down her notes. 'We appear to have two Ezekiels, two Reverends, wouldn't you say? So I'm wondering which Reverend was at the Feast of Fools, sinner or saint?'

Forty Three

'I was just here for the wipe-out!' said Virgil Bannaford eagerly.

'I'm sorry?'

'Here for a jolly good laugh, nothing more honourable than that, mea culpa.'

'So the therapy?'

'A complete gas!'

'You didn't take it seriously.'

'Not into any of that nonsense!'

'You've had bad experiences?'

'One therapist, yonks ago, complete charlatan, told me to wear an elastic band around my wrist – and to ping it when I felt myself needing to control a situation.'

Virgil laughed at the absurdity of it all.

'You like to control things?' asked Peter.

'Apparently!'

'And did it work, the elastic band?'

'Hah! Of course it didn't work, I'd broken the damn thing by lunch time, snapped it out of its stupid little existence.'

Peter nodded.

'Well, I'm sure your therapist had their reasons.'

'Their mortgage, most like!'

'And I do agree – we need to deal with the forces within rather than play games with them.'

'Stupendously ridiculous.'

'But we also note you'd broken the band by lunch time, which at least exposes your issues with control … even if it doesn't heal them.'

'No comment.'

'So you gave Barnabus a hard time?' said Tamsin, picking up the story.

'As that old rascal Freud once said, 'Sometimes a cigar is just a cigar!'

Peter: 'Fair point, though presumably in saying that, he was also saying that sometimes it isn't.'

Virgil would lean forward and then back: forward to attack, back to assess. Now he leant back.

'You can look into things too much, if you ask me.'

'Looking into things frightens you?'

'Not in the least! It just bores me. Therapy's little more than a dubious commitment to gazing in the navel direction! And what if you then discover – and here's the thing – what if you then discover there's nothing bloody there, that you're empty, that you don't exist?'

'Is that what you fear?'

'That wouldn't be so clever! No, life's too short.'

A slight pause.

Tamsin: 'So the Feast of Fools was just one big laugh?'

'Gladiatorial combat with therapist, followed by Saturnalian orgy with clowns! What could be better?'

Unless interrogators were careful, they could find themselves pressed back by the body-energy in this man. Peter peeled himself off the dark-panelled wall, and decided on fresh direction:

'You clearly miss the Bullingdon Club, Virgil.'

'Impressed with your research.'

It was Bella he should be impressed with, the woman who'd found out more about Virgil than was apparent in any police records.

'The Bullingdon Club?' queries Tamsin, looking to both. Virgil gives Peter the floor with the words, 'Ignorance before experience.'

Peter explains: 'The Bullingdon Club, 200 years old, is essentially a Dining Club at Oxford University for the sons of royalty, sons of nobility and these days, sons of mere money.'

'Well, it's a sort of equality, letting the nouveaus in!'

'Club uniform smart: tail coats of dark navy blue, matching velvet collar, ivory silk lapels, mustard waistcoat and sky blue tie, which they wear to drink large quantities of champagne and to destroy whichever premises has the misfortune to be hosting them.'

'We always paid for damage done.'

'Membership is by election and may involve approaching a homeless man with a £50 note, only to burn it in front of him.'

'I never did that – or at least I don't remember doing that!'

'New members are expected to consume the entire contents of a tin of Colman's powdered mustard,' continues Peter, 'after which their room is trashed.'

'There seems to be a lot of trashing in the Bullingdon Club,' says Tamsin.

'Oh my God, listen to yourselves!' exclaims Virgil. 'Are the country's elite no longer allowed to behave badly, before assuming their dutiful place as leaders of nation and empire?'

Tamsin wonders which empire he refers to, and asks how an Abbot from the desert knows quite so much about the Bullingdon Club?

'Brother Torquil was a member in his wild youth, son of some Scottish lord. But he's now responsible for novitiates at the monastery of St. James-the-Less, so he trashes less than he used to. But he'd tell stories of astounding destruction while we worked in the monastery garden.'

'With a large dollop of nostalgia no doubt!' says Virgil. 'And has this got anything to do with the case in hand, because if not, I'm off.'

'We don't know if it's got anything to do with the case,' says Peter. 'How could we know?'

'Sounds like a load of socialist envy to me, the old green-eyed monster stalking my past.'

'Not necessarily. At the beginning of a case, no one knows what contains significance. As with a jigsaw, we can only sit down and get the pieces out of the box. What will fit where, is still something of a mystery. This may not fit anywhere at all. But you have to look at all the pieces first.'

'You sound like my nanny. Beastly woman.'

'My experience is that every piece fits somewhere, even if it's only background.'

'She wasn't all bad, Nanny Stokes, stale breath of course, but one mustn't speak ill of the dull.'

He looks for a laugh which doesn't come so he tries to build bridges:

'And of course I'm a great supporter of the police.'

'How reassuring for us all,' says Tamsin.

'Absolutely.'

'And you've nothing else to add, Mr Bannaford?'

'Nothing. My pockets are clean!'

'So you were just here at Henry House for the laugh?'

Forty Four

Like a lizard in the sun, Martin Channing sat still, relaxed and alert. And he knew how to open with an attention-grabbing line, as he reflected on the Feast of Fools:

'Well, I thought it was an unmitigated success,' he said.

'Really?'

'Like an evening of commedia dell'arte, with the Harlequin, Columbina, Pierrot, et al! Marvellous!'

'An unmitigated success apart from the murder,' said Peter.

'A plodding and pious response, Abbot – you've wandered into bland.'

'Thank you.'

'And not a camera in sight.'

'I'm sorry?'

'Cameras bring bland as sure as night follows day. Put an authority figure on TV, and it draws from them considered words, official words, judiciously chosen – and authentic as spray-on tan, words designed only to beguile or anaesthetise the public.'

'Quite a speech.'

'But am I wrong?'

'I was simply pointing out the fact of murder.'

'And so what?'

'Well, it's not without importance,'

'But does the world have to stop?'

'The world pauses perhaps.'

'Then there would have been some very long pauses in Medieval England, Abbot!'

Tamsin attempts to re-focus: 'We're trying to find out what happened here last night.'

'Creation is red in tooth and claw,' says Channing, ignoring her, 'always has been, we just forget.'

'At least now we investigate the claw's damage,' says Peter.

133

'Do you like Dorset, Abbot?'

Where was this going?

'I don't know it well.'

'You'd love it, everyone loves it, Portland Bill and all that, everyone loves Dorset.'

'I'll take your word for it.'

'But presumably you read the piece in the *Silt* last week?'

'I may have missed it.'

'They've found fifty-one decapitated skeletons there, an execution dating from the early eleventh century.'

'I'm sure the Dorset police are on the case.'

'You see, we should never pretend we're a civilised species, Abbot, that's what I'm saying. We all contain the appalling.'

'The *Silt* contains it every week,' says Tamsin, keen to get back to the Feast of Fools.

'As do you, Detective Inspector, and even the holy and habited Abbot!'

Peter says he isn't sure anyone is pretending to be civilised, but the lizard sweeps smoothly on:

'The executed of Dorset suffered multiple wounds, inflicted by a sharp-bladed weapon to head, jaw and upper spine. All a little unnecessary – the violence, I mean – but then humans will be humans, delighting in savagery, and all of it watched and applauded by a very large crowd. The massacre was entertainment!'

He paused before finishing.

'So really, we should be thankful it was only Barnabus on Friday night, with an audience of just one.'

'Certainly not fewer than one,' said Tamsin, 'though maybe more, who knows? Perhaps you know, Mr Channing.'

Martin, conspiratorially: 'Mind you, the executed of Dorset were only Vikings, trespassers in the area, so we shouldn't be too sad. Not Swedish are you?'

'Do I look Swedish?' asked the black-haired, olive-skinned Tamsin.

'Freedom of movement around the European Union was allowed in those days – but only if you had a large number of sword-wielding friends.'

Tamsin feels it's time to move on from Dorset ... and the Vikings.

'So why were you here in Henry Hall?'

'Professional interest. A local event on Halloween night ... could make a decent story. And I wasn't wrong, was I?'

'Do you usually send yourself?'

'Flaky features editor pulled out.'

Peter and Tamsin sift the words for truth.

'And the evening itself?'

'As I say, a rather charming success from beginning to end … well, almost the end. All very bizarre, of course, the clothes, the voice pills, the stage shoes – but really, wasn't bizarre the point? And I was so looking forward to my second session with Barnabus. Plenty of material to reflect on!'

'Perhaps Frances will stand in for Barnabus?'

'Perhaps.'

He wasn't keen.

'And the Lord of Misrule?' asks Tamsin.

Give us some help, thinks Peter.

'Not me, sadly, I would have been a great deal more wicked!'

'Some might say that as editor of the *Silt,* you're the Lord of Misrule already.'

'I take that as a huge compliment.'

That figured.

'And so no idea who it was, the Lord of Misrule?'

'No idea at all, but they had a certain panache, I'll give them that. Rather distinctive stylised movements throughout, negating all individuality, a cross between mime and ballet.'

Martin Channing can't resist a little demonstration, a strangely compelling sequence of moves.

'Are you sure it wasn't you?'

'I'll tell you who it reminded me of,' says Martin.

'Who?'

'Picasso's 'Seated Harlequin'.'

Tamsin looks blank as Martin explains:

'Who some say was his alter-ego, the sad man with a painted smile, traumatised by the suicide of his friend Casagemas.'

Pause.

'We'll bear the art history in mind,' said Tamsin.

Forty Five

'So yours was a different vision of therapy, Frances?'

'A rather more practical one, perhaps.'

Frances had alert and lively eyes.

'Barnabus wasn't practical?'

'I believe in quick results from therapeutic intervention.'

'And Barnabus didn't?'

Frances sighed.

'Barnabus said healing took time, and the trouble is, time's something nobody has … or not something they can be bothered with, at least.'

'The murderer will have time – when this is all over,' said Tamsin.

A pause, broken by Peter:

'And perhaps that's the reason why they're ill.'

'How do you mean?'

'People unwilling to offer time to the healing process. They seek the quick fix and the easy mend.'

'Distraction junkies, unable to focus on the important?'

'Not unknown,' said Peter, but Frances is unconvinced:

'Rake up the client's past,' she said, 'and you're lost in a swamp with no exit. It's like the eternal onion, layer after layer removed, but never reaching the heart of the matter.'

Peter says: 'You prefer something more cognitive?'

'Hijack the mind, get the old box of tricks working for you – of course! Why are you depressed? I don't want to know – and neither do you frankly. But let's at least get some positive thought going. Six sessions max, wham bam, thank you, Sam.'

'Think yourself fit?'

'Good slogan. We could use that at *Mind Gains*.'

'Feels a little like papering over the cracks,' said the Abbot.

'And papering over the cracks is fine.'

'It is?'

'What's your problem with papering over the cracks?'

'The cracks, I suppose.'

'Cracks are okay! People can happily live in a house for years with the cracks papered over. It looks nice, which is what most people want. And as long as the holes don't get any bigger, nothing unmanageable at least, what's the issue? Nothing wrong with a bit of papering over – if it saves rebuilding the entire wall!'

'That's a take on therapy I can understand,' said Tamsin.

Peter: 'But Barnabus liked to rebuild the wall?'

'There was a pseudo-spirituality in his work, which I always felt was misguided.'

'Because?'

'Why encourage people in their delusions? I wish to promote realism, not psychological infantilism.'

'So religion, however described, is opposed to the goals of mental health?'

'No question. I say to people: where is there any evidence God exists? Prove to me that any supernatural being cares a hoot for you, or ever will? Freud believed religion was rooted in a child's sense of helplessness in a dangerous world.'

'And you agree?'

'Of course.'

'So the human is less a soul and more a machine?'

'Clearly! So yes, attend to the hurt, identify the harmful consequences of the hurt, identify strategies for coping, discuss the benefits of moving on, the benefits of releasing past grievances, establish ways this process might be supported – it's not rocket science and it sure as hell isn't spiritual. It's just the re-orientation of our psychology. The "whys" don't matter – the only thing that matters is: "what now?".'

'So your creed is something like: "Don't stir the water – just build a bridge over it"?'

'That's what I used to say to Barnabus.'

'But he didn't agree?'

'He could be very stubborn.'

'And so could Bella,' says Tamsin.

'Bella?'

'She pulled out of the Feast of Fools after an argument with you. What was that about?'

Frances breathes deeply and speaks slowly:

'She wanted to be the Lord of Misrule. She'd organised the event and felt she was owed that.'

'But you didn't?'

'I didn't what?'

'You didn't feel she was owed that?'

'It was a ridiculous idea.'

'Explain ridiculous.'

'Simple. At the heart of the event, the pivot of unpredictability on which it sat, was the random nature of that appointment.'

'And so that was that.'

'I run *Mind Gains*, not Bella.'

'No.'

'Are we done?'

'And now, of course, there's no Barnabus to share that leadership,' says Tamsin. 'Will you miss him?'

'It was terrible what was done to him, unforgiveable, although in some ways – and don't take this the wrong way – he was like a sick dog put out of its misery.'

Forty Six

'It's a bit like the four gospels,' said Abbot Peter. 'Same story, different versions ... only this time, without any names.'

They remained in the Long Room, mulling over the evidence amid a creeping chill. As in the arctic, it was best not to stay still in Henry House.

'But we do know the evening started with a welcoming glass of sherry in the hall.'

'And no one yet in party clothes.'

Peter was definitely cold.

'Could we light the fire – or is that still evidence?'

'I believe the grate has been thoroughly vetted.'

'Then let me do the honours.'

Peter soon had a good fire burning.

'You're quite competent at lighting fires,' said Tamsin, surprising herself with this piece of praise.

'The Bedouin are the best teachers.'

'Really?'

Sarcasm.

'If you can light a fire in the desert, you can light one anywhere.'

'Underwater?'

'Now you're being silly.'

'I'm just rebelling against these ridiculous desert myths.'

'And the interesting question is: why?'

'To work,' said Tamsin.

Peter nodded.

'Present at the Feast of Fools were Frances Pole, director, Barnabus Hope, director and Pat Strong, cleaner. That was the *Mind Gains* staff and then the four clients, Kate Karter, Virgil Bannaford, Ezekiel St Paul and Martin Channing.'

'And Bella Amal, the administrator, should have been there, having organised the event. But Frances had a row with her, after which Bella walked out in a fit of pique – about two hours before guests were due to arrive.'

'She then apparently spent the evening at home and later at *The Smugglers Arms*. Needs checking obviously, but it would be an unwise lie.'

'But Bella's template for the evening was carried out as far as we can tell. After sherry in the hall, more than a glass or two apparently, the participants came up here to the Long Room, where there was wine and nibbles.'

'Sherry downstairs, wine upstairs. Did they want them all drunk?'

'That was the idea. In the gospel according to Frances, excess, disguise and the removal of rules bring with them the psychological liberation of the clients.'

'And here in the Long Room, eight screens, behind which people's clown outfits were laid out.'

'They'd been told about these downstairs.'

'They were reminded by Frances that the challenge was complete disguise throughout the evening. If no one could say what you did the following morning, then you were a success! Sounds rather fun in a way.'

'Sounds a complete nightmare,' said the Abbot. 'But people made a brave attempt at conversation. Virgil said that Pat seemed very tense downstairs – "like a deer on a rifle range", was his phrase – which was apparently unlike her. Not her normal self at all, he said.'

'Interesting. Though really, what in her short life could have prepared her for a night like this?'

'It seems Kate held the floor with some slightly hysterical behaviour. Once she saw a piano, she tried to organise everyone into a choir.'

'The wine was talking.'

'Or singing.'

'And then Frances brought them to order, they swallowed their voice pills, after which she explained that shortly, the lights would go out, and they knew what to do.'

'The lights did go out – the gardener earning some overtime – and under cover of dark, everyone retired behind their screen to change.'

'The consensus is that Bella's screen was still there, as it would be, given the late nature of the withdrawal – but not used.'

'They then emerged from behind their screens in full disguise: show shoes, masked, gloved, a merry band of harlequins.'

'The lights returned and the bowl of election was produced.'

'This was to decide who would be the Lord of Misrule.'

'In the bowl were seven folded cards, one of which would declare its owner the Lord of Misrule.'

'People made their choices, until one of them – I wish we knew who – held up the card which gave them power for the following hour.'

'There was a meal at the table, during which the Lord of Misrule began to use their power, ordering people to perform duties and tasks of a variously fun or mischievous nature.'

'The one that everyone remembers, apart from Kate who wasn't sure, was the farm animal game.'

'And then after the meal, the Lord announced a game of Sardines with terrible repercussions for the loser.'

'One participant is sent off to hide, the others have to find them, and the loser is the last one to do so.'

'So they all count slowly to fifty while the hare seeks a secret place. And then the search of Henry House began. No lights on, so a little spooky but they went their separate ways, though one or maybe two – some disagreement there – tried the office door and discovered it was locked.'

'So they banged on it loudly asking if there was cheating going on.'

'Meanwhile the hare, who turned out to be Virgil, curled up on the four poster, was gradually being found. Those who found him had to lie there with him, squashed together.'

'Like sardines.'

'Indeed. It does bring my Christmas Past to mind.'

'And the last clown to find him, who was Kate, was then forced to kiss the feet of all participants and apologise for her stupidity.'

'Frances then took control again, ordering everyone to find a dark place, change out of their clothes and gather again in the Long Room. This they all did in cheerful mood; Frances, trying to speak as normally as the pills allowed, thanked them all for their spirit of adventure. It was then noticed that Barnabus was missing.'

'But Frances, "suspecting he'd left early in a mood", she said, made light of it, encouraged everyone not to be late for their sessions on Monday – and ordered Pat to return to being a cleaner!'

'Pat then said something like: "I hope, with all my heart, that is possible".'

'Odd.'

'They then left the building in varying degrees of merriment, with the teetotal Ezekiel the only one unable to loosen up.'

'Not a spectacular surprise.'

'Frances checked the office, found the door open, assumed Barnabus had simply gathered some things before leaving – and then left herself.'

'With Ezekiel as chauffeur.'

'She'd drunk the cellar dry, likes a drink apparently, while Ezekiel had imbibed nothing but orange juice. So she locked up and went home.'

'And the clothes?'

'All bagged up and left outside, as pre-arranged, to be collected by the cleaners Saturday morning.'

'And Henry House quiet at last.'

'As quiet as a tomb.'

'And that was that, until an anonymous phone call from the *Mind Gains* pay phone on Sunday morning, to say that the dead body of Barnabus Hope was in the office cupboard.'

'Not the murderer presumably, informing on themselves.'

'No. So someone else was here that morning, someone other than the murderer.'

It was then that a detective poked his head around the door.

'Yes?' said Tamsin.

'Sorry to disturb you, Ma'am, but one or two developments concerning Pat Strong.'

'Nice girl,' said Abbot Peter, by way of nothing at all.

'What about Pat Strong?'

'The address she gave when employed here is a false one; there's no such place as 11 Regency Villas in Stormhaven.'

'Suggesting a rather casual employment regime.'

'Or a desperate one,' said Peter.

'And the other development?'

'She appears to have gone missing, as far as we can tell.'

Tamsin took this information in with a smile.

'Nice girl, Abbot?'

'That was my impression.'

'Or did you just fancy her?'

Peter sat impassive.

'Abbot Peter's psychological profiling comes up trumps again,' she adds.

'I may have been slightly hasty,' he says.

A victor's smile from Tamsin.

'But then again, I may not.'

'Find Pat Strong and bring her in, Constable … while Abbot Peter and I take a look at the clown in the cupboard.'

Forty Seven

'Well, this does rather change things,' said Martin Channing.

He was sitting with Frances Pole in a coffee shop, five minutes from his office, in the ancient and well-heeled town of Lewes.

'I don't see why we couldn't have met in Stormhaven.'

Martin had summoned her and she didn't like being summoned, you didn't summon Frances ... but she had obeyed.

'Because there isn't a coffee house there without grease on the walls.'

'You're such a snob, Martin.'

'And you aren't?'

Frances sniffs with disdain, as Channing continues:

'It was very clear, for instance, who the cleaner was at the Feast of Fools.'

'What do you mean?'

'When the evening was over and normality returned, you made things very plain, shall we say? "You do realise it's past midnight, Cinderella?" '

'There was cleaning to be done.'

It was clear the girl needed to get back to work, what was his issue?

'Everyone has their place with you, Frances.'

'You could have come round to mine,' she says, still resentful.

'I'm not sure that would have been a good idea.'

'You don't imagine I still want you.'

'I wouldn't be so bold, Frannie dear. But how does it look?'

'What do you mean, how does it look?'

'Two suspects gathered in secret court to get their stories straight?'

'I don't know what you're talking about.'

'And now I'm being tempted by one of those cakes. Would you like a cake, Frannie?'

143

'Frances.'

'Indeed.'

'Do you ever feel anything, Martin?'

'What should I feel?'

'Recent events.'

'It's a very particular tragedy, of course it is.'

' "A very particular tragedy".'

'What do you want me to say?'

'How about a complete nightmare?'

Martin Channing sips his peppermint tea.

'A nightmare of sorts, Frances.'

'I didn't know they came in different flavours.'

'You surprise me. I thought dream analysis was stock-in-trade for shrinks. Didn't Freud call dreams the royal road to the unconscious?'

'I've never really believed that.'

'But I bet you don't tell your patients.'

Frances was non-committal.

'Of course not,' said Martin. 'Think of the special power that bestows on you – the one who understands dreams! That vital sense of mystery to justify the rather large fee.'

Frances was enjoying her latte, but little else. Martin's cynicism could entertain, but not today.

'There is truth to be found in dreams,' she said.

'So what were yours last night?'

'Mine?'

'That would be interesting.'

'But dreams also feature the last meal you ate.'

'So it may be the cheese rather than your subconscious?'

'It's not always easy to distinguish.'

Martin was not interested in dreams, he couldn't care less, he was here to talk about money. But Fran was proving her old intransigent self this morning. She remained an attractive woman, someone who'd maintained her looks, a little harder in the face perhaps … and too strict a diet had removed any gentleness in her features. But they would not have worked as a couple, he knew that.

'So where does the nightmare end and the dream begin for *Mind Gains,* Frances?'

'I see no dream beginning, none at all.'

Frances was now a sulky girl.

'I mean, where does this leave the clinic?'

'Very much on the front page, I'd say,' said Martin.

'Exactly.'

'And you know what they say about publicity.'

'Remind me.'

Channing smiled.

'Show me a celebrity who doesn't prefer a bad word to no word.'

'No, Martin, that's a lie you journalists cling to, after another hatchet job on someone.'

'A pound every time.'

'I'm sorry?'

'I wish I had a pound every time I'd heard that tired little line. Do you rehearse these old arguments in front of a mirror? I know it can be hard to drag you away from there.'

Frances took another sip of her latte.

'Perhaps it helps you sleep at night,' she said. 'Imagining your spite has actually done them a favour.'

'I sleep very well.'

'Really?'

'If I'd wanted to run Oxfam, I'd have applied for the job.'

The coffee house was busy, competition for tables just managing to stay polite.

'It costs 13 pence to make a cup of coffee,' he said, aware he'd got little change from the £5 note he'd handed the barista. 'That makes this pretty close to robbery.'

Frances was unconcerned about the mark-up on coffee.

She says: 'Meanwhile, I'm imagining a word association game sounding something like 'Henry House – murder! – Mind Gains – grizzly death! – therapy – danger!' Why would I want any of that?'

'I wasn't saying you did.'

'No, well I don't.'

'You're sounding very prim, Frances.'

'I don't need you today, Martin.'

'You needed me last week.'

'As I say, I don't need you today.'

There was a silence between them, only broken by Martin posing the question he'd meant to ask all along.

'You didn't kill poor old Barnabus, did you?'

'No, I didn't, Martin. Did you?'

Forty Eight

Bella Amal, the administrator – or rather, Director of Administration – saw everything in Henry House. Everything noticed and logged, not in a book but in her head ... and it hadn't been a policeman in the shadows upstairs.

Since her arrival that Monday, after the delay at the gates, she'd watched the last of the forensic activity play itself out beneath the Elizabethan beams, old rooms scoured by new technologies, finely combed, dabbed and photographed. But since the morning interviews, the house was open again, all except the office, where the body had been found and apparently still lay, which was too morbid.

But returning to the matter in hand – and Bella always did, never one to let a matter drop – that had been no police figure in the gallery shadows, the movement too hasty for forensics, too furtive, a body in search of obscurity. The figure had moved quickly towards the bedrooms, away from her gaze, but Bella could move quickly too. And she was recovering herself, she felt that, recovering from the events of the day. Slowly, Henry House was feeling like her kingdom again and whoever was up there, they shouldn't be, and Bella would let them know. She'd told the constable she'd monitor visitors while he nipped out for a sandwich – bad boy, really – and she'd monitor this one now.

She crossed the hallway and climbed the stairs. The polished wood of the gallery floor was covered by worn carpet, enough to quieten her steps as she moved towards the arch which led into the bedroom corridor. At the end of the corridor, at the front corner of the house, was the master bedroom, awaiting VIP's. Nearer, was the bedroom used by Barnabus, and it was here Bella sensed a human presence, slight breathlessness behind the door. Who was it? And what were they doing in Barnabus' bedroom? The door stood ajar, wedged on the uneven floor.

'Hello?' says Bella.

There's silence and then a noise, something knocked, a knee against a bedside table?

'I need to know who you are,' says Bella. 'And what you're doing.'

Again, no reply.

'I'm coming in,' she says, and pushes at the door. It sticks at first, more pressure applied, and suddenly it's flying back on its hinges. Bella steps inside.

Forty Nine

Bella turns to see Virgil sitting on the bed.

'No need to panic, old thing,' he says with cheery challenge.

'What are you doing here?' asks Bella, flustered.

'I'm sitting on the bed.'

'Why?'

'Are you the police, old girl, or just a nosy busy-body?'

Bella looks around like a concerned sparrow. She looks for something disturbed, something to explain his presence in the room. There is nothing obviously changed.

'Virgil, I need to know what you're doing here.'

'You need to know what I'm doing here? Well, that's a laugh and a half! The real question is: what the hell you're doing here?'

Aggression.

'I work here.'

'Not in this bedroom, you don't.'

'I work in Henry House.'

Virgil smiles with derision.

'Lots of people have worked here, Bella, lots of servants like you down the years – but none of them have owned it.'

Bella is thrown.

'I never said I owned it, but I have a responsibility – .'

'You're passing through Bella, a mere employee, "downstairs" as they say, and soon there won't be a clinic here, not after what happened last night. *Mind Gains* is finished and good riddance!'

'I think you'll find – .'

'And then you'll be back at the job centre with all the other oiks, instead of bursting into bedrooms like you own the place.'

'There you go again, implying – .'

'You're what they call a "temp", Bella.'

'I'll call the police.'

'You'll call the police?'

The rage in Virgil is overwhelming, like a tidal surge through a bamboo village.

'I'll have you evicted!' she says, backing away as he moves towards her. Already off balance in her platform shoes, Virgil's deliberate shoulder sends her flying against the chest of drawers, before falling to the floor. He moves now towards the door, but blocking his way is Kate Karter.

'What are you doing here?' she cries out, as he pushes past.

'Ask yourself the same question,' he shouts, disappearing back to the gallery. 'What are any of you doing here?'

'Rude man! Have you no manners?'

Kate enters the room and sees Bella on the floor, struggling to get up.

'What was that about?' she says. 'I hope you didn't upset him.'

'The man's a maniac,' says Bella, smarting.

'I thought he was a bit restless at the Feast.'

'Well, I wouldn't know, would I?'

'No,' says Kate, 'you wouldn't. But when we threw our costumes into the laundry basket at the end, he said, 'Well if that's the best *Mind Gains* can do, I don't anticipate a long stay here in Stormhaven.' He said it as if nothing would make him happier. Strange fellow.'

'Barnabus did intimate he could be difficult,' says Bella. 'So are you going to help me up?'

They struggle and slide a little, but once Bella is standing, she pulls away, brushes herself down and goes to the mirror to recover her face.

'So what are you doing here?' she asks.

'I was interviewed.'

'That was earlier.'

'And then I decided to hang around a while, go for a walk.'

'A walk?'

'It's not a crime.'

'Can't see the point.'

'And I was in the hall collecting my bag, when I heard your voice.'

'There are still police around,' says Bella, touching up her lipstick.

'Well, there would be, wouldn't there?'

'I'm just saying.'

'And you'll have to put up with them, even if they do get in your way.'

'None of them wipe their shoes.'

'You'd think forensics would.'

'Would what?'

'Wipe their shoes.'

'None of them.'

'But probably good at washing up … no evidence of bolognese sauce unnoticed on the saucepans.'

Bella's lipstick is sorted and her face restored.

'I just wonder what he was doing here?' says Kate.

'Who?'

'Virgil. Yours, I think.'

Kate has found Bella's missing earring but receives no thanks.

'Virgil? I have no idea,' she says, ready to go. 'As far as I can see, he was just sitting on the bed. I'll tell the police obviously.'

'Have they found Pat?'

'Pat?'

'I heard from the young policeman she's gone missing. He sort of implied it.'

'It's time you were gone, Kate.'

'Didn't you know about Pat?'

'Don't worry about me, Kate. I know all I need to know.'

'I was only seeing how you were.'

'And I'm fine, so lead the way, I have things to do.'

And with that, the two women left the room, returned to the hallway and without a further word, parted company.

Bella watched as Kate got into her car and drove off. She didn't like her, she was an unsettling presence, hysterical and stupid, and Bella was restoring order to Henry House. She was getting things back on track, back in place, as if nothing had happened and no murder had occurred, because that was the way forward.

But now Abbot Peter and Tamsin appear in the hall, led towards the office by an excited constable.

'We found them in the cupboard, Ma'am … though no one knows what they mean.'

'What exactly have you found, Constable?' asks Tamsin, as they disappear into the office.

And being Director of Administration, and perhaps a nosy busybody, Bella is wondering the same.

Fifty

Your thousand limbs rend my body this is the way.

The ten words, in spidery script – 'way' is particularly pained – had been found as they prepared to move the body from the cupboard. They were written in black biro on the inside wall, where the crumpled form of Barnabus the Clown still lay. Tamsin had deliberately withheld the body from Peter's gaze before the interviews.

'We'll look at the corpse after the interviews,' she'd said.

'But you've already seen it.'

'I have, yes.'

'So the delay is on my behalf.'

'We don't have the time.'

'We always have time for what we want to do.'

'And you want to see it?'

'No.'

'Well then.'

'I'm just wondering about motive here.'

'The murderer's?'

'Yours.'

'Mine? Well, I just think it would be better.'

'Because?'

'Because I do.'

Tamsin hoped Peter was making life as difficult for the murderer.

'It's not because you care about my feelings,' said Peter, 'so why?'

How had the conversation gone? Tamsin had said Kate Karter, the first of the suspects to be interviewed, was waiting for them, true as far as it went … she had been. But she knew her uncle was right, Kate hadn't been the reason, and no, it wasn't because she cared, or not in the traditional sense of the word. She didn't care for the feelings of others, because why would anyone do that? Who'd ever cared for hers? But she did care about the success of her investigation. And although the Abbot claimed Barnabus was not a friend, and claimed it repeatedly, Tamsin viewed the dead man as the closest approxima-

151

tion to a friend her uncle had. His murdered body, the crumpled clown, would lodge in his mind, this is how she'd been thinking, and she'd wanted his mind clear during the interviews ... and at its listening best. Otherwise what was the point of having him along? And so, yes, she'd delayed the showing.

But now, led by an excited constable, Peter and Barnabus were finally to meet, meet for the last time, with as much intimacy as tape, lights and plastic baggery would allow. Peter looked down, said 'My God,' and then simply stared at the battered clown, a spent figure on cold knees, lurched sideways across the cupboard, head down, right arm reaching forward.

'Stab wounds to the neck and stomach,' said Tamsin.

Blood stains were clear on the wall behind, like the dry drips left by an inexpert decorator ... and blood on the red and yellow of the twisted harlequin silk, though where red dye ended and blood began, was hard to tell.

'But death arrived by two blows to the skull with a heavy metal object,' continued Tamsin, 'almost certainly the poker from the fire.'

She pointed to it, now wrapped in clear packaging. Peter nodded.

'So are those his lines?' asked Tamsin.

'How do you mean?'

'Did he write those words – on the wall.'

Peter hadn't given the words a thought.

'I can't really see them.'

He remained a few feet away, hesitant.

'Well get closer, for God's sake! You were the one who wanted to see the body.'

'No, I was the one who wondered why you weren't letting me see the body. There's a difference.'

'It's eluding me.'

Pause.

'But with hindsight, Tamsin, it was a wise call.'

'Thank you.'

'I might well have been distracted in the interviews.'

'So is it his writing?'

Peter edged closer, close enough now to touch the chilling flesh.

'I don't know,' he said, tucking his habit behind him as he knelt down. 'He usually emailed.'

'But are they the sort of words Barnabus would write?' persisted Tamsin.

'You're asking for rather specialised insight there. To know what someone would write when dying – .'

'But do they ring a bell?'

'Strangely, they do,' said Peter, gazing on the uneven scrawl. 'But it's a distant bell, only faintly heard across the valley of time.'

'Can we take the body, Ma'am?' asked one of the team, impatient to be off.

'In a while, Joseph, but first do something cultural.'

'Ma'am?'

'Go on a tour of the historical Elizabethan kitchens – keep it brief – and while there, make us a cup of tea on the best bone china available.'

'Yes, Ma'am.'

He seemed pleased to have something to do, even it was just making tea.

'The human needs to work,' she said.

Peter's head was still in the cupboard.

'Appropriate,' he said.

'What's appropriate?'

'The crockery. You do know that bone china first came to Europe during the reign of Elizabeth?'

'I didn't.'

'Oh,' said Peter, faintly disappointed.

'How have I got as far as I have?' said Tamsin.

'Available only to royalty, nobility, rich merchants – so very probably to the Rowse family who lived here.'

'Everyone else drank straight from the kettle presumably?'

'And, of course, in those days it was actually made from bones. '

'As the name suggests. '

'Which gave the delicate pottery its surprising strength.'

'The crockery industry is not having my body.'

'Oh? I quite fancy the idea of being drunk from and washed up every day.'

'Then our ambitions differ.'

There was a pause as Peter returned to the matter in hand.

'The skull took a good battering,' he said, contemplating the encrusted blood in the dark curly hair.

'I'm wondering if the murderer left the words.'

'Some sort of signature?'

'Yes.'

'Seems unlikely. Apart from anything else, the angle's all wrong.'

Peter got up to impersonate the murderer leaning down to write. It wasn't working.

'The thing is,' he said, 'if Barnabus did write them, and it looks like he did, it means – '

' – it means he was in the cupboard alive for some length of time,' said Tamsin. 'The thought had crossed my mind. He certainly didn't write them after the assault with the poker.'

'And so the next question: why was he put in the cupboard half-alive and then re-visited later – we don't know how much later – for the killing?'

Tamsin went to the window.

'He wrote those words,' she said, as if the matter was settled.

'I think I agree.'

'Couldn't you just agree without the caveat?'

'No.'

'Because?'

'Because I don't agree without a caveat, so why lie to help you feel better?'

'What better reason to lie?'

'They do feel like a message, that's the thing. And if they are a message, then he wrote them to help us.'

'So why didn't he just write the killer's name?'

Peter pondered for a moment.

'Perhaps he knew they'd be back and so used a code they wouldn't understand.'

There was a pause.

'But which you would!' said Tamsin.

'Sorry?'

'But which you would! That's it!'

'Me?'

'Why not? I suddenly feel like a gooseberry here, a strange feeling, but I do. This is one bloke to another. He knew you'd read this.'

'I struggle to see how.'

'What did you talk about when you last met?'

'Nothing of great consequence.'

Tamsin gave him a look.

'Well, I suppose he was very interested in the dead vicar at St Michaels and my small part in the investigation.'

'Precisely. All the more reason to attempt communication with you. He guessed you'd be involved.'

'Possibly.'

'What else did you talk about?'

'He wanted to write a book.'

'I hope you advised against it.'

'I did.'

'We need a purge not an increase.'

'But apart from issues here at *Mind Gains*, I can't really remember much else.'

Tamsin was now on a roll.

'Well, what do you have in common?'

'What did we have in common?'

Peter remembered Barnabus on his arrival in the desert, such a troubled soul, so fresh from a failed marriage, so guilty, so vulnerable. But somehow he'd found new life in the dry air, and refreshment in the sparse heat.

'We had the desert in common, I suppose.'

'Start there.'

'The desert's a big place.'

'Where's the tea?' said Tamsin with some force, after which she left the room to harass the constable. Peter pondered the twisted figure before him.

'So, my friend, what are you trying to tell me? *Your thousand limbs rend my body this is the way.* The funny thing is, I can hear you saying it … perhaps once you did say it to me … but why are you saying it now?'

Fifty One

'Why do you not love me as a woman should love her husband?' said Ezekiel.

He was pacing the room, a small man in his green silk suit, precise, contained but rigid with rage.

'I do love you as a woman should love her husband,' said Rebecca, sobbing by the empty fireplace.

'But you want to disobey me.'

'I don't want to disobey you.'

She did want to disobey him.

'Then why do you question me?'

Why did she question him?

'Is it disobedience to love your daughter?' she said.

'I love my daughter.'

'I know you do.'

'But I love her with a holy love.'

Distinction drawn.

'Do you think I do not love my daughter?' continued Ezekiel.

'Of course you love her.'

'Do you think I don't know what's best?'

There was hesitation from Rebecca, the sin rising in her again: the sin which said he didn't know best, that she knew best, that he was mad, that she hated him and hated what he was doing to her and her children. Shame on you, Rebecca! Oh, when would she be free of such terrible thoughts? She was younger than Ezekiel by twelve years, and still learning, so much to learn. He'd worked hard to make her a good person, and here she was, aged 37, with so much sin in her. How could he ever forgive her?

'You are still a spiritual child.'

'I know.'

'You understand little of the ways of the Lord.'

'Help me, Ezekiel.'

It was a relief to hand over responsibility, to accept once again that in the divine order of things, the man was the head of the household. And Ezekiel was a good man, he did not drink as her father had done, and neither did he go after other women as some men did. There was much to worship and obey as her marriage vows demanded of her.

'You know what's best, husband.'

And then remembering the words of Mary, when told she was to give birth to Jesus:

'Let it be unto me according to thy word.'

He'd like that and part of her was cunning enough to feed him what he wanted.

Ezekiel's chest expanded with honour as he looked down on the girl he had plucked from the youth group to be his wife, under God.

'She will come back to the true path,' he said, 'but she's a wayward girl and best not indulged.'

The trouble was, Rebecca still admired her daughter's spirit and hoped it would never be crushed.

Never!

Fifty Two

It was Frances who told them about the ghost of Henry Hall – though as Tamsin said, who believes in ghosts these days?

They met Frances in the hall as they were leaving, the first day of the investigation complete.

'And does Henry Hall have a ghost?' Peter had asked.

He'd heard some local tale about a haunting.

'Oh, please!'

Tamsin was incredulous.

'Of course we have a ghost,' said Frances briskly and Tamsin asked if she'd seen it.

'Every old house has its ghost,' said Frances, 'and particularly Tudor houses.'

'They're more ghost-ridden than others?'

'They were violent times, times when many lives ended prematurely, and – well – horribly.'

There was a pause as they stood in the dark hall. Violent times, premature deaths, some horrible, she'd said – like clowns being bludgeoned to death with a fire poker?

'So much more civilised now, of course,' said Peter.

'I'll just get my coat,' said Frances.

'The ghost of Ann Boleyn is said to haunt both Hever Castle and the Tower of London,' remarked Peter, almost expecting a ghoul to appear from a doorway, holding its head.

Tamsin says: 'I didn't realise ghosts could divide their time.'

'But then you don't believe in them.'

'Of course I don't.'

'No mystery allowed in Tamsin's world.'

'They're like Father Christmas – something we've invented for our own entertainment.'

'More common in times of recession,' said Frances, returning. 'At least sightings are.'

'Is that so?' said Peter.

'Apparently. When we're wealthy and masters of our universe, we don't bother so much with dubious possibilities. But when the veneer of control is removed and the world a more frightening place, we begin to see mysterious things in every dark alley.'

'And every dark gallery perhaps?'

They all looked to the gallery above them

'Well, that is where the ghost wanders, according to Dr Minty. He told us about him during our negotiations for the property.'

'The ghost appears up there?'

'The place where he was noosed and pushed over.'

'What?'

'He kept fighting apparently, fighting the tightening rope, he'd freed his tied hands, a struggling puppet to entertain the drunken crowd, here in the hallway, on the stones where we stand, not a quick death.'

Tamsin thought to change the subject.

'Perhaps the doctor was just trying to raise the price: 'Attractive period property in extensive grounds – with en suite ghost.''

Frances sniffed.

'I'm not American.'

'So you weren't impressed?'

'I just noted his delusional tendencies and got on with the negotiations, which to be fair, were not hard.'

Tamsin: 'Do you believe in them, Frances?'

'In what?'

'Ghosts. I'm sure psychologists have the whole thing explained.'

'It is like he's here sometimes.'

'Like who's here?'

'Edward O'Neill. That was his name.'

'The ghost of Henry Hall is Edward O'Neill?'

Fifty Three

'O'Neill was his birth name, but he was known professionally as the Irish Harlequin,' explained Frances in the dark hallway. 'It was one of the reasons I went for a clown theme at the Feast of Fools.'

'It was your idea?'

'Well, Bella had input as well.'

'And so what was O'Neill's story?' asked Peter, as they moved towards the door.

'Do we really need to hear this?' asked Tamsin.

'I do,' said Peter.

Tamsin sighed as Frances returned them to the past:

'The Irish Harlequin was good copy, as Martin Channing might say, something of a favourite among the Elizabethan aristocracy. The Earl of Essex discovered him when he was sent to Ireland by Elizabeth to subdue the Irish.'

'That's gone well.'

'These days, he'd be called a satirist; but in those days, he was a jester, a constant thorn in the side of the powerful. And he dressed as a harlequin, an early example of branding – hence the name.'

And now Peter was seeing Barnabus again, sprawled in the cupboard, his smashed skull.

'So why was this disturber of the peace a favourite of the aristocracy?' asked Tamsin. 'Sounds a rather irritating man.'

'Oh, he was. But the powerful like a little self-flagellation … as long as it's obsequious and dependent.'

'And then one day Edward O'Neill forgot to be?'

'He was invited by Sir Dudley Rowse, owner and builder of Henry Hall, to provide the entertainment here on New Year's Day in 1600. He was a popular figure by this time, notorious and dangerous, a man who feared no one and said whatever he wanted.'

'Hubris.'

'And he used this particular celebration to mock the English with some venom.'

'In their own backyard?'

'Yes, he called for them to begin the new century by leaving his homeland, referring to the occupation as "the abduction and rape of another man's wife – which I've always been against myself, but the English are different, I know".'

'I can see he was edgy.'

'It didn't go down well. But it was the plague that did for him.'

'The plague?'

'The Black Death was a delicate subject in this house.'

'Why so?'

'There were many outbreaks in Elizabethan England and it wasn't pleasant, as you know: swellings in the armpits, legs, neck and groin, high fever, delirium, vomiting, muscular pains, bleeding in the lungs and mental disorientation – not a happy list.'

'And not obviously comic material.'

'Shakespeare was terrified of the disease.'

'Who wouldn't be?'

'The plague caused the closure of the Globe theatre for months at a time, had a huge impact on society ... but it was more than that here.'

'You mean Henry House? But I thought the plague was a city thing.'

'Far from it. Farmers, like Rowse's family, were vulnerable in such close proximity to animals and their fleas. And it was during the epidemic of 1593 that this house became a Plague House.'

'A Plague House?'

'Every home that housed the illness was declared a Plague House, locked and bolted from the outside, no one allowed to enter, no one allowed to leave. It was a death warrant for all those inside.'

'So how did they eat?'

'They vomited and died more than ate. But a watchman was assigned to the plague houses and victims would lower baskets from upper windows for the them to put food into.'

'So Rowse was locked up inside here – yet survived?'

'Somehow yes, it wasn't unknown. But he witnessed the wretched deaths of his wife, his mother and four of his children under this roof.'

'Terrible.'

'All of which made it unwise of the Harlequin to speak of the benefits of the plague.'

'Families aren't a universal blessing, I suppose,' suggested the Abbot.

Frances agreed, but said the Harlequin had been rather more political in tone, taking his listeners back to the fourteenth century, when the Black Death first came to England. The savage death toll had social consequences. With nearly one half of the population killed, a shortage of labourers ensured an economy based on serfdom broke down and workers, suddenly in demand, could ask for better conditions and higher wages. For the first time in their lives, they weren't hungry!

'Good, surely?'

'Not for the rich, who preferred their work force on the edge of starvation, made them more compliant, said the Harlequin – and he was right. To those with status and wealth, a world in which workers weren't hungry seemed particularly threatening – they even took the matter to court to hold wages down. "'So I bless the plague with every breath in my body", declared the Harlequin. "I bless it for killing Englishmen! And I bless it again for placing money in the pockets of the poor!".'

'And that was the final straw.'

'Sir Dudley Rowse, a man famous for his temper, went berserk. His one remaining son had been killed in the fighting in Ireland – as if he needed another grievance – and in a fit of drunken rage, he had the Harlequin hanged for treason.'

'Hanged?'

'Dragged out into the hallway, marched up the stairs, noosed-up in the gallery and hanged.'

'No trial?'

'Hanged from the balcony there,' she pointed across the hall, 'in full costume. New Year's Day, 1600.'

Stunned pause, broken by Peter:

'So the murder of Barnabus is the second murder of a clown in Henry Hall?'

'It would appear so. Shall we go?'

Peter and Frances turn toward the entrance, where a lone policeman keeps watch outside. It has been a long day, time for home and then a scream behind them, and they're both spinning round to see Tamsin in a state of shock.

'I saw the ghost!' she exclaims.

'Where?'

'Up there on the landing! He was there, I swear it, looking down. I saw the Irish Harlequin!'

Act Three

I have found little that is 'good' about human beings on the whole. In my experience most of them are trash, no matter whether they publicly subscribe to this or that ethical doctrine or to none at all. That is something that you cannot say aloud, or perhaps even think.

Sigmund Freud

Fifty Four

Tuesday 4 November

It is unusual to receive post from a dead man, though it does happen.

Abbot Peter sat with his colleague in the front room of Sandy View, his small beachfront home, set on the shingle coast of Stormhaven. It was an ironic name, there was no sand, which amused some and irritated others who thought it a teenage stunt, hardly appropriate for an Abbot. But then people think things all the time; they think all kinds of things and most of it unverified nonsense. Howling beneath their mental moons, impressions become opinion, opinions become judgements and judgements become death for someone. So Peter stood unconcerned this morning in *Sandy View*, watching the rise and fall of undulating pebble, as it received the morning's incoming tide. He and his colleague had other matters to consider, and most pressing, the case notes made by Barnabus after the therapy sessions with those taking part in the Feast of Fools.

'So here,' declared Peter, holding them in the air, 'are the thoughts of the murdered on four of the chief suspects.'

Silence.

'Unusual,' he said. 'Definitely interesting.'

Frances had told them most therapists keep records of sorts, though she'd given them a warning: 'The client's record of the meeting will be entirely different from those of the therapist. We all hear different things and no doubt Barnabus mostly heard Barnabus.'

His client notes, discovered in the drawer in his bedroom, were brief, written in fountain pen and a clear hand.

165

'So here we go,' said Peter, putting on his glasses. 'I'll just read them out as they stand. And we start with Kate Karter, who was perhaps the most distraught in our initial interviews. Speak to us, Barnabus.'

Kate Karter: Like some fading film star, a rather affected and mannered individual; alienated from her true self and sending some fictional figure out to perform on her behalf. Maintains avoidance of inner discomfort by keeping herself busy – fearful of silence and sadness. Her husband is a teacher and she shows ambivalent feelings towards him, admiration, concern and disdain. Without a physical mask when we met – apart from a fake sun tan – but her emotional mask was a brittle, frightened and resistant thing. Felt distance.

The Abbot left a pause, no response, time to move on.

'And so onto Virgil Bannaford, whose company Barnabus did not enjoy!'

Virgil Bannaford, lecturer in higher education, history I think, a slightly scruffy ball of restless energy and rage. He seemed to come for a fight, resentful even before he sat down. Therapy was his choice, but also his hate and he assaulted both the idea of it and me. His wife has thrown him out. Is this why he's angry? Possibly but seems angrier with therapy than with his wife; it felt quite personal against me. Simple transference? Didn't feel like it. His rage is a sea of molten lava but he speaks of himself as peaceable – and put the problem firmly on me! 'I don't get angry. I'm a peaceful guy,' he said.

It was at this point that Abbot Peter noticed his colleague sticking a pen in her ear, which was a bad idea.

'I'll tell you what, Poppy – I propose an exchange. I take the pen but as compensation, I give you the *Owl in the Tree* book – which looks a good deal more interesting than the biro. Fair?'

It wasn't fair, he knew that, she preferred the biro. The *Owl in the Tree* book was quite dull and if she'd wanted the owl story, which she didn't, she'd have picked it up instead of the pen. But she accepted the exchange with grace, Peter hid the biro deep in his habit, where things stayed for years, and returned to his homework. Tamsin would be along soon and she'd be demanding coherence.

'So now, Poppy, we get to the finely named Ezekiel St Paul, who you somehow know isn't going to work in a betting shop. Difficult meeting by all accounts, so what's new there? And rather poor Barnabus than me:

Rev Ezekiel St Paul (can't be his real name), Pastor of the Seraphimic Church of the Blessed Elect in Uplifting Glory. Phew! His polite and precise manner belies the savagery of his inner workings, expressed through fundamentalist religion. Asks by what authority I speak? Caught me out there. He speaks with God's authority of course. Believes his daughter is possessed by demons and there was a moment of connection between us when his eyes watered at the thought of further and unpleasant rites of exorcism being carried out by the church elders. But he then locked me out again with the remark: 'The godless cannot help the godly.' Suddenly I'm redundant ... no worse, something malignant.

'Well we all know that feeling, Poppy,' said the Abbot and at the mention of her name, she smiled. It was possible that until this moment, Peter had never really pondered the simple trust and present joy of a child's smile; they'd simply never come his way – or perhaps he'd never come theirs. But on this Tuesday morning of 4 November, it was a thing of such hope and beauty that Peter, for a moment, quite forgot the twisted figure of the clown in the cupboard. And quite forgot his own redundancy, two years ago now, when like a stranded star fish, he was left homeless and jobless in the desert ... after his not entirely peaceable exit from the monastery of St James-the-Less.

'Suddenly I'm redundant,' wrote Barnabus, and Peter knew the feeling.

'And finally, Poppy,' he said, returning his mind to Stormhaven, 'we have my old friend Martin Channing. Martin "The Fox" Channing, whom you trust as far as you can throw a large whale and whales are big anyway, even small ones, you can't throw the small ones any distance at all, so a large one ...'

The energy for picture language deserted him and he returned to his brief:

Martin Channing: Editor of the Sussex Silt and as a friend told me, 'the only reptile on earth who wears a bow tie.' Some connection with Frances it seems; I don't know what. Cool, distant, clever customer. Uses mental analysis to avoid true emotion; he could only cope when he was interviewing me. Had problems with idea of listening to his life, rejected it firmly. Wary of attack, spiteful in riposte, a man well-protected from his pain.

So there we are, Poppy! Four of the suspects kindly described for us with some accuracy, and no doubt some inaccuracy, by the victim. No illustrations to match *Owl in the Tree*, but insight nonetheless. So what do you make of them?'

Poppy's strained face and a pungent waft spoke of interests closer to home, matters more immediate and pressing than any police investigation.

'Of course there are other suspects, who don't appear in Barnabus' records,' said Peter, 'because amazingly, it's not always the client who kills the therapist. There's Frances Pole, the other director *of Mind Gains*. She's uncomfortable at the moment, no doubt about that: firm, brisk but uncomfortable. Why? And then I suppose there's Bella Amal, the receptionist – or rather the Director of Administration, as she calls herself, self-aggrandisement through title … rather like me calling myself an Abbot …though, as you're no doubt about to observe, Bella wasn't actually at the Feast of Fools, but in a pub, for some of the time at least, certainly the early part of the evening. But then again, with all the costume nonsense, who knows who was who, and who was where that night?'

Poppy looked at him as though she did know, as though she knew everything, even the size of whales, a very wise look, like an owl in a tree.

'So have we got the wrong end foremost here?' pondered Peter. 'Bella Amal might just be very clever. Some people are very clever, Poppy, and the clever are not always the kind. But top of our list of suspects, at the moment, is Pat Strong, the cleaner who was there that night and has now gone missing, having given a false address to the clinic. So we don't know who she is, and we don't know where she lives. I hope it isn't her, obviously, because I like her. That's unprofessional and to be kept between you and me. But there it is, and I'm not a professional anyway, I'm a retired Abbot who knows nothing.'

Poppy was straining again.

'And there are issues.'

Peter found it helpful to think out loud.

'Pat was there at the end of the game of Sardines, and there when everyone went off to get changed – but seems to have disappeared soon afterwards, leaving the premises quickly. And she's now been out of contact for over three days. So why disappear? Whether killer or victim, it's not good however you look at it.'

The doorbell rang and Peter got up to answer.

Tamsin: 'Oh my God, what's that smell?'

Poppy looked troubled by the loud stranger, her face crumbling a little. Peter moved to explain that it wasn't a monster, not strictly true – but at least a monster who'd not harm her. Peter would keep her on a tight leash, he promised.

'I'm sorry, I didn't see the child,' said Tamsin, putting her bag down.

'She's called Poppy,' said Peter.

'I'm sure she is, but please don't ask me to look at any photos. It's okay to detest other people's children.'

'Seen any more ghosts?'

Tamsin sighed.

'I saw what I saw.'

'And screamed as you screamed.'

'I saw the Irish Harlequin.'

Tamsin looked at Peter.

'Why are you smiling?' she asked.

'We must all frame our fears as best we can, Tamsin. Some call them ghosts, while others – '

'Coffee?'

It was a pleasing turn-around to find himself as the hard-bitten realist and Tamsin, the credulous innocent. He didn't deny the possibility that she might have seen a ghost; but equally, he enjoyed the uncomfortable squirming of a rationalist in shock. Certainly they'd found no one at home when they went upstairs to look. They had looked, looked everywhere and not a soul, he was sure of that.

'You haven't opened your post,' said Tamsin, as the kettle boiled.

It lay on the side, forgotten, having coincided with Poppy's arrival. Sarah had been in a fluster, Poppy had needed her bottle, one thing had led to another but nothing had led to the post … until now. It was a dramatic appearance however, because looking at the clean white envelope, something was immediately apparent to Peter:

'That's Barnabus's writing.'

Fifty Five

'It can't be.'

Tamsin was suddenly interested in the post.

'I've just been reading his client reports. That's his writing. And same pen.'

'Well open it.'

Peter took hold of the envelope, peeling the flap carefully. He drew from it a white card, on which a poem was written in Barnabus's hand, no question.

'It is Barnabus.'

'What does it say?'

Tamsin had forgotten the smell.

'It's a poem.'

'A poem? Did you speak in verse together?'

'Not to my knowledge.'

Peter was elsewhere, gazing at the words before him.

'So read it then.'

'It looks uncomfortably pertinent:

What will the burial of my body be?
The pouring of a sacred cup of wine,
Into the tender mouth of earth.
And making my dear sweet lover laugh one more time.

And then the words, *Happy days, Peter!*

'And that's it?'

'That's it.'

'Nothing else?'

'No.'

'It's like he knew he'd die.'

'Possibly.'

'So who was his lover?'

'I have no idea – he never spoke of one to me.'

'Looks like she – or he – was the killer, doesn't it?'

'Possibly.'

'Can you say anything other than "possibly"?

Abbot Peter raised his eyebrows.

'And what's the "Happy days, Peter"?' she said.

'I'm not sure.'

'You're on good form this morning.'

'You'd prefer me to pretend knowledge?'

'Maybe.'

'That's worrying,' said Peter.

Tamsin took the card.

'It's like he expects you to know.'

'I'm aware of that.'

'So it can't be difficult.'

Again Peter heard the distant bell of recognition ... a distant bell ... and knew that in silence he would make the connection. But Tamsin did not offer silence, always pushing too hard, too insecurely for silence to settle anywhere nearby. It was an irony, noted by Peter, that the demand for results frequently ensured none appeared. And then the phone call, answered immediately by the DI.

'Okay,' she said, 'Okay. We'll be right there. Just keep him happy, give him some tea – fresh water in the kettle – and we'll be there in twenty minutes.'

'We're going to Stormhaven Police Station,' she said, definitively.

'You're going to Stormhaven Police Station,' said Peter. 'I'm here with Poppy until Sarah collects her in about half an hour.'

'Sure you don't want six months' paternity leave?'

'Who's the big draw?'

'Doctor Minty, used to own Henry Hall. He says he has important information.'

'I'll join you in a while.'

'Well, you may miss the action.'

'If you're trying to punish me, it isn't working.'

'I'm just saying.'

'And so am I, Tamsin. I'll be with you shortly.'

The policewoman took her leave in some irritation. She didn't like it when there was a job to be done and other people's plans did not coincide with her own.

'And remember to change her nappy. She stinks.'

The door slammed shut.

Fifty Six

And it was shortly after Tamsin's exit that Abbot Peter took a call from Bella. His attention was only half on the conversation, for he didn't want Sarah returning with things as they were. Peter was hardly a man in the grip of moral compunction, he sometimes wished for more; but written deep into the laws of the universe, engraved in rock on some distant star, was the one about mothers returning to a clean nappy. And it was far from clean at present.

'I'm concerned for Pat,' said Bella.

'We all are,' replied Peter.

How did she know?

'And I understand it's none of my business.'

'Well, we all carry each other in a way, Bella; it's not a crime to be concerned.'

Being nosy was different, that was an appalling crime, but on this occasion, he'd give Bella the benefit of the doubt.

'I ought to declare an interest,' she said.

'Which particular interest?'

'Pat and I, we were friends.'

'Of course.'

'I mean close friends, if you see what I mean.'

'Well, possibly.'

Various images passed through Peter's mind.

'She was a close friend who gave you a false address?' he said.

'She was like that.'

'It doesn't sound like that close a friendship.'

'I always knew there was a hidden side to her.'

'That's quite a lot to hide.'

'She'd been badly treated and trust did not come easily.'

'I understand. But friend or not,' – and Peter wasn't too sure – 'the evidence is stacked high against her, Bella.'

'Oh don't be ridiculous!'

172

'So why is she so afraid to come forward?'

'I don't know.'

'No.'

'Pat didn't murder anyone, Abbot, and when you find her, you'll discover that for yourself.'

'If she's alive, of course.'

Abbot Peter was not inwardly hopeful.

'If she's alive?'

'We have to prepare ourselves for all possibilities.'

'Why would anyone want to kill her?'

'I was hoping you'd tell me, Bella. You see everything at *Mind Gains* from your hideout in the hall.'

'Hardly a hideout.'

'A recess, then.'

'And I don't imagine this is anything to do with *Mind Gains*. She was only here 25 hours a week. Who knows what she did with the rest of her time.'

'Well, if a close friend doesn't know –.'

'Like I say, there was much that was hidden; we didn't meet away from the place.'

'So where did you meet?'

'Henry House has various rooms, Abbot.'

'Quite.'

'She never spoke of any enemies.'

'But perhaps she saw something, found something or knew something. If she hid her home life from you, she might have been hiding something else.'

'I don't think so, no.'

'Or perhaps she had an enemy she didn't know about.'

Bella paused.

'Are you OK?' asked Peter.

'Yes, it's just a frightening thought, someone close by who –.'

'The hidden enemy?'

'Oh, don't!'

Bella seemed genuinely disturbed.

'Well, Bella,' said Peter glancing at the clock. 'This may sound strange, but I have a nappy to change; not mine, I hasten to add, I'm still managing to steer clear of incontinence – but we can talk more when I next see you.'

'I understand,' said Bella, gathering herself as one determinedly cheerful through the tears. 'But you will let me know if you hear anything?'

'I'll do my best.'

'I mean, I know you can't reveal things but, well –.'

'I'll do my best.'

'I just want to know she's okay.'

'As I say, I'll – do what I can.'

'That's all I want to know.'

Would she ever get off the phone? And of greater weight, would Pat ever be found? The belief that the missing will one day return is natural – but often mistaken.

Fifty Seven

'You sold Henry House at a very reasonable price, Doctor.'

Tamsin sat with Doctor Minty in Interview Room 2 at Stormhaven Police Station. Though not entirely clear, it was the room that least smelt of Dettol – or Poundland's version of it.

'I'd earned a very good living being a not very good doctor.'

'Wasn't this every doctor?' thought Tamsin.

'It seemed the least I could do.'

Tamsin disagreed. The least he could do was take the money and run. Why were people occasionally charitable? It seemed so against every animal instinct and left Tamsin confused. There must be a scientific explanation for altruism but it wasn't immediately apparent.

'And remember I was down-sizing to Wales, not moving to Knightsbridge. I didn't need the money.'

'So Frances and Barnabus sold you the idea – and you sold them the house?'

'Well, it was Frances, really.'

'How do you mean?'

'Barnabus wasn't in the picture at that time. He was brought into the equation for the money, as far as I could tell, because Frances didn't have it.'

'I see.'

Tamsin saw a whole new line of enquiry opening up.

'Very nice man though, Barnabus; never looked the banker sort to me.'

At this moment, Peter knocked on the door and entered.

'Out of the frying pan and into the fire,' he said, smelling the Dettol substitute. 'And given the choice – .'

'This is Abbot Peter, Doctor Minty. He's a Special Witness on this case.'

'I'm not sure I know what that means.'

'We all wonder sometimes.'

'But I have seen you around, Abbot. You're not hard to spot in Stormhaven – though I'm not a church goer myself.'

Why did people feel obliged to say that to him? It presumed an interest in the issue that simply wasn't there.

'Doctor Minty was just telling me about the sale of Henry House to *Mind Gains*; he was saying that Frances needed Barnabus for his financial resources.'

'Interesting,' said Peter, catching his habit on the splintered formica on the chair.

'And was that what you wanted to tell us, Dr Minty?'

'I'm sorry?'

'You said you had something you wished to speak to us about.'

'Ah, yes.'

'I was wondering if it was the financial arrangements of the purchase?'

The doctor seemed to be drifting off. Never work with animals, children – or pensioners.

'Oh no, that's quite by the way,' he said, and seemed happy to leave it at that.

'And anyway, it was just an impression – and maybe a wrong one. A misdiagnosis, as they say! I've made a few of those!'

'You mean about the money?'

'About the money, yes.'

There was a pause.

'So what did you want to tell us?' asked Tamsin, patience strained.

'I read about the case in the *Evening Argus*.'

'Not the *Sussex Silt?*'

'Toilet paper.'

The distaste in the words was almost physical: 'Used toilet paper,' he added.

The energy in his disdain showed life had returned, a relief to Tamsin:

'You read about the death of Barnabus?'

'A former neighbour sends it to me; the *Argus,* I mean. It's a way of staying in touch with my old territory.'

'Of course.'

'I lived here for 35 years, you know.'

'35 years?'

Tamsin could not imagine living anywhere for thirty five years, and certainly not Stormhaven.

'Which makes me 97 per cent sea water, of course.'

He chuckled at his joke.

'That's a good length of time,' said Peter, reflecting on his own move from the desert. He'd have enjoyed news of his old haunts but the *Daily Desert* had yet to reach the news-stands. And his closest neighbour had been fifty miles away, so no strong links there.

'Though I have to say,' said Doctor Minty, 'the news that consumed me while I was here, seems a funny little thing from afar.'

'Local news can suddenly look very – well – local!' said Peter.

'Precisely.'

'One earth – but we inhabit different planets.'

'That's exactly how it is, Abbot! I moved planets.'

Charming gentlemen's chat and all that, but Tamsin wished to re-focus:

'You came here to tell us something.'

This time she would get it out of him.

'My son,' he said.

'What about him?'

'It's just that you may not realise who he is. I mean, you've interviewed him but he probably didn't tell you he was my son.'

'Why wouldn't he?'

'He's not enormously proud of the fact.'

'I'm sorry, who are you talking about?'

'Virgil – Virgil Bannaford, as he now calls himself.'

'He's your son?'

'Yes, he took his mother's name when she walked out, or however you like to describe it, left me, whatever.'

'He went with his mother?'

'Rather hurtful really – but he could be like that.'

'And how old was he when he left?' asked Peter.

'Fifteen.'

'So much unresolved at that age.'

'Maybe; that's not my territory. I suppose his mother and I never offered him a very happy home at Henry House, and he was always a rather disappearing boy … who knows where he went off to. But he went with his mother when finally she left.'

'And why do you think this is important?' asked Peter.

Doctor Minty looked him straight in the eye.

'The only communication I've had with him since then, and that includes Christmas, was when he wrote urging me not to sell the house to *Mind Gains*.'

'Did he want the house?'

'I don't know – but he certainly didn't want them to have it.'

'And what did you do in response?'

'I didn't reply to him. He wasn't speaking to me so I didn't bestow a great deal of authority on his plea.'

Harsh, thought Peter ... while Tamsin nodded in approval.

'I don't know if that was right.'

'But now you're concerned?' asked Tamsin.

'A little'

'You really think that's a motive for murder?'

'I'm not saying that. I'm merely saying that Virgil is not a casual client, as one newspaper report suggested.'

'He told us he was just doing it for a laugh.'

'Well, maybe, he is a bit of a loose cannon. But *Mind Gains* has taken over his old home and while he didn't want it while I was there – .'

'Maybe now you're not there, he does?'

'As I say, it could be nothing.'

'It's hardly nothing.'

'You don't know if these things are important.'

'Was your son ever violent, Dr Minty?' asks Tamsin.

'Oh, I don't think so, no. Enthusiastic when stirred, loved rugby at school, throwing himself at people, broke his nose on four separate occasions, plenty of fights – but not violent, as such.'

'You've been very helpful, Dr Minty.'

It was a dismissal, which the doctor failed to notice.

'Will you be visiting friends while here?' asked Peter, rising from his chair. Now the doctor noticed.

'Er, no, I'll be getting the train back to London – and then heading west,' he said, rising himself. 'There's nothing for me here but sadness.'

'Oh?'

'Things that might have been better. Wish I could do it all again!'

'Perhaps you will,' said Peter, who never believed anyone's story to be over.

There were tears in the doctor's eyes.

'You seem upset, Dr Minty.'

Abbot Peter touched his shoulder.

'I don't want to go,' said the doctor, a quivering eight-year-old all over again, hunched on his bed, telling his mother he didn't want to go to school because everyone there was horrid.

'You miss Stormhaven?'

'I miss Henry House.'

Fifty Eight

'Well, he was a bundle of laughs,' said Tamsin as they sat alone in Interview Room 2.

'Probably not destined for the London Palladium.'

'But interesting.'

'I liked him.'

'You would, he was a loser … just your type.'

'He seemed like a man in a dream, a soul cast free from its moorings and wondering who or what it is now.'

'Spare us the autobiography.'

'Very insightful, Tamsin.'

'Thank you.'

'I should pay for a session with you.'

'No, I'd just be sitting there wondering whether our first visit should be to the previously insolvent Frances, or the less-than-honest Virgil. I like it when the lies start to appear.'

'Information withheld.'

'The lies, yes.'

'Bella said she found him in Barnabus' bedroom,' said Peter.

'Who?'

'Virgil.'

'What was he doing there?'

'Previously a mystery, but no longer. I'd imagine it was his bedroom in former times. Do you remember where you slept as a child?'

The question brought both to silence and it was in that brief eternity of space that the link came to Peter.

'Hafiz,' he said.

'I beg your pardon?'

'Hafiz, he's our link.'

'Whose link?'

'The link between myself and Barnabus.'

'Hafiss?'

'Hafiz.'

'Is he local? Can we speak with him?'

Fifty Nine

⌘

Freedom beckoned for Behrouz – freedom at last! So why was this not good news?

He stood in relentless sun, gazing through sweat, on the high walls that rose out of the rock – and yes, he sensed his journey's end. A three-day camel ride from water, here was freedom, freedom from his long-carried cargo. And it was also despair.

He'd heard of this place from passing Bedouin. They hadn't been happy about it, not in the least. A great deal of haughty tut-tutting, evident suspicion, they spoke of this monastery as a stranger in town, a parvenu, an Abdul-Come-Lately. After 600 years, you were still a new-comer in these parts. But then who was surprised? For as the pyramids were comprised of stone, the Bedouin were made of suspicion, the nomads' suspicion of the permanent; and there was the feeling in Behrouz, something new to his soul, that perhaps he should become a nomad himself, the temptation to walk on, travel on from this place, pass on by these rough walls and disobey his master.

The truth was, things had changed. His master – or former master – was not here. He'd even told Behrouz he was his master no more, he remembered that, he used those words ... and not having seen him for eighteen months, authority fades, relationship fades, Hafiz back in Shiraz across many desert miles and Behrouz here in Egypt. Sometimes he struggled even to remember the poet's face. He carried literary gold in his sack, he knew that. So why would he hand it over to another? It felt like cutting off his hand.

It was possible he wasn't alive ... Hafiz that is, entirely possible. He'd heard different stories from travellers. People spoke of a purge in both court and city, a hanging of heretics, a mutilation of malcontents. The brother of a seller of frankincense claimed to have been in Shiraz when Hafiz's hands were removed, chopped from his wrists and thrown on the ground to be eaten by the birds, unorthodox hands now severed from the sinner. And the last act of Hafiz's hands, so the brother of the frankincense seller said, and he seemed very convinced – though it turned out he wasn't there himself – was to throw his poems in the fire! Well, why was Behrouz surprised? Hafiz had feared that outcome, had he not? That was why he'd sent Behrouz away, packed him off through the window with a small bag of provisions and vague instructions to travel west, with the story he was looking for work. But he'd never been looking for work, he carried his work with him, every day of the way, the poetry on his back, that was his work, keeping it safe, and which – if the brother of the frankincense seller was to be believed – was now the only record of the poet's labour.

Everything was terrible. It was a terrible weight, a terrible honour, a terrible importance. And thrown into the fire by his own hand? That wasn't right and thank God he hadn't been there, it would have been too bad, really too bad, but how it grieved him that he wasn't there. He would have given them a piece of his mind, no question. It was possible at least.

But now, Behrouz must decide, decide about the poems and what to do with Hafiz's instructions. He'd spoken of a monastery, not specific, just something about the crazed loon St Anthony and the outbreak of desert monasteries he oversaw. He'd told Behrouz to aim for one of these, to make for the deserts of Middle-Egypt and to seek an Abbot, not a Caliph, and this he'd done. Here he was, looking at one now, an edifice which appeared to rise out of the rock, complete union, so that where one started, and the other ended, was hard to tell. It didn't look right without a minaret, looked deficient somehow, like a mouth missing teeth. He could teach the Bedouin a thing or two about suspicion.

But were these rough walls to be the end of his journey? And perhaps more pressing, did he, Behrouz, want the end of the journey? There were his feelings to consider. These poems had held him together for the past eighteen months, given him both reason and direction. So was he, the copyist, the calligrapher – no small labour, these were joint works in some way – was he now happy to leave them in the hands of an unknown other? They were as much his children as those of Hafiz, not quite but nearly, and like a painter unable to sell his work, Behrouz wanted freedom ... but not at the expense of these poems.

These were his feelings. It was not in a man's nature to give treasure away – and what of life beyond this place, beyond this privileged possession? Today, he was Behrouz Gul, the carrier of wonders. Tomorrow, he would be Behrouz Gul, copyist and yes, a fine hand, but there were many other fine hands. He spoke dismissively of his peers but he was not so different, not so superior, indeed quite equal, just one in a crowd. Only these poems gave him difference, gave him the sweet inequality he craved.

But then his master's words and the reason for travel. You can sometimes forget why you set off on a particular path, your clarity overcome by the mist of desire. And Behrouz now felt like an icon of lost clarity … for this journey had never been about him and his needs. On his back, he carried the work and witness of Hafiz, a fragile keeping for such glory, for if he slipped and fell, what then? Or if attacked by brigands or found dead in the night cold, what then? The satchel was engraved on his back, part of his body and at one with his soul; but he must wrench himself free, let go, give it up, this is what Behrouz must do, strange how decisions are made. Amid the sun-baked rocks, Behrouz was coming to his senses, slowly, slower than a camel on a crutch, but was it time to hand over the poems of Hafiz, offer them into more stable keeping? Was it time to find protection for these children, to make them safe – safe from those against love and laughter and in favour of fear? He looked at the strong walls, a holding more secure than his own. It was time.

He walked wearily towards the gate, approached by a sharp incline to dissuade those with a mind to attack. These were the walls of a fortress built to withstand weather – and Bedouins; built to remain and remain in this unforgiving wilderness. He stood before a beaten, battered door and a bell on the end of a rope as old as the moon, knotted at the end. He pulled at the rope, a tinkling of unenthusiastic metal and then a wait, not unfamiliar in the desert, one long wait of sand and rock in Behrouz's experience.

Movement the other side. Was someone there?

Sixty

A slit in the monastery door opens and a face peers out.

Behrouz says: *'I come in peace.'*

The eyes through the slit continue to gaze and he feels the need to expand:

'I'm a traveller who seeks hospitality.'

Eyebrows are raised through the slit.

'Pray tell me, what manner of fortress is this?' continues Behrouz.

The slit slams shut, there is brief silence, the door then opens, aching hinges, and a weather-beaten face above a brown habit, greets him:

'Welcome, my friend, to the monastery of St James-the-Less.'

'I bring a gift.'

'A gift?'

'I hope you will consider it so.'

'I'm sure we shall, for gifts do not come every day. Not through the front door at least.'

'You're not easy to find.'

'Good.'

'But I believe I bring a blessing.'

The doorkeeper looks long and hard into his eyes.

'And yet you look sad,' he says.

And now his eyes are watering.

'I am sad,' says Behrouz, surprising himself. These were not words he'd spoken before, never had he allowed these words. But their truth could not be denied, here at the monastery gates. *'I am the saddest man on earth.'*

'To be the saddest man on earth, that is a hard calling.'

'It is, yes.'

'Let me take your load.'

The doorkeeper reaches out towards the bag Behrouz carries on his back. Behrouz makes to push him away, an involuntary movement, but then changes, relents, allows the weight to be taken from him and kneels down in the sand and cries.

'It is good sometimes to water the sand,' says the doorkeeper.

'I'm sorry,' says Behrouz.

'Sorry for tears? That's not an apology the desert understands. But we can find ourselves a cooler place to sit.'

Behrouz nods and rises slowly to his feet.

'First things first, we must raid the kitchen on your behalf,' says his host. 'Some physical refreshment, and then we can talk. Yes?'

Behrouz nods again … like a man in a dream

The door keeper picks up the cargo, swings it onto his back – how strange it looks on another man's back! – shows Behrouz through the gate, closes it behind them and leads the way across the court yard.

'It is a heavy load you have carried!' he says.

'A good load,' says Behrouz, suddenly light on his feet.

'My name is Brother Gabriel, by the way – sadly not the angel.'

Though later, as Behrouz ate and drank at a table in the kitchen, the saddest man in the world, cheering slightly, begged to differ.

Sixty One

'So who or what is Hafiz?' asked Tamsin, as they drove along the sea front.

They weren't hungry, that was for sure. They'd bought fish and chips and eaten them with wooden forks, sitting in the car, looking out to sea.

'We'll make a pensioner of you yet,' Abbot Peter had said cheerily.

'It's only the cold. Otherwise I'd be outside.'

'Yes, that's what they say as well.'

It was cold. A bitter wind blew across from Newhaven harbour, though not cold enough to worry fishermen casting on the shore, dark silhouettes against the low wintry sun. Oblivious to the elements in their thick waterproofs, they made the most of the high tide, as squawking gulls swooped overhead. And in the end, and after some in-car dispute – each hoping the other might feel the urge – it was Peter who got out, habit a-flap, and braved the gusts to dispose of the wrapping in one of the concrete bins. He'd thrown a few remains to the birds on his way, cold chips caught by beaks in flight, before returning gratefully to the vehicle, still pungent with the legacy of vinegar.

'Enjoying the case?' he'd said, closing the car door with relief. 'Nice to be back in Stormhaven?'

Tamsin had thought before responding.

'I find working in Stormhaven peculiarly embarrassing.'

'Embarrassing?'

'There's simply nothing in me that wishes to be associated with this place. Is that terrible?'

'A bit harsh maybe.'

'But true.'

'Fair enough.'

'Sitting in a car eating fish and chips is about as good as it gets.'

Peter thought for a while as the car pulled away from the kerb and turned west.

'It's been unlucky as a town, perhaps.'

'Stormhaven?'

'Yes.'

'You make your own luck.'

'Sometimes. And then sometimes an author like Jane Austen walks along your cob – as she did at Lyme Regis – while writing *Persuasion*, includes it in the manuscript and suddenly you're interesting. That's luck.'

'So the only problem with this bleak town is that Graham Greene didn't stroll across the pebble beach, see a couple of boys fighting and decide to write a book called *Stormhaven Rock*?

'We've under-performed with celebrity endorsements.'

'"We?" You've only been here two years.'

'Home is where I lay my hat, Tamsin. These are my people now.'

'Those left alive.'

They were making for Henry House, where they were due to meet Frances at 2.00 p.m.. But before that, she wanted to hear about Hafiz.

'He was a Persian poet in the fourteenth century,' said Peter.

'So how does he link you and Barnabus?'

'Born in south east Persia, now Iran, around 1320. Two years before the birth of Geoffrey Chaucer and a year before the death of Dante.'

'Is this what we call "background"?'

'Context.'

'How very university.'

'And remarkably, he's still Iran's favourite poet.'

'Remarkable because?'

'Have you seen his poems?'

'Not knowingly.'

'He writes from the Sufi tradition of Islam.'

'Explain.'

'It's the mystical stream in that great river of a faith. Hafiz, for instance, believed that humans could be so overwhelmed by God's love that they became God themselves, became one with God.'

'Sounds a bit presumptuous to me.'

'It's a pretty offensive idea to most religions, not just Islam – they all like to keep God and humans separate. But really, why can't God give himself to someone entirely?'

'He'd have to exist first.'

Peter allowed the atheism as the car heating, tentative at first, began to make an impression on his chill hands.

Atheist to believer: 'I'm still waiting for the link.'

'It was a poem by Hafiz that Barnabus sent me.'

'That odd verse you got in the post? That was Hafiz?' Tamsin was interested.

'I knew it, but didn't know why I knew it.'

'So you know the poems of Hafiz?'

'He's like an old friend I've somehow lost touch with.'

'So now we have Peter, Barnabus and Hafiz.'

'Indeed.'

'The Three Musketeers.'

'Hardly.'

'And the connection?'

'The desert.'

'The Three Deserteers!'

He'd remember that phrase.

'We all met at the monastery of St James-the-Less. I should have remembered. I told you that when Barnabus came to stay, he spent most of his time in the library. But what I didn't say, what I'd forgotten, was that he spent most of his time there reading Hafiz. We owned a full set of his poems.'

'A Christian monastery harbouring Islamic poetry? How so?'

'Truth goes wherever she's made welcome.'

Tamsin felt a moment of unease. She had an odd relationship to truth, the idea both intriguing and frightening. For now, however, with traffic to consider, she chose a change of subject beneath a grey sky flecked with blue, and lit by the last of the afternoon sun.

'Frances,' she said.

'What about her?'

'Let's hope she's as welcoming, as we explore the *Mind Gains* finances.'

'It's going to be tricky,' said the Abbot.

'I don't see why.'

'It'll sound like an accusation.'

'It is an accusation.'

'No, it's a question and the best questions don't accuse – they merely seek the truth.'

'This is when I begin to enjoy it,' said Tamsin, ignoring the moralising. 'When the cage-rattling starts.'

They turned again through the old gate and started up the drive, dark and closed in by rhododendron and evergreen. With a corner turned, however, gaunt trees on mown grass appeared to their right; to their left, cold horses in wet fields, longing for the summer, and in between – the still façade of Henry House.

Sixty Two

'It's no secret that Barnabus' money was of considerable help,' said Frances, as they sat together in one of the dark-panelled counselling rooms. She'd been irritated by their intrusion, 'as if I don't have enough things to do at the moment!'

'As if we don't,' Tamsin had added, and once seated, she'd moved quickly to the matter in hand: money.

'You can see why we might be interested.'

'Not really,' said Frances. 'You do a good thing and then find your motives questioned.'

'And what is the good thing you're doing?'

'*Mind Gains*, of course. A much needed mental health resource in the area. Before we came –.'

Tamsin interrupts: 'Much needed by whom exactly? I mean, you were hardly busy.'

Peter glanced at Frances, who looked down into her lap, while Tamsin continued: 'I'm told the Feast of Fools was a publicity stunt, and to that degree successful – I mean, you're certainly in the papers.'

Cruel.

'But you can see, surely, how the relationship between a struggling endeavour like *Mind Gains* and financial investment, might just feel like an important line of enquiry.'

Frances looked up with some venom.

'We were just starting. These things take time. You're so stupid.'

Heartfelt but not wise. Calling Tamsin stupid generally had consequences.

'We understand that nothing would have started here without the financial resources of Barnabus,' said Tamsin.

'He invested significantly, yes.'

'And did you?'

'Did I what?'

'Did you invest significantly?'

'I didn't have the cash to hand that Barnabus had.'

'So the answer's "No".'

'But I had the business brain and the therapeutic experience.'

'Of course.'

'So it wasn't as if Barnabus was throwing good money after bad. We were a team, we complimented each other and I'd no doubt we could make a decent profit.'

'So *Mind Gains* is more a business than a public good?'

Frances sighed visibly.

'It has to work as one to be the other. You can't run a charity on grass cuttings.'

'Oh, so you're a charity?'

'Not exactly, no.'

'It's a business?'

'It's a business, of course – but a helping business and we deserve a proper salary for our helping skills. I assume you get paid to keep the peace?'

Tamsin returned with a further observation:

'So we have this public good, this "helping business", which is all very wonderful.'

There was a 'but' in the air.

'But we also note, Frances that so far, the only member of the public who seems to have benefited is yourself.'

'I don't see.'

'Well, to put it crudely, you now have Barnabus's investment safely gathered in – and no Barnabus to claim it back.'

Abbot Peter moved uncomfortably as Tamsin continued:

'If we were being cruel, we might say a more truthful name for *Mind Gains* would be *Frances Gains*.'

The reaction was immediate.

'That's grossly insulting, utterly ridiculous, you should be ashamed of yourself, Detective Inspector!'

Frances had sprung from her chair, furious.

'But your hysteria isn't proving me wrong,' says Tamsin.

'Are you going to defend me, Abbot, as a trustee?'

Peter said: 'No one is condemned by a question, Frances, and the question is this: will you benefit from the death of Barnabus?'

The director *of Mind Gains* breathed deeply and returned to her chair.

'I may benefit financially from this tragedy, I don't know; it hasn't been an issue much on my mind.'

'And that simple fact, the fact that you are a beneficiary in this death, is of interest to the police in a murder investigation.'

Frances was calming down.

'I would never have killed Barnabus.'

'Why not?'

'I needed him.'

'I think we've established that,' says Tamsin.

'No, I needed Barnabus the man, Barnabus the therapist.'

'Why? You're better qualified. You're much better qualified.'

Frances blushed a little.

'It's not a crime to be qualified,' said Peter.

'No.'

'And by all accounts you found his pseudo-spirituality "misguided",' continued Tamsin.

'I did.'

'So why would you miss him?'

'He had things I don't have, I'm very happy to admit that. We must all be accountable.'

'And these things were?'

'I don't have his patience, his, well … love, I suppose.'

'Love?'

'I hate most of my clients.'

Pause, but no change of mind as she continued:

'That's rather a strong word, but why beat about the bush?'

Peter considered the role of hatred in the life of the therapist and decided it didn't really have one.

'The "worried well" I call them,' she continued. 'I just want to get them and their whining little lives out of my face. So I needed Barnabus the therapist much more than Barnabus the money man.' And then a pause before she added, like someone in a soap opera: 'His real value to me hadn't come to an end – it was in fact just beginning.'

'A fine speech,' said Tamsin. 'Shame there's no jury to hear it; I could imagine them being moved.'

'You don't believe me?'

Frances was mortified.

'You've spoken very clearly, Frances,' said Peter. 'We just need some substance behind your oratory, a few supportive facts.'

Frances was quick to respond:

'Martin Channing offered me more money than Barnabus ever could.'

Suddenly, another window, with fresh views, was opened.

'Martin Channing wanted to invest in *Mind Gains*?'

'Yes, he did. I didn't need Barnabus's money.'

There was noise in the hallway, a commotion outside, the scraping of feet on the black and white marble.

'I want to see someone!' shouted a female voice. 'I'm not going until I see someone!'

'A client?' asked Peter.

'Could be,' said Frances. 'The nature of the work is that visitors aren't always at their best on arrival. Bella will handle it.'

'You don't want to see her yourself?' asked Peter.

'Bella will handle it,' said Frances firmly. 'When you own a dog, you don't need to bark yourself.'

'I wasn't thinking of you barking,' said Peter. 'Just a friendly word.'

'It's all right' said the reassuring voice in the hall. 'Come and sit down over here.'

'I want to know what happened!' cried the voice again, in some despair.

There was now the sound of another tussle.

'There's no one else in the building,' said Bella, using a familiar ploy. 'Perhaps if we went to the kitchen I could make you a cup of tea? And then I'm sure we can find an answer to your problem. But first you must tell me your name ...'

Sixty Three

'I never leave Henry House without feeling I've missed something,' said Tamsin, indicating right as the car passed out of the old stone gate. 'And it's not just the dark interior.'

'When it was built, of course, everyone would have wondered at its light not the dark,' said Peter.

'Only the moles.'

They were returning to Stormhaven with a plan in mind, but Peter was still thinking of light.

'Panes of glass were the big new thing in Elizabethan houses.'

'Wuppy-doo.'

'Is that a put-down?'

'It's my normal response to history.'

Peter sat with this for a while.

'They replaced wooden shutters which had made things so claustrophobic.'

'It still is.'

'But they had to work for their light, the Elizabethans, because making a pane of glass was a painstaking process.'

'And you'd know of course.'

'A blob of glass was blown into a cylinder-shaped bubble.'

'You do know!'

'The cylinder was placed on a cooling table and cut in half. A small piece of glass was produced, and gradually, these small pieces were joined together with lead to make a window.'

Tamsin laughs: 'You actually know how the Elizabethans made their windows?'

'I do.'

'You should get out more.'

'To what end? So I can know less?'

'No, so that you can know something worth knowing.'

'And what would that be exactly?'

193

They drove on in silence.

Awaiting Peter was a conversation with the entrepreneurial investor Martin Channing, who'd kept very quiet about his attempt to buy into *Mind Gains*. Tamsin, in the meantime, would speak with Virgil Bannaford. Just how angry was he that *Mind Gains* had taken over his old home? And when he said he was just along for the laugh, was he really telling the truth?

The conversation with Hafiz would have to wait.

Sixty Four

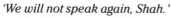

'We will not speak again, Shah.'

'No.'

It was a resigned 'no', one of acceptance, without attempt at disagreement.

'The hours left to me are fewer than the fingers you redeemed, this is my sense,' said the dying poet. He looked again on his hands, translucent skin and stiffening joints which hadn't written for a while. 'You can do nothing for me now.'

'So even rulers have their limitations?'

'Rulers are perhaps the most limited of all, Shah Shuja.'

'I agree. I saved your hands but cannot now save your life.'

'It's called old age, I believe.'

The Shah sat with the frail Hafiz in the fading light of the day. It was a final going down of the orange orb and the poet did not expect to see its rising. And welling up inside the Shah, and surprising him, the need to unburden himself, for what did it matter now? He was speaking with a man only hours away from eternity. So what rules of conduct mattered anymore?

No secrets had passed between them down the years – it hadn't been that sort of relationship. There'd been mutual respect – most of the time at least, respect can come and go – but they hadn't shared a cup of thick black coffee in their forty years at court, nor pondered the sky together … and certainly shared no secrets. But then for a ruler, who is there but himself? There are no friendships, there can never be, for every friend is a political move, a means rather than a joy. Only the common people have friends …but the Shah wanted a friend now.

'Each day,' he said, 'each and every day, Hafiz, I am a man who tries to stay standing on sands that shift beneath my feet.'

'Leadership is a hard calling.'

'Each day a different stumble, a different threat, a different adjustment. And this is what men call power!'

Years of difficulty and distance melted away as he spoke – the intimacy of two men who had simply known each other a long time … of shared water under the bridge, much water, many bridges, two men clinging to the same lifeboat, the lifeboat of life, so much now unimportant.

Hafiz says: *'I have enjoyed my hands for these extra years.'* He flexes them weakly once again. *'I am grateful for your arrival in the market place that day.'*

He remembered it well, and he remembered it now, remembered the tugging rope on his wrists, jerking him towards the cutting block, darkly stained with apostate blood … and the curved sword of Dr Saad, the court doctor, his call to healing on hold, the weeping in the crowd, the flames – his poems were still burning as he stood by the block. And then the confident call from Mubariz to proceed, the whispering breath of Karim in his ear, 'Why did you think you were different?' – until from the blue, from somewhere, the command to halt!

A slow looking up, a hesitant Doctor, his arms raised, caught between authorities, lowering the sword and then angry words exchanged, the rage of Mubariz, leaping down from his platform towards Hafiz, the quiet fury of Karim, Dr Saad grabbed – if he wouldn't do it, Mubariz would! And Hafiz tethered like a goat, he'd prefer Dr Saad … and then court guards intervening, thank God for the court guards, he didn't say that too often, but the Shah had come armed, unsure his mere word would carry the day, for he was wise in that way. As Mohammed said, 'Trust in Allah – but tether your camel.'

'Your word against Allah's?' Mubariz had raged and the crowd cheered.

Memories now.

'You must not just remember the battles, Hafiz.'

'Good words, Shah.'

'The schemes and the sniping – .'

'They are nothing to me now, believe me.'

'Really?'

'Really. The ghosts, the fears, the empty plots, all the grudges and sorrows, they have passed.'

'I am glad.'

'Who knows where to, I knew them well at the time, but they are strangers to Hafiz now. Perhaps they never really existed.'

'May Allah be praised!' said the Shah to Hafiz.

'May Allah be praised,' said Hafiz to the Shah. *'And the thing was, I always thought of my writing hand as God's friend, as a call to prayer.'*

'You have always been a call to prayer for me.'

A further intimacy and Hafiz seemed buoyed by the remark.

'You forgot to mention that, when you exiled me.'

'You were a difficult and rude call to prayer.'

There was little to say to this indubitable truth. And now the Shah had a worldlier question on his mind: 'So tell me, Hafiz, are you still in love?'

Hah! The dying poet turned his face towards the window and the minaret skyline. It was so long ago, a smitten baker's boy and fifty years between; but yes, he thought of Shakh-e-Nabat every day, the one not given.

'She stole my past from me, Shah, stripped it bare, left nothing but longing, nothing but dissatisfaction. Of course I am still in love.'

'Then you made good out of your dissatisfaction.'

'Maybe I did.'

'Good rather than hate, hope rather than gloom. Not that I wish to appear congratulatory.'

'Be as congratulatory as you like! Hafiz can cope with that. I trust I have not been gloomy, I prefer light – it is truer.'

He was watching the disappearing sun sink beneath the Musalla Gardens. Going, going, gone. Would he really never see the sky fire again?

'It is in loss that we find life.'

'If you say so, Hafiz.'

'I do, I do. But loss still haunts, still lingers.'

A pause.

'And do you fear the, er, change?' asked the Shah.

What is a polite word for death?

Hafiz thought maybe he did. Soon even the maggots and worms would tire of his body and these things are not easy to grasp, despite a life-time of preparation.

'Maybe I do … to trust in love at the edge of the abyss is a difficult calling … and a sad one. I do not want to let go of my fat body, you see. I realised that in the market place, it is too sacred, too full of God.'

'It is words like those which get you into trouble.'

'Not now, not anymore.'

'So you say.'

'I am too short-lived for trouble.'

'So what now?'

'Now, Shah? Now I become the flame that needs no fuel and the spirit that needs no body.'

'The flame that needs no fuel?'

'That will be me!'

The quiet was so comfortable and so calm, unusual for the Shah, that it was a while before he realised Hafiz had gone, had left the room, passed on, passed away, no longer in need of his body. The Shah rose slowly, not young himself, bent down and kissed the poet's cooling *forehead. They'd not been friends, something impossible for a man such as himself, in a court such as this, in a region such as Fars and an empire such as Persia. Though if things could be stated in this way – and begging tolerance for any nonsense perceived – the poet lying before him, known as Hafiz, had been the best friend he'd never had.*

Sixty Five

'Of course you do realise you're making a prize ass of yourself,' said Martin Channing. He sat in his minimalist warehouse office with a clean shirt of Cambridge blue, and was king of all he surveyed.

Tamsin had dropped Peter on the outskirts of Lewes. She'd said the walk into town would do him good, despite his six mile run before sunrise. She clearly felt more 'good' was necessary.

'I'll see you later,' said the Abbot.

He was happy enough with the arrangement; few things in life gave him quite so much pleasure as mindful walking … no thoughts, just the experience of one foot in front of another, the world unfolding around him. He'd made his monkish way to the offices of the *Sussex Silt,* found on the industrial estate by the river Ouse, the tidal waterway which cut the ancient town in two. On the opposite bank was a large supermarket, which reminded him that he needed baby wipes and milk. But not before catching a few words with Mr Channing.

Their relationship went back a couple of years to his arrival in the town – though really, did the word 'relationship' ever apply to Martin? People were entertaining to him, a means to an end, but a relationship? In the early days, Channing had suggested Peter write a piece about his desert experiences. He'd worked hard to produce something good, wondering if one thing might lead to another – only to see it a few days later on page seventeen, under his name but altered beyond recognition and a quarter of the length. Martin had called it 'minor surgery', Peter 'a massacre, with not a single line left standing'.

Like many people, the Abbot was interesting to Martin, but to be kept at an appropriate and playful distance.

'Do you like the office?' he asked, as Peter settled.

'Very warehouse.'

'They used to make rather solid and dependable river boats here,' he added. 'But now I steer a rather different ship.'

'A Destroyer?'

Channing's smile was urbane and self-congratulatory, as Peter returned to the matter in hand.

'No one makes an ass out of themselves by posing a question, Martin.'

Peter had simply asked Channing how eager he'd been to buy into *Mind Gains* – and been declared an ass for his pains.

'They do if it's a stupid question,' said Martin.

'And is there such a thing? Surely the crime lies in not seeking rather than not knowing?'

'Very wise, I'm sure, Peter. In fact, I was thinking of doing a "Thought for the Day" in the *Silt.'*

Peter is surprised but Channing is not done:

'I mean, it's cheap, easy and gives the impression of honour. But then I thought, is anyone really helped by that grandiose nonsense?'

'I didn't realise you were trying to help people.'

'I should definitely employ you, Peter.'

'In what capacity?'

'Would it matter?'

'I have no wish to be a quirky addition to your staff, Martin.'

'And there I was thinking you were touting for a job.'

'No.'

'Really?'

'I merely want to know if you were serious about investing in *Mind Gains* and how you felt when – or if – you were turned down.'

Martin stopped swinging in his chair.

'Frances and I used to have sex,' he said.

Ah. Peter wished Tamsin was here.

'You were lovers?'

'No, we just had sex. No love. I don't think either of us would have wanted that, or known what it was. Indeed, I still don't. And it's ages ago, a very old story. University and all that.'

It felt like a new story to Peter.

'And you stayed in touch?'

'Heavens no. Definitely lost touch, no touch at all, until we bumped into each other in Lewes High Street, thirty years on.'

'A chance meeting?'

'After which a very interesting cup of coffee followed.'

'And she told you about her ideas for *Mind Gains*?'

'Among other things. Allow me a private life, please!'

'Nothing much is private when murder comes to call.'

Abbot Peter shifted in his seat.

'I know what you want to ask, Abbot, and the answer is "No" – it all seems rather childish now.'

Peter nodded.

'And you offered money?'

'I did.'

'Are you not busy enough?'

'I get bored very easily, Peter. You can hear my confession, if you like. I'm bored of this job, I need more stimulation in the office. Work on a national in London and there are at least one or two intelligent folk filing copy, a controversial columnist, a greedy MP, a bitchy Oxford professor, all thoroughly unpleasant – and in the professor's case, pure acid. But all bright and amusing nonetheless, good company. Here in the provinces however – .'

His face mimicked despair.

'I apologise on behalf of dull provincial people everywhere.'

'I mean, I'm getting bored of you, even as I sit here, Abbot! I was delighted to see you, always a pleasure, but the novelty soon wears off. Nothing personal.'

'If it's any consolation, Martin, I'm still quite interested.'

'I wish I could join you.'

'And I'm especially interested in your feelings towards Barnabus, when Frances passed you over for him.'

'I wasn't passed over.'

'I think you were.'

'She wanted a shrink, that's what she really wanted, though God knows why.'

'She wanted someone qualified to do the job?'

'Therapy is a profession where qualifications mean nothing – particularly at Henry House!'

'You don't like Barnabus.'

'Believe me, whether or not I like Barnabus has got nothing to do with it.'

Peter considered for a moment.

'So you bear no hard feelings towards him – or Frances?'

'What a strange world you inhabit, Peter.'

'Why so?'

'To imagine there could ever be hard feelings about something like that.'

'Something like rejection?'

'It was just business, entertainment! I think religious folk struggle with bitterness more than the rest of us!'

'So when Frances said no, everything was good?'

'We need not over-egg the pudding, Peter. But pretty much so, yes.'

His phone then rang.

'Hello?' he said, while waving goodbye to the Abbot. Their time was clearly done and Peter gathered his things.

'And who's speaking?'

'It's Rebecca, Mr Channing.'

'Ah yes, well I think I once met your husband at Henry House.'

'Yes, you did, Mr Channing.'

'So how can I help, Rebecca?'

Peter would have liked to have heard more. He'd have liked to have heard both Rebecca's problem and Channing's solution, but the editor's gestures were clear enough; he was being dismissed and was soon on a bus back to Stormhaven, having forgotten both baby wipes and milk.

'Damn.'

Peter was still coming to terms with the need to shop. You don't shop in a monastery: all that you need is already there, and if it isn't there, it's probably out of reach, a couple of deserts away. But here in Stormhaven, and presumably other towns in the west, nothing is there unless you go and get it. Some people like going to get it, and they are called 'shopaholics'. But Peter was not one of these. He hated going to get it.

But he did like the bus and had found a window seat on the top deck, half way back. The light was fading but he clearly discerned the flinty silhouette of Lewes prison, a Victorian addition to the landscape at the top of town. It's most famous inmate down the years was probably Eamonn de Valera, incarcerated there after the Easter Rising in Ireland in 1916. He was a man who interested Peter: a man sentenced to death by the British government and then reprieved because of his American birth; but even more interestingly – for Peter at least – a Republican politician who asked to be buried in a religious habit. It was not a desire Peter shared, a religious habit for eternity? Exciting perhaps for a politician, but less so for an Abbot and as the prison disappeared from sight, he wondered: would this be where the murderer of Barnabus spent their first night in captivity? Only if male, and more pressingly, only if found. How near were they? And what wall of fire stood between them and the truth?

But what most focused Peter's mind as they accelerated down the A27 was the fact that he'd heard the same woman's voice twice that afternoon: once at Henry House in the hall, demanding to know what was happening, and then again on the phone to Martin Channing, seeking his help.

Her name was Rebecca and she was clearly in some distress.

Sixty Six

'Well of course I lied about my intentions! I was hardly going to tell the truth!'

Virgil's forceful defence put Tamsin on the back foot, when she should have been on the front.

'Lying to the police is a crime.'

Lame, Tamsin, very lame – you can do better than that.

'I didn't lie anyway,' says Virgil.

'You just said you did.'

'Hyperbole. You never asked me whether I'd lived in the house as a child! Did you ever ask me that?'

Tamsin stares. For a posh boy, Virgil lives in a very small house, covered in papers and piled with books, photos on the mantelpiece of smartly dressed college days, a louche, golden haired youth amongst others born to rule.

'Had I been asked that, asked whether Henry House was my family home – and a perfectly fair question it would have been, let me add – I would of course have given plod an answer of unimpeachable truthfulness.'

'Instead of the lie you did give us.'

'You're rather one-tracked, aren't you?'

'Some call it focused.'

'And perhaps you have to be one-tracked to be a plod.'

'You talk as if you're somehow superior.'

'Don't know about that!'

'It's how it sounds.'

'I'm multi-tracked, me – I see seven things at once, sometimes more, superior possibly but damnably irritating!'

'So shall we get back to the subject?'

'And what you call a lie, this is my point – we're getting there, across unpromising terrain, I grant you – what you call a lie, I call the tilting of my sails to the changing wind.'

Tamsin found him strangely believable. He wasn't lying, of course not; he was simply tilting his sails towards the changing wind. It was self-evident, surely? Note to self: 'Tamsin, get a grip.'

'So here's a question: are you a murderer?'

Virgil laughed.

'I'm a rogue – but a loveable rogue!'

'You're a rogue.'

'Total rogue, hands-up to that, no defence.'

'And what makes you a rogue?'

'Questions, questions!'

'It's what I do. I want to find out about you.'

'Exactly. And I don't want you to find out about me! I like me covered over.'

'So why are you a rogue?'

'Look, I rather abuse trust … terrible abuser of trust, is that good enough?'

'You abuse people's trust?'

'And people don't like that, not a good idea, "Abusing trust is a very bad plan, Virgil!" ' he says, in a voice other than his own.

'So you abuse trust.'

'Mea culpa.'

'Anyone's trust in particular?'

'No one I'm telling you about.'

'So shall I take you down to the station for further questioning?'

Virgil subsides.

'Well, old wifey probably hasn't seen the best of me.'

'Your wife thinks you're a bastard?'

'Totally my fault of course, well partly hers, but the largest serving of blame is on my plate, definitely, large portions, though she hardly helped things, all that roaring about, like some deranged lioness.'

Tamsin felt as one walking in mud, slipping and sliding, no grip and little progress.

'So you're a rogue but a loveable rogue, you say?'

'Absolutely!'

'And who says you're loveable?'

'Who says?'

'I don't see a queue.'

Virgil gives a naughty grin.

'I say I'm loveable, damn it!'

'I'm not sure that counts.'

'I won't let you *not* love me! Everyone loves Virgil!'

'Barnabus struggled to love you. A pretty hard session you had together, by all accounts.'

'He was like a fancy fly half on the rugby pitch, and I mashed him, battered him totally … I mean in the session, not with the poker.'

'You're sure about that?'

'I think I'd remember.'

'Only if it suited you.'

Virgil is frustrated.

'The man's in my house, for God's sake, in my bedroom! He's sleeping in my bedroom! That's definitely bad form.'

'Your old bedroom.'

'Who ever forgets their childhood bedroom?'

'I've done my best, but you seem to be struggling.'

'It was my bedroom.'

'The bedroom you walked out on before embarking on a long and drawn-out tantrum towards your father, who remained at Henry House.'

'That's completely different.'

Sixty Seven

A fire burned in the hearth of Sandy View and the Abbot and Tamsin sat as close to the flame as possible. Peter was perched on the old herring box and Tamsin enjoyed the chair.

'You could always get another chair,' said Tamsin.

'I keep meaning to.'

'That's a statement that lacks conviction.'

'No, I definitely keep meaning to.'

'If you wanted a chair you could have one the following day; you could have a new chair tomorrow.'

'It's on my list.'

'Is that the imaginary one you never look at?'

Peter raised his eyebrows at this sustained intrusion into his private life.

'It has a slightly notional feel, I grant you.'

It was good to recognise the truth sometimes: he didn't have a list.

Tamsin poses a leading question: 'Do you fear that two chairs would encourage more people to drop in?'

'Anyone's welcome here,' says Peter.

'Really?'

'Open door.'

'But that isn't the message of the furniture.'

'What do you mean?'

'The furniture doesn't speak of welcome or an open door. It says 'Why are you here?'

'You're in a comfy chair, aren't you?'

'Yes, but you're on a herring box.'

Outside was a cold clear night, as the tide withdrew slowly across the shingle, leaving shiny stones in the light of the moon. Both held a generous glass of whisky in their hands.

'So what have we got?'

They'd decided that a review of the case was in order.

Tamsin: 'We've got a spooky house, a murdered clown –.'

'Psychotherapist.'

'Same thing. And we also have what looks like seven suspects.'

Peter went through the list:

'Frances Pole, Kate Karter, Martin Channing, Virgil Bannaford, Ezekiel St Paul, Pat Strong – and you're including Bella Amal?

'I know she wasn't there, but her name has to be in the mix. She's too involved.'

'And the cleaner Pat Strong has gone missing in suspicious circumstances, after giving both a false name and false address to her employers. So who is she? Where is she now? And is she dead or alive?'

'And if she's dead, who killed her?'

'Or what drove her to kill herself?'

'Anything else from the notes Barnabus took after the meetings? Any unmentioned moments of revelation?'

'I was most struck by Ezekiel St Paul.'

'The Reverend.'

'I just couldn't see why he was there at the Feast. His particular brand of belief would regard therapy as little less than satanic. His attitude would be: why see a therapist when you can pray?'

'And my attitude would be: why do either?'

'He said himself that the godless cannot help the godly. So why did he choose the godless to speak to? I don't understand his place in all this, it's not making sense. And then there's Kate Karter – .'

'I've had my fill of her today.'

'Really?'

'She's rung me three times to say that she believes her life is in danger.'

'From whom?'

'She doesn't say. She spills her fears in a torrent of words and then makes a joke of it. So perhaps it doesn't matter.'

'Not necessarily. A joke for her is an escape from reality, a step away from her true feelings, a way to deflect attention from pain.'

'You mean fear might be the truer emotion?'

'Possibly. This is what Barnabus said about Kate: 'Without a physical mask when we met – apart from the fake tan – but her emotional mask was a brittle and resistant thing.'

'And Martin and Frances?'

'Interesting.'

'They once had a relationship, you say?'

'They once had sex.'

'The two are not entirely separate.'

'I'm merely giving you Martin's take on the matter. He was clear about the sex but against any mention of love. He did, however, want to invest in *Mind Gains*.'

'But Frances went for Barnabus instead, the no-mark, poorly-qualified Barnabus, which can't have gone down well.'

'Martin says it meant nothing.'

'And you believed him?'

'I'm not sure. He does the careless veneer very well. And Virgil?' he asked, aware he hadn't heard from Tamsin about her visit. 'He gave Barnabus a wretched time when they met.'

'He was a bit of a lamb with me,' said Tamsin. No need for the Abbot to know how difficult she'd found the interview.

'But he didn't like *Mind Gains* being there?'

'He hated *Mind Gains* being there. Well, in his shoes, who wouldn't?'

'Are you his PR woman?'

'I'm just saying!'

'Not everyone clings to their past,' said Peter.

'Really? Well, what do you think of the Abbot who replaced you in your desert home? A tiny bit resentful perhaps?'

'Funnily enough, I was speaking to him on the phone today.'

'They have phones?'

'Surprisingly good line. He could have been in Eastbourne.'

'Maybe he was.'

'I didn't hear any retired couples in the background.'

'And you like him?'

'The new Abbot?'

'Yes.'

'Well, we're hardly friends.'

'Precisely!'

'And obviously he's destroying the place.'

Tamsin laughed and Peter spouted some nonsense about people doing what they can until they can do it no longer.

'And what's that supposed to mean?'

'He's a gifted man, but made small by his perceptions.'

'And how does that work?'

'A discussion for another time, perhaps.'

'I don't think I'll be passing this way again, so it's now or never.'

Peter is reluctant but the whisky is warm in his belly and the fire so fine it could seduce a nun. 'We only begin to understand how our perceptions create our reality once we've been through some sort of change or crisis in our life, and been broken by it. Perhaps something collapses or we're faced with new circumstances, where nothing that used to work for us works any longer. We're then shocked into noticing how warped our perceptions have been to this point, how blinkered.'

Tamsin was struggling, but Abbot Peter knew his destination: 'Abbot Donald, however – or Abbot Donaldo, as he calls himself, for fear of sounding like the cartoon duck – he hasn't passed that way yet, hasn't been broken, hasn't allowed himself to be. So he's still in the grip of his old perceptions, insecure perceptions, still trying to achieve success, nonsense like that.'

Tamsin pulled a face.

'It isn't a crime, Abbot.'

'What isn't?'

'Success.'

'Indeed. But neither is the pursuit of it an interesting way of life for the adult human.'

Tamsin looked into the fire and sipped her whisky.

'Sounds like you haven't let go, Uncle.'

Sixty Eight

Uncle? How strange that sounded on Tamsin's lips. So long in the world alone and now the hint of connection, the rumour of belonging.

'I have twenty five years to let go of,' said Peter, regarding his whisky as though it was a prism of revelation. 'That's a lot of existence, and it takes time to pass through, even amid the undoubted wonders of Stormhaven.'

Tamsin was looking at some notes.

'Not that he'd ever shown any affection for the place himself.'

'Who?'

Peter had been back in the desert.

'Virgil,' said Tamsin, getting them back on track.

'No, that's right. From the notes left by Barnabus, he hated his childhood from beginning to end, left Henry House as soon as he could, and never returned.'

Tamsin questioned why he should now change his mind and Peter said it was called ambivalence, longing for something we hate, hating something we long for. And then along comes *Mind Gains* and cuts off the path to resolution, the path back home.

'So rage at his parents is now transferred onto the *Mind Gains* staff,' says Peter.

'Skull-fracturing rage?'

'He enjoyed rugby as a boy.'

They pondered the flames before Tamsin moved on.

'And then there's Bella: the heart of the place or a nosy busybody?'

Peter was putting a couple more logs on the fire, driftwood from the beach. He also splashed a little more whisky into both glasses.

'She intimated to me,' he said, 'that she'd enjoyed a "close friendship" with Pat.'

'And what's that supposed to mean?'

'I don't know much about these things. I saw it expressed only in a concern for her safety.'

'No one saw her from the beginning of the event to the end, and for some of the time at least, she sat and read in the pub.'

'Slightly alibi-seeking behaviour, don't you think?'

'What if it is just an alibi, pure and simple?'

'Possible, obviously. She didn't ask the landlord for the time after spilling her drink over his head?'

They both chuckled. The deliberate creation of alibis remained a surprisingly unsubtle business.

'It wasn't unusual for her to sit in the pub apparently. She has a seat in the corner and reads romances with a gin and tonic and a "do not disturb" aura.'

'She'd organised the Feast of Fools and wanted to be the Lord of Misrule, but Frances wouldn't have it,' said Peter, as much to himself as his companion.

'Frances said the appointment must be left to chance to maximise the psychological chaos – which makes sense of a sort.'

'But Frances must have felt very strongly about this, to alienate the wonderful Bella over the matter. Bella was very much her appointment according to Barnabus.'

'And of course no one has admitted to being the Lord of Misrule; and in a way, why would you?'

'The Lord of Misrule was the murderer,' said Peter.

'So you say.'

'By some means,' continued Peter, 'the supposedly anonymous figure of Barnabus was isolated in the office by our mystery Lord during the game of Sardines, where he was stabbed – but possibly not killed. Strange.'

'People do all agree that the disguises were good.'

'Blood stains show he was attacked by the desk and fell to the floor there.'

'And Frances says there was no one in the office when she left. I think you'd notice a body on the floor, even after a glass or three of wine.'

'So the body was in the cupboard by then, though not dead, still able to write.'

'*Your thousand limbs rend my body this is the way.* He was killed later.'

'Sometime around midnight.'

'So someone came back to finish off the job – or never left the building.'

'Everyone was seen leaving, except for Pat, the cleaner, who disappeared and Frances, who locked up by herself – though with the Reverend Ezekiel St Paul in attendance somewhere, warming up the car.'

'And presumably Bella wasn't still reading in the pub at midnight?'

'No one can quite remember when she left, but it was some time before then.'

There was a pause. Tamsin yawned followed by Peter, and with permission given, both suddenly felt tired.

'It's late,' she said.

'It is,' said Peter.

'Can I stay the night?'

These were not words he wanted to hear.

'Two whiskies in a car could threaten my career,' she explained.

Peter noted that it wasn't her life she was worried about, but her career.

'You're very welcome to stay,' said Peter. 'The spare room is as you left it, I believe.'

'But that was eleven months ago. Has no one been since?'

'You may be mistaking me for a guest house.'

Her last stay at Sandy View had been something of a camping experience, after which she'd brought both sheets and a bedside lamp for the spare room. But apparently the floodgates of hospitality hadn't opened since. With sleeping arrangements sorted, however, the two made their plans for the following day as teeth were cleaned and hot water bottles filled. Abbot Peter would start with Ezekiel, and Tamsin would catch up with Bella. She wanted to hear more about her relationship with Pat, professional interest only. Abbot Peter's first meeting, however, was with Poppy – and he wanted Tamsin out of the house before she came.

'She's quite unsettled by visitors.'

'Then this is a good place for her,' said Tamsin.

'You have a cruel streak.'

'That's no streak, that's all of me.'

'I beg to differ.'

Abbot Peter was not keen on self-condemnation. It was always destructive and always mistaken.

'I'll be gone early anyway. I have a meeting with Chief Inspector Wonder at 9.00 a.m.'

'Something I know you'll be looking forward to.'

'He's an idiot.'

'And we can meet again tomorrow evening.'

'It'll have to be late. I'm at a leaving bash, pretending I care about the departing Mick Norman, a revolting man.'

'That's the good thing about monasteries.'

'What is?'

'People didn't leave – they just died.'

'How cheering.'

'I'd take a funeral over a leaving party every time.'

'I almost agree. It – and he – will be appalling.'

'Then perhaps we'll make other plans.'

'You could stay up until it's over.'

'No, there's little I can sensibly do after 10.00 p.m. on Guy Fawkes Night, other than go to bed and long for the first light of dawn.'

Sixty Nine

At about the same time as Peter and Tamsin talked, there was a knock on a door across town. It was answered by Ezekiel St Paul.

'I'm sorry to bother you,' said a well-wrapped Kate Karter, 'but can I come inside a moment?'

Ezekiel looked bemused.

'You may remember me from the Feast of Fools? Kate Karter?'

'We will do our business where we stand,' said Ezekiel, barring her way. 'It's late, and I don't want my household disturbed.'

'Absolutely, Ezekiel.'

It would have been wise to call him Reverend, if she'd wanted to progress further.

'It was just that I was passing and I know a bible has been found at Henry House with no name inside – and I wondered if it might be yours.'

'It isn't.'

'Whether you'd perhaps left one there inadvertently? Are you sure I can't come in?'

'I would know if I had lost my bible, Mrs Karter; and I would have noticed it rather sooner than this.'

'Of course, a treasured possession … or perhaps one of your family? Your wife, son or daughter? It couldn't be one of theirs, could it? No one can think who it belongs to!'

'It does not belong here, Mrs Karter, that I know – but I hope it's returned to its owner soon. It is God's word that they have lost!'

'Indeed, God's word, as you say.'

'And now, good night to you.'

'Yes, yes, good night Ezekiel.'

And with that, Kate hurried away into the night.

'Mad as a hatter,' she thought.

But it hadn't gone as planned. She'd failed.

Seventy

Wednesday 5 November

'*The Sussex Silt* seems damn quiet on the matter!'

Chief Inspector Wonder exuded bluff jollity behind his desk in the Police headquarters at Lewes. Tamsin had no interest in this overweight man being happy; but she'd take this, over his nervous insecure carping when a case was taking its time.

'That may be because the editor, Martin Channing, is one of the suspects.'

'Martin Channing caught up in this malarkey?'

Tamsin nodded.

'Well, that's a turn-up! Oh, that's very good, that is.'

'There are six other suspects.'

'Well, we must all hope it's him.'

'You don't like the man?'

Tamsin managed to sound suitably distant, as one who lived above the rough and tumble of human conflict and transcended the daily spite.

'That man, Tamsin, is a slimeball. And don't tell me you don't agree.'

'People do what they can until they can do it no longer.'

Wonder's head turned.

'And what in Beelzebub's name is that supposed to mean?'

Tamsin couldn't remember what it meant, if she ever knew; the Abbot had explained, but she hadn't listened and didn't care now anyway – the effect was achieved.

'So is it him?'

'I don't know. It's all smoke and mirrors at the moment. Everyone saw the murderer at work but no one saw them, if that makes any sense.'

'None at all.'

Tamsin explained events around the Feast of Fools, an event which left the Chief Inspector baffled.

'You couldn't make it up!' he said. 'I mean, what did they think they were doing?'

'Who?'

'Well, all of them. I mean, what d'you reckon to this therapy stuff?' he asked leaning back in his chair and bursting one of his shirt buttons.

'I don't use it myself.'

'I've got this psychotic fellow asking if he can offer half hour sessions to people who work here at HQ.'

'I think you mean psychotherapist.'

'Possibly. I'm not up on all the terms, old school me. He says they'll benefit from a listening ear amid the strains of life, that it will help them to be more motivated. Of course I just say, "Problems? Man up and grow a chin, you big girl's blouse!".'

Wonder enjoyed his comedy while Tamsin wanted to cut the chummy chat and get back to the case. But both Wonder and his chest were in expansive mood:

'And then what will the unintended consequences be?'

'The psychotherapist?'

'The psycho bloke, yes. Have you thought of that?'

'Why would I? It's not my job.'

'Very nice for the officers to have free therapy in company time and all that, but what if they suddenly "find themselves" and want to go off and start a donkey refuge in Venezuela? What then?'

Tamsin felt this was unlikely.

'Knowing your officers as I do, Chief Inspector, I don't think there's great danger of that. The donkeys in Venezuela may need to struggle on alone for a while longer.'

'No, but it makes you think, doesn't it?'

It made Tamsin think her boss was a waste of her time.

'Well, keep me in the loop, Tamsin.'

'I will.'

'And the old monk fellow's helping, is he?'

'An extra pair of hands, certainly.'

'The Special Witness post is meant to be a little more than that, Tamsin. It's about value added. Are you getting value added?'

Tamsin struggled to offer a complimentary word about Abbot Peter. The traditional motivational sandwich of 'praise, reproof, praise,' was simply not her bag. She tended to offer just the filling while keeping the praise for herself.

'It was a good choice of mine to appoint him, if that's what you're asking.'

'Not really.'

'Then I'm not sure anything else is relevant right now.'

Tamsin sometimes forgot that this man was her boss.

Seventy One

'Now that is a wondrous thing, Poppy!'

Abbot Peter gazed with awe at the computer screen in his study …
while Poppy considered an empty milk carton on the carpet.

Wondrous: it wasn't something he often said about e mails, but
today was an exception. Here was a wondrous email, one of two
missives waiting for him on this Guy Fawkes Day morning. The first
came from a Paul Heron who wrote to ask him if he was the same
'Abbot Peter' who used to teach Maths and occasionally PE at Winter
Hill Court Preparatory School? Sensing a court case in the air, Peter
was relieved to be able to reply in the negative. He'd been 4000 miles
away during the decade in question. But it was the second email
which gripped him, an email covered in sand and bringing to his dark
study – the builder of this extension had not been a fan of natural
light – a most precious desert cargo.

In theory, Poppy's presence in the study made her a trespasser. It
was a house rule at Sandy View: wherever else they went in the
house, no one was allowed in Abbot Peter's study. But he'd bent the
rules for his small companion and Poppy seemed to understand,
seemed to grasp that here was a place of quiet. She sat now on the
blue carpet in a state of enchantment with the recycling box, brought
in from the kitchen for this very purpose. Peter had quickly noticed
that whatever toys her mother left for her – colourful toys, clever
toys, cuddly toys – she'd gravitate with strong inevitability towards
the recycling, an ever-changing treasure trove of cereal packets,
plastic bottles, old marmite jars and tin foil.

'But obviously you must tell no one,' he'd warned her, 'no one, you
understand? Or they'll think I'm going soft and start imagining
they're allowed in my study as well … and they're not, you see – only
you.'

And if Poppy had treasure, so did Peter, as with one click on the
keyboard, he opened up a library of poems by his old friend Hafiz.

They'd been delivered to St James-the-Less by his copyist, Behrouz Gul, fearful for their survival in Shiraz. And there they'd sat for 600 years, largely ignored, but occasionally discovered and one of the explorers had been Barnabus Hope, who'd never been the same thereafter.

'He cracked the world open for me,' Barnabus had said. 'And light flooded in!'

But it was only last year, and how fortunate, that these poems had been digitalised by the thrusting new Abbot. Abbot Donaldo may be destroying the place, but he understood technology and, in his words, was 'keen to make St James-the-Less a global influence.' It would no doubt be called St James-the-More soon in a further re-branding exercise. But, in the meantime, he'd been only too pleased to send Peter some of the monastery's treasures – and what strong feelings arose inside him as he read.

Peter had been moved by these poems twenty five years ago ... no, melted – better by far than moved. Moved is some brief emotion quickly left behind, but melting is change, reconfiguration with nothing the same thereafter. These poems had melted Peter all those years ago, but can you be melted twice? And perhaps more pressingly, would these lines shed light on the one who smashed the skull of his friend? Yes, perhaps friend was the word, he still wasn't sure, but before starting on the poetry, Peter read through Abbot Donaldo's brief message. Greetings in Christ's name, brotherly love from the desert, blah blah blah, and then he signed off with St Paul's famous lines from the book of Corinthians, popular for royal weddings, he'd heard: 'And now these three remain: faith, hope and love. But the greatest of these is love.' And of course being Donaldo, and being eager to show how much he knew, he'd had to write them in Egyptian.

Always the showman.

'Here goes, Poppy!' said Peter, scooping her up in response to her outstretched arms. 'Do you want to read the first poem with me? Yes? And don't panic, they're all sensibly short. Hafiz knew we'd be busy people. And then we'll get straight back to the *Owl in the Tree*.'

With Poppy settled on his lap, he started to scroll down to the first piece of verse. And as he did so, something leapt like fire into his consciousness.

When the hounds see the fox, and Peter just had, the chase is nearing its end ... and all thanks to Donaldo.

Act Four

What we call happiness in the strictest sense comes from the (preferably sudden) satisfaction of needs which have been dammed up to a high degree.

Sigmund Freud

Seventy Two

Peter took the phone call at 7.00 p.m., as the first of the fireworks fizzed into the night air. By 7.20 p.m. he was in a taxi. He'd tried to call Tamsin but her phone was turned off. He then remembered the leaving do, an appalling policeman's send-off , with Tamsin pretending to care … it wouldn't be a great impression. Peter had left a message – though who could tell when she'd pick it up?

Kate Karter had sounded distressed on the phone, genuinely distressed, and begged him to come quickly. No doubt she'd already tried Tamsin and had no luck. She was at Henry House, she said. Why Henry House? asked Peter. She would explain everything, she said, it was a long story but he must hurry, 'Everything depends on it, Abbot, everything!'

The taxi made quick progress out of Stormhaven, and why not, this was hardly Bangkok.

'So what's at Henry House tonight?' asked the driver. 'Not another murder?'

'Oh, just seeing a friend.'

'You mean someone lives there? I read in the paper it was a place for nut jobs now.'

'It's a therapy centre called *Mind Gains*.'

'*Mind Games*?'

'*Mind Gains*.'

'Sound the same to me.'

'I think that was the idea, a play on words.'

'Of course I remember it when Dr Minty lived there.'

'Ah yes. Good memories?'

'Rubbish doctor, but at least no one died at his hands – not on the premises anyway.'

'If you could just drop me here, please.'

The taxi pulled up outside the gates. Something in Peter did not wish to herald his arrival. He paid the cabbie – could he claim expenses and how did you do that if you did? He watched him swing the car round and drive back towards Stormhaven, back towards safety, that's how it felt, in a way. As the car disappeared around the corner, Peter turned and stepped beneath the Tudor rose, through the stone gates, passing from one world to another, from one time to another, a more dangerous time. He walked slowly along the cratered drive in the night shadows of evergreen and rhododendron. Puddles glinted in the moonlight as he turned the bend which brought Henry House into view. He'd never been so struck by the chill isolation of this building, from Plague House to *Mind Gains* but always somehow itself, and quite beyond any rules. Impassive, that was the word, like the white make-up worn by upper class Elizabethan women, by the queen herself, a mask of indifference, but a killing mask.

Why these facts came to mind now, Peter couldn't say as he approached the grandiose pillars around the entrance and noticed the front door ajar.

He thought again of the quivery writing in the office cupboard. And as bangers exploded in distant air, and bonfires consumed guys – Lewes was famous for its Protestant fire – Peter was thinking of the quivery signature of the original Guy, Guido Fawkes, after four days of torture in the Tower of London. It didn't need a graphologist to see the pain in those letters. After his discovery and capture with gunpowder, in a building adjoining the House of Lords, King James had suggested the gentler tortures to begin with, to encourage information. But when those proved too kind, he authorised something that was not – the rack. On the fourth day, resistance tired of its courage, and the names of fellow conspirators spilled from his screaming mouth. And then the court judgement: that Fawkes and his companions in high treason would be dragged by a horse backwards to their death, head near the ground. They would first be hanged – hanged until choking but not dead – after which they would be taken down. Their genitals would then be cut off and burnt before their eyes, their stomach cut open and their bowels and hearts removed, with them conscious throughout. They would then be beheaded, with the dismembered parts of their bodies displayed, so that they might become prey for the fowls of the air.

Why did Peter think on these things as he stepped into the dark hall of Henry House? And it was then that he saw a light in the study.

Seventy Three

'I'm going out,' said Rebecca, getting up.

'You're going nowhere at this time of night,' said Ezekiel.

'I'm going out.'

'Stay!'

There was remarkable power in the voice of this small man, there always had been.

'I'm going to the Police Station and I'm going to tell them what's happened.'

'Do you see the sin of Eve, Michael?'

Michael looked up from his homework.

'The sin of the woman who thinks she knows best!'

Ezekiel's son and heir did not respond as he should; but Ezekiel would stay strong in his household leadership:

'You will stay, Rebecca, and that is my final word on the matter.'

'I don't care about your final word, Ezekiel. I'm still going.'

Rebecca stepped into the hallway to get her coat. There was both terror and fire inside, as Ezekiel moved towards her.

'Let her go, Father.'

'I beg your pardon?'

Ezekiel spun round towards his son, Michael, who had first preached in church at the age of 16, who had always known right from wrong, whom many felt anointed by God's spirit for fruitful ministry. But his words now were words of disobedience.

'The Police Station is the best place, Father, you know it is. It can't go on, none of us can, we need to bring this to an end.'

Rebecca was torn, raging inside, but worried for Michael. She knew her husband and his ways, and hesitated in the hall. Ezekiel grabbed her arm, pulling her struggling back into the front room. She resisted, wrenching to get away, but he was forcing her back down on the chair, back where she should be, until the anointed one, Michael, the boy-preacher, was up from his seat in quick easy moves and screaming 'No!'

It's now Ezekiel being jerked back, pulled away, pulled down by a seventeen- year-old-boy feeling power in his body for the first time.

'Go, Mum, go!'

'Will you be all right?'

'Go, for God's sake, go!'

He was struggling with his father, half on top, trying to hold him down, breaking years of control with rage for energy.

'*Go!*'

Rebecca made for the door and hurried out into the firework night. Ezekiel had never liked her trainers, they were not feminine shoes, not appropriate for a woman and he'd like them even less tonight, as she ran in short bursts, these were freeing shoes, shoes with spring in their step, so she ran then walked, walked then ran, bangers banging, looking behind, making for the Police Station. She was worried for Michael, worried for herself – but most of all worried for her daughter.

Not too far now.

*

Kate Karter was standing on a bench in the middle of the office with a wire noose round her neck, her hands pulled up behind her head, like one lying back in the sun. But these hands were tied, hard plastic cuffs cutting into the skin.

'Oh, Abbot Peter!'

'It's all right, Kate. I'm here.'

'Quick, he's gone out, but we don't have much time. Get me down – but please be careful.'

The bench was well chosen by the murderer, an unstable affair.

'You'll need a knife to free my hands. Then you can get to the noose.'

'I'll be back,' said Peter.

He stepped into the hallway and it was then he saw the ghost. It was the ghost of the Irish Harlequin, up in the gallery, disappearing into the Long Room.

Peter stood transfixed.

*

There was one bonfire still to be lit in Stormhaven, though now was not quite the time. This would be too early, given the state of play.

But it was a good pile, the gardener had done a fine job, well, you'd expect it … if a gardener can't build a fire, what hope for anyone? It now needed only last minute attention, a little petrol poured around the base, quite a lot in fact, it's hard to stop when you get going, a generous soaking for the wood and old newspapers crumpled and stuffed in the gaps.

And this would be their goodbye to Henry House, though hardly tearful, a beautiful house, but never more than a stage for revenge, so no love lost, not towards the building, though love lost was all they knew.

It would be a fine fire, shooting flames into the night sky, a suitable backdrop for hell, and they would do what they must do, it was deserved and then they'd be gone, everything sorted.

Seventy Four

Peter disappeared to the kitchen to find a knife. The ghost could wait. He fumbled in drawers without light, watching the shadows, watching for harlequins, feeling with his fingers for the sharp edge he needed. That would do, that was sharp and now back across the hall to the office.

'Please, my arms, they're hurting!' said Kate, wobbling slightly.

She was a pathetic figure, this object of hate.

'It's okay,' he said, 'I'm going to have to climb onto the bench.'

'Don't do that!'

'It's the only way.'

Kate was frightened. A slip would do neither of them any good, but especially her.

'For God's sake, be careful!'

Peter gingerly stepped up onto the insecure stage, gathered himself and his balance, and then began gently to cut at the handcuffs, no sudden movements allowed, while a terrified Kate watched the door like a hawk.

'Hurry, please.'

The knife was a vegetable cutter, serrated edges, a good choice but dangerous around Kate's wrists, necessarily exposed by the angle of the arm. He cut and he cut, slowly, slowly.

'We're getting there,' he said.

And then her hands were free.

'Oh thank God!' said Kate, 'and I mean that.'

They stood cautiously on the bench together.

'Will you say a prayer for us as we stand here now, Abbot? We're going to need God's help to get out of this, believe me. Hands together, Abbot, for the both of us.'

Peter was surprised, but compliant.

'A simple prayer perhaps,' but no words came out, for in the moment he bowed his head and offered praying hands, the deed was

228

done. From her cleavage, Kate produced another set of plastic cuffs, slipped them tight onto to Peter's praying hands, and then transferred the noose from her neck to his. Kate stepped carefully down from the bench.

'I last did that routine twenty years ago at the Theatre Royal, Brighton.'

Peter was still in shock.

'It was a thriller called *Money for Old Rope*,' she said, 'and that's exactly what it was, believe me, not the best of plays – but there was a scene like the one we just played out.'

'A great shame I missed it.'

'Most people missed it, as I recall.'

Kate had collected her coat from the corner and now stood looking up at Peter, still rubbing her wrists.

'I have never had to practice any routine as much as that one,' she said.

'Practice makes perfect.'

'It did tonight.'

'And do you still practice prayer?'

'I never practiced prayer, never quite got the hang of that. But you do … your downfall, I suppose.'

'You could let me down, of course,' he said, feeling the uncertainty of the bench beneath him.

'No, I can't.'

'I don't believe you murdered Barnabus.'

'I didn't.'

'Quite. And I know this isn't your quarrel. So why involve yourself?'

'This isn't my quarrel, as you say, Abbot – but it's our future, you see, and with this, my bill is paid.'

'Which bill is that?'

'Gerald and I, we'll be free now, quite free.'

She put on her thick winter coat, fur-lined and then drew from the pockets a purple woollen hat which she placed on her head.

'Goodbye, Abbot Peter.'

She closed the office door behind her, then a pause, followed by the shutting of the front door. Kate Karter had left the building, leaving Abbot Peter alone.

Though hardly alone; Peter knew well enough that company was close at hand. And was that a bonfire being lit outside?

Seventy Five

The Reverend Ezekiel St Paul arrived breathless at the Police Station, tugging at his jacket, attempting sartorial order. But his collar remained askew and there was swelling round his eye, from when his head had hit the table.

'Been in a fight, sir?' enquired the desk sergeant.

'I wish my wife returned to me,' he said with a polite smile.

'I beg your pardon?'

The new arrival was in bit of a state, but then the sergeant was not a picture of competence himself, a party hat on his head and streamer paper on his shoulder.

'I know she is here.'

The music from the canteen made conversation difficult, but they struggled on.

'You know who's here?'

'Rebecca St Paul, my wife. I understand she's here.'

'And why do you think she might be here?' said the desk sergeant leaning forward.

'She left the house a short while ago, saying she was coming here.'

'Then she must be the invisible woman.' And then a thought. 'Unless she knew Mick Norman, of course.'

'I'm sorry?'

Louder: 'Did she know Mick Norman?'

Straining: 'Mick who?'

Very loud: 'Mick Norman. It's his leaving do through there. Thirty years in the force and still standing – just. Are you sure you haven't been in a fight?'

The Reverend was done with the Police Station.

'I would like to be informed if she comes here tonight.'

The desk sergeant indicated he couldn't hear.

'I would like to be informed if she comes here tonight!' he repeated.

Request understood, but no obedience promised to this strange little man.

'It was a free country when my shift started, Reverend. And unless anything's changed, I'm not obliged to inform anyone of anything unless a crime's been – .'

But Ezekiel St Paul was already walking towards the door.

*

'How did you bloody well find me?' asked Virgil Bannaford, genuinely confused.

'Your name was in her address book.'

'Whose address book?'

'My daughter's.'

'But I don't know your daughter!'

'Well, isn't that strange?'

Rebecca had made for the police station initially, but chose another path, given what she'd said before leaving. Ezekiel would come after her, she knew that, he'd come for her but she didn't have to give him directions … and suddenly 56 Johnson Road had sprung to mind. She'd got as far as the porch but no further, blocked by the substantial frame of Virgil.

'I have no idea who or what you're talking about.'

She wasn't in the mood for another man full of shite.

'Oh believe me, it's there, written in her book. Patience saw you as a way out.'

'Patience?'

'You might know her as Pat, Pat Strong, the cleaner at Henry House.'

'Oh!'

Recognition.

'Well, I did meet her briefly, nice girl, but I don't know why she'd have my address.'

'Really?'

Rebecca believed a mother should never search the bedroom of her daughter. It was a betrayal of trust, an intrusion on something sacred. Her own mother had trampled over the sacred repeatedly, and Rebecca had no wish to follow. But when daughters disappear, the rules do too. The diary, found quickly – perhaps she'd wanted it found – had made painful reading, a record of young unhappiness. Patience referred to her father simply as 'Mad'. 'Mad in a bad mood today' or 'Mad is planning something with the Benders.' Rebecca understood this to be a reference to the elders of the church. But she didn't escape the girl's wrath either, usually referred to as 'Weak'.

'Weak on usual form.' Though the entry Rebecca particularly remembered was in green ink and said 'Why doesn't Doormat grow some balls. It's pathetic to watch.' But if the diary was easily found, the address book was different, hidden away at the back of the drawer.

'Beside your address Mr Bannaford were the words: 'Possible escape?''

'I don't understand.'

'My daughter was planning on leaving home, this is clear. Perhaps she saw you as a refuge. Perhaps she's here now? Was there a relationship between you?'

'No, there damn well wasn't, thank you very much! I mean, pretty girl, very pretty girl, but none of that malarkey.'

'She's been missing for three days, Mr Bannaford – and I'm now going to the police. They will search this place, so you might as well tell me: is she here? Because if you've hurt her –.'

She felt like an avenging harridan, hugely powerful. Where had this strength come from?

'I have no knowledge of your daughter's whereabouts, Mrs St Paul.'

'Oh I think you do, Mr Bannaford.'

'You can imagine what you like, no really, you can imagine the moon's made of cheese, but your thoughts are egregiously mistaken, and a damnable blot on my honour, so if that's all you have to say – .'

He began to move his large frame forward, edging her back. But Rebecca clung to the door frame.

'Why else would she have your address?'

'I have no idea. And now you better go.'

'She's been missing for three days, Mr Bannaford. Do you know what that feels like?'

'Very troubling, I'm sure, dashed troubling, but there's not a lot I can do.'

'So I've decided to find her.'

'Well I hope you do, believe me.'

He softened.

'Really – I hope you do.'

Virgil didn't know whether to be furious or kind, while Rebecca felt sick at the thought he might be telling the truth, that he could be an innocent man.

She had one last shot, a long shot high in the sky, like the fireworks overhead, but something Ezekiel had let slip.

'Tell me, Mr Bannaford: do you know anything about Henry House? Anything that perhaps no one else knows?'

Seventy Six

Abbot Peter stood stationary in the dark. And if he didn't remain so, he would die.

His hands were beginning to numb and his feet ached to move, but with his head in a noose, balance was all that kept him alive and his feet must stay still. He thought of Tamsin and his message on her phone. The leaving party had hours to run, so no cavalry tonight, none that was sober at least. And he was thinking of Guy Fawkes, crippled by torture and facing awful death. His friends had been dealt with first, hanged to choking, taken down, castrated and then the long knife brought into play, the chest opened, this way and that, quartered and disembowelled, hands reaching in and pulling out, the body ransacked until the sweet relief of beheading, the axed neck, the spurting blood of oblivion. And as Guy Fawkes watched, each agony and scream was his, a particular torture lived again and again, waiting for his own, the seconds ticking, coming soon, always best to be first in the queue.

But then, as he'd waited on the scaffold, waited for the hangman, he'd asked for one last hurrah from his broken body, one more push, and gathering what strength remained, he'd thrown himself from the scaffold, breaking his neck in the fall. Freedom! He'd done what he could, spared himself the awful end. They still quartered him, he wasn't getting off that lightly; but they quartered the dead, not the living.

Peter contemplated similar themes, thin wire round his neck. Would it be wise, like Guy, to opt for worse ahead of much worse? One brave leap from the scaffold ...and then he was thinking of Poppy, playing on his study floor ... Poppy with arms outstretched towards him, waiting to be picked up, waiting to be swept up into the air and held safe. His eyes watered. How he longed now to stoop low and whisk that little body skywards and see those joyful trusting eyes. These were not familiar thoughts, strangers to his psyche but

233

overpowering, why had he not had children of his own? Perhaps he needed only the children of others, that was enough, more than enough but far away now, his hands bound, held in the grip of tight plastic and the wire noose keeping him straight – straight like a soldier on parade, like a puppet on a string, awaiting the puppet master.

And then the shock of the flames, a bonfire on the lawn, sudden conflagration, petrol-fuelled heat. Hungry flames ripped skywards and visible on top, the silhouette of a burning guy, punished again for high treason … as now the flames lit the office, dancing with hellish delight through the room, this way and that, that way and this, dark and light, light and dark, now you see me now you don't, an opening door and standing across the room from Peter … a clown.

Seventy Seven

'And finally, I'd like to say thank you to my wife: thank you for not being here tonight and ruining the evening, you bitch!'

'Mick Norman as tasteful as ever,' whispered Chief Inspector Wonder to Tamsin.

'He's always been repulsive.'

Mick Norman – 'thirty years in the police farce!' – delivering the speech he'd made a few times in front of the mirror. But he'd been sober then, less soaked in alcohol, which can affect performance and did tonight, with too much bitter in so many ways. He over-estimated his comedic talent, and under-estimated communal weariness towards his unhappy marriage, which had consumed him for almost as long as his resentment at not making the rank of Inspector. So there was laughter throughout, but the half-hearted variety, the embarrassed sort, because boorish isn't funny, a bit close to the bone old Mick, the one about his wife, not nice, and really everyone unhappy until it was over and the music resumed in the canteen of Stormhaven Police Station ... but only after Mick Norman had called on everyone to 'get some more down yer and don't miss me too much 'cos I sure as hell won't miss you!'

Tables had been cleared to the side, but there wasn't a rush on to the dance floor, groups staying close to the alcohol, paid for from the social fund, so no reason to hold back.

'Perhaps not the best way to end his time with us,' said Wonder to DI Tamsin Shah, who'd been trying to leave for some time. 'I met his wife once.'

'Poor woman.'

'She was really rather nice, not the picture he paints at all, but who knows what goes on behind closed doors?'

'I'd leave the door open if Mick Norman was with me.'

'There speaks the ice queen!'

What a ridiculous, stupid bloody male response, thought Tamsin.

'Always a bitter man,' she said.

'Decent copper.'

'But never an Inspector and he couldn't cope with that.'

Tamsin knew well the negativity towards fast-track promotion girls like herself.

'I didn't realise you had to have tits to be promoted,' a sergeant had once said to her.

'So why haven't you been?' she'd said, lightly touching the man boobs stretching his sweaty shirt.

'Tart.'

Tamsin had looked at him, lost for words and walked away. But she'd get her revenge; he was still in the area, and she'd get her revenge.

'I think I'll be off,' she said to the Chief Inspector.

'So soon?'

'If I don't leave now, I'll have to resign.'

'You do know that you're a good cop, Tamsin,' he said.

The music was too loud for talking but she heard clearly enough.

'Yes, thank you.'

'Bloody good cop.'

Why did men get like this when drunk?

'And a bloody attractive cop to boot,' he continued, 'shouldn't say it but there we are!'

Oh dear.

There's more: 'And it's not the wine talking, Tamsin, but the truth talking! You have no right to be so bloody good and so bloody attractive! And if I was a younger man – .'

This was getting worse, with an embarrassing silence on the cards at their next meeting.

'Good night, Chief Inspector.'

'Er, yes, goodnight, Shah – whatever you call yourself!'

His arms and lips moved towards her in a vague lunge but one avoided with an evasive spin and Tamsin stepped with relief from the half-light of the canteen into the neon-lit foyer. The desk sergeant was alongside her.

'Ah, I was just coming to find you, Ma'am.'

'You should have come sooner.'

'There's a couple want a word.'

'A couple?'

'Well a man and a woman, Ma'am. And they very much want to see you.'

*

236

'You must have had something good on Kate,' said Abbot Peter from his uncertain scaffold.

'Oh, the bèst,' said the clown. 'Her husband's a paedo, the lowest of the low.'

'Fighting off strong competition.'

'Or he *was*, in the West Country, a few years back, fifteen-year-old girl, case dropped in the end, and doesn't seem to appear on any records now – apart from mine. And if his present school found out, of course ...'

'And why this?'

The clown paused.

'Why you standing there with a noose round your neck, soon to hang?'

'And don't say it's nothing personal.'

'It's entirely personal.'

This wasn't good news.

'Victims are sometimes told not to take it personally,' said the clown. 'I believe I've been told that in my time. And perhaps occasionally it's true, but not tonight, not at all. I want you take this most personally.'

'I did know it was you.'

'Know?'

'Suspected.'

'More truthful.'

'No, I knew. Barnabus was too smart.'

'Barnabus is dead. How smart is that?'

'Did you not notice the writing in the cupboard?'

Slight hesitancy.

'No? Shame – it had your name all over it.'

But only a brief wobble from the clown, who is now confident again:

'I spoke to your DI, today. Tamsin whatever, busily chasing red herrings this afternoon. I suspect your half-baked suspicions will die with you.'

The clown moves nearer.

'I'm coming to stand closer, it's the Lord of Misrule's prerogative. I'm in charge.'

Peter feels vulnerable, the clown now a few feet away.

'I don't envisage being interrupted, but perhaps it's better if I'm away from the door, should anyone enter. I mean don't worry, we're locked in, so we should be safe – but you can't be too careful in these old houses.'

'It has a ghost you know, a real Harlequin, I just saw it, on the balcony.'

'And what if the ghost was me, Abbot Peter?'

'Abbot Peter' was spoken with some malice.

'Well, that's possible.'

'And what if I'm half a second away from kicking the bench from beneath you?'

Peter remembered Guy Fawkes in his last moments, still fighting against the odds, the tortured body making something from nothing. All Peter had was time, the need to make time, more than half a second.

'This is a magnificent grudge,' he said.

'You took Barnabus from me.'

'I'm struggling to remember how.'

'I'm not.'

'I remember him travelling a long way to escape you.'

Now the clown moved closer and stopped to place their foot on the bench. Peter felt slight movement beneath him. One more push and …

'It's a good fire, isn't it?' said the clown, moving towards the window. 'I wanted the feel of hell for you, but I didn't realise quite how fiery it would be. It really could be a stage set, with you as the guy.'

The clown danced a little in the firelight, a cross between mime and ballet, just as Channing had performed in interview.

'And now your final scene. We'll tarry no more.'

Peter gave up his struggle for escape, there being nothing more to do. He had only time, and his time was done, not even fists beating on the front door were any help to him now: 'Open up, open up – it's the police!'

But there were no fists and no beating – just silence, mad firelight and a clown. He closed his eyes and heard the harlequin's feet come closer, returning to his left. He felt the foot once again against the side of the bench.

'Into your hands, O Lord, I – .'

A terrible scramble on the floor beside him, he opened his eyes, two clowns fighting on the floor, dangerously close to his scaffold.

What the hell was going on?

Seventy Eight

'It might have been good if you'd told us this before,' said Tamsin.

She'd just listened to Abbot Peter's phone message and was concerned she'd heard no more. Her return calls were getting no reply.

'I'm sorry,' said Rebecca. 'I had my reasons.'

'So did Ivan the Terrible,' said Tamsin, 'so let's rehabilitate him as well.'

After a lethal cocktail of boredom, noise and a drunk boss who should know better, Tamsin was not in a forgiving mood.

'I know where she is!' said Virgil suddenly. 'I only know where the little dear is!'

Shocked silence.

'You do?'

'Well, I know where she might be.'

'That's not quite the same.'

'She'll be doing what I used to do as a child.'

'How do you mean?' asked Rebecca.

'My car – you've drunk too much, Detective Inspector.'

*

Shortly afterwards, an aggressively driven mini minor set off towards Henry House with a desperate mother, a post-party copper and an energised man-boy at the wheel. Police back-up would be along, when some sober police officers, with no party hats, could be found and organised.

Seventy Nine

'Bella!'

'Pat!'

After initial contact, the masks had come off as they hit the floor with waving arms and rolling bodies. The two combatants saw their opponent in a flickering fire-lit moment of shock and surprise, before struggle resumed, with savage intensity. Peter shuffled on his scaffold, his bench four feet from the action, as Bella inched slowly back towards the execution, the heavier and the older, the wily warrior against the youngster, single-mindedness and the power of hate inching slowly towards the bench ... and then Pat forcing her back again, inching her away – but for how long? And above his noose-held neck, so many questions rushing through Peter's mind: where had Pat appeared from? And were they not friends? Suddenly Pat is on top.

'I know who you are, Bella Amal.'

Pat was astride her opponent, the spread-eagled Bella, clown astride clown, breathless victor looking down on subdued loser; neither had the energy for more.

'Whore girl,' said Bella. 'Pierrot! Did you really think you could take him from me?'

'He loved me.'

'At least the past tense is correct.'

Pat felt sadness, exhaustion as her jerky breath settled.

'Still, you've got me now,' said Bella with resignation.

'It looks like it, Bella.'

'Trumped.'

'Pat look out!' whispered Peter, with a terror that was too late.

He'd seen the vegetable knife on the floor a moment after Bella, but a moment too late, the blade handle grasped, swung up through firelight, a swift rocket of metal, ascending then descending steel, sunk deep in Pat's shoulder and gasping, she rolls off, rolls away, hands reaching up and back, shock and pain, bloodying clothes, Pat staggers to her feet and then stumbles to a halt. Between her and Peter stands Bella with the knife in her hand.

'Who to kill first?' she says. 'A genuine choice. Both of you obviously – but who first?'

'You know it has to be me,' said Peter.

'Always want to be first in the queue, Abbot. I hate pushy people.'

'Pat may never have seen a hanging, Bella; part of every girl's education, to see a monk swing, surely?'

The knife-jabbing Bella was edging the whore girl back towards the window, a moment she'd waited for since she'd seen them kiss on the stairs on Halloween morning, confirming every suspicion ... she knew anyway, lost soul Barnabus and the whore girl, her husband and the whore girl.

'You must tell me, cleaner bitch, how did Barnabus feel about me working here?'

Bella couldn't stifle a sniffle of delight and amusement.

'He just said you were mad.'

'You should have seen his face when I walked through the door that morning.'

'You had no right – .'

'I was prepared to start again, forgive and forget, well not forget, you don't forget, do you? But offer him a second chance.'

'And he, you ... but not as a wife.'

Pat was beginning to whimper, to sob, to buckle.

'Home-wrecker.'

'I would never wreck a home, never, I – .'

'Whore girl searching for halo.'

'You didn't have a home, Bella, not with Barnabus.'

'Mrs Hope to you. Amal! Egyptian for "Hope"!'

Yes, that had been Donaldo's clue, there in his blessing at the end of the email.

'Fifteen years of water under the bridge, Bella. That's what Barnabus said.'

Pat steadied herself with her good arm, reaching down to the desk.

'Not under my bridge,' said Bella. 'Nothing's passed under here. Now get on your knees.'

Peter watched as the drifting, fainting, slurring young clown slowly obeyed. A savage kick in the stomach, nasty, Pat sprawling, choking on the floor, reaching for her screaming shoulder, crawling towards the door.

'You'll need the key,' said Mrs Hope. 'If you could just wait a moment.'

Bella now turned round to face Peter.

'Where did she come from Peter?' she asked calmly.

The bonfire in the garden was quietening, like a drunk nearing sleep. The hysteria of petrol, cardboard and wood was over, the flame sated and sedate; with the dancing light of youth now done, the blaze settled into the late middle age of embers and ash. Henry House was dark once again, only shadows outside and in.

Peter spoke quietly:

> *'Your thousand limbs rend my body*
> *This is the way to die:*
> *Beauty keeps laying*
> *Its sharp knife against me.'*

Recognise it?'

'Shall we start your countdown?'

'It was Barnabus, speaking through Hafiz. 'Beauty – as in "Bella" – keeps laying her sharp knife against me. Clever, that – too clever for me, until today.'

'So I stabbed him to death? It's not a crime … well, it is a crime, but not one that will be pinned on me. So how about one minute, that's sixty seconds, before your neck feels the tightening?'

She walked round in front of him, as Peter puzzled with the words just spoken.

'But before we do all that nonsense, the hanging and everything – not that your death is nonsense, but you know what I mean – I repeat my question: where did she come from, Abbot?'

'Who?'

'The whore girl, Pierrot. Where did she come from? '

Eighty

'I don't know,' said Peter.

Where had Pat appeared from? He hadn't a clue.

'I'm happy to place a blade in your calf in pursuit of knowledge, Abbot. Painful I'm told. Where did she come from?'

'I don't know.'

'One more chance.'

'Bella, I closed my eyes with one clown about to execute me. I opened them, to see two clowns on the floor.'

An alliance of confusion, something shared, we're in this together, any alliance was good, however brief. And then his puzzlement understood.

'Did you say you stabbed him to death?' he asked.

'Don't distract, Abbot, it won't help. I'm holding every card in this room and I want to know where she came from. Was she in the cupboard?'

'You do know Barnabus didn't die of stab wounds.'

Abbot Peter wanted to make this clear, but Bella wasn't interested:

'She was in the cupboard, yes?'

'She may have been.'

'That's all I needed to know, Abbot! Wasn't so hard, was it? And you're spared the knife – if not much else.'

'You didn't murder Barnabus.'

'And I didn't murder you – it was suicide!'

With dainty ballet steps, she approached the condemned and his scaffold, and would have finished the short journey but for a force of nature which removed her from her feet.

Eighty One

'I should have thought of it,' said Peter.

'You should have thought of what?' asked Tamsin, on entering the kitchen.

She was a late arrival, Virgil and the Abbot already settled at the table, hands holding cups of strong tea with two sugars. She'd overseen the removal of Bella Amal to Lewes police station; and Pat, or Patience as her mother called her, to Brighton Hospital. Rebecca had accompanied her there.

'A priest hole in Henry House,' said Peter.

'It was all those damnable Catholic plots against Good Queen Bess,' said Virgil.

'A monarchist in our midst?'

'Too bloody right I am,' declared Virgil.

'The Abbot's still adjusting to a land without pharaohs,' said Tamsin.

But Virgil is stirred:

'And Elizabeth was way too lenient, giving them all that benefit-of-the-doubt nonsense.'

'Not something her sister Mary had done,' said Peter.

'God, no! But the papists got their comeuppance in the end!'

Tamsin coughed.

'Is there a beginner's version available – for those who don't subscribe to *Obscure History Weekly*?'

It was Peter who spoke:

'To understand the origins of priest hole in English society, you need know only this: under Elizabeth, the saying of the Roman Catholic Mass was made illegal. So if Catholic households wanted to continue the practice, they had to take precautions.'

'Precautions against what?'

'Sudden and unannounced searches by priest-hunters.'

'Avoiding priests I can understand, but seeking them out?'

Peter says: 'Whatever you think of their beliefs – and you think nothing of them, I know – you couldn't fault them for courage.'

'Fair point,' added the monarchist Virgil. 'It was a damnably risky business being a Roman priest in those days. Today, and no disrespect, a Mass is just a Mass, but in those days, it could be fatal. In 1591, a priest was hanged outside a house in London, where three months earlier, he'd conducted an illegal service.'

'Unbelievable.'

'So if you wanted a priest in your house, you needed to be able to hide him and hide him jolly well! False walls and all that, some very clever builders, creating secret space, not only for the priests but also for all their religious tat – chalices, copes and candlesticks, the whole caboodle.'

'I was at East Riddlesden Hall last year,' said Peter, rubbing his neck unconsciously. He could still feel the wire and perhaps he always would. 'The priest hole there is an offshoot of the chimney, which as we now discover, is the same in Henry House.'

'But here in Henry House,' added Virgil, 'it's larger than most, much larger – which was just the best discovery for a boy like me, in need of another world to escape to.'

'Your very own Narnia.'

'It was in a way. I mean, generally the priest holes were small, seriously small, no fresh air, no toilet, cramped and dark; and with searches sometimes lasting two weeks, it was pretty hellish for the poor priests stuck inside.'

'A lonely vigil.'

'And sometimes a fatal vigil. It wasn't uncommon for priests to die of starvation or lack of oxygen.'

Tamsin seeks clarification: 'So the government knew about the existence of the priest holes?'

'Oh yes, they knew about them,' said Virgil. 'That's why the search would take so long: they'd know they were there, but could they find the damn things? And the answer was, no, they couldn't always. They'd rip out panelling, tear up floors – with the terrified priest perhaps just a foot away, behind a wall and scared to breathe.'

Abbot Peter took up the story:

'Nicholas Owen was the most famous builder of priest holes. He built the hideouts at East Riddlesden Hall, the one I saw, and at Chesterton Hall, where he incorporated it into a water closet.'

'And from what I remember,' said Virgil, 'the government thanked him with a river trip to the Tower of London where they tortured him to death on the rack.'

It was something of a conversation-stopper.

'We need to get on,' said Tamsin. There was only so much history and torture she could endure, and much work to be done. But Peter had a little further digging to do.

'You clearly became fascinated by history as a child, Virgil.'

'Well, living here, it was hard not to be,' replied the force of nature who'd flown out of the wall, and smashed and crashed into the Lord of Misrule, now nursing five cracked ribs in a police cell in Lewes. 'Especially after I found the hideout, which my parents knew nothing about. History was my escape, no pun intended.'

'And my saving tonight.'

'Pleased to be of assistance, Abbot. So three raucous cheers for Nicholas Owen and the hole-builders!'

'I remember your father calling you a "disappearing child".'

'And I was, it was such a great hole, and unusual of course, providing not only a hiding place but also a laddered chute down to the floor below, coming out in what is now the office – but used to be the morning room.'

'The "morning room"?' said Tamsin. 'What on earth is that?'

She'd not grown up in a large country house.

'The room you go to in the morning,' said Virgil.

What else would a morning room be?

'Why?'

'Why? Well, you'd go to read the paper, receive guests, write poetry, that sort of thing.'

Tamsin thought you should go to work in the morning, rather than sit around wasting time.

'So it's not surprising that Bella didn't see me coming.'

Peter: 'She saw everything in this place, except the priest hole.'

Virgil: 'Who said the study of history's worthless, eh?'

This was aimed at Tamsin.

'Virgil, we may need to speak to you again,' she said. 'But thank you for your night's work.'

'Hear, hear!' said Peter.

It was the cue for the saviour to leave.

'Not at all,' he said, jumping to his feet. 'It must be good to know the investigation's over. Wretched business, of course.'

Abbot Peter walked with Virgil into the hall where he suddenly seemed on edge.

'Would you mind if I just took a quick look upstairs, Abbot?'

'Well, I suppose not.'

'It's just the room I'd like to see.'

'Yes, of course.'

Peter felt embarrassed at his hesitation, and this was the trouble with murder: it nurtured suspicion and destroyed the trust from which all good things grow. He was meant to be guiding Virgil to the exit, seeing him off the premises, a crime scene once again. But what harm a quick look upstairs? How could you deny a man one last glimpse of his childhood bedroom?

'You go up,' he said. 'I'll tarry awhile, as they say.'

Virgil climbed the wooden stairs and disappeared down the corridor. Peter climbed slowly behind him, not wishing to intrude – but aware of the police presence. He stood in the gallery, loitering, there but not there, like a prison guard when his hand-cuffed escort must relieve himself by the side of the road. He looked around the darkness. It was here in the gallery, of course, that Tamsin had seen the ghost of the Irish Harlequin, and he was remembering her hallway scream ... when suddenly he was brought back to the present, a heavy sobbing, the sound of choking, jerky tears. It came from down the corridor, the sound of a male lament, heaving grief followed by silence. Peter waited. A further minute passed, and then Virgil appeared from the darkness, returned to Peter's side and together, they descended the stairs and walked out to the car in silence.

'Hard for you to leave?' said Peter.

'Very,' said Virgil, looking down at his feet, as he fumbled for his keys. 'But we won't open that can of worms, nothing good to be achieved by that, what's done is done.'

With eyes that could neither look on the house, nor say goodbye, he got into his car and drove away.

Eighty Two

Peter watched Virgil go ... and remembered his own childhood bedroom: a bland room, in a bland house in a bland road. What would he do now if he were allowed back? And what would he say to the boy who once slept there, suffocated there, hoping against hope for something better?

Needing cold air and solitude, he wandered round to the side of the house where the bonfire had burned on the lawn. It was like going back stage after the play, when the machinery of performance is revealed.

'So that's how it was done!'

Of the terrible conflagration, there was little left now, just a rim of untouched wood around the edge, blackened by flame but not destroyed; and the heat, smouldering still in orange embers beneath the settling veil of ash.

Twice saved from the noose tonight, a prisoner two-times reprieved, the events of the evening remained fresh and chaotic and he wanted the chaos to leave. He listened to the breath he had no right to breathe, and felt both the panic and calm of the scaffold. Had Hafiz known such things and survived? He smiled as he remembered more lines from the Persian craftsman:

> *Now that all your worry*
> *has proved such an unlucrative business,*
> *Why not find a better job?*

So much had happened, and so intensely, he'd almost forgotten how the evening had begun, with a phone call from Kate Karter. And such a fine performance from then on, a performance he hadn't seen coming, and better than many he'd endured at the Theatre Royal. But now? Now everything for thespian Kate would change. He wasn't meant to be alive, this had not been her plan. So had the police knocked on her door yet? Had they interrupted the household calm and asked if Mrs Karter was in? And had they yet mentioned that they were arresting her for being an accessory to attempted murder on two counts, and that she did not have to say anything but that it may harm her defence if she didn't mention when questioned something which she later relied on in court – and that anything she did say may be given in evidence? Perhaps they had, and perhaps she'd left with them quietly, telling her husband she'd done it for him, done it for them, love you!

And in the silence of the empty house, would he finish his half-drunk hot chocolate? And would he keep the TV on for company or turn it off and cry? And how would he feel about no more parents' evenings, no more marking, no more rude and ungrateful young people, no more reason for living? A supply teacher would be taking his classes tomorrow, every downfall good for someone, every disgrace a joy for another. And what would the headlines say and would there be pictures, and would he be recognised, and how now to speak with his neighbours and what to say to his friends?

*

'We'll be all right now, Gerald,' said Kate. 'Believe me.'

She sounded confident in the safety of their front room.

'How so?'

'I've sorted things.'

'You've sorted things.'

Why could Gerald not believe her?

'Yes, I've sorted things, not easy but I have, so for God's sake sound a little grateful at least!'

Pause.

'How did she know, Kate?'

Kate had finally told him about the threats Bella had made. She hadn't told Gerald the full story of events since then, just that she'd sorted things.

'I don't know how she knew, but she did know.'

'And where were you tonight?'

'Sorting things.'

Silence, a weary quiet … some news programme but neither of them listening.

'I'm tired of this,' he said.

'You're tired?'

Gerald could be so self-obsessed sometimes, like he had any reason to be tired!

'I'm tired of the chase.'

'There's no chase now, that's what I'm saying.'

'There's always a chase, Kate, the past is a tracker dog, always getting closer.'

'And who's to blame for that?'

There was no answer, there'd never been an answer, not a good one, just the exhaustion of the fox at the end of the run, aching lungs and weak-legged, staggering from one hide to another, the baying hounds and the dull terror of a future closing in.

'What makes us free, Kate?'

'Not getting caught, my dear old fool.'

There was a knock on the door, and then another, harder.

'I'll go,' said Kate. 'Love you.'

*

Peter looked across the lawn, back towards Henry House, towards the office window, events lived once again.

Bella, the terrifying Bella, with three scores to settle, three suspects tried and found guilty: the husband, the lover and the monk – the monk adjudged guilty of 'unnecessary assistance in the desert'. Barnabus had left his marriage for the desert and somehow never returned. The blame would be spread evenly and cruelly.

And how was Pat tonight? The fighting, hurting, fainting Pat, receiving treatment after her office heroics. She'd been deceitful herself, false identity and address to keep her life free from her father's gaze. Her account of events would be heard soon enough. And Bella's role in an evening she didn't attend would be interesting to hear as well. But now? Now something was gnawing at Peter's peace.

'It must be good to know the investigation's over,' Virgil had said, as he left the kitchen.

But it wasn't over, Peter knew that. The investigation was advanced but not over. Bella had stabbed with intent to kill, but she hadn't caved his head in with the poker. The killer of Barnabus Hope was still out there, preparing for bed, sipping their tea, watching the same sparkling explosions now lighting the Stormhaven sky.

So who would that be?

Eighty Three

'So what happens in therapy, Uncle?'

Peter and Tamsin sat on the small sofa in the hallway of Henry House. After the drama of the evening, they sought vague conversation, musings of a wandering nature. Tamsin even tucked her arm inside Peter's. They could have been father and daughter.

'It isn't rocket science.'

'Well, that's a relief.'

'Above all else, a therapist is simply a witness to your story, a companion in your search for the truth of your life.'

'But how does that happen?'

'It varies. But the client tells their story as best they can, they share their pain, their hopes, their nightmares.'

'And the therapist?'

'The therapist simply mirrors their truth back to them, so the client can better see it.'

'That all sounds very passive.'

'No, good mirroring is active and the result of active listening which can be exhausting.'

'But it's still an unequal exchange.'

'It's an unequal exchange in terms of information shared. It's not a normal conversation. Apart from anything else, it's a conversation that must always stay on the territory of the client. The therapist isn't there to talk about their own problems.'

There was a pause in the dark hallway.

'Still wouldn't be my first port of call.'

'It's not anyone's first port of call, is it?'

'I suppose not.'

'In fact, it's usually the last resort, when nothing else has worked. No one crawls onto the therapist's shore, unless their boat is full of holes – or sunk.'

'So people walk in and spill their secrets?'

'They'll probably want to test the therapist out.'

'Make sure they're competent?'

'To make sure they're safe. To enter into the world of the client, the therapist must first receive an invitation, and that has to be earned. They have to prove themselves safe.'

'How?'

'By listening … by never believing the label the client – or anyone else – has put on themselves … and by paying careful attention to the life and mystery behind the label.'

'Well, it's a nice idea.'

'No, for most people it's a pretty scary idea, the idea of being discovered.'

'You can always bluff.'

'No one can bluff. People's words reveal who they are.'

'Words can deceive.'

'Not for any length of time.'

Pause.

Peter: 'You really don't trust therapists, do you?'

'No.'

'Why not?'

'Whenever I see the word, I see two words, "the rapist".'

'Savage.'

'It's how it is.'

'And that's probably a story in itself,' said Peter.

There was no way Tamsin would allow anyone a peep behind the scenes of her carefully constructed life, absolutely not, this she knew.

'And I certainly wouldn't come here,' she said, 'no matter how many qualifications Frances has. I mean, would you tell her anything?'

Abbot Peter could not hold back a yawn.

'No, Barnabus always reckoned that the well-qualified Frances would be a better administrator.'

'Well, there is now a vacancy for that position.'

'I suppose there is.'

'Henry House seeks dynamic people-centred individual to build on the work of psychotic predecessor. Grudge-holding knife-murderers preferred. Must also be able to tie a noose.'

'That was Kate.'

'How is your neck, by the way?'

'Feeling very lucky.'

*

And the murderer's name came to Peter at about 2.00 a.m. that morning.

Tamsin had dropped him off at Sandy View, but didn't stay. She needed her own bed to recover from the evening's events, particularly the leaving-do of Mick Norman, which sat in her psyche like a bucket of cold sick.

'I understand the noose must have been frightening,' she'd said, as the Abbot got out the car. 'But believe me, the leaving-do was worse.'

'I suggest you don't go into trauma counselling, Tamsin.'

Peter had gone inside, poured a glass of whisky and sat down in his comfortable chair. He decided against lighting the fire, he'd had enough of fires tonight. He eventually picked up a book and started to read, but read nothing. He was reading but not reading, reading but not receiving, re-reading lines, re-reading paragraphs once and then twice, and then again until he gave up and put it down. The book was simply too busy with one set of words when his mind searched for another set, words spoken over these last few days, words spoken by Tamsin just this evening, words spoken by himself.

He fell asleep to the sound of the waves on the shingle shore, the timeless splash and heave in ascendance again, the whizzing rockets stilled. Other sounds came and went, but the sound of the sea remained. And he dreamed of huge clues being trailed, trailed before him, and Peter chasing, trying to catch up and everyone laughing.

And then he was following a stream, and then another stream and then another stream until at 2.00 a.m., the three streams joined and became a river and he woke up with sleep-denying clarity – and knew the murderer's name.

Eighty Four

'We think it's best if you go home now, Mrs Simple.'

'It's Mrs St Paul.'

The nurse heard no difference, but then she wasn't paid to listen, not by her reckoning at least. She did nursing shifts to earn money, not save the world.

'It's best if she sleeps now, Mrs Simple, and there's nothing to be done until morning.'

'I just want to be with her.'

'She'll be fine.'

'She was attacked with a knife.'

'And everything has been done for her. There's certainly nothing you can do.'

'I can be with her.'

'And I'm saying that it's best that you go home, and return in the morning.'

'I don't really want you telling me what to do.'

It was at this moment that the Reverend Ezekiel St Paul arrived in the AMU ward of the Royal Sussex County Hospital in Brighton.

'And you are?' asked the nurse.

'I am this girl's father,' he said.

'Well, I was just telling this woman – .'

'That woman is my wife, and the girl lying here is my daughter. '

Ezekiel spoke assertively, hard to contradict, and for once, due to their target, Rebecca rather enjoyed his words.

'I was just saying to your wife, Mr Simple – .'

'And why is she still dressed as a clown?'

There was something unnerving about the hospital attire of his daughter: a hospitalised harlequin. It was how he'd last seen her, on that revealing evening at Henry House, but that had been five days ago.

254

'The medical team thought a change of clothes would disturb her too much tonight.'

'She came in like that?'

'And if you could please keep your voice down, Mr Simple.'

'I will explain, Ezekiel,' said Rebecca.

'Oh, there's no need to explain.'

'And as I was saying to your wife, it would be best if you went home now and returned in the morning.'

'Go home?' said Ezekiel, amused. 'I have only just arrived.'

'These are not visiting hours.'

'The Sabbath is made for man not man for the Sabbath.'

'I beg your pardon?'

'Visiting times are there to help people like me.'

'No,' said the nurse, 'visiting times are there to help people like me, people who have a job to do.'

'My daughter is your job.'

'And so is everyone else on this ward, and I don't have time for discussions like this.'

'So what do you have time for?'

'I'd like to continue this conversation outside please,' said the nurse with finality.

'You can continue the conversation wherever you like, but we'll be staying here while you do.'

'Then I'm calling security.'

And with that the nurse strode off down the ward and out of sight.

'You must tell me what happened,' says Ezekiel, standing at the end of the bed.

Rebecca sits quietly for a moment.

'Well?'

'It's over,' she says, hoping she had strength for more.

'What is over?'

What does she mean? Has the doctor told her something?

'I'm not going back to how it was, Ezekiel … and nor is Patience. We talked.'

Ezekiel stays silent, breathing deeply, swaying a little.

'Where's Michael?' she asks, as a fresh wave of weariness strikes her.

'You ask questions of me?' Ezekiel is furious. 'After tonight, you ask questions of me!'

'Ezekiel, I'll ask whatever question I like from now on.'

Firm but calm.

Ezekiel is now swaying again.

'He's at home,' he says.

'I left you assaulting him.'

Ezekiel is uncomfortable.

'Is he okay?'

'He is fine.'

'Getting stronger, is he? Fighting back?'

There's a pause. Rebecca now becomes conscious of the disturbance their voices are causing to other patients, who groan or sigh in the dark. One says 'Shut up with your talking!'

'Do you understand why we're here, Ezekiel?' she whispers.

'Because our daughter has been attacked. Why else would we be here?'

'One day you will need to wake up.'

'Unless the Lord builds the house, the labourer builds in vain.'

Rebecca puts her head in her hands, as one quite spent.

'What's that got to do with anything?'

Ezekiel is not immediately sure.

'We're here tonight, Ezekiel, because you are a bully and I am weak, and I don't know which is worse. But that's why we're here tonight; not because of a mad woman with a knife, but because you and I have crucified our children.'

Ezekiel begins rocking again, back and forth on his heels, holding on to the bars of the bed.

'Will you stop doing that? You're disturbing Patience.'

Ezekiel pulls his hands away from the bars. Rebecca is wondering how far she can go.

'I can't stop you being a bully,' she says, voice low. 'But I can stop being weak. I'm going to the foyer to ring Michael, and then we'll go home. We'll leave Patience to sleep. If you want to wait for security – .'

She looks down on the sleeping form of her daughter and bends to kiss her forehead. The moment she does, Patience opens her eyes.

'Well said, Mum,' she whispers. 'Ten years too late, but well done.'

A half-smile crosses her face before she drifts back into medicated sleep.

'Did she speak?' asks Ezekiel.

'She did, yes.'

'What did she say?'

'We can talk about that. But now we get back to our son.'

*

It was strange to be leading the way to the staircase, strange for Rebecca to be leading.

Eighty Five

Thursday 6 November

'It was like three streams joining to become a river,' said Abbot Peter, as the car drove through the sea fog that had swallowed Stormhaven this morning. Passing headlights were smudges of light in the murk, as Peter told Tamsin of his dream. The detective was sceptical.

'There's no Dream Squad in the police force for one very good reason: they're nonsense.'

The drive continued for a while.

'We will have support?' asked Peter.

'It's all in hand. But I need you to tell me more ... much more than you've managed so far.'

'It started with something you said last night.'

'And what did I say last night?'

*

'We'll run the story in our evening edition' said Martin Channing to his editorial team, gathered for the morning briefing. The editorial team was another name for Martin, but also present were Rupert Brooke, his deputy editor, and Fortune Chivas, the paper's lawyer. 'The *Evening Argus* has had free rein for much too long.'

The on-going investigation into the murder at Henry House had been on the front page of their Brighton-based rival for the last three days. And he hated their Brighton-based rival.

'Its coverage has been pretty good,' said Rupert Brooke.

Martin said their coverage had been appalling, absolutely appalling, and made another note – if another note was necessary, with so many already made – to get rid of his old friend Rupert Brooke, as soon as the chance arose.

'I disagree,' said Rupert, because he did disagree, and wanted to say so. The *Evening Argus* had done a responsible job.

'Always remember that I'm the editor, Rupert.'

Unknown to Rupert, the wheels of dismissal had been turning for a while. Martin had been speaking to younger journalists, sounding them out; he liked youth, fresh blood from university, hungry to succeed and cheap to employ, grateful for the break rather than questioning how he ran his empire. Rupert had been too long in the game, had a mind of his own, not helpful, it clouded his professional judgement. And perhaps, on reflection, Rupert had never had newspaper ink in his veins, that was possible – and that's where it had to be to survive in the trade, the dark ink pumping through your veins, keeping you scrabbling on the treadmill of the moment.

But whether he had or he hadn't, in the land of today, Rupert was a newsprint corpse and only his burial remained to be sorted. His redundancy was being worked on by Mr Chivas sitting opposite, an ex-London lawyer of no fixed belief, beyond the trinity of pounds, shillings and pence. When everything was done, Rupert would be out. He, Martin Channing, was the editor and Rupert best remember that.

'I understand the supremacy that role gives you in our professional setting,' said Rupert in response.

'Good,' said Martin.

Rupert would have walked out then and there ... but for his mortgage.

Martin's restlessness extended beyond the failings of Rupert Brooke, however. His own part in the Henry House murder story had been irritating and not without irony. The one story he knew about, he couldn't print; the one story he wouldn't have to invent – a circumstance as rare as a white crow – he wasn't allowed to tell. Instead, he'd had to watch the *Argus* pick at the scraps like a grateful hyena. But no more: with yesterday's arrest of Bella Amal for murder, Martin was going for broke.

'We'll print nothing to pre-judge the trial of course,' he said, with a knowing wink towards legal guru, Fortune Chivas. 'But we'll pay a rather more colourful visit to Henry House than the *Argus* has so far managed.'

The door then opened and a junior appeared.

'The police are refusing to confirm that Bella Amal has been charged with murder, Sir.'

258

'Well she isn't being questioned about her flower arranging.'

Chivas smiled darkly as Channing continued:

'And I'm hearing pretty lurid accounts of what happened there last night. A kind friend at the Royal Sussex rang to say a harlequin was brought in with severe shoulder wounds, after being attacked by Bella Amal. The clown in question was Pat Strong, so you don't have to be Poirot to see a pattern here. Of course she'll be charged with the murder of Barnabus Hope.'

Rupert and Fortune Chivas stayed silent.

'They say that with regard to the murder,' continued the dogged junior, 'the investigation is still on-going, and that further arrests may be made shortly.'

'Ridiculous,' said Martin, but he felt unease pass like a ghost through his thin soul.

He wasn't looking for further arrests. He had the truth; he didn't need the whole truth and nothing but the truth.

Eighty Six

Henry House appeared only slowly from the mist, the surrounding trees and fields lost in the wandering haze.

Tamsin parked the car and turned off the headlights. As it turned out, with regard to the murderer's name, it hadn't just been a dream. Peter had offered further explanation on the way:

'It started with something you said last night.'

'And what did I say last night?'

'You said you'd never go to Frances for counselling.'

'True.'

'Reminding me that Barnabus once said she'd be a better administrator than therapist.'

'You've told me this.'

'So I began to wonder about Frances's credentials.'

'I don't see why.'

'I have my reasons.'

'My Chief Inspector would be better employed as car park attendant. It doesn't mean he didn't pass the Inspectors' exams.'

One thing had become another in Peter's mind, streams joining. He'd remembered, for instance, a conversation with Barnabus, the outlines at least. It had been when he first told Peter about the *Mind Gains* adventure. Peter had celebrated him finding a well-qualified partner and such historic premises, 'a twin blessing!' Barnabus had simply replied, 'It isn't all it seems.' At the time, he'd thought Barnabus was speaking generally, that nothing's ever quite as good as it looks.

'But then I thought: what if he was speaking specifically? What if something I'd said wasn't as it seemed?

'Okay.'

'And if that were so,' he continued, 'there was only one possibility: no one's doubting the antiquity of the building.'

'Not yet.'

'Which just leaves the qualifications.'

'Okay again,' said Tamsin, sounding bored. This was her case, not his, she'd focus on her driving, adding only: 'Not gripped, but okay.'

But like an explorer in deep snow, Peter battled on.

'And then there was my conversation with Martin Channing. We were discussing his attempt to buy into the business, but he was also managing to question the efficacy of therapy.'

'Do you make these words up?'

Peter paused, a cold pause, and feeling uncomfortable, Tamsin says he's made his point.

'Psychotherapy is a relatively new discipline,' he continues.

'Well thank God you're not calling it a "science". That's a joke.'

'For God's sake, Tamsin, just listen for a moment, will you?'

Genuine anger. Tamsin pulls the car over to the side of the road.

'I am listening.'

'No, you're behaving insecurely and the insecure can't listen.'

'Carry on.'

'The thing is, no one quite knows what qualifies someone to be a therapist.'

'I'm saying nothing.'

'And then I remembered what Martin said, "It's a profession where qualifications mean nothing – particularly at Henry House".'

'Barnabus.'

'My thought at the time, yes, and I said that, to which Channing replied, 'Believe me, whether or not I like Barnabus has got absolutely nothing to do with it."'

'So if it isn't about Barnabus?'

'Exactly.'

'Then Frances Pole MSc, PhD might simply be Frances Pole? Well, that would be very funny.'

'Not for the person who found out.'

'And that might have been Barnabus?'

'Quite possibly. What if he became suspicious, who knows why, and rang around the various professional bodies – only to discover that no one knew of Frances Pole MSc, PhD?'

'It's supposition.'

'But worth a punt, given that Frances was the last person in the office on the night of the murder. As Bella told us as much in the kitchen, remember?'

'No.'

'We were talking about job titles, and she said, "Frances likes to appear professional".'

Tamsin's resistance was crumbling.

'The sober Ezekiel was with her when she left. She wasn't caving in anyone's head then.'

'He was outside warming up the car. Frances had told him to leave while she set the alarms. It was perhaps a spontaneous murder, not planned. She saw him in the cupboard when collecting her coat – perhaps the cupboard door was open and she went to close it – and there's the body of Barnabus, semi-conscious, dying of knife wounds. And she thinks 'Why not?' She had his money, didn't want him holding her to ransom over the qualifications issue – and here was a happy way out. I suspect she knew about Barnabus and Bella, and guessed what had happened.'

'Speaking as a professional, it is all circumstantial.'

'And speaking as a monk, it's worth a conversation.'

They drove the final 500 yards to Henry House in silence, got out of the car and stepped beneath the Tudor rose into the hallway, where the duty policeman lay sprawled on the ground, unconscious.

And coming from the kitchen, the faint smell of gas.

Eighty Seven

Earlier in the day, around 7.00 a.m., they'd interviewed Bella Amal at Lewes Police station, famous for its coffee machine, which both Peter and Tamsin enjoyed at this early hour.

As Tamsin confirmed, 'You don't get that quality of bean in Stormhaven.'

The interview was a mixed bag, the curate's egg as they say – good in parts. It was a conversation in which they learned everything about the night Barnabus Hope was murdered – except for the name of the murderer.

Bella had not proved a tough nut to crack and was all the more pitiful for her strange attire.

'We're trying to get you a change of clothes,' said Tamsin.

But in the meantime, they were interviewing a clown.

'As it started, so it ends,' thought Peter. 'Commedia dell'arte.'

'Bella Amal, did you murder Barnabus Hope by caving in his skull?' asked Tamsin.

'No.'

'So where were you at midnight, on the night of the murder?'

'I was in bed.'

'Good answer.'

'I *was* in bed!'

'Don't do the hysterical thing on me, Bella, I'm not doubting you.'

Bella calmed down, soothed by the removal of misunderstanding. She didn't like being misunderstood, never had, misunderstanding hurt her grievously. She liked to be precisely understood, just as she precisely misunderstood others. Tamsin now continued, with Peter content to watch. He desired distance between himself and his tormentor. Distance and some coffee; they were good beans.

Tamsin expanded a little: 'When I say good answer, Bella, I mean you're telling the truth.'

Bella nodded.

'We know you were at home at midnight on the night in question – CCTV – and so we know you didn't kill Barnabus.'

Bella sits puzzled and cagey in her harlequin clothes, both trapped rabbit and watchful fox … but no mime or ballet now, no posturing in the firelight.

Tamsin says: 'So that's two good answers, Bella, and if you continue with your good answers, it could help you, who knows?'

Peter knows – knows it won't help her at all, but Tamsin likes the hunt and the tease, intimidation and friendship, offered and withdrawn, now you see it, now you don't.

'It was your intention to murder Barnabus – that was your plan.'

Bella stays silent.

'So we won't make a saint of you, Bella, just because you failed. If anything, your sentence should be increased for incompetence.'

Bella looks like a told-off little girl as Tamsin continues:

'Abbot Peter here, he makes saints out of failures, it's a weakness he has – though perhaps he'll make an exception in your case, given your last encounter.'

She looks at them both, but neither looks at the other.

'But for me, Bella, failures are just that – failures, and I'm sorry if you feel judged.'

'I would never have done it.'

'You would never have done what?'

'I would never have killed him.'

'Stay with the believable, Bella, always best.'

'Can't do right for doing wrong!' she exclaims.

'Still not taking responsibility?'

Bella never looks at Peter, not once throughout the interview. But Peter does now look at her, and more as time goes by, he's ready again, ready to look on her, safe from the cheese-wire noose and the flickering light of hell, seeing her afresh, beyond the fear, a tad overweight in her tragic clothes.

'But as I say,' says Tamsin, 'we've established you didn't kill Barnabus Hope, your former husband.'

'He was still my husband, we never divorced. He was still under contract to me.'

'How romantic.'

'And the Pierrot girl was a whore.'

Tamsin pauses.

'You mean Patience?'

Bella nods.

'Rather harsh.'

And as Professor of Harsh, Tamsin should know.

'She's in hospital, Bella, since you ask, condition stable, and should be all right, should be absolutely fine.'

Bella gives a 'why would I care?' look.

'Any ideas who might have killed Barnabus, by the way?'

'No.'

'It wasn't Kate, was it?'

'I don't know.'

'Because Kate was your patsy for the evening, wasn't she?'

Bella says nothing.

'Ask her to jump and she merely asks 'How high?''

Again nothing.

'It was a bit of a find, wasn't it? Those paedophile charges against her husband Gerald in the West Country, dropped for some reason, after which they disappeared from view.'

'Yes,' says Bella, quietly. 'I'm good at finding things out. It's good to see everything.'

'And that's what we're trying to do, Bella, trying to see everything, with your help obviously, so let's reflect on the Feast of Fools for a moment – a remarkable event and from where I'm sitting, guided by a hand of some genius.'

'Good move,' thinks Peter. 'People love explaining their genius.'

'You weren't there, of course.'

'No.'

'Or rather you weren't supposed to be. Were you there?'

A crossroads, a Rubicon, one of those moments: would she pull back in to silence? Or would she finish the story and explain how it was done?

Eighty Eight

'It was important I wasn't there – or that people thought I wasn't there, it made things easier.'

She's going to tell. Relief.

'So you made it happen.'

'I set up a row with Frances before the event.'

It was a boast.

'It was that easy?'

'Very easy, too easy.'

Oh, wonderful, a bit of showboating as well.

'You insisted on being the Lord of Misrule?'

'I knew she wouldn't give in on that, just knew it; she was all uptight, said it had to be that way, her way. Everything had to be her way.'

'She could be like that?'

Fishing for dirt.

'She didn't appreciate other people's views – and I knew she wouldn't appreciate mine.'

'Oh? I thought she was a fan of yours?'

'I never felt I belonged there,' she says, like a heartbroken diva. 'It was always her show.'

'I suppose you were just the administrator.'

Bella shrugs.

'So you pulled out of the Feast in a tantrum – but still pulled every string.'

Bella now looks coy. Like an April sky, instant and changeable, but she really does want to explain her genius, this is quite clear, so Tamsin lures her in with more flattery:

'Remarkable work, Bella, I have to say that. Ever thought of a career in the police?'

'It all hung on the disguise … which meant I could take Kate's place when the lights went out.'

'And so fresh from your public reading in the pub, you came up to Henry House, slipped into the Long Room when the lights went out, while Kate crept out and everyone changed into their clown costumes?'

'That was the plan. It left Kate a free agent; free to guide Barnabus into the office when we played Sardines, and free to keep him there on some pretence until I arrived. And it left me the Lord of Misrule.'

'You knew who everyone was?'

'Of course. Each costume had a small colour tag at the neck. Invisible unless you were looking for it.'

'And the short straw that made you the Lord of Misrule?'

'There was no short straw in the jar. The short straw was in my sleeve; no one could have been the Lord but me.'

She's as pleased as Punch, whom she resembles in a way. And now Tamsin turns cold:

'No offence, Bella, but I've always found circuses rather dull and clowns the dullest act of all, so if we could move on, we're in something of a hurry this morning.'

Hurt flashes across the face of Bella. She feels the freeze.

'Places to go, people to see,' says Tamsin. 'That's us, Bella, not you. You've got nowhere to go now, and I have to say – and I speak as a fan, well, former fan – your previous brilliance rather deserted you when it came to the killing.'

Bella is close to tears.

'Kate's told us what happened, but you might as well colour in the gaps. Under the cover of Sardines, you cornered Barnabus.'

'Columbina!'

It's said with passion.

'I'm sorry?'

'No matter.'

Tamsin glances at Abbot Peter, who looks knowing.

'So you cornered Barnabus in the study, but didn't finish the job,' she continues.

'There were people banging on the door.'

'The locked door.'

'They thought that was suspicious, that someone might be hiding, might be in there. They kept banging.'

'Yes, Kate pretended she was one of them.'

'She wasn't one of them.'

'No, she was with you. But I think everyone else was rather excited. Or rather drunk.'

'And Kate said he was dead anyway.'

'And you believed her.'

'No reason not to.'

'No reason not to? Kate's an actress not a doctor, Bella! How would an actress know? What do you need to know about anything to spout other people's lines every night?'

'I think they're all called actors now, even the women,' says Peter.

He wants Bella to acknowledge him, but she doesn't.

'I think she just wanted to get away, don't you, Bella? She was frightened by the banging and wanted to get away, so yes, he's dead, Bella, I'm sure of it, job done and now can we get out of here please? They're knocking on the door, for God's sake!'

'It was a concern.'

The showboating is over.

'A concern? A terror more like! The social disorder of the Feast of Fools was coming back to bite you. They were like animals out there!'

Bella sits quietly, reliving those moments in the office again, the struggle with Barnabus, the look in his eye, the knife and the blood, the hard bite of the blade, crunching, the body going down like a Caesar in March, those moments of panic, Kate's stupid fear rubbing off on her, the terrible banging and the need to believe he was dead, such comfort in Kate's words, it was over, finished.

'We dragged him to the cupboard and put him inside. That was always the plan.'

'Back on track, Bella, well done. Panic over.'

'He could then be found on Monday morning and we needed to re-join the game or rather, Kate did. I was thinking clearly.'

'Of course you were.'

'I was.'

'So no self-recrimination then? A small if crucial breakdown mid-project, but it happens to the best of us.'

'I climbed out of the window and made my way home. It should have been fine.'

'While Barnabus got on with his poetry writing, there's commitment for you, no paper to hand, so he used the cupboard wall to record the evening's events.'

'*Your thousand limbs rend my body this is the way*,' says Peter.

'And there, sadly, his bleeding body had to leave it,' adds Tamsin, closing the folder in front of her.

'He was full of nonsense,' says Bella, 'better off dead, better off out of the arms of the whore.'

She looks for reassurance, that it was all right to speak as she did.

'I think that's all for now, Bella and you must be tired. I'm aware how exhausting it can be, cataloguing one's own failures. Interview terminating at 7.37 a.m.'

'She could never have made him happy.'

'I'm sure the judge will bear that in mind.'

And with Bella gone, back to the holding cells, Tamsin turns to Peter.

'So what was she talking about?'

Eighty Nine

'How d'you mean?'

Peter was genuinely puzzled.

'You know what I mean.'

'I really don't.'

'Who the hell is Columbina?'

'Ah yes, Columbina.'

'Well?'

'I should have spotted that connection a little earlier.'

'What connection?'

'After all, Martin Channing gave us the clue when we first interviewed him. The fatal triangle.'

'Are you going to explain? I'm being exposed to dangerously high levels of smug.'

'I'm not smug, Tamsin – more ashamed.'

'Tell your face.'

'Remember Channing described the evening as something out of the Commedia dell'Arte?'

'Vaguely.'

'And one of the classic story lines in the Commedia is the love of the Harlequin for Columbina – a love thwarted by the clown, Pierrot, who's sent by Columbina's father to break them up.'

'So Barnabus was the Harlequin and Bella his Columbina.'

'With poor Patience cast as Pierrot. As I say, the fatal triangle. '

There was a companionable silence.

'You did very well,' says the Abbot.

'Thank you.'

'Very savage.'

Tamsin liked to do well, but liked doing better than others even more.

'And the other thing,' says Peter, 'I was enjoying looking at her.'

'Really?'

'Looking at the one who wanted me dead, at the one who terrified me – but who terrifies me no more.'

'Planning some discreet revenge?'

'She danced in the firelight like a marionette, so happy at my approaching demise.'

'You are allowed hateful thoughts.'

'I know, I know.'

They got up from the table.

'And my savagery was not just about my desire to win.'

'No?'

'I was savage for you, Uncle, after what the bitch did.'

'Vicarious aggression and I'm grateful. But today I could do nothing but look at her crumpled clothes, bereft of the back-lighting, and feel how good it is to be alive.'

'Why can't you just scream: "I hate you!" – I'd feel more comfortable with that.'

'Hate has come and gone, I'm afraid.'

'So tell me about an Abbot's hate – before it goes.'

'How about I tell you the name of the murderer instead?'

Ninety

They stand in wary silence in the hall of Henry House, gazing on the stricken policeman, PC Lister, sprawled on the cold marble floor.

Tamsin confirms with a thumbs-up that he's alive. He appears to have been crawling towards the entrance, when he finally collapsed.

'There's gas,' mouths Peter.

Tamsin looks quizzical. Peter holds his nose and mouths 'gas' again. Tamsin knows there's gas, she doesn't need telling and mouths 'I know!' pointing to the kitchen door, ajar. They walk slowly towards it, Tamsin stepping through first. The room is empty but the source of the smell soon clear, the oven door open with a quiet, insistent hiss. On closer inspection, Tamsin's head down, there's a budgerigar lying in the oven. She pulls back and Peter takes her place.

'It's Jung,' he whispers.

'Sorry?'

'The *Mind Gains* budgie, he's been gassed in the oven … Ah, and the gas controls removed. This looks like a plan.'

Tamsin directs his attention to a canister at the other end of the room, releasing its own brand of poison into the stale air. As they both move towards it, the kitchen door closes behind them. They look round to see Frances Pole, seemingly unsteady on her feet. And at the same time, Peter notices tape around the windows.

'Stay exactly where you are,' he whispers to Tamsin.

She senses him moving awkwardly and looking strained. What's he doing? Is the gas getting to him?

'I'm sorry about Jung,' says Frances. 'Very sorry. But he'd had a stroke, and it seemed the kindest thing. He wasn't enjoying life.'

'And have you been, Frances?' asks Peter.

'Have I been what?'

'Enjoying life?'

Their eyes move as one towards the gin bottle on the table, largely consumed.

'I've had better days.'

'And a little early to be drinking, perhaps?'

'Is there a too early?'

'Five o'clock has always been my rule.'

'I used to have eleven in the morning as mine, but really, is nine so different? It's still just a silly rule.'

'And you've been under a lot of pressure, Frances.'

'No more than usual.'

Tamsin's feet are growing cold. Is the gas now getting to her? Is this the first effect? They needed to do something … other than talk.

'But pressure nonetheless,' says Peter. 'Trying to get a business going, trying to look after people – and who cares for the carer?'

Carer? Frances?

'Alcohol has always been about annihilation for me,' she says. 'Wonderful annihilation, everything blown away! Isn't that why we drink?'

'We all have our reasons,' says Peter. 'And yes, there are days when annihilation seems strangely attractive. As Van Gogh said, "When the storm gets too loud, I take a glass too much to stun myself".'

'How understanding of you, Abbot – almost Barnabus-esque.'

She sways slightly.

'But we'll need to turn the gas off, Frances or there's going to be an accident.'

He's beginning to feel sick.

'Are you afraid of annihilation, Abbot?'

'I don't seek it, if that's what you mean.'

'But aren't you meant to be cheerful in the face of death, off to a better place and all that?'

'So they say.'

'Oh they do, they do. Some of my favourite lines from Tudor history, spoken by Bishop Latimer to his friend Ridley shortly before they were burned at the stake by Queen Mary.'

'You like your history, don't you?'

'I have a history degree.'

'Really?'

'Really.'

'So many qualifications.'

'Such fearless words: "Be of good cheer, Master Ridley and play the man; we shall this day light such a candle in England, as I hope, by God's grace, shall never be put out!" Wonderful.'

'They were brave words.'

'An example to us all,' said Frances, feeling for something in her pocket. 'Words of hope from a time when hope still lived.'

'It still does, Frances.'

'For the religious in the room, perhaps … which rather narrows it down to one!'

Abbot Peter feels eyes on him:

'When death cannot be avoided,' he says, 'then we accept it. But this is not such an occasion.'

'But will you like death?'

'I don't know if I'll like death, Frances, I may do, hard to tell, evidence being sparse – but I do like life.'

'You sound a bit of a fraud to me, no different to the rest of us.'

'I also look after a little girl called Poppy. I'd miss her – perhaps she'd even miss me.'

Frances laughs: 'Bloody hell, what's this – a Great Ormond Street Special?'

She's holding a box of matches in her hand, and adds:

'You'll be asking me to give generously next.'

'No, I think it's you we should be supporting.'

'I'm a very lost cause, Abbot Peter,' she says, taking out a match from the box. 'And while not wishing to be ungrateful, I have to say I've grown rather tired of this place.'

'It's not been the best of times for you?'

'It's been the worst of times. Seemed such a good investment, it really did, but now I'd like nothing more than to give it all back to that appalling doctor.'

'Appalling?'

'Weak, like my father, another male disappointment.'

'I'm sure a sale could be arranged.'

'Where's an estate agent when you need one?'

'I know he'd love to buy it back off you, we spoke about it, he said how much he missed the place.'

'Oh, so *you're* the estate agent!'

'And perhaps a fresh start would be good for everyone.'

'At her Majesty's pleasure, for the murder of Barnabus?'

As Frances speaks, Tamsin watches only her hands and the match she holds.

'Though I merely hastened the inevitable – I mean, it was hardly murder.'

'A dog put out of its misery,' thinks Tamsin, but Abbot Peter still wants to be friends.

'I agree,' he says, 'strong case for leniency in my book.'

'How do those Arthur Hugh Clough lines go?' said Frances. "Thou shalt not kill – but need not strive officiously to keep alive".'

'You like his cynicism, Frances, I can understand that.'

'Really?'

'He allows the bleak in you a voice, gives permission to the despair.'

'Are we having a session?'

'No, we're just talking.'

'If we are having a session, I should warn you, you won't be getting paid.'

'We're just thinking about fresh starts,' says Peter.

'Never believe anyone who offers you a fresh start.'

'Oh?'

'One of the great marketing lies.'

'Wasn't that somewhere in the *Mind Gains* publicity?'

'You say what you have to say.'

'Then let's do something very specific: how about a start free from all those pretend qualifications?'

Frances reddens in the face as Peter adds:

'You don't need that nonsense now.'

'That's what the little prick Barnabus said: "In the ashes of our imagined qualifications will our true self be found".'

Frances moves towards the oven.

'I prefer annihilation over fresh starts,' she says, 'annihilation is the best fresh start of all, and we should be standing in enough of a bomb now.'

'Why us?' asks Tamsin, her feet freezing, as the gas does its work. 'Why include us in your death-wish?'

There's a pause. Frances looks at them blankly.

'Because I don't want to die alone, you can come with me.'

But Tamsin doesn't want to go with her. She says that everyone dies alone, we're born alone, we die alone, and though Frances looks shocked, Tamsin isn't done in that sealed kitchen:

'It's like those narcissistic fathers, who kill their children and then kill themselves: "Come and join me in my self-obsession, no really, you must, little Johnny!".'

Frances looks contrite, but decided.

'I'd still enjoy company as I enter the unknown,' she says.

'But it's not going to work,' says Peter.

'We'll just have to see.'

'This is a unique Elizabethan jewel.'

Frances laughs.

'Please don't bring the National Trust into it.'

'It has very particular features.'

'Oh I know, believe me. I've already heard from that nice constable about the priest hole off the chimney. Very clever.'

'Well, there's that, and – .'

'Fascinating, no really, fascinating, but that's enough, let's do this before your police friends arrive. And I bet you God doesn't exist. Winner takes all.'

Frances strikes the match.

Ninety One

Tamsin flinches at sparking ignition.

Flame!

Nothing.

Frances fumbles inside the box and strikes another.

Flame!

Nothing.

' "This is the way the world ends",' she says lighting a further match, but with less intent. ' "This is the way the world ends, this is the way the world ends, not with a bang but a whimper".'

Frances looks suddenly frail.

'The uniqueness of Henry House,' says Peter 'lies in its *two* priest holes, the second behind the water closet and leading to the garden. Just here behind me.'

'I'm so bored of the history,' says Frances. 'Someone said history is the new sex and that so isn't true.'

Tamsin looks round to see the hole, worked open earlier by the Abbot's feet, and large enough for an adult and much fresh air to crawl through. Her cold feet had not been due to the gas.

'Virgil showed it to me last night on a little tour of his old home … and thankfully revealed how to open it, with his foot.'

Frances turns and runs from the room, into the hallway, the front door slamming behind her. Tamsin makes to move.

'I think you can leave her, the place is surrounded,' says Peter.

'That's a police line, and not always true.'

'Eerie figures in the mist. I was watching through the window while we spoke.'

Tamsin's raised eyebrows say 'Bully for you.'

'Why so shocked by police competence?' says Peter, and after opening a window and throwing the gas canister through it, he suggests tea in the fresh air of the Long Room.

'I'll bring the milk,' he says, looking inside the fridge. 'We can bury Jung later.'

'I'm not sure he's dead,' she replies. 'He's twitching.'

Tamsin reaches inside the oven, removes the ailing Jung and carries him in a cradling palm to the porch where she kneels down, lays him on the ground and kills him with a rock.

'Are you all right, Ma'am?' asks a constable.

'Better than Jung,' she replies aimlessly, to a face of puzzled horror. An explanation is needed. 'He was the *Mind Gains* budgie, Constable, but he wasn't well.'

'Right, Ma'am.'

More explanation necessary.

'He'd had a stroke and was then gassed. In the oven.'

Why is she getting involved in this conversation?

'Right, Ma'am.'

'Not by me, obviously. By the therapist who runs this place.'

'Glad she's not looking after me then.'

Fair point.

'You can carry on with your duties now, Constable.'

'Yes, Ma'am.'

'When you've buried Jung.'

'Me, Ma'am?'

'Yes, Constable.'

'Right, Ma'am. I can do that. I'll find a trowel.'

'You do that.'

'Anywhere in particular?'

'Oh, somewhere nice. Among those trees perhaps, beneath the pine cones.'

'Yes, Ma'am'

'Thank you.'

'And his name was "Jung", you say?'

'Does it matter?'

Impatience is creeping in.

'I like to say a few words, Ma'am.'

'You do this sort of thing a lot?'

'I once had a rat called Derek, Ma'am. Sad day when he died.'

'I'm sure.'

'He had to be put out of his misery as well. Not certain as to the manner of his death, my brother performed the act, I couldn't do it myself, he was my older brother, braver than me … may have used a stone, I don't know – perhaps I should ask him one day.'

'Perhaps you should, Constable.'

'But then something inside me doesn't want to know. Funny that.'

'Funny peculiar, perhaps.'

'But I did say a few words over the grave, and that might be nice for Jung.'

Frances is being guided to a police car while PC Lister, formerly drugged on the hall floor, walks in a dazed fashion across the fog-bound lawn. It's a slightly surreal scene. Presumably there is a paramedic close by; this is a competent police operation after all, no party hats.

*

The Abbot waited on the stairs while the mercy-killer washed her hands. She returned in a subdued mood.

'Out, out damn spot!' said Peter.

'Not funny.'

'Macbeth wasn't a comedy.'

'It had to be done.'

'That's what Lady Macbeth said.'

Tamsin was unsettled and Peter softened.

'I am joking. I know you had to do it.'

'I did.'

'And you should be feeling proud, Tamsin. I couldn't have done that.'

She needed those words, needed quiet reassurance.

'I've never been in a mental health unit before,' she said, looking towards the office.

'Be grateful.'

'But it does concern me that two out of three staff members – that's 66 per cent of employees – are psychopaths. Let's hope this isn't a national statistic.'

They made their way towards the Long Room.

'Where better for a tree to hide than in the forest?' said Peter.

Ninety Two

Henry House
Six months later

'I suppose it's about closure,' said Dr Minty.

He stood in the Long Room and was fumbling for his lines.

'Dreadful word, closure – and not really true anyway, because this isn't about closure, it's the opposite really – or at least it's not only about closure.'

'Get on with it!' shouts Virgil and his father obliges, though without great confidence. He's not good on his feet, and why should he be attention-grabbing and smart with his words? He was a doctor, not an estate agent and while he looked out on friendly faces – he wasn't sure about the editor fellow, you could never tell with his face – they were not necessarily faces he knew well, or indeed wanted to know well.

'This evening is really a thank you, I suppose.'

'Well, make your mind up, you old ditherer!'

The venue was Henry House, the Long Room, and gathered here, those who knew something of the journey – no, not 'journey', he'd said, 'I'll sound like one of those awful reality shows, but you know what I mean.' And people did know what he meant, a doctor who'd made a mistake, left home before he was ready and had now come back with fresh energy to see what could be done. So perhaps his leaving had not been a mistake after all, this was his take on the matter. And some were here to wish him well with his new venture, while others were here because they'd suffered while he was away, caught up in the tragic Feast of Fools.

Peter was offering Tamsin a running commentary:

'Note the longing in Virgil: the son who walked out on his father at the age of fifteen, the son aching for a fight, yet aching also to come home.' Virgil had remained on the side of friendly so far, but it was a close thing. 'He wants to get back, wants to find something in his father he hasn't found before – but he's a man with large quantities of what is generally known as baggage.'

'I just don't see this baggage everyone talks about,' says Tamsin.

'Most dangerous when unseen.'

And, for his part, Virgil was glad the Abbot fellow was here tonight, even if he did have a mysterious plane to catch.

'I do have a plane to catch' he'd said, which seemed a little unlikely, an Abbot in a plane? But Virgil hadn't pressed, because you have to allow people their excuses – God, he'd told some lies in his time to get away from dull evenings.

And next to the Abbot was that saucily attractive DI Tamsin Shah – certainly a looker, no question! – and then an older man, drifting to fat, who was apparently the Chief Inspector who oversaw the case that ended in jail sentences for Frances Pole, Bella Amal and Kate Karter: the case now known in the media as 'The Feast of Fools Murder'. Typical, bloody typical!

But Virgil was less pleased that Channing was present, odious man, truly odious – but to be fair, tonight was about gathering those touched by the events in some way. And he'd been here that night, in the commedia dell'arte as he called it, and caught in the wash like everyone else.

'And as I think you all know,' continued Dr Minty, 'I have decided to come back and attempt something new here in Henry House.'

'Ever thought of central heating?'

Virgil again, enjoying the banter, enjoying the attention and not wrong. Much had changed in the world since the reign of Elizabeth I, including space travel and the diminishing popularity of pig's head for tea, but the heating in Henry House had remained locked in time, where it was either big fire or big chill.

'Well, anything's possible,' said his father, laughing.

'Apparently he had a buy-back clause in the contract,' whispers Rebecca to Ezekiel. 'I've been following the story. He obviously wasn't sure about the decision to leave.'

'It's a mistake to travel too far in retirement,' says her husband. 'It is hard to make new friends.'

Ezekiel remained fragile, still in shock after his banishment from the church. The elders had not taken kindly to his request that Patience be allowed to go her own way, without exorcism or any other extreme practices.

'So we give her as a prize to Satan?' they'd asked.

And he didn't even know if he believed in his request. They were his words, spoken by him at a difficult meeting with the Benders – that's what Patience called the Elders, apparently, wilful girl – but it had been Rebecca's ultimatum.

'Stay married to them and you won't stay married to me.'

Prompt and ruthless banishment from the community of grace had followed.

'You understand you leave us no choice,' said friends.

'I believe we all have a choice.'

'Oh, you mean we might choose to embrace the devil, Ezekiel?'

Was he, Ezekiel, now the devil?

The Roman Catholics excommunicate well, but Catholics, as Peter said, don't do it nearly as well as Protestants … and in particular, the Seraphimic Church of the Blessed Elect in Uplifting Glory. Life-long friends of twenty years now looked away as they passed Ezekiel in the streets of Stormhaven; dinner invitations stopped in a moment. Yet Patience and Michael were both with him tonight, his children were with him by choice, and how many of the Benders could say that? So while strong pillars had collapsed, leaving him numb in the ruins and frightened, there was some treasure to be found in the rubble.

Dr Minty continued: 'So hopefully it's about closure on a set of events triggered by my foolish departure.'

Peter also disliked the word closure. That was for individuals to find in their own time, not something you could announce from the front.

'But maybe sometimes we have to leave a thing, to discover its value!'

Murmurs of general approval.

'So I've asked Patience – Patience, where are you? That's right, step forward a little! – I've asked Patience, funded by the newly-set-up Barnabus Fund, to research how we might continue what Barnabus started. Lewes has therapists by the dozen, dripping from every golden drainpipe I'm told, but what about Stormhaven? Bit of a desert in my experience, especially for the young. So I'm thinking about a centre for children and young adults affected by trauma, a refuge centre for the emotionally abused. Patience already has some interest in that direction. New life for Henry House?'

Applause.

'Now, no more rambling from me.'

'Hear, hear!'

Virgil again.

'Now if anyone else would like to offer a word, please do. Virgil, you seem eager to start – though in a way, you've never really stopped!'

'If I may just intervene,' says Martin Channing, moving smoothly forward and assuming control. 'Because I'm sure I speak on behalf of us all, Dr Minty, when I say how good it is to have you back in Stormhaven and to have Henry House returned to hands that are fit to run it.'

Restrained approval, with no one feeling this was the time to settle old scores.

'Why do you print so many lies?' asks Virgil, feeling free to wander from the script. Martin remains charming:

'Lies? Strong word, Virgil. Where's my lawyer?!'

He's joking.

'Just answer the question.'

'Well, I think it was the psychoanalyst Jung – .'

'Jung?'

It's Patience.

'Jung, yes.'

'That was the name of the *Mind Gains* budgie! He was called Jung!'

Martin seizes the opening provided:

'Indeed, whom Frances tried to gas in the oven.'

'What?' says Rebecca, who hadn't read anything about this. 'How could anyone do that?'

'That's exactly the question we asked in the *Sussex Silt*,' says Martin, 'being tireless campaigners for animal rights. Though for accuracy's sake, it was the DI here who actually killed the bird – making the decisive strike with a rock. Isn't that so, Detective Inspector?'

Aghast eyes now look at Tamsin.

'I had to kill the bird, it wasn't well.'

The remark doesn't sound as caring as she'd hoped.

'Then we must all hope the Detective Inspector never takes up a career in nursing,' says Martin with a smile.

Laughter.

'But to return to Jung – the psychoanalyst not the budgie – it was he who said that "What is truth for us in the morning is often a lie by the afternoon".'

Some dismay.

'What's that supposed to mean?' asks Rebecca.

'Truth and lies,' says Martin, 'these things are perhaps more complex than we imagine, more closely related even.'

Stubborn Virgil returns to his question: 'So why do you print so many lies?'

'Well, I can tell you one thing for sure,' says Channing, 'We will be the most supportive of papers towards all that goes on here in the

283

re-born Henry House. And I can today announce a £5000 donation from the *Sussex Silt* towards the Barnabus Fund!'

'Ooohh!' noises.

'Thank you, Martin' says Dr Minty, surprised. 'Much appreciated.'

Though he's not sure if it is, tainted gold and all that.

'Not a grant you want made public,' mutters Tamsin under her breath, still smarting from the bird-murder allegations.

'I'd like to say a few words,' says Patience, stepping forward.

'You have the floor,' declares Minty gratefully.

'Because this place has changed my life.'

Genuine approval. This is what the punters want to hear, innocence and energy, words to suggest that life means something, that light can shine in darkness, that darkness is not the end – that, simply put, it's worth everyone getting up tomorrow morning.

'As you know, I was formerly a cleaner here – .'

'A secret cleaner,' murmurs Ezekiel.

'Yes, a secret cleaner, Dad. I had to be. We've had our problems as a family, still have our problems, which family doesn't?'

General acknowledgement.

'But this place was a refuge when I needed it.'

Ezekiel is still not sure that she did need it. Did she really need it? A child should not need to take refuge from her parents, if they're godly. He hadn't taken refuge from his parents, he'd taken the punishment without complaint.

Patience continued: 'I hid for four days in the priest hole over there, which I discovered, quite by chance, when cleaning.'

She paused. Did people really want to hear this? She'd never spoken in public before.

'Tell it,' said Abbot Peter quietly. 'Tell us your story, Patience. It would be good to give it some air.'

Ninety Three

And so Patience did tell her story, confessing she didn't know Bella planned to kill both her and Barnabus at the Feast of Fools, which was a good way to get everyone's attention ... though she then felt stupid and said that of course she didn't know, how could she have done, because murder is rarely announced, apart from in declarations of war. And so death was the last thing on her mind when, after the Feast, she went downstairs to change: 'I was on cloud nine, I was in love!'

'So sad,' said Peter to Tamsin.

She then went on to describe how Kate asked her into the office, in a most insistent way, like it was really important, and once inside the room told her that everyone was in danger, there was a madman around, and how she then put a knife in Patience's hands for her protection. It all happened so fast, and then Kate was saying no, she was too young and told her to put the knife down and come over to the cupboard where she showed her the body of Barnabus, at which point she broke down and started to cry, it was terrible, and then Kate had said she'd get help, and it didn't cross Pat's mind to wonder what sort of help but when she looked round, the door was locked and the knife gone and she knew she was in trouble, instinctively knew, with her hand print on the knife, she said she felt like 'a goat tethered outside the slaughterhouse'.

Shock around the group, who'd been expecting something more innocent from these young lips, more hopeful, something less smeared by human evil.

'I also knew that my father – I must be honest tonight – had only come to the Feast because he suspected I worked here. I don't know how he found out, but I was aware that whatever else I did, there was no going home.'

Nervous eyes glanced across at Ezekiel, who stood in a trance.

'So I disappeared,' she says, 'like Virgil tells me he used to disappear as a child.' And she recounted how trapped in the office, she escaped into the priest hole, hoping no one else knew of it: 'Please, God, please!'

She'd told no one, it had always felt like a secret, a secret she shared with the house alone. She then heard Bella come in, with Kate, and she heard Bella asking where Pat was, and Kate saying she'd definitely been here, and must have got out the window, and Bella was furious and couldn't see how I could have got out the window, and then manage to lock it after me, and Kate said that I must have dematerialised, which was hardly likely, and Bella called her something and then they left and there was silence.

There was also silence in the Long Room, apart from Virgil saying 'Sick cows' under his breath.

Patience continued: 'A little later, I heard the door open again, which I suppose was Frances making her final rounds – .'

'Hardly Florence Nightingale – .'

'And then I heard a noise, somewhere between a crack and a thud, which must have been, must have been when ...' And for a moment she could get no words out, and her mother was holding her, tears, sobbing and then strong again, pulling herself free, and talking about the long night that followed, how she made her way up the ladder, which brought her to the first floor where there was space to sit, and how terrified she was she'd be found, not knowing who could now be trusted.

Rebecca started to cry, and Michael consoled her with an adolescent arm, now old enough to protect.

'It's difficult to describe it now. Tonight, I stand here with a fire burning, with friends and a glass of wine – but believe me, on Halloween night, it wasn't like that.'

'A remarkable story,' says Martin Channing.

'Put your cheque book away,' says Virgil.

'He can't help himself, can he?' says Tamsin to Peter.

'Who?'

'Either of them.'

'And so I lived here for the following five days, sealed in by day but able to roam a little at night.'

'The Detective Inspector thought you were a ghost,' says Peter.

'I didn't think she was a ghost.'

'I think you did.'

'I didn't realise you believed in ghosts, Tamsin!' says the Chief Constable.

He's grasping at straws, of course, still making his way back, six months on, from his embarrassing words at Mick Norman's party. He

286

now regretted his unguarded flirtation and had tried to put the whole thing to bed – 'unfortunate simile, but you know what I mean, Tamsin' – bluff apologies which accompany the morning after every works do: 'Drink, eh?' he said. 'You probably don't remember much!'

But Tamsin remembered everything, every word and inflection and, like a ship holed beneath the waterline, her boss had never quite recovered, never got back to the port called authority. Not that Tamsin ever mentioned the evening, but then she'd never had to: why mention the obvious when the obvious is there without mention? They don't talk of snow much in Greenland.

Patience explains the ghostly appearance: 'You caught me out. I needed the loo and I thought the building was empty, and then suddenly I see figures in the hall. I was more frightened than you! So I hunched a little, hoped you'd believe I was a ghost – I knew I stood where once the Harlequin had – but I never imagined you would!'

'I didn't.'

Peter: 'She did. I saw her face.'

And then Patience described how she'd survived on the kitchen supplies and midnight press-ups, sit-ups and stretching, until her life-saving entry into the murder room.

'I'd been listening to everything: Bella's voice was not hard to hear, though I couldn't always make out the Abbot's words.'

'Like most clergy, he struggles without a microphone,' says Tamsin, keen for revenge.

'You think I had a microphone in the desert?' replies the Abbot under his breath.

'In the desert, you were talking to yourself, which doesn't count.'

'And I had a noose round my neck at the time. You must try it sometime; it does tense the throat a little.'

'You seem very defensive.'

'And I did have my back to her.'

'People stood behind Martin Luther King, but they still got the gist of his dream. Why are you wriggling?'

'I'm not wriggling.'

'Face it, your diction is disappointing.'

She liked to win.

'I'll be forever haunted by your remarks,' says Peter.

Meanwhile Patience is wrapping things up, describing how Bella had been stronger than she thought; how, despite the press-ups, she found an unexpected steel and strength in her opponent, the pain of the knife wound, the feelings of giddiness and how she couldn't believe it when Virgil suddenly flew across the room.

'I knew she'd be hiding there, just knew it, had to be, spent half my childhood in the same place – and then I get to save the Abbot's bacon too!'

Laughter and 'good old Virgil' feelings, how he glowed in the gathered love and the wave of acknowledgement from Peter, almost a blessing, and then conversation breaking out as the Abbot slipped out into the night, best avoid the goodbyes. Goodbyes made him cry and so they became rigid, distant affairs. Be hale and hearty – or just creep out the door, and he crept out tonight, case packed, taxi soon to arrive, the pilgrimage starting here.

Tamsin thought he was mad to set off in further pursuit of the dead.

Ninety Four

Stormhaven had come to London but not for the shopping. This was true for Abbot Peter, but true also for Frances, Bella and Kate.

HM Prison Holloway, also known as the Holloway Castle, sits red bricked and modern in London's Camden Road. It's new build, newer than the original of 1852 and single sex since 1903, needs must, for where else to put suffragettes, poisoners and war time fascist sympathisers – not that they're the same, not at all, but each in need of a good locking up here in north London, where five judicial hangings have taken place. Not for a while, of course, the last – the famous last – being Ruth Ellis in 1955, whose remains still lie on site in an unmarked grave, there was a film about her ... though superseded in the headlines by other fatal women like Myra Hindley, Brady's assistant on the torturing Moors; Françoise Dior, niece of Christian, French socialite, Nazi sympathiser and burner of London synagogues; and Maxine Carr, more Soham than socialite, and giver of false alibis to the child-murdering Huntley.

But not one of Holloway's guests down the years had ever come from Stormhaven – until now, when suddenly, like the red buses that offer travellers a free glimpse – 'That's Holloway prison there, no really, and it has a fantastic swimming pool apparently' – three from Stormhaven all came at once: Frances Pole, Bella Amal and Kate Karter.

They'd done their best to avoid each other, both on remand and since conviction. Beyond memories of Henry House, what on earth did they now share? And avoidance was possible. With each on a different landing, they were spared each other's company during evening 'Association', when cell doors were open and convicts could roam – a time for showers, phone calls and gossip with the thirty others who shared your space. But the work day was different, and the whole day was work in Holloway prison, morning and afternoon, paid work but unpredictable, you couldn't be choosy about companions on your shift. And there was a day that spring, perhaps it had to be so, when Stormhaven met, when each was assigned gardening duty, less supervised than kitchen or laundry, a sign of trust. And there in the garden tea room, as they took a break from planting, it was a table for three, the Stormhaven Three, the meeting each had avoided yet each had known must occur – and perhaps wanted, who knows?

All of them 'lifers', slowly getting used to the word, but the meaning varied, with different minimum sentences: Frances and Bella not less than twelve years and Kate not less than eight. She'd be the first back to the sea, if she still fancied a dip.

'Well, here we all are,' says Frances, different in her overall, her polished skin even more polished.

'Don't know what the big deal is,' says Bella, quite excited, quite frightened.

'Sorry about Gerald,' says Frances to Kate.

'That's life,' she replies, and it sounds stupid as soon as she says it.

Bella: 'A weak man.'

'Made weak by you,' says Kate.

'Oh yes, blame me, babe.'

'Yes, I do. Oh I do. He was free, making good, in his way.'

'He was a kiddy-fiddler – who's crying?'

'Do you ever take responsibility?'

'Not for perverts.'

'You're repulsive.'

'Perhaps you're looking in a mirror.'

The tea break hadn't got off to a good start.

'Do you never give up? asks Frances, who views Bella with disdain, a poor appointment, no, a bad appointment by her, how stupid she'd been, how unforgivably stupid, the woman was a complete bitch, though really, Kate should get a grip, stop moping, something of a lost soul since her arrival in Holloway, as though she wasn't here, that's how it looked, as though Kate had left Kate and, since Gerald hanged himself, almost full time in the chapel, a place where the emptiness echoed her own.

She'd asked Abbot Peter to come and see her after Gerald died. She'd written to him, pleading. And he had come, travelled up on the train to Victoria and then by tube to Caledonian Road. And he'd passed through the checks and bolted doors, and sat with her in a visitor's room, in a habit that Kate felt needed a clean. But it hadn't gone well, quite apart from his clothes, it hadn't gone well, hadn't achieved what she wanted. He'd said how sad he was at the news of Gerald's death, and how angered he was by the hounding which led him there, a hounding led by the *Silt*. But she discovered she didn't want his sadness, or his anger, what good were these, she wanted to move on, to find a new interest, to which Peter had simply said:

'You can't say goodbye to something until you've first said hello to it.'

And this wasn't what she'd wanted to hear … why say hello to sadness or anger, she wasn't the sad type, and not the angry type, though she wasn't now sure what type she was. And they'd sat in silence for a while … and she wasn't saying sorry to him, because she hadn't had a choice that night, she'd had to leave him strung up on the bench, so how could she say she was sorry? She remembered the quiet, before Peter wished her well and took his leave.

And of the three – and in a strange way they were a three, not friends but a three through circumstance, the Stormhaven Three – Frances had settled most easily into this ordered life, impressing staff … almost viewed as one of their own and merging quickly with the prison's posh circle, those in for fraud, office types with arts degrees caught shifting money around on a screen. They were a bit of a club, the elite, while the rest were mainly theft, supermarkets and clothes, low-life with a habit to fuel; and there were killers, not many but a few, partners in the main, revolting partners, partners knifed in rage, and really, with their stories told, it was hard to say they were wrong. Bella hung around the edges of the thieves, unable to belong anywhere, but adept at finding the vulnerable to sit with and knowing which staff to approach, keeping busy and noting who was with who.

'Anyone missing Henry House?'

Someone had to ask and it was Kate.

'No,' says Frances.

'I don't miss the cold,' says Bella, 'that cold hall!'

'Nice marble floor, very classy,' observes Kate.

'But cold. Prison in January's not all bad.'

Holloway was warm, no question.

'And I don't miss the ravens,' adds Bella.

Kate is surprised.

'You didn't like the ravens?'

'What's there to like about ravens?'

'I always thought of you as one of them,' says Frances.

Bella blushes a little.

'Scavenging on the lives of others, opportunistic killers of the small and vulnerable. I think you were very like the ravens of Henry House, Bella.'

Immediate offence taken.

'And you weren't?'

'Oh, I take responsibility. But I'm not a raven.'

'No,' says Bella, 'you were the cock of Henry House, if you know what I mean,' – she was suddenly girly, nervous giggle – 'ordering everyone's time but not as bright, in the end, as the other animals imagined.'

This time Frances blushes, heat in her face.

'No offence,' adds Bella.

Frances feels the darkening, the black hole, she'd felt it since the first mention of Henry House and how powerful it was. The light prison space, the respect of guards and peers, the history course she'd started. Without knowing, she'd begun to imagine herself half-decent again, right and not wrong, good and not bad, until mention of that place, the deceit and ruin it stood for, her own tomb as much as that of Barnabus. And now self-pity as well, my God! How she missed the alcohol, missed the annihilation, the oblivion of the three-day bender. Social drinking? What was the point of that?

'I do miss its history,' says Kate.

'The history of the place was awful,' says Frances. 'Unremittingly awful.'

Kate explains herself:

'The sense of being part of something other than myself, a bigger story.'

'There was only unhappiness to share in, believe me.'

'Someone must have been happy at Henry House down the years!' Kate wanted to be cheered up.

'Yes – Pat,' says Frances, with a reluctant chuckle.

'I don't think she's happy,' says Bella, playing with the small milk carton.

There was movement around them, another shift coming in for tea.

'It's good to know someone more bitter than me,' says Frances.

Bella shrugs.

'I heard she's almost running the place now,' says Kate.

'Hardly,' replies Bella.

'That's what I heard.'

'Well, she couldn't be running it, she hasn't the qualifications. What qualifications has she got?'

There's an awkward silence.

'Perhaps the happy are qualified,' says Kate, who'd exchange her second class English degree and Equity membership, for whatever it was to be content, to be happy.

'The happy?' says Frances. 'What hope for anyone if that's the qualification required?'

And that was that, as it worked out, because there was now an officer by their table.

'The lilies and gladioli will not plant themselves, ladies. And then what will we look at in the summer?'

The Stormhaven Three rose from the table, left the tea room and each other. One day at a time, think only in days, and summer would come in its own time, like the lilies and gladioli, one summer and then another.

And then another.

Ninety Five

The lights were still on in Henry House long after the speeches were finished. Abbot Peter had left in a taxi, whisked away into the mysterious night, something about a plane, but the evening went on, Dr Minty the tearful host, so happy again, happy at the talk, the laughter and the hope around him, such conversations, he could hardly keep track! And certainly not privy to every encounter in his home that night – like the one currently unfolding in the master bedroom, where a small man now stands in the doorway looking in.

'What are you doing here?' he asks.

Patience had returned to the master bedroom. The last time she'd been here was the morning of 31 October, the dawn of Halloween.

'Just remembering,' she said dreamily.

Truth be told, and she did tell it now, she'd come here for a little quiet. The evening had been joyful, perhaps she'd felt an adult for the first time, valued for the first time, but full of noise and now she wanted peace … and memories.

'Remembering your days as a cleaner,' said her father, more instruction than question.

'No,' says Patience.

Ezekiel is uncomfortable.

'I was a lover here, not a cleaner,' she adds, looking at the four poster.

Ezekiel's hands become tense fists by his side. He would not call her a whore, he was learning that sometimes it was best not to speak; but then he struggled for another word.

'It's better that you know me, Father, rather than invent me – much better. Barnabus and I would have married.'

'Over my dead body!'

It just came out, parental authority, he knew no other way. But the man who'd frightened her once, did so no longer.

She says: 'Do you really imagine your body, dead or otherwise, could have stopped us?'

And now she's smiling, can't help it, there's pity in her eyes, looking at her father in the doorway, a suited bundle of terror, so frightened in the world, in the real world where his word wasn't law. And she's imagining the conversation as the organ blasts the wedding march and cameras click and flash:

'Who's that on the floor, half way down the aisle?' asks Barnabus, in his smart grey wedding suit.

'Oh, it's my father,' she says, in her creamy dress, veil tossed back.

'Is he all right?'

'He insisted we marry over his dead body.'

'Well, if that's the family tradition …'

And then she's sad, sad for the day that will never be, for the life that will never be.

'Could you leave me now?' she says to the small man in the doorway.

Ninety Six

'Well, just ask him,' said Rebecca.

'I can't just ask him … can I?'

'What's the worst he can do?'

What was the worst Channing could do? Michael knew:

'He could laugh at me.'

Sometimes the man, and sometimes the awkward teen, still cautious in the world, waking slowly to his strength.

'It's time for bravery, Michael.'

And so he had just asked him, and how things unfold, neither planned nor considered, but he caught him on the stairs, Martin Channing, editor of the *Sussex Silt* – the 'bad mag' as his friends called it – on the stairs at Henry House, you remember these things when you get your first job, because that's what he'd asked for, and here's the thing: Martin Channing didn't laugh at him at all.

'Do you know what young people want?' said Channing, pausing for a moment.

'Of course I know.'

'And can you write?'

'I don't know.'

'Fair enough. That probably would have been Shakespeare's reply at your age.'

'I'm better than what you've got.'

'Really?'

'Loads better, no question.'

Rebecca, listening at close distance, is uneasy. Why rubbish his current writers, Michael? You're going to blow it.

'And the story is god,' says Channing.

'I'm sorry?'

'You must remember the story is god.'

Channing surveys the boy with snake eyes, aware of the challenge laid down. The story is god? Before him, Michael sees Satan in a pink

296

shirt, demanding his soul. Does he give it? Rebecca's thinking he should give it, definitely, for the moment at least, a temporary handing over of the soul, just to get started, just to get his first job.

'No, the truth is god, Mr Channing.'

The editor smiles, he likes the boy's spirit.

'As long as it's a good story, Michael, as long as the truth dazzles.'

'The truth always dazzles, Mr Channing.'

The editor's face is hard to read, though Rebecca's having a go and thinking 'Careful, Michael, you don't know who you're dealing with here – so why don't you just bow a little? Sometimes bowing is helpful.'

'Monday, 9.00 a.m.,' says Channing. 'You know where we are?'

Rebecca's thrilled. Monday 9.00 a.m.? A job? Wonderful! Just say yes, she thinks, just say 'Of course, Mr Channing' and well done Michael, she'd buy the editor flowers.

'I should do,' says Michael, 'I once threw a brick through your window.'

Pause. Forget the flowers. Why did he say that?

'So it was you?'

'It was me.'

'I remember its arrival,' says Channing.

As a car on ice, loss of control and Rebecca knows a frozen moment of terror. What chance of a job now? Channing speaks, sounding like the magistrate he'd never be, he says it was very fortunate no one was hurt, really very fortunate, a grossly irresponsible act.

'I trust it won't become a habit?'

'You'd printed lies about a friend, bad lies.'

'I can still hear Cheryl's scream, Michael; but of course you never thought of Cheryl. It's always the small people who are hurt by protest.'

Channing's phone is ringing.

'Monday, 8.00 a.m. Don't be late.'

'You said 9.00 a.m.'

'And you threw a brick through my window,' he says by way of dismissal, the phone already to his ear, though mouthpiece covered. 'And you'll need to apologise to Cheryl on reception, she was hysterical, bring chocolates or something.'

He carries on down the stairs, mouth now to phone. 'Chivas! How are things? Rupert still clinging on you say? That's fine, but we'll need him gone by the end of the week ...'

*

'You mean you're finally going to introduce us?'

They stood in the gallery overlooking the hall. Virgil had suggested Suzanne come and meet his father – and she'd laughed.

'Well, why not?'

'I can't imagine, Virgil – but then it isn't me who's kept the two of us apart for the last however many years.'

'We weren't talking.'

'You don't say.'

'So how could you talk with him, if I wasn't talking with him?'

'Very easily – if your tantrum wasn't such a global event.'

'Look, I don't see why you're being so snotty about it. I only suggested you come and say hello, thought you'd be pleased.'

'So you are talking now?'

'I had the old bugger round to supper.'

'Really?'

'I mean you can't go back – but at least, well, you can talk.'

'I think that's brilliant, Virgil. Late in the day but brilliant.'

Suzanne gives him a kiss.

'He apologised.'

Pause.

'And Abbot Peter says that's all any parent can do.'

'Abbot Peter?' says Suzanne.

'He was the one in the habit.'

'I got that far.'

'He had to go, something about a plane. But he said all a parent can do is apologise.'

'Okay.'

'And not some general "Oh yes, I was terrible, I was to blame for everything, wasn't I?" nonsense.'

'My mother exactly.'

'But specific things, specific apologies – and then it's up to the child to make their way from there. That's what the Abbot said anyway.'

'Abbot Peter.'

'Good bloke – bit of a religious codger, obviously, but a true blue.'

'And a famous family man, obviously,' said Suzanne, laughing.

'Well, he must have been a son to someone.'

'I'll take your word for it.'

'And you do know that detective is his niece?'

They looked down into the hall to see Tamsin talking with their daughter Emily. They sat in the recess where Bella had once ruled.

'Well, thank God she isn't his girlfriend. Older men shouldn't, you know.'

Virgil did know, but still couldn't help himself.

'I mean, she's a bit of a Grade One stunner obviously.'

Suzanne looks at him.

'Like you, of course, like you! I mean, it's not as if you stop looking at other women. You just don't – .'

'Virgil, I'm afraid I may die before you both make it.'

His father had arrived beside him.

'We were just coming, Father, this is – .'

'Very good to meet you, Dr Minty, I'm the missing Suzanne.'

They grasp hands and in his watery eyes there's a meeting place already, it sometimes happens.

'It's so good that you and Virgil are talking again,' she says.

'It is good, isn't it? Very good. Isn't it good, Virgil?'

He looks to his son, who looks awkward.

'Don't get embarrassing, Father.'

'And we won't allow him between us again,' says Suzanne firmly.

'So what do you do?' he asks. 'When you're not spending a dull evening at Henry House.'

'You mean income?'

'I suppose so.'

'I trained as an Educational Psychologist … and I'm just getting back on the bike.'

'Interesting. You don't expect that sort of thing in Stormhaven.'

'Amazing what you find under stones.'

Dr Minty is wondering if she might help the new ventures here at Henry House.

'I'm going to show Emily my old bedroom!' says Virgil.

'Don't over-estimate her interest, dear.'

'But it's my bedroom!'

'Precisely. I'm sure she'd prefer to see the priest hole, as indeed would I.'

'Show you the priest hole?'

'Why not?'

Virgil is bemused.

'But that's my secret!'

'You don't need your secrets now, Virgil. You needed them once, but you don't need them now. So will you show us?'

Ninety Seven

While in the master bedroom, later that night, Pat sat on the four-poster, listening to the voices on the stairs, to life in the building, good sounds, this was a Plague House no more, she'd make something of this place, she'd continue his work, Barnabus's work. Abbot Peter spoke so well of him and she'd made contacts already ... and then there he was, standing by the window, impossible, the clown she loved, standing there, looking at her. Heart-stopping.

'Barnabus!'

'Hello, my dearest.'

Feeling for words.

'What are you doing here?'

She was up off the bed.

'Just passing through,' he said, 'just saying goodbye, my love.'

'Barnabus.'

Was this a dream?

'Goodbye, my precious.'

'Barnabus, don't – .'

'And know this – you were my Shakh-e-Nabat!'

'Who?'

'The life not given ... our life ... but had it been ...'

His voice fading.

'Barnabus.'

She reached towards him.

'I am gone, my love, going.'

'You can't go!'

'I'm drawn away, drawn forward.'

'Come back to me!'

'So brief, but do this ... I'm waning, like the moon, remember? ... but do this, my sweet lover, laugh one more time.'

'I can't laugh, Barnabus.'

'Laugh for me one more time, for we laughed, didn't we?'

Such warmth, and they had laughed. But she was crying, though maybe laughing, so sad but happy as well, no sad, sad and sobbing as her hand passed through his fading face, and then desolate and then dancing, dancing as she'd once danced for Barnabus, dancing with the disappeared, dancing into the pain with her tears, with the future, dancing in Henry House.

Epilogue

Peter's flight from London Gatwick to Istanbul took four hours, and then a six hour wait in the hades of the departure lounge, before boarding the plane to Shiraz.

Avoiding the horrors of in-flight entertainment, Peter returned to his final conversation with Tamsin, as they'd stood together waiting for the taxi outside Henry House, flying towards Shiraz, but for now, gazing on the building with Tamsin, aware of its power once again, silhouetted against the darkening sky line.

'So Henry House finds a new identity,' he'd said.

'You mean the children's thing?

'The "children's thing", yes.'

The ravens were crowded and chatty on the chimneys, mimicking the noise within.

'Why don't they just shape up like the rest of us had to?' said Tamsin, now looking down the road for the taxi.

'Who?'

'Well, people are always doing this and that for children, like it's something great.'

'It is great.'

'Gets on my nerves. Am I allowed to say that?'

'As long as it's true.'

Tamsin cut a desperate figure.

'Is it your own childhood that gets on your nerves?' asked Peter.

'I didn't have a childhood, so how would I know?'

'No.'

'But I survived.'

'It's the time of our lives when we're most shaped, though.'

'It's just like any other time, in my book.'

' "Unrememberable but unforgettable", as someone once said.'

'Meaning?'

'Well, we can't consciously remember any of it, not the earliest, most formative times, not a scrap.'

'Exactly.'

'But our body does, our body remembers everything and holds these truths, sometimes painfully, until we're ready to collect them.'

The lights inside Henry House glowed bright in the deepening dark. And there were peals of laughter inside, a guffaw from Virgil.

'What if we're never ready?' said Tamsin.

Peter smiled.

'Doesn't even the smallest part of you wonder what truths your body has held for you all these years?'

'I'm too busy, Uncle, too busy to wonder.'

'And that's that?'

Fear in Tamsin's face, a tightening.

'I don't have time,' she said, 'and nor do you, by the looks of it.'

Car headlights were swinging round the corner.

'That's your taxi and you have a plane to catch.'

'I do.'

'Thank goodness it's on time.'

'Maybe on this occasion it suits you more than me.'

'I don't know what you're talking about!'

*

Back in the present, high in the sky, peering down through the small window, and below him, Iran's first solar power plant, so well done Shiraz ... not the poetic ferment you once were, but life is change ... and then not much to report of the journey until the charmless taxi driver at the airport, who despised both Peter and his habit in one seamless reaction. The Abbot did stand out in Iran, he was not unaware, a walking monastery in a way and a fox among hounds. But was it really so different from the robes that busied themselves around him, with suitcases and dreams very like his own? And Shiraz was a tolerant city, this was the tradition and a city which even today, in different times, hosted a Jewish synagogue, a Baha'i community and two Christian churches.

But if the city was tolerant, the driver was not, an embodiment of religious loathing; and things worsened as they tried to fix a price. Peter disliked haggling, organised acrimony from start to finish, a wretched descent into lie, gamesmanship and grievance, worse even than Monopoly. There were no happy endings in the haggling game, and none this afternoon in Shiraz. But it was the driver, not passenger, who was sorer than a wasp bite when the deal was done; for while Peter hated haggling, he was very good at it. After twenty five years in Egypt, where every pint of goat's milk was a negotiation, forget meek and mild - here was a haggle-hardened veteran of bitter consumer wars. He looked the driver in the eye, knew him from the inside out and didn't give him an inch.

The car jerked away from the kerb with Peter barely seated, his suitcase tumbling, and then drove with speed into the traffic, sometimes quite literally. Peter didn't mind the speed, speed was good, they would at least die together and he was in a hurry. Beyond the dust of the car window, the sun was setting in a serene blue sky, as in the chaos below, they made the wild drive to the North East of the city, his final destination. On arrival, he thanked and paid the sullen driver and stepped from noisy street into sudden quiet – the quiet of the Musalla Gardens.

*

At last! He stood for a moment, breathing in and breathing out, putting the travelling behind him, he was here. He luxuriated in the scent of the orange trees, and slowly he began to walk, treading the labyrinth of little paths among the clear pools, streams and flowers.

The Tea House was closing, waiters washing tables and sweeping around, but open enough for a frosted glass of rose sherbet, the last of the day, 'You lucky, Sir!' And then for this Englishman abroad, the deep pleasure of thick petal syrup, chilled with ice. As Lord Byron had once declared in these parts: 'Give me a sun, I care not how hot, and sherbet, I care not how cool, and my heaven is as easily made as your Persian's.'

On this matter at least, the Lord and the Abbot agreed.

And he gazed on it now as he drank, there in his eye-line, a small island of columns and dome across the flag stones. He'd seen it as soon as he entered the Gardens, seen it from a distance, but had chosen the circular way, the slow approach. He'd come to Shiraz for its ghosts, for conversation with the dead who could on occasion be wiser than the living.

But he wanted the conversation alone and quiet, something great sites of pilgrimage struggled to offer. He'd almost been trampled to death on the Mount of Olives by a coachload of pilgrims whose commitment to loud prayer blinded them to the needs of all other souls present. He'd arrived for quiet meditation, and left harassed and judgemental, something he'd no wish to repeat in the Musalla Gardens, home of the tomb of Hafiz.

This was why he had come late. A popular attraction for locals and tourists alike, Peter had timed his arrival to avoid them all. It was nothing personal, he simply didn't wish to see them. He desired a private audience with this magnificent spirit, this startling master of words.

'A poet,' Hafiz once said, 'is one who can pour light into a cup, then raise it to nourish your beautiful parched mouth.'

And Peter's mouth was parched.

He sat at his table, watching evening arrive, another cycle of the sun complete, the darkening sky of purple and blue. They call it 'The Blue Hour' in Shiraz, as public illuminations cast a gentle yellow on the greenery around him, the dome now a fluorescent glow. And in the embers of this day, he thought of Barnabus, because in truth, he didn't want to be alone, why did he imagine he wished to be alone, it simply wasn't so, for he wished to be here with Barnabus, would have liked to be here with Barnabus and Hafiz, the Three Deserteers as Tamsin called them. They should be drinking together! So much he could only say to them, so much only they could laugh about.

Lost friends.

And slowly, his breathing made him sane as the air passed through him, up and down, in and out, breath deepening, the madness of travel ebbing away, the planning, the rush, the in-flight hospitality, the hatred, the haggling all ebbing away and the quiet arrival of sane … and he wanted to be sane, now of all times.

He treasured the final drip of iced syrup, from tongue to throat, rose from the wooden table and walked across the flagstones towards the copper dome, bright with light, the shape of a dervish hat, and, according to the guidebook, supported by eight columns ten metres tall and built by the French archaeologist André Goddard in 1935. But there'd been a tomb for Hafiz since 1410, here in the Musalla Gardens, in life his favourite place on earth. So if you were going to meet him, if you had to pick a spot to speak with his ghost, this was surely it?

Peter felt nervous as he approached the tomb and shocked at the impetuous nature of his visit. Why had he come? It was just a tomb after all. Or did he really believe in ghosts? Did he really imagine Hafiz to be waiting for him, knowing him in some way, knowing his life in some manner? He climbed the five small steps and stood under the strange awning. Above him, a mosaic of tiles – gold, blue and white – in beautiful Arabian symmetry. Looking out, Peter saw a sunset Hafiz himself must have seen. And looking down was the tomb of the man who became a pen in the sun's hand.

To Peter's left was a leather-bound book. It surprised many to learn how popular Hafiz was in Iran, still the country's favourite poet, with his tomb a place of guidance for people, even fortune-telling. Visitors in their thousands still made the pilgrimage to this place, still came here to understand their future better by picking a random page from the leather tome before him, the works of Hafiz. They would open the book and the poet would speak again, speak into their life. He would tell them what to do, how to live, how best to proceed from here. Was that the same as believing in ghosts?

Grateful to be alone in the warm evening breeze, Peter slowly opened the book. And now, unbidden, the smashed skull of Barnabus returned to his mind, dark curly hair encrusted in blood, he'd never quite escaped the crumpled clown in the cupboard these past six months, reaching out to write on the wall, an unlikely copyist for the Persian bard, before the poker crashed down at midnight. He'd tried to get to the living Barnabus, but came back again and again to the dead.

Before him on the page are two lines:

The impermanence of the body should give us great clarity,
deepening the wonder in our senses and eyes.

Reaction? Peter is disappointed, this is his initial feeling. The impermanence of the body had given him only pain these past few months; he knew the theory of clarity but for now, the reality was pain ... and a sinking feeling, a sense of being let down by the guru. Had he come all this way to hear that? Was this all the ghost could manage? He wanted something new, a burning bush of revelation, some lightning to split his cloudy spiritual sky – and this wasn't it.

So why keep on hoping, was hope mankind's greatest folly? Freud was realistic – bleak but more honest than religion, selling nothing more in his Viennese front room than the shift from misery to ordinary human unhappiness. And really, why expect more?

Feelings of self-pity swamped Peter, a desire to cling again to tragedy. He'd come here to let go but how could he ever let go? How could Hafiz speak of wonder in the face of blood-encrusted wounds? And now anger, yes, Peter watched anger pass through him like a hot flux. And some self-importance, if he was honest: these were not words for the wise Abbot Peter, not words for one who'd seen what he had seen!

He watched the dismal procession of reactions pass through, and then nothing ... nothing in the Musalla Gardens, a numb nothing at the tomb and a wasted pilgrimage, as he listened to distant traffic and caught the orange scent and ... arrived home, in that moment, he came home, like a desperate survivor crawling ashore, some chink of light, some melting, a small sapling sensed in the dry ground of his heart, the strength of life, impermanence but glory, the impermanent but ever-deepening wonder.

The gate keeper is loitering. Peter smiles and the gate keeper smiles back, a public servant well-used to the pursuit of personal revelation in this place. It's why people came, and why he had a job, and why the orange trees and pools were so beautifully maintained, when other space in the city was being sold off, taken away screaming and violated with new build. So for the gate keeper, revelation in the morning was good, revelation in the afternoon was good but revelation at closing time – revelation which caused customers to pause awhile before leaving – this was not good ... but he would still smile!

Peter acknowledges him, acknowledges his desire to get home and glances again at the book, one more time, a brief farewell, what would the poet say? And there, six words of fading text in the half-light of dusk, Hafiz's last hurrah.

Six words.

It's time to go. Peter bows his head in gratitude, steps down from the shrine. He walks back to the gate, a return to the noise and bustle of the street. He pauses as the sun slides beneath the Zagros mountains like dropped egg yolk, bulbous orange sinking in the west, out of sight and in Peter, a sense of letting go, a peaceful end to something undefined, something put down, something finished, sinking like the sun and left here in Shiraz. Perhaps his desire for answers ...

He'd spend the night at the Chamran Grand Hotel on the north side of the city and fly back to Istanbul in the morning. More immediately, he'd argue with the taxi driver now pulling towards him at speed.

'How much to the Chamran Grand Hotel?'

Five minutes later, an irritated driver pulls out into the traffic and Peter watches as the city passes by and listens again to the words:

The impermanence of the body should give us great clarity, deepening the wonder in our senses and eyes.

How he longed to get back to the deep wonder of the crashing waves, the shingled shore, the fish and chips, the possible purchase of a second comfy chair, Tamsin had a point there – and to the fragile impermanence of a little girl called Poppy, reaching up for him, demanding to be swung high in the sky.

And then, as if now ready, he brought to mind the six words he'd read before leaving the tomb ... mad words really, not for polite conversation, but how strange – he could almost hear the poet saying them to some incredulous soul:

Could that be so? Could that really be so? Death ... a favour?

'Maybe it is, my friend,' said Peter, as the Chamran Grand came into view. But as the last of the Three Deserteers left standing, he had a proposal: 'Let us call it a favour postponed ... for now, I want to live!'

Author's Note

As you may be aware, Hafiz was a real person, and along with the poems quoted, many of his original lines are reflected in his dialogue in this story. He lived in Shiraz, accurately described here, for most of his sixty-five years, 1325 – 1390. There are large gaps in our knowledge about his life, but he left behind many poems and some facts do emerge through the mists of Persian time. His birth name was Shams-ud-Din and his coal merchant father, Baha-ud-Din, died when Hafiz was in his teens. He married in his twenties and had a son, there are references to both events in his poetry. He outlived them both, however, though we don't know how or when they died.

He became court poet in his twenties, after the experience, as a seventeen year old, of delivering bread to the house of Shakh-e-Nabat, with whom he fell hopelessly in love. She became for him a symbol of the creator's beauty and her image remained with him throughout his life. There is no record of him ever having spoken with her, however.

As court poet, he was the victim of various power struggles. Shah Shuja, his most reliable patron, overthrew and imprisoned his own father, to regain power. At this time, Hafiz wrote mostly protest poems. He reportedly upset the military genius and mass slaughterer Tamerlane, when he was rude about Samarkand, the great man's capital, and Bokhara, his kingdom's finest city. Hafiz was duly summoned to explain himself, so the story goes – but so disarmed Tamerlane with his charm, that he was dismissed and sent home with gifts.

Hafiz continued to drift in and out of favour with Shah Shuja throughout his life. On one occasion, for his own safety, he had to flee to his birth place of Isfahan for four years. He did not live in settled times.

He did learn the Koran by heart, and his spiritual teacher was Muhammed Attar, perhaps a man not dissimilar to the figure portrayed in this story. He is buried in the Musalla Gardens in Shiraz, on the banks of his beloved Ruknabad river and his tomb there is as described in the final chapter.

He wasn't always a spiritual writer. He wrote Ghazals, a poetic form with strict structural requirements, used also by Rumi the century before. Common themes for this poetic form were loss, the pain of loss and the beauty of love despite that pain. We can guess where he got his material from.

I have taken two liberties with his life in *A Psychiatrist, Screams*. The first is the timing of the vigil which he keeps. The story of the vigil is an important part of Hafiz folklore, including the vision of the angel and the return afterwards to Muhammed Attar. But I have placed it earlier in his life than was probably historically the case. He wrote prolifically after the experience, adopting themes of union between God and humans.

The second liberty, perhaps more obvious, is that his poems were never smuggled out of Shiraz to the fictional monastery of St James-the-Less. But this story line is based on the known fact that Hafiz did face threats from strands of Islamic fundamentalism that appeared in Shiraz at this time. We have no evidence, however, that Muhammed Attar was harmed by them; only that he was secretive in his activity, and probably with good reason.

If you would like to meet Hafiz for yourself – and really, why wouldn't you? – I warmly recommend the translations of his poetry by Daniel Ladinsky.

*A series of macabre murders in a bleak
English seaside town, each with a cast of suspects
with secrets of their own to protect.*

*But who can hide from the man who sees
our inner truths?*

ABBOT PETER
A HABIT FOR CRIME

'Abbot Peter is a true original.' *Daily Mail*

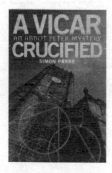